Tom McNeal was educated at the University of California and Stanford University, where he was the Jones Lecturer in creative writing from 1987 to 1990. His prize-winning short stories have appeared in numerous periodicals and anthologies. *Goodnight, Nebraska* is his first novel. He is married and lives in Fallbrook, California.

Goodnight, Nebraska

Tom McNeal

Doubleday

LONDON · NEW YORK · TORONTO · SYDNEY · AUCKLAND

TRANSWORLD PUBLISHERS LTD
61–63 Uxbridge Road, London W5 5SA

TRANSWORLD PUBLISHERS (AUSTRALIA) PTY LTD
15–25 Helles Avenue, Moorebank, NSW 2170

TRANSWORLD PUBLISHERS (NZ) LTD
3 William Pickering Drive, Albany, Auckland

Published 1998 by Doubleday
a division of Transworld Publishers Ltd
Copyright © by Tom McNeal 1998

All of the characters in this book ar fictitious,
and any resemblance to actual persons, living or dead,
is purely coincidental.

A catalogue record for this book
is available from the British Library.

ISBN 0 385 41017 4

Typeset in 11/13pt Garamond by
Hewer Text Composition Services, Edinburgh

This book proof printed by
Antony Rowe Ltd, Chippenham, Wiltshire

In memory of Samuel Thompson McNeal
and Barbara Christine Duckworth. And for Laura.

The author would like to thank Leslee Becker, Peter Fish, Ehud Hava Havazelet, Patricia MacInnes and Brent Spencer for their critical assistance; Jack Duckworth, Lee Hughson, Bill Miller and Ted Vastine for their expert consultation; and John L'Heureux, Peter Matson and Cathy McNeal for their steadfast kindness and support.

Everything comes to him
From the middle of his field. The odor
Of earth penetrates more deeply than any word . . .
The thought that he had found all this
Among men, in a woman–she caught his breath–
But he came back as one comes back from the sun
To lie on one's bed in the dark, close to a face
Without eyes or mouth, that looks at one and speaks.

– Wallace Stevens, from 'Yellow Afternoon'
from *The Collected Poems of Wallace Stevens*

Chapter One

THE SUPERNORMALIST

I

WHEN RANDALL HUNSACKER WAS THIRTEEN, HIS FAMILY MOVED FROM SALT Lake City to a canyon in the foothills, into a stilted five-room house perched above the tightest in a series of tight turns in the canyon's sharply descending road, so that from their front porch Randall's family often got a good view of cars pushed to the limits of control. The screech of tires, followed by the acrid, and – to Randall's nose – exhilarating odor of burnt rubber, was an everyday occurrence. Randall himself hoped that one of these cars would spin out and perhaps roll over. He didn't exactly hope for human carnage, but he knew that in such cases it was sometimes unavoidable. Occasionally, if he was alone as a car passed by, Randall would make the *ka-chunk ka-chunk ka-chunk*ing sounds he imagined a rolling car would produce.

When a Buick Riviera carrying two people actually did miss the curve, Randall was disappointed he was not there to see it. It was an early July evening. He and his father were working late, painting somebody's guest house in Federal Heights. His mother had already begun her shift at the Ten Pin. His sister Louise was in the back of the house with a girlfriend, sitting at the kitchen table, thumbing through *TV Guide* and *Glamour*, talking about boys and haircuts. The man driving the Buick Riviera missed the curve completely, shot pell-mell up the embankment and without braking slammed through the spindly posts that supported the front porch, which dropped like a table-leaf.

By the time Louise and her girlfriend rushed out the back door and came sliding down the bank, the driver, an oil man from Wyoming, and his passenger, a young woman wearing Levis and dangly silver earrings, were laughing like maniacs. The driver's comic perspective of the event did not, however, keep him from filing legal actions one week later against Wasatch County, the builder of the house, and Randall's parents for approval, construction and occupancy of a substandard structure within the county's required building setback. (In regard to the county, there were several ancillary charges involving such things as 'inadequate signage precedent to a mortifyingly dangerous curve'.)

From August to December, while this matter inched toward resolution, Randall's family either entered the house by scrambling up the side of the hill and coming around back or by climbing an ancient extension ladder to the front door (to improve stability, Randall's father strapped the ladder to stakes at its base and to the house above, but nonetheless, at its midsection, the ladder had the unnerving feel of a suspension bridge).

'An oil man, out sightseeing with a girl half his age, knocks out your front porch, then sues the bejabbers out of you,' Randall's father said to Randall one day out of the blue as they were finishing up a job. He swung his characteristic half grin toward Randall. 'Don't ever tell me it ain't a screwy ol' world.'

Randall's father was a large, hearty man with a pink scalp edged with just a horseshoe of silky brown hair, a man who smelled pleasantly of sweat and sawdust and cigars, a man who had shed his optimism gradually and with regret. He took on whatever odd jobs turned up, and Randall liked tagging along. Randall carried tools, and ran back to the truck when others were needed. He lugged away whole rolls of old carpet. He mixed perfectly uniform batches of concrete. He painted carefully. He didn't know which came first, his liking the work or being good at it, but both were true. Whenever someone praised Randall, his father always said the same thing. 'Yep, he's my little supernormalist,' he would say, a reference to a joke he'd heard long ago, and then he would append an explanation: 'The boy thinks he can do anything.'

In January, Randall's father signed a side agreement proposed by the oil man's insurance company, which held harmless both Randall's father and the driver, and in addition provided Randall's father with a check for $200 to cover the direct expenses of buying the piers, posts, planks and paint required to rebuild the porch.

'Two hundred smackers,' said Randall's mother in a squeezed-tight voice, and then, turning a bitter smile to Randall and Louise, 'Your father finally hit it big.'

ON THE DAY HIS FATHER DIED, RANDALL HAD GONE ICE-FISHING WITH A friend. Randall thought of staying home to help with the porch, but his father said that all he was going to do that day anyhow was line up materials and maybe just get started. The meaty part would begin tomorrow. Meantime, his father told him, ice-fishing trips didn't come along just every day.

Louise was the one who found him. Louise was not quite sixteen. Before returning home, she'd spent the afternoon with a girlfriend. When she heard her father's portable radio playing beneath the house, she called out that she was home. 'It's me,' she said, peering into the dimness. At her girlfriend's house Louise had drunk some cola with rum in it, but whatever giddiness she'd been feeling vanished as she followed the muted sound of the portable radio to the body. She wondered if she ought to try to get to his mouth to do resuscitation, but when she experimentally touched his hand she understood from its stiffened nature that he was dead without doubt. Louise withdrew in stupefaction. She climbed the extension ladder into the house. She washed her hands twice with soap, then she called her mother at the Ten Pin, and informed her of the facts.

By the time Randall got home, they'd removed the body. First the jack and then the cribbing his father had built to support it had given way. He was pinned beneath the timbers. When Randall was alone with Louise, he began asking questions. What did he look like? Did he write anything in the dirt? Louise said maybe he was trying to say something because his mouth was open. His body had already begun to stiffen, she said, and his tongue was gray. From the wild marks in the dirt and the state of his pantlegs, his feet had flailed around even while his chest was pinned down. She stopped as if unsure whether to go on.

'What?'

'Nothing,' Louise said finally.

'Tell me, Weasel. Tell me what else.' (As a child, Randall had called Louise Wheeza, which, at about age ten, he'd altered spitefully to Weasel, which had then undergone a more mysterious translation, from malice to affection.)

'No, that's it,' Louise said. 'There is nothing else.' Randall could see she didn't think he believed her, and he didn't. So she said, 'Except it seems like a terrible way to die, without even two minutes to prepare for it.'

When he had the chance to slip away, Randall crawled under the house. He thought he might find blood, but he didn't. What he found were the gouges and scrapings in the dirt his father's boots had made. There was no order or pattern to them at all, and it was easy to imagine the violent thrashing of his legs as the house pressed the last air from his father's chest. His father's flashlight lay to the side, switched on, its beam barely visible. The silence under the house was as deep and complete and discomposing as cave silence. It seemed to compress so tightly from all sides that it suspended Randall within it. For a long moment he couldn't move. Finally, as Randall scooched away, he saw something else. A few feet downhill from the scrapes and gouges was the stubby, half-chewed cigar that had been in his father's mouth at the moment the cribbing gave way.

That night Randall lay in bed wondering how he could feel so different. It was as if a hand had reached inside him and taken his heart and begun gently to squeeze. His heart was tender at first, then raw, then it hurt, actually hurt, with every beat. This went on. Even when he awakened in the night from sleep, it was there waiting, the dull, painful, rhythmical throb.

The memorial service was short, with a hired stranger from the mortuary saying words that meant nothing. Besides Randall's sister and mother, the only others in attendance were two waitresses from the Ten Pin. Randall's mother was not herself. Her cynicism had slipped away and left her disoriented. When the service was

over, Randall had to touch her elbow and lead her stiffly outside
the chapel to join the others standing in the bitter cold. Nobody put
his arms around anybody else. No one knew what to say. One of the
waitresses said it was the coldest winter she ever remembered and
the other waitress said, 'Coldest and longest.' A silence followed.
Randall's mother in a small voice said, 'He always joked that he
preferred winters like this. He said it helped keep the riff-raff out.'

Six weeks later, on Randall's fourteenth birthday, his mother laid
two identical revolvers on the kitchen table in front of him. 'Your
father took these in pay from a widow-lady and cleaned them all up.
The idea was he'd keep one and give you the other for your birthday.
He thought you'd both take up partridge hunting or some ridiculous
thing.' The hardness was gone from his mother's voice; she seemed
in fact about to cry. Randall didn't want to see it. He pulled one of
the long-barreled pistols closer to him on the table. It was a Ruger
– a bird with a dragon's head was set into the wood handle. He
lifted the pistol; it felt like three pounds easy. 'I'm pawning one,'
his mother said, 'but I thought you might want the other.'

Randall shoveled snow for neighbors up and down the canyon,
and when he'd earned the money, he bought a gray felt case for the
pistol, and slid it into the back of the bottom drawer of his dresser.
A month or so later, he bought a box of .44 magnum cartridges
that he arranged neatly next to his father's last half-chewed cigar
in a Roi-Tan box that fit snugly beneath a loose floorboard on the
back porch.

II

A FEW MONTHS AFTER THE FUNERAL, RANDALL'S MOTHER CAME HOME WITH
a man. She didn't introduce him to Randall and Louise. She let the
man stand there and do it himself. 'I'm Arnold,' the man said. Instead
of extending a hand, he kept rubbing his scalp. He was a tall man
and had just conked his head on the living room chandelier. Randall's
mother looked at Arnold and then at Randall and Louise. She seemed
at a loss. 'Look,' she said when Arnold excused himself to use the
bathroom. Her voice and manner were wobbly. 'Your father's gone
now. I wish he wasn't, but he is.'

The line of boyfriends was a long one that ended with Lenny.

Lenny was four years younger than Randall's mother, but looked younger yet – his face seemed always to have the flushed, pleased look of a bully who's just won a fistfight. He dressed in unbelted Levis and clean white T-shirts with a thin-width cuff rolled at each sleeve. He reminded Randall of a weird mix of Fonzie from the old TV show and the little killer Perry in a movie he'd seen called *In Cold Blood*. Lenny had never married, but was engaged a few years before to a woman whose photograph he still carried in his wallet. One night at Hardy's Restaurant, he pulled the picture from its plastic sleeve and laid it on the table before Randall, Louise and their mother. While they regarded the woman in her revealing bathing suit, Lenny talked. 'My fiancée had no attention span whatsoever,' he said. 'I'm hungry,' she'd say and we'd stop some place nice and three bites into a plate of spaghetti she'd just let the fork fall from her hands. "I'm full now," she'd say.'

All at the same time Lenny folded up his wallet, laughed and shook his head. 'I like it when a woman knows what she wants,' Lenny said, winking at Randall's mother. 'Better yet, I like it when *I* know what a woman wants,' and then he said, 'Better yet, I like it when I know what a woman wants a little while before she does.' This time he winked at Louise.

Louise gave him a look of heartfelt revulsion. Lenny smiled and adjusted the roll on his sleeve until it was just so.

It occurred to Randall that Lenny took pleasure in believing that most people were a little afraid of him. Whenever Lenny flashed his self-pleased smile on Randall, a wet pricklish fear spread over Randall's neck, a fear that brightened Lenny's eyes.

Most of a year passed. Lenny didn't marry Randall's mother, but one Sunday, without much preparation, Randall, Louise, and their mother moved into Lenny's house in the Rose Park section of Salt Lake, on the dwindling side of I-15. 'My house is like me,' Lenny said. 'It's big for its size.' It was a basic one-story brick house, but Lenny had built his bedroom into the attic and had begun remodeling the basement. This was where Randall and Louise were to sleep. Lenny had installed a tiny corner bathroom with a fiberglass shower enclosure, and had begun separating the rest of the basement into two dismal rooms. He'd framed the dividing wall, but hadn't yet gotten to the insulation or sheet rock. It felt to Randall like a honeycombed cellar, something you'd normally enter only in a bad dream. Louise tacked up sheets for privacy while Lenny stood by and talked about how cool it was down here in the summer, and how warm it stayed in the winter.

'And I should just think of all the mouse punks as chocolate chips,' Louise said, and Lenny, pretending she meant it as funny, laughed hard.

Mornings, Lenny worked out with free weights in the front room, cooked and ate a six-egg omelet and, if the weather was good, washed his truck, all before he went off to work at 7.30. It *was* a truck, as far as Randall was concerned – but Lenny called it a tractor. He pulled trailer-homes with it, though Lenny liked to call them mo-biles (he elasticized the final syllable, so that it rhymed with *trials*). Some were fourteen-wides, and some were twenty-fours and twenty-eights that came in two sections. Lenny pulled them into place, set them on piers, made the sewer, electrical and propane connections. The set-ups were the easy money, but he filled in with skirtings and awnings. Randall didn't offer to go out on jobs with Lenny and Lenny didn't ask. It was Randall's mother who pushed it.

So one wintry day, against his will, Randall found himself bouncing along in the high, closed cab of Lenny's truck, the cassette deck playing gospel music loud. While Lenny drove, Randall shuffled through the plastic cases on the seat. Mahalia Jackson. The Clara Ward Singers. The Gospel Harmonettes.

'Two things colored women do better than whites and one is singing,' Lenny said over the music and the truck noise, then tossed a goggle-eyed smirk at Randall, who glanced away and felt his neck moisten with sweat.

When they got to the Taggin' Wagon Trailer Park, Randall did what he was told. He crawled headfirst under the trailer, breaking spider webs as he went. He bellied about as Lenny, peering in from an access panel, directed. Randall worked the redwood pads into the dirt, set the metal piers on top of the pads, attached the locktops to the I-beams. There were places so tight he had to hold his breath to wriggle through.

'Fine,' Lenny said that night when Randall's mother asked how he did. They were all riding in Lenny's Subaru – Louise, Randall, their mother, and Lenny, who said, 'The kid's built perfect for the work. He's like a little salamander.' Lenny, as if pleasantly surprised by both the astuteness and sly malignance of this appraisal, let out a sudden laugh. Randall's mother laughed guardedly. They were on their way to the Hi-Spot Lounge. This was the new routine. Lenny had lined up Randall's mother with a day job at a lunch counter so she could have her evenings free. She sat up front with a pizza box in her lap while Louise and Randall sat in back. 'How about you?' Randall's mother said, turning to him in the back. 'How did you like it?'

Randall, who'd hated the day, didn't know what to say. Louise seemed to sense this. 'Who cares how the retard liked it?' she said so he wouldn't have to respond.

When they got to the bar, Randall's mother passed the pizza back to him and Louise. Do all your homework, she said, and, Louise, you help Randall when you're done with your own. Some of this was genuine concern, but Randall sensed that the sickishly sweet flavor of it was introduced for Lenny's benefit. Louise opened the pizza box and said, 'Fatty meat? You ordered a fatty-meat pizza? After you knew I was vegetarian now?'

Lenny and their mother strolled across the parking lot toward the bar.

'Did you even *look* at this fatty-meat grease?' Louise screamed at them from the back seat.

Once Lenny and their mother disappeared into the Hi-Spot Lounge, Randall climbed into the front seat, ate, and then just waited until Louise was done with her work so the light would go out. He liked it with the light off and one of Lenny's tapes turned low, as if the women's voices were coming from somewhere friendly and warm and just a little ways off. Sometimes Randall and Louise would doze and, upon reawakening, talk in ways they never otherwise would.

'I dream about him all the time,' Randall said, of his father. 'Just now I dreamed I was working with him under a house and I kept scooching close so I could smell him and be sure he was really there. What's weird was, I *could* smell him. In the dream I was smelling his smell.'

Randall could feel Louise staring at him in the dark. 'Was it a good dream though?' she said.

'Yeah, it was. It was like he'd been here for a visit.'

After a little while Louise changed subjects. 'Know why we have to stay in this car and can't stay alone in Lenny's house? – because Lenny's afraid we'll steal his things, I heard him telling Mom.'

'What things?' Randall said.

'That's what makes it so hilarious. Lenny doesn't have anything worth stealing. So here we are, doing our homework in a Subaru.'

The first week or so of their evenings in the car, Randall's mother came out periodically to check up on them, but as these evenings accumulated, she visited Randall and Louise less and less. They got used to spending the nights alone in the Subaru, Randall generally in the front seat, Louise in the back. One night, Louise got out of the car and came back with cigarettes, which she and Randall smoked.

The next night Louise said he could come along on the cigarette run if he wanted. She went to a car with the window down, leaned in and rifled the glove compartment. She did this three or four times before heading back to the Subaru with cigarettes, several dollars in change, a *Star Wars* pocketknife and a dirty magazine. 'All the good stuff must be in the locked ones,' she said. The magazine was called *Raunch*. She held it out in one hand, the pocketknife in the other. 'Your choice, Kiddo.'

Randall took the magazine, but after looking through it wished he'd taken the pocketknife. 'Can I trade back, Weasel?'

To his surprise, Louise let out a laugh and slid the pocketknife onto the back of the seat. 'I overindulge you, Randallkins,' she said.

A week later, he'd forgotten this favor. Louise, bored from sitting in the car, wanted her back scratched. This was a familiar request. She would stretch out on the back seat and roll up her shirt to the shoulder blades. That was all right, but she made Randall undo the brassière, too, which gave him a funny feeling. 'Naw,' he said.

Louise sighed and offered a number of bribes, all of which Randall declined. She'd found of box of Dots in somebody's car and studied one now for freshness. 'Okay,' she said, popping a black candy into her mouth, 'how about if I explain to you what fellatio is?'

'What's that?'

'Only a certain kind of sex act every youth ought to know about.'

Randall thought it over and shook his head. Finally she said, 'So what if I tell you something I never told you about the body when I found it?'

Randall was suspicious. 'Like what?'

'You'll scratch my back if I tell you?'

They sat in the dark for a while. There were crickets working and from somewhere a woman's high laugh carried. 'Yeah,' Randall said.

'He peed his pants.'

All at once Randall closed up into himself. 'I just knew you were going to say some big fat lie like that.'

'He did though,' Louise said. 'Peeing his pants was one of the last things in the world your father ever did. I saw it. It's also on the medical report if you'd care to look it up, under *Other Observations*. It says, "Deceased's trousers damp with urine." '

Randall slid down to the floor and snugged up under the seat. If he could find a certain position, he fit there like a foot in a slipper. In a sulky voice he said, 'He was your father, too.'

Louise in a low serious voice said, 'No, he wasn't,' and thereafter rushed on as if she'd just gotten over a barbed-wire fence. 'She's my mother, I'm sorry to say, but there were so many men she herself couldn't say who my father or yours was. You look like him. You feel bad about him. So I guess he's your father. But I've decided he was definitely not mine.'

Randall, inhaling, flattened himself against the car floor. 'How do you know there were other men who might be our father?'

'How do you think?'

'I don't know,' Randall said. 'Why don't you tell me?'

'I *saw*. With my own two eyes. In our own house. While you and your father were off on some odd job.'

Randall lay quietly in the dark. His fingers came upon something on the floor, something small and flat, a Necco wafer maybe, or a metal slug. He laid it on his tongue – its taste was faintly oily – then he swallowed it whole.

III

TWO YEARS LATER, SITTING IN MRS KY'S STUDY HALL LOCATED IN THE OLD
Home Ec Room of West High, Randall discovered Anna Belknap.
For a while she was simply one of several girls he furtively observed.
Then, one windy afternoon in October, with shadowy light playing
at the high windows, Anna Belknap, while doing her trigonometry,
took the back of her hand and lifted her long brown hair away from
her white neck, and held it there until the lacy, creamy-yellow light
teased across her skin. Then, letting her hair fall, Anna Belknap
turned and tossed a quick, coltish glance toward Randall.

Randall and his father had once painted a house for a man who
owned a dog and a rabbit. The rabbit lived in a long low hutch
behind the garage and the dog spent its days watching the rabbit.
The rabbit munched carrots and rattled around her cage, oblivious
to the dog, but the dog was haunted. It was like a spell, and he
became almost a statue of a dog, absolutely still, staring longingly
at the rabbit, unable to pry his eyes away. This was how Randall
felt while watching Anna Belknap, like that enchanted dog.

Each day as he walked into study hall, Randall's heart seemed to
lodge between his ears, where it pounded so fiercely he wondered
that others couldn't hear it. Mrs Ky, the proctor, was an older,
full-bosomed woman whose successful management style boiled
down to vigilantly presuming the worst.

Randall sat near the center of the room, bent forward with his
arm curled under his neck and over his shoulder, staring past his
grammar book at Anna Belknap. He knew almost nothing about
her, except that she wore nice clothes and was in college French
classes and went with a Mormon tennis type named Jason Wilson.
One of Randall's favorite daydreams involved his coming upon a car
wreck in which Jason Wilson had already perished, but when Randall,
with unexplainable strength, raised the car by himself, Anna Belknap
miraculously wriggled free, looking very shaken and grateful and
beautiful, although her blouse was badly torn.

'Mr Han-zicker!' Mrs Ky's sharp voice split the stillness. 'You
have a book on your desk, correct? Then that is where your eyes
belong!'

Nearby sniggers, made mean by boredom. Randall's skin blazed and, for one long moment, Anna Belknap turned her complacent, creamy-smooth face his way.

QUIETLY AND METHODICALLY, RANDALL BEGAN ACQUIRING INFORMATION. ANNA Belknap lived in a big house in the Avenues. Her phone number was 364–3238. She drove a fashionable blue Volkswagen convertible, which she parked every morning in the east lot. She was not a Mormon. After school, on nice days, she sat on the grass near the tennis courts sunning her legs while doing homework and waiting for Jason Wilson to finish tennis practice. She smiled at Randall in the hall, or at least seemed to, he was never 100 percent sure. He wrote her notes with the idea of slipping them under the wiper blade of her VW, but he never did. He dialed her number and hung up when she answered. Fantastically, he hoped that she hoped the caller without a voice was him.

In school, Randall's marks were just good enough that the teachers would leave him alone – Cs, C–s, an occasional D. The only teacher he liked was Mr Steiner, who taught shop. Mr Steiner was a wiry, short, and slyly funny man who wore large flesh-colored glasses and drove an ancient Land Rover of a type Randall had only otherwise seen on *Wild Kingdom*. He had a sign on the wall behind his desk that said, EVERYTHING IN LIFE IS SOMEWHERE ELSE, AND YOU GET THERE IN A CAR. – E.B. White. The previous year Randall had taken Small Engines, a prerequisite to auto shop, and had liked it at once. He liked walking into the large Quonset that smelled of oil and had ramshackle lawnmowers and chainsaws and snowblowers tagged and pushed together in a corner, with high wooden stools snugged under the lines of high metal benches where each boy, after a quick demonstration from Mr Steiner, would perform some task on the little, four-stroke Briggs and Stratton they'd been issued. Always Randall started when, at the end of the hour, Mr Steiner broke into the busyness with, 'Okay, gents, fun's over. Let's clean up.'

Mr Steiner had taken a liking to Randall. He had him show others how to rebuild a clutch, boil a carburetor. And this year he'd given Randall more advanced projects. One cold afternoon in January, Randall was hanging around the auto shop, fiddling with a practice carburetor when the tinned doors opened and Mr Steiner towed in an aged Pontiac LeMans. Randall slid under the bumper to unchain it, then walked a slow circle around the car. "65?' he yelled over to Mr Steiner, who was at the side sink washing up.

"64.'

'But not the GTO.'

'Close.' Mr Steiner walked over drying his arms. 'Body's the same as the GTO, but this has got the 326 instead of the 389.'

Randall popped the hood. 'What's wrong with it?'

Mr Steiner had his pocketknife out, peeling away the thin layer of sludge from beneath his nails. Without looking up from this work, he said, 'Why don't *you* tell *me*?'

Two days later, Randall did. 'Head gasket, but the block's not cracked.'

Mr Steiner smiled. 'Not bad for starters.'

Randall was wishing he'd looked further. 'There's more to it, I guess.'

Mr Steiner said there usually was. He kept his gaze steadily on Randall. 'Let's say I was to supply the parts. Would you be interested in fixing the heap up for me?'

Randall stared at the old muscle car. A LeMans was not a GTO, but, still, it was huge. Randall was drawn to the red paint and cream-colored seats (it reminded him of the Cadillac his father had ridden west in with a couple named Carlton and May – his father had prized a particular picture of that Cadillac, with him and Carlton and May sitting happily on its fender).

'We'll make it your term project,' Mr Steiner was saying, 'plus I'll pay you a little something for your time.'

Randall started work the next day. He didn't try to hurry. He worked systematically without stopping. He drained the radiator, removed the air cleaner, vacuum hoses, and fuel lines from the throttle. Mr Steiner, who'd brought him a thick handout on engine rebuilding, said, 'Okay, you're on your way. Yell when you get lost.'

In late January, a smothering inversion layer moved into the Wasatch Basin and stayed. The smog dimmed the sunrise, and turned the sunset a flaming orange. There were woodburning restrictions; the auto shop stove stood closed and cold. Randall bought a quilted vest at Desert Thrift and kept working. One day in February, when it was getting dark before five, Mr Steiner walked up to Randall while he was gunking rocker nuts. Mr Steiner adjusted the shop light for him. 'How much longer?' he asked.

Randall, seeing that Mr Steiner was out of his coveralls and wearing street clothes, said, 'I can quit whenever.'

Mr Steiner regarded Randall for a long moment, then began working a key off its ring. 'Lock it after me when I go. Don't let anybody male or female in here, nobody.' He presented the key to Randall. 'Something goes wrong here and a couple of those gentiles over in administration will have my dingus in the wringer but good. *Comprende, amigo?*'

Randall, who liked to tell the truth, said he did, more or less.

Evenings, Randall returned home as reluctantly as he entered school each morning. There were almost no arguments in Lenny's household because Randall's mother almost never disagreed with anything Lenny said. The years since the death of Randall's father had made his mother smaller somehow, with less meanness to her, and meanness, it turned out, was what had tightened her grip on the world. To Randall, she looked frailer all the time. She'd begun taking naps when she came home from her lunch shift. Randall and Louise no longer had to wait in the Subaru while Lenny and their mother spent evenings in bars, but they still shared the basement with their twin beds on opposite sides of a curtained wall. Overhead, late at night, they could sometimes hear certain loud noises from Lenny's bedroom. They knew what it meant when Lenny and their mother came home laughing and bumping into things, their mother's laughter thin and brittle, Lenny's rich and clamorous, both soon swallowed by the pulse of Lenny's gospel music.

'Here comes Mahalia,' Louise said to Randall from her side of the curtain, trying to make a joke out of it.

Randall didn't say anything. He just lay in the dark trying not to listen. To him it was like too large a man climbing on too sick a woman. 'I hate Lenny,' he said one night in a low enough voice that, when Louise didn't initially respond, he supposed she hadn't heard.

Finally out of the dark, Louise said, 'Who doesn't?' She was quiet for a few seconds. 'One day when I was alone in the car with him he says, "Louise, excuse me for saying so, but if I was stranded on a desert island, you're the person I'd want to be stranded with." '

A dark mass of strange hatred fisted up inside Randall. Dots floated behind his eyelids. 'Lenny said that to you? What did you say back?'

Louise chortled. 'I told him it was about the kind of idea I'd expect from a peacock with a peabrain.'

This pleased Randall, who said, 'You should tell Mom what he said to you. Maybe she would leave him. Maybe it would get us out of here.'

A bitter laugh burst from Louise. 'Mom leave Lenny? That's a big rich notion. In case you haven't noticed it, our mother's been de-boned for some time now.'

Randall pulled his pillow to his chest and curled into a tight ball. For a moment the overhead music stopped, but then resumed. Suddenly, out of the blue, Louise said, 'Who's Anna Belknap?'

Randall lay perfectly still, trying to pretend he hadn't heard right.

'Other than some girl you've got the hots for,' Louise said.

Randall felt cornered and snappish. 'How would you know that?'

'I've got my wily ways.' Louise softened her voice. 'So who is she?'

In a sullen voice Randall said, 'Just what you said. Some girl.'

'When are you with her?'

Randall didn't answer.

'When do you talk to her?'

Randall kept curled tight around his pillow. 'Don't.'

'You don't talk to her? Ever?'

Randall didn't answer.

'But you *do* write to her.'

Alarm shot through Randall. On the other side of the curtain, Louise turned on her light and was rattling papers. Then her voice crept through the curtains.

'*Dear Anna Belknap*,' she read. '*You standing today with bare arms in half sun next to the quonsits was something somebody should paint.*' Louise laughed softly. 'My little crazy-ass brother waxes poetic.'

Randall, twisting quickly, reached under his bed for his Roi-Tan box. All of his unsent letters to Anna Belknap were gone. The old cigar was there. The .44 magnum cartridges were there. The *Star Wars* pocket knife was there.

Louise was again reading aloud. '*Dear Anna. From upstairs in Mr Daly's room I looked down and saw you mad at Jason Wilson, if you ever need help with him maybe you should call me.*'

In blind fury Randall slashed the knife through the dividing curtain.

Louise, bare-breasted, sitting up in bed with the letters spread about her, laughed and loosely pulled up the covers, but not before Randall, in mortification, had averted his eyes.

IV

IN HER SENIOR YEAR, AFTER TWO SUSPENSIONS FOR ALCOHOL ON CAMPUS, Louise was transferred to the continuation school on State Street, just south of the car dealerships. 'I like the curriculum,' Louise said to Randall. 'We do Mathpaks, Litpaks, and Six-packs. The last is my personal fave.'

Randall's mother took the news of the transfer without comment, but Lenny had things to say. 'Consider us,' he said over dinner through a mouthful of food. 'Consider your mother having to go to bed at night thinking, Yes, my daughter has become the most classic kind of fuck-up.'

Randall glanced at his mother. Her face was colorless, her eyes were cast down. With her fork she separated one pea from the others.

'I'll get my diploma,' said Louise, who seemed to be enjoying the attention, 'and I'll nail it to the front door on my way out of this hovel.'

Louise had started disappearing at night, Randall didn't know where. 'Where're you going?' he would ask. 'Anywhere,' she would say.

He followed her to the overpass, where she was picked up by kids in a rusty Ford Econoline with AL THE LOCKSMITH painted faintly on the panels. She returned late at night and always, before climbing into bed, Randall heard the creaking of her bureau as she slid something into it.

Randall didn't like staying in the house alone, so after his mother and Lenny left in the evening, and after Louise went out with her friends, Randall rode the bus downtown, where he transferred from route to route. He would've liked to have had his own car, but he was comforted by the buses. He was among people without having to talk to them and, except for No. 33, whose windows wouldn't close, the buses were all warm. Randall liked looking into the tall, lighted office buildings and, further out, into the muted yellow light of snug-seeming homes. He liked looking down into the cars that drew alongside, seeing people alone and singing to the radio, sometimes spying a woman's white skin or dark cleavage. Occasionally, either from a distance or in the faint light of dusk, he thought he glimpsed Anna Belknap, or, at other times, his own father. (Once, he glanced down from the bus and for an instant saw his father in the pinkish bald man, who, while waiting for the light, had stretched a dachshund up to the steering wheel, as if to steer.)

Whenever he grew bored, Randall got off the bus and set out walking. He liked to look under the hoods of the used cars in the lots on South State, and he liked to browse in the mall jewelry stores imagining he was shopping for something Anna Belknap might like. One night he was eating a chili dog in the Trolley Square food court when a voice said, 'Well if it isn't Randall Han-zicker!'

It sounded for an instant like a slightly drunken Mrs Ky, but, turning, the face Randall instead saw, beaming prettily from among a group of pretty girls in stylish ski outfits, was Anna Belknap's. Randall couldn't say anything. He raised himself from his chair and just stood there, grinning feebly, feeling his throat tightening and color climbing up his neck and spreading over his face.

'Hey, you guys,' Anna Belknap said to her friends. 'This is the guy I told you about from first-semester study hall. I could feel his eyes studying me all study hall long.' She grinned at Randall. 'Or was I just imagining that?'

Within Randall's mouth, sitting lumplike, was his last bite of white bun and chili dog, which, upon seeing Anna Belknap, he'd stopped chewing, and so constricted was his throat now that he couldn't swallow or speak. His eyes swam from Anna Belknap to her girlfriends, who stared back as one.

Anna seemed to misunderstand. 'Oh, sorry!' she said. 'My mom's always saying, "Introduce! introduce!" and I never remember. These are my friends, Tina, Amy, Pamela, and Trish. And this is Randall Hunsacker.' She turned to Randall. 'Did I pronounce it right?'

Randall nodded.

Anna Belknap said, 'I hated it whenever Mrs Ky yelled your name in study hall. She said it all wrong and made it sound so – *weird*.' She laughed. 'Anyhow, it's really a very distinguished-sounding name.'

She stopped then and waited for Randall to speak, but he stood absolutely mute. One of Anna Belknap's friends, the one in a bright yellow coat and black ski pants who wasn't interested in this conversation in the first place, said, 'We're going downstairs to the Gap, Anna. You going to stay here with the mummy or what?' and another girl, to Randall, said, 'Anna made cheerleading today, is why she's acting so stupid,' and another, less loud, but loud enough that Randall could hear, said, 'So what's his excuse?' and Anna Belknap, still smiling at Randall, but carried along by a current of laughter moving away from him, called back, 'Bye, Randall Hunsacker!'

RANDALL WAS STILL AWAKE WHEN LOUISE SNEAKED IN LATER THAT NIGHT. HE heard the bureau creak, her clothes fluff to the floor, the metallic fretting of the bedsprings as she settled into bed. He waited a minute or two. Finally he said in a low voice, 'Weasel? You awake?'

'Nope,' she said, an old joke of theirs. 'How come you are?'

He danced around the subject for a few minutes, then told her of his encounter with Anna Belknap. He was worried Louise would laugh and poke fun, but she didn't. 'You really didn't say a single word?' she asked.

'Not one. Pretty pathetic, huh?'

Louise didn't answer. She was perfectly silent. Randall presumed she was bored, which annoyed him. He moved onto the next topic. 'So where does the money come from, Louise?'

A long second passed. 'What money?'

'The money in the yellow socks in your dresser.'

'I count that money, in case you've got any ideas.'

'Like I'd steal from my sister,' Randall said.

'Like you'd root around in your sister's dresser,' she said.

Randall ignored that. 'So where does the money come from?'
She didn't speak.

'Tell me, Louise.' He waited. He knew that she knew he wouldn't let it go. He couldn't stand secrets. He had to know everything. It wasn't that you could ever put your own order on events and circumstances, but without knowing everything you couldn't even try. It was like cows from a feedlot funneled onto a freight train. It might not make much difference, but you'd still like to know where the train was headed. 'Louise?' he whispered.

'From acquisitions,' she said in a bursting bitter voice. 'Acquired from houses owned by people with more things than they can keep track of.'

After a while, Randall said, 'I also saw that tin box behind the socks.' The box held some kind of stash – pills of all sorts grouped by color in individual unlabeled baggies. 'What do you do with all that stuff?'

'Nothing you're ever going to learn from me,' Louise said. Then, in a wearier voice, 'I use them to go elsewhere, Randallkins, which is about all I ever want anymore.'

Randall sensed that this was an issue that was completely beyond him, so he switched to a problem more within reach. 'Well, don't you think you ought to be more careful hiding the pills and stuff?' He was thinking of how he'd found a new hiding place in the garage for his own Roi-Tan box.

'What's to hide?' Louise said. 'I knew you'd find out no matter what, because that's your nature, to find out everything. And I knew Mom wouldn't *ever* find out because she doesn't want to find out *anything*.'

'What about Lenny?' Randall said. 'What if he goes snooping around in your dresser?' Randall wasn't sure why, but it was something he could imagine Lenny doing.

A sharp laugh burst from Louise. 'Lenny? Going through my stuff? Not if he appreciates the status quo around here.'

For a time Randall lay with his eyes open in the dark. Then he said, 'I'm almost done with the LeMans.'

Louise said nothing.

'I'm going out for football,' he said, which was true, although, until that moment, he'd only been thinking about it.

'Football?' she said. 'As a junior? Shave your head and shit to play just one year?'

'Yeah.'

'Why?'

Now Randall didn't answer.

'Because Anna Belknap is a cheerleader?'

Randall lay there quiet.

'Jesus, Randall, it's like there's no limit to what you're crazy enough to hope for.' She waited a moment. 'So is this Anna Belknap Mormonoid or not?'

'Not. Why?'

'Because if she was Mormonoid you'd really be barking up the wrong tree,' Louise said distractedly. A few seconds passed. Then she said, 'Maybe I could help out with Anna Belknap. Want me to help out?'

'That's a joke,' Randall said, and then when Louise said nothing, and he could almost feel her dreaming up ideas and moving them around in her mind, weird ideas probably and probably involving her scummy friends, he said, 'No, Louise, and that's a definite no.'

V

FOOTBALL SUITED RANDALL. HE WAS FAST AND STRONG AND HE LOVED THE RAW throb of the game, the recklessness, and during his first days of spring practice he came to understand that he was less afraid of pain than other boys. Still, he'd come late to the sport. From a distance, football had always seemed simple to him, but, from within, it was an angry form of chaos, a confusing blur of mass and motion. Randall enjoyed it, but he couldn't sort it out. He ran full-tilt into blind-side blocks, he tackled backs without the ball, he was fooled by the quarterback's worst pump fake. But he never quit or slowed down and by the end of the first month of practice, the coach's approval of Randall seemed evident. He called on him first to block punts and crack the wedge on kickoff returns.

To Randall, it suddenly seemed a sunnier world. The coach and the principal and even some teachers greeted Randall by name in the halls. Football players said, 'Hey, 'Zacker.' Girls looked him over, not many, but a few. Randall, whose beard was heavy, began to shave more often and more carefully. Over in Mr Steiner's auto shop, the separate parts of the LeMans 326 slowly turned into an engine. The new timing chain was installed, the flywheel mounted (twice, first with the old bolts then with the new ones Mr Steiner provided), the head installed and torqued.

'What's *cavitating*?' Randall said, staring down at the book.

'It's what you do all day long, Randall,' Mr Steiner said grinning.

'Which is?'

'Sucking air.' He grinned and headed off. 'You'll lock up?'

Randall nodded and watched Mr Steiner go.

One evening while he was working on the LeMans, Mr Steiner's telephone began to ring. Randall ignored it, but it continued ringing. Randall lifted the receiver and listened.

A girl's voice, or maybe a woman's, said, 'Is this Randall Hunsacker?'

Randall, unsure what to say, said nothing.

'It's me, Anna Belknap.'

Randall was surprised, of course, but a small part of him, the small, muscular, unreasonable part, was not. Still, he felt his throat tightening and drying up. 'This is Anna Belknap?' he said.

Anna Belknap let out a light laugh. 'It sure is.'

Randall, to say something, said, 'How'd you know to find me here?'

She laughed again. 'Pretty good, huh? It's my inside sources.'

Randall made a dry laugh and was trying to think what to say next when she said, 'The reason I'm calling is I was hoping you'd take me to the spring dance. It's not girl-ask-boy or anything, but I'm asking anyway.'

What Randall wanted to say was that he'd like to take her, but he didn't know how to dance. He said nothing.

'I know it's short notice,' Anna Belknap said, 'but would you like to?'

'Yeah, I would,' Randall said.

'Okay then,' she said. She sounded happy. She gave him her address, they arranged a time. 'Are we going to go in that car you're fixing up?'

The car was uninsured. He couldn't drive it. He'd promised

Mr Steiner he wouldn't. 'Yeah,' Randall said, 'I don't see why
not.'

RANDALL'S NEXT TEN DAYS WERE FRANTIC. TO FINISH THE LEMANS HE WORKED
until two or three each morning. He followed a strict regimen, and
was surprised at how much he liked giving his own order to days
that had never before seemed his own. He hardly ate and hardly
slept, but he was never hungry and never tired. He floated through
school. He slammed and banged through football practice.

'Zacker's got a date with Anna Bellknockers, kids,' one of the guys
sang out in the shower after Tuesday practice, and it drew a chorus
of hoots.

'Zacker does dates?' a boy from the far end of the shower
yelled.

'What *don't* Zacker do? Somebody tell me what Zacker don't
do?'

'Tell you what Bellknockers won't do. Jason Wilson's gone with
her for over two years and never even got into her pants.'

'She is *cold!*'

'Refrigerated!'

'Non-combustible!'

Randall, quiet and blushing and soaping himself down, felt a
strange undiluted happiness streaming over him.

On Wednesday, using the hoist, Randall lowered the engine and
transmission back into the car and replaced the drive shaft. By
Thursday, he'd installed the exhaust pipes, muffler, radiator and
fan. Friday afternoon, while Randall was replacing the hood, Mr
Steiner walked over. 'I road-tested it today.' He pulled out his wallet
and handed Randall three $50 bills. 'It ran like a top.'

Randall looked down at the money. He wanted to ask Mr Steiner
if he couldn't borrow the car for just one night, because he knew
Mr Steiner would want to say yes, but Randall didn't ask, because
he knew Mr Steiner would have to say no. 'Thank you,' he said.

By seven Saturday morning, Randall, following his handwritten
schedule for the day, had begun waxing and detailing the car. As
he worked, he went over the evening's little details – how to smile
when he picked Anna up (calmly), what to talk about in the car

(her cheerleading and what kinds of things she did in the brainy classes), what to order at the restaurant (chicken cordon bleu, was Louise's advice), how to sit and act and talk (confidently, he told himself, but not overconfidently), what story to tell while they waited for the food (his father's old supernormalist joke), what to order if they went by the Roasting Company afterwards (cappuccino), on and on and on. Sorting through the little details helped – every fear that surfaced was quickly beaten back by some smartly calculated, if imaginary, countermeasure. By midafternoon, Randall had made several pre-planned purchases at Trolley Square, and then met Louise in their basement quarters back at the house. Louise had gotten a new tape player from somewhere and put on some of Lenny's Sarah Vaughan. The idea was that Randall would get comfortable with the slow dancing, which, Louise said, would be enough to get him by. 'Okay, Randallkins, it's Arthur Murray time,' she said, extending her arms.

Randall positioned himself as he thought best.

'Jesus, Randall, she's going to think you prefer guys.'

He shored up his embrace. It wasn't just that it was the first time in years he'd had someone's arms around him. It was also the strangeness of her chest against his. 'Okay,' she said, 'here we go. Yeah, that's fine. That's good.' She snugged closer. 'That's good. See how easy this is. Relaxed intensity, that's what you're after here. If you kiss her, make it light, maybe to the neck, almost so light she'll think she might've made it up. Relaxed intensity. Everything calm, nothing abrupt. Then, later, a couple of dances in, you drop your hands –'

Randall broke off, stepped backward.

'What?' Louise asked.

'Nothing,' Randall said, moving away, 'it's just that I think I got it.'

AS RANDALL WHEELED THE RED LEMANS OUT OF MR STEINER'S AUTO SHOP THAT night, he was almost ill with excitement. His stomach tumbled and gurgled. His head throbbed. He stopped at a lax 7-11 for beer and Binaca. He kept thinking he was forgetting something. He checked the box on the back seat. He checked the console and glove compartments. Everything was there. Everything was set.

Except tickets. He was halfway to Anna Belknap's house when he thought of the red tickets zipped into the pocket of the backpack he'd left lying on his bed. It was okay, he told himself. He was early, he had plenty of time. He reversed direction and headed home.

Lenny's truck was parked at the curb, so Randall parked a full block away. It was a mild spring dusk, the shadowy hour when people withdrew from the street, and houses began to fill with yellow light. Randall looked in on a boy twirling a basketball on a forefinger while watching *Hawaii Five-O*. He smelled grilling onions, heard somebody yelling, 'Edie, where's my Tabasco?'

There was a harshness to the sounds coming from Lenny's house that Randall became aware of reluctantly, as he would of a fire. A woman's voice, stretched so thin it kept breaking, was screaming at Lenny about his crazy little go-anywhere pecker. Lenny returned with something in a menacing cold voice too low to carry. The voices were coming from the basement. 'You know what?' the woman said, loud but no longer screaming, 'there isn't a single feature about you I don't hate.' In these lower tones, the woman's voice was distinguishable as Louise's.

Randall crept close to the bricked lightwell outside the basement window and, careful not to dirty his good clothes, got an angled view of the basement. He couldn't see anyone, but he could hear Lenny's soft crooning voice. The argument had entered a reconciliatory stage. 'I'm sorry, Kumquat,' Lenny said in a coaxing, sugar-coated voice. 'I mean it. I am.' Somewhere off to the side Louise was crying, a soft recuperative kind of crying.

Randall went to the garage, took off his sportcoat, laid the stepladder against the wall, and climbed to the cubbyhole he'd made for the Ruger. It was there, and the cartridges, too. He brought them down. He loaded the pistol. He entered the house through the side porch, the one door that didn't creak. He removed his shoes, moved slowly toward the basement stairs, through the dining room and into the living room, where he stopped short.

His mother, dressed in her old peach-colored robe, lay curled up on the sofa, her knees tucked up, her head clamped between her arms. She didn't move, even as Randall slowly passed through her field of vision. She stared ahead with fixed unblinking eyes, as dead as a live person could be.

At the head of the basement stairs, Randall stood and waited. Music was playing down there, Sarah Vaughan, and there were no other voices. He eased down the steps in his stocking feet. Lenny and Louise were dancing. He had his arms around her. She had her arms around him. She was wearing a yellow dress, but with one hand he'd lifted the skirt so that her black briefs were visible. That was where his hand was.

'Lenny,' Randall said in a low voice. A strange and pleasing calmness had overtaken him. For a long time, certainly since he'd come to Lenny's house, and probably since his father's death, Randall had been waiting to find someone worthy of the hatred he'd been nursing. Lenny, hearing his name, turned. An odd, confused grin crossed his face. Randall felt like someone about to receive a gift that, until that moment, he hadn't known he coveted. Your right is his left, he told himself. He aimed for Lenny's heart and meant gently to squeeze the trigger just like Lenny himself in target practice had taught him to do, but something – cowardice? pity? – made him pull too hard. The skin near Lenny's collarbone tore open to raw wet flesh. Lenny rocked back, his mouth a lopsided, elongated *O*. For a moment, before he clamped his hand to it, an artery squirted blood. It was a second or two before either Lenny or Louise seemed to understand what had happened. Then Lenny sat heavily down. 'No!' Louise shouted. She gathered herself around Lenny and, turning to Randall, bloody herself now, her yellow dress sopping up blood, shouted, 'No!' again. She began sobbing and cradling Lenny's head with bloody hands and covering his face with kisses.

For what seemed like a long time, Randall stared at this scene, trying to make sense of it. He'd shot Lenny, but he hadn't killed him, and he didn't feel like shooting again. Louise was screaming at him. He lifted the backpack from his bed. He went up the basement stairs. His mother was still lying there tucked into herself. 'There was an accident,' Randall heard himself say. 'Everyone's going to be okay, but you should call an ambulance. You shouldn't call the police. If anyone wants to call the police you should tell them it would be a terrible mistake.' The telephone sat on an end table beside the sofa. Randall dialed the number. He set the telephone into his mother's hand. He put on his shoes. He heard his mother say hello to someone and then give her name and address. Randall slid the Ruger into his backpack and slung his sportcoat over his shoulder. He tried to look normal as he walked down the street toward the Pontiac LeMans.

VI

WHEN RANDALL PULLED UP TO HER HOUSE, ANNA BELKNAP WAS SITTING ON A bench on the front porch, under a soft light, wearing a white strapless dress and sitting perfectly and beautifully still, like a full-sized figurine. In the darkness of the car, Randall found a rag under the seat and used it to daub at the sweat on his neck and face, but the sweat kept coming. He should drive off. In his bones, he knew that, just like he knew that he couldn't. He drew a long breath and reached for the box of flowers on the back seat of the car.

'Hello, Randall Hunsacker,' Anna Belknap said when he drew close.

'Hey,' he said in a low voice. He tried to smile but couldn't. He stuck out the box in her direction.

Anna gave out a pleased laugh when she opened the box to a dozen white roses. Before going off to put them in water, she turned to Randall at the door. 'Want to meet the pater?'

Randall didn't understand the question. He thought maybe she'd said *painter*, which made no sense. 'Why would I want to?' Randall said, quicker and sharper than he meant.

Anna shrugged and laughed. 'No reason,' she said and was off.

When Anna reappeared, Randall was standing by the LeMans, feeling like a wooden version of himself. He'd been trying to go over his plan, trying to sort through the little details, but they'd gone swimming off in every direction. He felt like he was going out alone on a stage to star in a play without knowing any of the lines. But when he gazed at her mutely, she was looking beyond him, at the car. She smoothed her hand over its waxed red finish and in a light voice sang, 'Chicks and ducks and geese better scurry.'

Randall opened the door for her, smelled her smell, kept himself from glancing down her white dress, and closed the door after her.

The engine jumped to life. He eased the car down the driveway in awkward silence. He touched a finger to his neck. It was even wetter than before. He imagined his collar was already brown with sweat. He said, 'I know that song.'

Anna, who'd been looking out the opposite window, turned. 'What song?'

'Chicks and ducks and geese,' he said and Anna gave him an encouraging laugh. 'My father used to sing it when we'd be going out on odd jobs.'

'Your dad did odd jobs?' Anna said.

'Yeah. He could do about anything. Concrete, carpeting, hot-mopping, rescreening –' Randall stopped. This was not what he meant to talk about.

'I guess you'd never get bored,' Anna said and resumed staring out her window. On a straight avenue, beyond earshot of the house, Randall to his own surprise accelerated sharply, burning rubber in second and third gears, the white bucket seat wrapping around him.

'Fast car,' Anna said when they'd come to a four-way stop, 'but I don't really like to drive fast.' She gave him a sweet look. 'Is that okay?'

Randall, retreating into himself, said that it was, but a strange sulkiness stole over him. He began to drive with exaggerated slowness.

Anna ignored the tactic. 'Where're we going to eat?' she asked.

'Le Caille.' It was the place rich kids went on prom night. Randall pronounced it correctly because he'd asked the man on the telephone to repeat it twice. 'I guess it's pretty good.'

The LeMans crept along the street. 'I was just thinking,' Anna said. 'I know a place in Cottonwood Canyon where they have these adorable little jukeboxes at each table and they serve the best steak sandwich I ever had.'

No part of Randall acceded to this idea. He was going to Le Caille, in the LeMans, with Anna Belknap. He said nothing and kept driving.

In a soft voice Anna said, 'Le Caille's awfully expensive.'

Before he could stop himself, Randall said, 'So?'

He was looking directly at her when he said it. She paled and turned, and he knew he should say something to smooth things over but he couldn't make the sullenness he was feeling recede.

'Look in the glove compartment,' he said.

Anna unlatched the glovebox. The door, like a square jaw, opened to reveal a small gift-wrapped box. Anna held it without unwrapping it.

'Open it,' Randall said. The LeMans crept up the I-15 onramp.

'What is it?'

'Open it.'

She did, and stared at the contents without removing it. It was a wristwatch, its face surrounded by a band of silver inset with turquoise.

'I'd noticed you liked turquoise stuff,' Randall said, 'and I saw you didn't have a wristwatch.'

'Randall, it's pretty, but –'

'Aren't you going to try it on?' Randall said, pulling slowly in front of a line of fast-moving traffic. Cars honked, swerved, and streamed around them.

Anna Belknap set the box on the dashboard. 'Look, Randall, I hope you don't think I asked you to this dance so you'd buy me stuff.'

Randall – he couldn't help himself – said, 'Why *did* you ask me to take you to this dance?'

Anna's creamy white skin took on a sudden rosy tint. 'I don't know,' she said. 'I guess I just thought it would be fun.'

Randall considered it. 'No, that's not why,' he said. He let his speed drop a bit. A horn screamed at them as two cars swung wide and shot past. 'I think you at least owe it to me to tell me why.'

Anna stared at him. 'Okay. Your sister called me up. She asked me to meet her at Snelgrove's. We ate ice cream and she showed me some of the notes you'd written me – so I could see what you were really like, she said.' A soft chuckle broke free. 'They were very funny,' Anna said. She glanced over at Randall. 'And endearing,' she said hurriedly. 'They were endearing, too.'

Anna's words came at Randall like a series of sucker punches. It took him a moment to get his breath and in that moment his sullenness hardened to anger.

'And for a while there,' Anna Belknap was saying, 'Jason and I were going through this awful phase and I just thought . . .' Her voice tailed off.

'You should try on the wristwatch,' Randall said in a stony lifeless voice. 'You should put it on.'

He could feel Anna Belknap's eyes on him.

Another car shrieked at them as it flew past.

'Everybody wants me to speed up,' Randall said in the same stony voice. He applied the first steady pressure to the gas pedal.

The speedometer climbed. Sixty, sixty-five, seventy. The engine hummed. This was what this car had been waiting for, Randall could feel it. This was why you called it a muscle car.

'Randall?' Anna Belknap said in her clear strong voice. 'Please don't let's ruin things.'

Eighty, eighty-five, ninety.

Suddenly he sliced the LeMans through three lanes of traffic and shot unbraking down a long offramp at the base of which stood a traffic signal.

'Randall!'

His eyes fixed impassively on the signal in front of him. It was red.

'Okay! I'm putting it on!' Anna said.

Randall's foot lifted from the accelerator and shifted to the brake. The Pontiac's wheels locked, keened left, skidded down the last 200 feet of offramp and, nosing a few feet into the intersection, came to a stop. Crossing drivers glared at Randall as they guided their cars around the LeMans. Anna Belknap, tightlipped, strapped on the watch.

'Do you like it?' Randall said, his voice once again his own.

'I guess,' she said without looking at it.

At the head of the winding drive to Le Caille, they were greeted by two college boys in flouncy shirts and black breeches. One opened Anna's door and the other opened his. Randall was circling the front of the LeMans when one of the boys said, 'We'll need you to leave your keys, sir.' Nearby, a well-dressed man, departing with his wife, was peeling off bills to give to one of the valets, and Randall, in his confusion, did the same, offering the attendant two one-dollar bills along with his keys, all of which the boy gladly took in hand.

The restaurant itself was expensively dark and warm, fragrant with cooked meats, alive with the tinkling of plateware and general goodwill. In the anteroom, stuffed rabbits hung from bound rear feet and deer heads protruded from the walls. The hostess led Anna and Randall through two rooms full of well-dressed diners to a far corner of one of the restaurant's larger rooms. It was a dizzying walk; with giddy pride Randall noted the way all eyes, and especially those of the men, were drawn toward Anna in her strapless white dress. Once he and Anna were seated in their cushioned wing chairs, water with lemon was immediately set before Randall, along with bread, though he'd ordered neither. He stared at the menu, trying to find chicken cordon bleu, but it wasn't there.

When he looked up, Anna Belknap was staring fixedly at him. 'So what happened back there, Randall?'

'You mean with those car-parking guys? I wasn't sure when –'

'No, I mean on the interstate. When you were driving . . . the way you were driving.'

He folded his menu and thought about it. 'Something weird went on just before I came to get you. That got me real tense and then, I don't know, I'd just thought out this date so much . . .'

In a calm voice Anna asked what had happened before he came to get her.

Randall took a gulp of his lemon water and looked around. 'This place reminds me of an eighteenth-century château,' he said, which was what the man taking reservations had said when Randall asked what the place looked like.

A waitress in a cotton peasant smock bunched around deep cleavage appeared. Anna ordered something that sounded like cocoa-vin with asparagus and Randall said, 'That sounds good. I'll have the same.'

After the waitress withdrew, Anna either closed her eyes or lowered them, Randall wasn't sure which, but without opening or raising them she said, 'You still haven't told me what happened before you picked me up.'

Randall stared at Anna Belknap's still, perfect face, then, disjointedly, in fits and starts, he told the story. Anna only looked up when he was done. 'You shot your stepfather for dancing with your sister?'

'They weren't just dancing. He had his hand somewhere.'

Anna was staring at the heavy wristwatch on her slender wrist. 'Is it possible that you killed him?'

For the first time that evening, Randall let out a short, snorting laugh. 'Not unless his heart's up near his shoulder blade.'

'But you shot him and he was bleeding?'

Randall nodded.

Anna sat back in her wing chair while a serving boy took away their salads, then she sat forward again. 'Do you realize that sometime tonight you're probably going to be picked up by the police?'

'Only if they call the police right away. Which I don't think they will.'

'Why not?'

Randall shrugged. 'Because it's my mother and my sister. And it would be messy for my stepdad.'

'But they called an ambulance, right? And if there's a doctor involved, I think they have to call the police.'

Randall, trying to act unconcerned, said he didn't know anything about that.

Anna sipped her lemon water. She seemed to be choosing her words. 'So where is the gun now?'

'In the LeMans,' Randall said. 'In the trunk.'

Entrées were served. Randall watched as Anna began to eat. For the moment neither of them talked. But Randall *had* been talking. He'd been able to say what he was thinking and from her interested expression he must've been saying interesting things. So maybe things were back on track. He reminded himself to order coffee if they ordered dessert. To tell the supernormalist joke. To ask about her cheerleading and school stuff.

'So what's it like being in all those brainy-type classes?' he said, but the question was lost. As he'd spoken, something had happened.

Anna, mid-bite, had cocked her head and made a quizzical look. 'Uh-oh,' she said and put down her fork. 'I think it's my period.' She spoke in a low voice. 'I think it's started, and I'm not really prepared.'

Randall, confused, asked what he could do.

'Nothing,' Anna said. 'I'm just going to go to the restroom. It'll be a few minutes so maybe you could get the waitress to put my dinner someplace where it'll stay warm.' She smiled at Randall. It was the same smile he remembered that first time she'd turned toward him in study hall.

The waitress took away both of their plates for warming. Randall drained his water, nibbled at his buttered bread and gazed uneasily around the room. From time to time he glanced back at the doorway through which Anna would again appear. Fifteen minutes passed, then twenty. Other diners began to steal looks at Randall, he could feel it. He sweated, a deep, suffusing, unstoppable sweat. When he pushed back from the table, his wing chair made a terrible screeching sound. He moved through the suddenly stilled room as if in a dream. Near the reservation board, the hostess stood under the animal heads. She spoke to him, but the words swam in Randall's mind. She put something into his hand. It was the turquoise-studded wristwatch, wrapped in a napkin, on which a note had been written. *Jason took me home*, it said. *I'm sorry for what we put ourselves through. Take care. Anna*

RANDALL DROVE SLOWLY AWAY FROM THE RESTAURANT. HE DROVE SLOWLY toward the high school, drove a slow circle around the campus, looking for Jason Wilson's Mustang, looking for Anna Belknap's long white dress. He drove by the auto shop, actually stopped for a moment, but then kept driving. Wendover came to mind. He had gas money, he had motel money. He could drive west across the salt flats to Wendover. It would be something to tell people, a story that would work its way back to Anna Belknap.

But the idea receded without Randall's even knowing it. All he knew was that he was suddenly driving east, toward the canyons, driving by feel. He'd never once been back to the old house, so it was a surprise when suddenly he came upon it. The windows were all broken. In the driveway a pile of wood and furniture, gathered for burning, had only blackened. A large sign posted in front of the property began, BY ORDER OF WASATCH COUNTY HEALTH DEPT. The front porch had never been rebuilt.

Randall's eyes rose to the canyon road. He began to drive it, taking the switchbacks in second and sometimes first gear. At the top, Randall turned the LeMans around and eased it onto a dirt area widened for parking. He got out, opened the hood, slipped the hoses from the brake reservoir. He took the beer and his backpack from the trunk, seated himself on the front fender, stared down the canyon through the newly leafing trees.

So this was where he was. He'd come back to the beginning and was like a stranger to his own memories. He was cut off. He'd gone nutso and shot Lenny. He'd royally screwed up whatever little chance he'd ever had with Anna Belknap. And now he was sitting on the hood of a stolen car with no brakes parked at the top of a steep canyon road.

The beer was warm and without taste, yet Randall had an urgent thirst for it. When he'd finished the fifth can, he lined it up on the ground with the others. He took the Ruger from his backpack, swung out the cylinder and pushed free the cartridges, including the spent one. He dropped one into each of the five cans. He looked at the last cartridge in his hand and, without much thought, put it into his mouth, let it slide to the back of the throat, and washed it down in a current of warm beer.

Randall got back into the car. He touched his foot to the brake pedal. It fell to the floorboard without resistance. He rolled up the windows. It was as if water were rising within him, filling all the empty spaces, sealing him off from sounds. He slid the white gearshift knob to neutral. He released the emergency brake. The car began to move. The silence of the movement both thrilled and calmed him – he knew in his bones he would survive this new form of travel.

VII

RANDALL HAD GOTTEN THE SUPERNORMALIST JOKE FROM HIS FATHER, AND HIS father had gotten it from a couple named Carlton and May.

When Randall's father was a seven-year-old boy living in Moline, Illinois, he'd stood in his front yard and watched men laying a wide span of the Lincoln Highway, which, according to a worker who stopped to drink from the metal cup that hung from the garden pump, would reach from one ocean to the other. Randall's father imagined the roadway sliding up wet from the Atlantic and then, a long time later, lowering itself dry and thirsty into the Pacific. Randall's father didn't mention this to his parents. They were dry, firm, fatalistic people who'd already decided theirs was not just a deficient boy but a lazy one. When Highway 46 was completed, Randall's father used it to run away from home. He was fifteen, but people believed him when he said he was seventeen and on his way west to live with an uncle who had work. He met hobos and tattooed truck drivers and three men from Cuba. And he rode one long stretch with a middle-aged couple named Carlton and May, who owned a red Cadillac with cream-colored seats. Carlton and May were the chipperest married couple Randall's father had ever seen. As they drove, they sang songs and played road games and told jokes. May owned a single-reflex Brownie Kodak and took pictures of everything. They called Randall's father Crackerjack and then just Jack. They let him sleep in the car at night, and use their motel toilet and tub in the morning, and they always waited for him before going to breakfast. For those few days, Randall's father slept harder and woke happier than he ever remembered. Of the several photographs May gave him, Randall's father saved just one. In it they all sit on the low-slung fender of the red Cadillac, parked in front of an Esso filling station. A green fedora half-shades Carlton's hearty, florid face. May has chosen for this occasion a butter-colored sundress with spaghetti straps, and she smiles friskily. Randall's father, wearing a white dress shirt Carlton and May had bought for him that day, is a round boy with a sure smile, a smaller, happier version of the man he was to become.

'Climb up front, Jack, between May and me, so you can hear this one,' Carlton had said over his shoulder one summery day as they drove the Lincoln Highway with the windows down. 'It's about a supernormalist and if you don't know what that is you'll soon find out.'

The joke was this. A supernormalist and his friend were walking in the woods one night. There was a slim moon. They carried a flashlight. The

supernormalist said there was no physical act the human mind couldn't accomplish if properly concentrated. The friend pointed his flashlight up and asked the supernormalist if he could slide up the lightbeam and touch the tip of the moon. 'Yes!' the supernormalist said. 'Yes I could!' The friend said, 'If you can, then you will.' The supernormalist gave this real thought. 'I'd like to,' he said finally, 'but I can't.' The friend asked why. 'Because,' the supernormalist said, 'if I got halfway up and you turned off the light, then where would I be?'

Carlton told Randall's father this joke as they rode along in the red Cadillac, and later, with strange pleasure, Randall's father related the joke to Randall, and, later still, Randall would tell his own children the joke, a poor joke, a forlorn joke, but it would travel that far.

Chapter Two

SEVERANCE

MR STEINER DIDN'T VISIT RANDALL IN THE HOSPITAL OR, LATER, IN JUVENILE *hall. Neither, of course, did Anna Belknap. Neither did Randall's mother. 'Lenny the asshole won't let her,' said Louise, whose visits were stiffness wrapped in rough jocularity. Louise never mentioned the shooting to Randall, but her feelings seemed to have shifted because of it. Like the court-appointed psychologist, like Randall's football coach, like the man from the district attorney's office, Louise kept a certain distance from Randall's bed. It was as if he were separated from the world by a clean sheet of glass.*

'Guess I don't look like a million,' Randall said and Louise said, 'How much less than a million does shit look like?'

Randall's body was a tender mass of bruise and abrasion and internal contusion. He'd cracked some ribs. He'd also lost the small and ring fingers of his right hand. The doctor described this disjunction as a rough severance and after that the words managed only a fitful connection to meaning. Fourth and fifth terminal digits. Crush injury. Granulation tissue. Undermined, folded over, stitched up. 'In layman's terms,' Randall heard the doctor say, 'the wound will clot and scab and turn into a gorgeous conversation piece.' Randall asked where his fingers were now. 'They looked for the digits at the site,' the doctor said, 'but they couldn't find them.'

Randall didn't mind going to juvenile hall. He wanted to take his punishment, then go back to school, go back to playing football, go back to feeling normal. When he mentioned these ideas to Louise or to his counselor, they would fall silent. Only his football coach offered any encouragement. 'Let's put it this way,' he said. 'Your status in society has changed some. Who knows, though? – keep your nose clean and anything can happen.'

For a time, the regular visits by his football coach afforded Randall a certain status at juvenile hall, and reinforced the feeling that he was different from the other detainees, who impressed him as losers. Randall kept to himself. He read the books his coach brought for him – The Vince Lombardi Story, The Paul Hornung Story, people he'd never heard of – and worked out long hours in the weight room, feeling his diffidence grow hard and muscular. It didn't matter that Louise's visits diminished. It didn't matter that his coach came less often. Oxygen pumped into Randall's bloodstream, his muscles hardened, and the days went by.

One Saturday, just at the close of visiting hours, Louise came and told him she was leaving. Leaving where? Randall asked.

A little silence followed. She hasn't forgiven me, and now she never will. That thought formed purely in Randall's mind.

'Morgantown, West Virginia,' Louise said finally in a faraway voice, as if she were already gone. 'You could write me care of General Delivery if you wanted.' She began jingling her keys, but suddenly muffled them within her fist. 'I never told you this, but Anna Belknap called me a little while after the accident,' she said.

When he'd lived in the canyon, there had been several neighbor boys who raised pigeons, racers mostly, but one boy raised pouter pigeons, with grotesquely distensible crops that they could inflate to what looked like burst point. That was the way Randall's heart felt now. He said, 'So?'

Louise deliberated a second or two. 'She said she was glad you were okay.' Louise opened her hand and stared at her keys. 'She also made me promise I'd never tell you even that much.' Louise's gaze rose to Randall's. The slightest smile formed on her lips. 'She thinks you're mad as a hatter,' she said.

A few days later Randall's football coach appeared. It wasn't visiting hour, but the counselor made what he kept telling Randall were special arrangements. ('Well then I especially thank you,' Randall finally said.) When Randall entered the dim deserted visiting room, his coach was sitting stiff-backed on one of the long benches. 'Smells in here,' he said when Randall was seated. The coach looked around. 'It's like when the people leave all that's left is the smells of their shoes.'

Randall knew not to say anything. He knew the coach was just collecting himself to speak, and in a moment the coach was speaking. 'Here's the deal,' he said. 'I have a college buddy who coaches high school football in Nebraska. A little town, but pretty, with great pheasant hunting. It's eight-man football, ideal for you, with your size and speed. My buddy's name is DeSarcina but out there everybody calls him Coach Dee. He's a good guy. I sent him a video of your work on special teams, including a couple of those lights-out tackles and the one blocked punt, and he liked what he saw. Bottom line is this. He'll assume custody of you. You'd live with his aunt, who's a widow, and he's got you lined up with a part-time job at a garage.'

Nebraska. West Virginia. Parts were flying off every which way. Randall said, 'Maybe I'll just move in with my mother when I get out.'

His coach tipped back in his chair and gave Randall a look. 'Your mother's gone, Champ. Your sister took off with your mother's boyfriend, and your mother went after them.' He gave this a moment to sink in, then sat forward again. 'If you go to Nebraska, the court will seal your records, meaning that if you don't get into trouble for the next five years, they'll cease to exist. Nobody will know anything about the shooting – not employers, not colleges, not the military, nobody. And most people will think of the car deal as just a joy-riding thing gone wrong. And besides you've paid your debt on that.'

Randall said nothing. He was trying to take the scattered pieces and reassemble them into something he could identify.

'Listen,' his coach said. 'I've personally been to the superintendent here and I've personally been to see the two most receptive members of the school board and there is flat no way in hell you'll play high school football here ever again.' He sat back and made a resigned palms-up gesture. 'Otherwise, I wouldn't be suggesting –'

Randall wasn't sure what the coach said after that. Randall had stopped listening.

Chapter Three

THE NEW BOY

I

JULY, NEBRASKA, SATURDAY AFTERNOON. MCKIBBEN'S MOBIL STATION WAS prudently situated at the intersection of Highway 20 and Main Street, which was Goodnight's single avenue of general commerce. Working within the shade and dieselly smells of the repair bay, Jim McKibben, the station's proprietor, unhurriedly shifted an inner tube through a tub of water, in search of a slow leak. Inside the Mini-Mart (a recent addition, constructed soon after Osborne's Market, located around the corner, and lacking highway exposure, had gone bust), McKibben's daughter, Gerrie, sat knee-up and head-down near the register, doing her toenails a new color called Plumsuch and listening to Casey Kasem counting them down. It was hot. Flies buzzed. Gerrie wore sandals, denim cut-offs and a black, Pogues World Tour T-shirt, beneath which a black Miracle bra, purchased by mail from Victoria's Secret, was making her breasts sweat. Down Main Street, within the cool gloom of the Eleventh Man Bar and Grill, Leo Underwood nursed along the afternoon drinkers and by means of a wall-mounted television kept an eye on the British Open (he was betting on Greg Norman). At the brighter stations – Sisters Cafe, Another Man's Treasures, Householder's Western Wear – patrons were making frugal purchases (or often, on second thought, none at all) while taking guarded positions on whatever topics were stirring (the wheeler-dealers down in the Unicameral, for example, or the current heat wave, or Tom Osborne's batch of new recruits). Inside the tiny community room of the Sleepy Hollow Trailer Court, several older women sat piecing together a jigsaw puzzle of a Carl Larsson housescape (category: very difficult) while exchanging whatever gossip they'd gleaned since the prior Saturday. (This week, like most weeks, it was considerable. Flossie Boyles had heard from Letty Hobbs, who'd heard from Edie Halston, who was related, that one of the Hemingford Furmans would be appearing buck naked in next month's *Playboy*, which, unusual for information of this type, was substantively true, though the appearance of the Furman girl in that magazine was several months away and her degree of nakedness would be more semi than buck.) In the cool dim parlor of her specimen Greek Revival home, featured eleven years earlier in *Nebraskaland* magazine, the widow Lucy Witt played a slow careful game of two-deck solitaire. And down on the flats twelve miles southeast of town, on a farm bounded by the Niobrara River and, beyond that, the sandhills, Lewis Lockhardt, forty-eight years old, wearing knee-high waders and using rubber siphon tubes, set water spilling from wide ditch to narrow furrows, taking at each stop an apprehensive half-moment to watch the water sliding easily between his long and less-than-robust rows of edible beans. While back at the house, his wife, Dorothy, thirty-five years old ('Thirteen full years Lewis's junior,' Flossie Boyles had noted more than once), sat at her quilting frame, positioned near an open window in hopes of a breeze, and sent her needle swimming through a turquoise cotton she'd purchased because its color suggested to her the Aegean Sea, as seen in pictures.

RANDALL'S BUE MOVED NORTH TOWARD GOODNIGHT, THROUGH A ROLLING patchwork of farms and pastures in greens, yellows and browns. Heat vapors rose from the two-lane highway. The drone of the bus was dull and monotonous. When the bus jogged through Alliance, the driver, a friendly, short-necked woman, turned to the third seat right, where Randall drowsed in the nearly empty bus. 'Goodnight's next,' she said. 'About thirty miles up ahead.'

Without quite meaning to, Randall began noting landmarks. A building that said, JACK'S BEANS. Another that said, MIRAGE FLATS IRRIGATION DISTRICT. Then, a little further north, a white clapboard one-room schoolhouse, then a tidy row of blue silos, then, on a knoll to the left, a cluster of antennas rising high above the small squat cinderblock broadcasting studio of KDUH-TV (*Serving the Black Hills to the Sandhills*, the sign said). There were other scattered signs. HEREFORDS – MORE CALVES, MORE POUNDS, MORE PROFITS. THE WAGES OF SIN IS HELL. GOODNIGHT, POP. 1,680 HOME OF THE FRIENDLY FESTIVAL JULY 2-3-4 (which was ten days past). Randall gazed beyond a rocky ball field toward a hedged plot of single-wide trailer-homes, with a weatherworn sign at the entrance that said SLEEPY HOLLOW TRAILER COURT and featured a spreading shade tree silhouetted against a yawning cartoon moon.

When the bus eased to a stop, Randall stood, shouldered his bags and, for the benefit of the half-dozen or so other travelers, nipped snug the half-glove that sheathed the missing part of his right hand, a neat trick he'd practiced to perfection. Then he banged his way down the aisle. 'Happy landings,' the driver said as he passed by her, but Randall was too fixed on his exit to reply. The bus doors hissed and accordioned open. Randall stepped out into the starkness and heat. From somewhere beyond his sight there came the raucous chatter of an air wrench on lug nuts.

Randall squinted at the gas station in front of him and began at once to read the signs. McKIBBEN'S MOBIL. TIRES, TUNE-UPS, PACKAGED LIQUOR. The sound of the air wrench suddenly stopped and from within the repair bay a bear-sized middle-aged man emerged and began striding Randall's way, his big body zipped into gray, oil-stained coveralls. The man, Randall noted, was fast for his weight class. He was covering ground.

Another hiss and, as Randall turned, the bus began to roll away. He started to raise a hand, but immediately saw the uselessness of it.

Gravel crunched close behind him, and Randall, pivoting again, was face to face with the man in the coveralls. 'You Randall Hunsacker?' the man asked.

Randall nodded.

The man extended his hand; Randall did the same, then waited for the man's face to register response to the half-hand he was shaking. It didn't. His healthy reddish face held steady. 'Well, I'm Jim McKibben and this is Goodnight, Nebraska.' His smile expanded to a grin. 'If you didn't expect much you won't be disappointed.'

Randall's eyes shifted from McKibben's brimming face. Within the Mobil station, someone – a girl – stood at the door staring out. Randall moved his eyes to the next storefront, a gray cinderblock building with a sign that said GOOCHS BEST FEEDS.

Randall said, 'No, I'm glad to be here.' Which was in the narrowest sense true. He'd finally reached the tiny black map-dot that for the past month he'd been pointed toward. Until he got here, he reasoned, he couldn't go someplace else.

Beyond introductions, little was said. Randall stood in the harsh sun with his bags hanging from his shoulders. When asked if he'd like to start work that afternoon, he said he would, sure. When asked if he wanted a ride up to Lucy Witt's, he said no, he'd been sitting too long as it was.

He began to walk. The downtown was only one long block, with a street wide enough for considerable traffic, but there wasn't any traffic. One car passed slowly, then, after a time, another. An older woman stepped out of the post office. An older man, sweeping the walk in front of his shop, glanced for the smallest fraction of a moment at Randall before disappearing inside. Randall kept walking. FRMKA'S SUPRETTE, FEATURING SHUR FINE FOODS. DRABBELS COAST-TO-COAST – KELVINATOR & MOTOROLA. THE ELEVENTH MAN BAR & GRILL. LLOYDS – THE FRIENDLY PHARMACY. CHAMBERLAIN MORTUARY. SISTERS CAFE – FAIR PRICES, GENEROUS PORTIONS – SUMMER HOURS MON. THRU SAT. 6-6.

Randall, sweating, turned right on Ash Street. He trudged past a mix of small homes, some with businesses attached (DR JOS. PARMALEE, DVM, NO PEER LOCK & KEY, WALKINSHAW'S BARBER SHOP); past a stretch of snug-seeming homes, the yards fenced and neatly tended; past three or four homes of real size until, finally, the address on the gable above a front porch matched the address in Randall's hand.

THE WIDOW LUCY WITT STOOD BACK FROM HER TRIPLE ROW OF CASEMENT windows, gazed out at the boy who stood poised at her yardgate, and wondered what in the world she'd gotten herself in for. Lucy Witt had grown up with six brothers and sisters, all of whom had married, just as she had (though none quite so well) and all of

whom had procreated, as she had not, so that over the years her
large home had provided refuge to a number of unmoored relatives
– a niece whose Air Force husband was stationed in Iceland, a sister
fleeing a rocky marriage, even a whole family whose money had run
out – and hers had occasionally been the winter home for a farmgirl
going to town school, but in all her years Lucy Witt had never had a
boy to board, and a wayward boy at that.

Though, she saw now with alarm, he didn't look so much like a
boy. His sturdy build and grim manner made him look more like
an actual man!

Beware the hired man. Her husband Dick had said that. Lucy had
thought he was being overly cautious, as was his nature (he'd been
a banker), but as the years passed the evidence had grown. There
was the hired man south of Alliance who, when kept from dating the
rancher's daughter, killed the entire family. There was the hired man
in Hyannis who turned on a family of four and killed them all with a
pitchfork (from the *World-Herald* she still remembered the phrase
'bloody and horrific perforation'). And there was of course Bobbie
Tidball over in Crawford, a widow like herself, who had befriended
and hired the man who subsequently came one night into her room
and strangled her with one of her husband's old neckties. Though
Bobbie Tidball was not yet fifty at the time, whereas Lucy Witt was
now seventy-four and so, she reasoned, had a lot less to lose, and,
besides, a necktie was certainly no worse than cancer or heart disease
or whatever other malady awaited you. The widow Lucy Witt swung
the door open wide and smiled as genially as could be.

'You must be Randall,' she said.

Randall nodded and was relieved she didn't mean to shake
his hand.

'Jim McKibben called and said you were on your way up. I'm
Lucy Witt. Hot out, isn't it?'

The house, when Randall stepped into it, felt cool and dim and
smelled to him like old letters, or at least like the little trunk his
mother used to keep old letters in. 'This is the vestibule, this is
the parlor,' Lucy Witt was saying to Randall, who for the moment
wasn't sure which was which. Everywhere the walls were lined
with expensive-looking panelling and furniture. A thick floral carpet

flowed down the center of the staircase. It reminded Randall of the funeral home his father had been laid out in, though he didn't say so. He merely followed behind as this soft, funny-smelling old woman showed him his room and his separate entrance and his separate bathroom, then led him back to the kitchen for lemonade and a roast beef sandwich. When he was nearly done with it, Lucy Witt said, 'So I understand you stole a car.'

Randall had both hands around his sandwich but his shoulders seemed suddenly to hunch. He put down the sandwich, wiped his mouth and formally, as if in a court of law, said, 'Yes, that's right.'

'And then you wrecked the car.'

'Yes.'

'And for you,' she said, nodding at his sheathed and diminished hand, 'was that the extent of the damage?'

Randall was again about to say yes when she preempted him. 'No,' she said, 'we'll assume for the time being that the answer to that is no.'

Randall waited for the next question, and when none came, he said he guessed he'd better head back to McKibben's and get to work. He got as far as the dining room when he stopped short and let his eyes climb the ornamental columns, capitals and volutes to a circular opening, on which rested a rounded, stain-glassed vault. Lucy Witt, regarding him from the kitchen doorway, nearly said, 'Cupola,' but didn't. She merely watched. Leaning far back on his heels, staring up actually open-mouthed, Randall in his transfixion lost his balance, and took a halting step backward, as – to Lucy Witt's eyes – a child might, and all at once her reserve against this boy entirely collapsed.

Prior to Randall's arrival, Lucy Witt had decided she would do no cooking for him. She would let the boy stay. She would make him cordially welcome. She would charge him only enough that he didn't feel like the recipient of charity (gratitude, she believed, generally grew into resentment). But she was too old to take up regular cooking again. That was what she'd decided and that was what she'd told her nephew, the football coach. But now, as Randall pulled open the front door to leave, Lucy Witt said, 'Oh! We'll have supper at 5.30 sharp, Monday through Friday. What kind of things do you like to eat?'

Randall turned as if in surprise. His eyes, wary to that point, possibly even crafty, dilated and softened.

'Beef stroganoff?' she said. 'Breaded veal cutlets? Spaghetti and meatballs? Chicken pot pie?'

II

THE DAY PASSED, THEN A WEEK, AND AT LAST RANDALL HAD MADE IT THROUGH July to August. He told himself to keep his nose clean and his eyes straight ahead. School had not begun, but football practice had. Randall enjoyed it, and played from within an obstinate sullenness that intimidated his teammates, whose names he never spoke. In late August he began school. He went to every class. Evenings and weekends, at McKibben's, he worked carefully and quietly. 'He don't give a lot of speeches but he knows how to work,' he overheard Jim McKibben saying. At the funeral parlor, as he'd begun privately to label Lucy Witt's place, he thanked the widow for whatever meals she prepared for him, and often she prepared his favorites – meat loaf, beef stew, ham and scalloped potatoes – though as good as these dishes may have been, nothing tasted to Randall as it might've. One night, when Coach Dee dropped by the filling station with some papers for Randall to sign (they made formal Randall's status as a first-term junior, thereby allowing him to play varsity football at Goodnight for two years rather than one) and was evidently stumped for small talk, he'd asked Randall what the widow had gotten him up that evening for supper, and Randall without thinking had said, 'Food.' Which Coach Dee, a wiry bantamweight whose tendency to strut was suppressed by his won-lost record (twenty-five and thirty-eight over seven years) and whose continued employment with District 3 had, in truth, less to do with his coaching ability than with his credentialed qualifications to teach algebra and chemistry, pretended to take for a joke. This, like so many other things about this town, unwarrantably annoyed Randall. It annoyed him, for example, that Lucy Witt routinely trounced him in double solitaire (the fact that they played only for nickels notwithstanding). It annoyed him when people said, 'You must be the new boy' and he had to give over his miniaturized, half-sheathed hand for shaking. It annoyed him that all anybody could talk about was Cornhusker football, as if BYU didn't even exist (he'd forgotten how little he'd cared for the Cougars while living in Salt Lake). At football practice, he somehow began to view his teammates as the enemy, and Coach Dee warned him increasingly about over-aggressive hits. 'Save 'em for Rushville,' he'd bark, or 'Save it for Hemingford,' and Randall while nodding somberly would take a secret luxurious pleasure in the anger he'd caused in Coach Dee and the revulsive fear he aroused in his teammates. And one midnight, after losing four straight games of double solitaire to Lucy Witt earlier in the evening, Randall lay in bed in the dark and took a slow, exact inventory of all the easily transported valuables that lay unprotected within the widow's fancy house.

All of it, all that he peevishly thought and all that he peevishly did, was an index of Randall's resistance to absorption into this small strange community. When a customer entered McKibben's Mini-Mart just as another departed, Jim McKibben, quoting the high school librarian, who had herself been quoting some book or other, liked jokingly to say, 'The door of egress is the door of ingress,' and then, if Randall were around, McKibben would give him a wink broad with knowingness, which of course annoyed Randall, though not quite as much as the fact that, presented with these words and this wink, Randall would grin like some bumpkin himself. The widow owned a dictionary, which, when closed, stood seven inches thick. One night, when he was thinking of it, Randall looked the words up and, two days later, in the midst of squeegeeing somebody's windshield, it occurred to him that in some ways someone as self-pleased as McKibben could use this ingress-egress funny stuff to shed a light on Randall's life. As he had exited one room (translate *life*), he was entering another. Except, Randall thought (he almost had to laugh), he hadn't and he wasn't. He hadn't fucking exited one life and he hadn't fucking started another one, and never would, not anyhow in a town as fucking pitiful as this one.

He wrote letters to his sister in care of General Delivery, Morgantown, West Virginia, short, dashed-off, slipshod letters on lined yellow paper, oozing with disapproval of Goodnight. *Greetings from Hicksburg*, he'd begin or *Greetings from ShitdeVille. Ain't we jist having us a wicked hot spell!* he wrote. *But seriously*, he wrote, *you should see the liquids they pour into a cup here and call coffee.*

Well weasel gotta scoot! he wrote. *Homework to do and maybe before final nod-off toodle my flute. Come visit why don't you? The Ladies Home Extension will demonstrate how to snap you a big bowl of beans.*

Though Randall had written twice to Louise, it was not until late August that he received his first in return. She wrote that she'd arrived what seemed liked weeks ago in West Virginia, but had only that day thought to check General Delivery. *Everything — hold onto your hat — is all fucked up,* she wrote. *I'm looking for work. Lenny's looking for me. Mom's looking for Lenny. The rich component is that if mom would go running off instead of chasing behind, Lenny would turn around and chase after* her *and I who am as sick as them would go running after* him. *Somebody should advise Mom but it won't be me. P.S. — just read above and see that solution-wise you weren't too far wrong in trying to shoot one of us.*

Not too far wrong.

Randall eased into this sentiment as if it were water from a hot spring. In her half-joking, who-the-hell-cares-now-anyhow kind of way, Louise was presenting Randall with forgiveness, a fact that suffused him first with gratitude, deep, warm, down-in-the-bone gratitude, and then — a surprise — with a sudden aching tenderness for his poor pitiful sister, as much lost, he guessed, in her foreign town as he was in his.

III

SEPTEMBER. SCHOOL HAD BEEN IN SESSION SINCE LATE AUGUST. RANDALL Hunsacker's cultivated disconnection from his teammates, other students, and the town as a whole afforded great blank spaces for others to fill in with their imaginations. Randall-rumors flew. In Utah, where Randall used to live, he'd been put in a juvenile hall for stealing and wrecking three cars, every one a red Pontiac LeMans. In Utah, Randall's stepfather had gotten Randall's mother and sister both pregnant. In Utah, Randall had gotten twin sisters (though not his own) pregnant. In Utah, after his accident and before passing out, Randall had put his two severed fingers in his mouth so they wouldn't get lost, but then had swallowed them.

Marcy Marlene Lockhardt listened to the rumors and laughed and sneaked looks at Randall in the cafeteria. Marcy was one of those winsome homegrown girls toward whom classmates always gravitate and in whom the older, more entrenched townsfolk always take pride – she was bright, open-faced, quick to smile, grin and laugh, with fair smooth skin that would with persistence freckle and darken in summer, and with straight dark hair that she could, according to mood, wear straight, braided or bunned, and with wide adventurous liquid-brown eyes that seemed ready to peer anywhere, and at last and of course, with a long-legged, full-breasted, perfect-seeming figure (which, other than girls in gym class, no one had actually seen in entirety, though her boyfriend, Bobby Parmalee, had seen some important parts of it). Marcy Marlene Lockhardt, even more than the Furman girl from Hemingford who'd gone to Wisconsin to study art and somehow got hooked up with a *Playboy* recruiter, was the premier regional candidate for innocent prurience, prized even more because, of the list of things a local couldn't imagine Marcy Marlene Lockhardt doing, removing her clothes to be photographed by a stranger for public consumption (and, very probably, tawdry private use) was toward the absolute top. Marcy Lockhardt was *nice*, and she went with Bobby Parmalee, a nice boy. They'd been sophomore royalty at last year's homecoming and they would be, it was certain, junior royalty this year. It was September, Marcy's arms and face were the freckled rosy brown of ripe apricots, and she'd just been made head cheerleader (As a *junior!* she kept telling herself). She was happy, and she was nice, and you could read those facts from the bounce in her step and the generous way she spent her smiles on one and all, high and low, skinny and fat. She seemed in fact so happy and so nice that no one gave much thought to the probability that she, like nearly everyone else in her age group, carried within her a small hothouse chamber where ideas she didn't yet know to think of as devious incubated in rich and splendid abundance. It was, in other words, more than mere instinct that warned Marcy Marlene Lockhardt against asking girlfriends about the new boy, against bringing up his name anywhere, against letting anyone know what she was as yet reluctant to admit to herself – that Randall Hunsacker aroused her interest.

IV

THE FIRST SUNDAY IN OCTOBER, THE WIDOW LUCY WITT ARRANGED FOR
Randall to take her out for a drive in her black, late-model Buick
Electra with protective plastic seat covers, full power, and, not
surprisingly, less than 3,000 miles on the odometer. (Once or twice
a week Lucy Witt would drive the Electra the few blocks it was to
Frmka's Suprette or even occasionally as far as Chadron, twenty-two
miles west, but far more generally the Electra stayed parked in its
ancient garage.)

'Where to?' Randall asked when they got to the corner of Main
and Millard, in the kind of tired, put-upon voice a student might use
to ask what pages a test would cover, not that Randall would ask
such a question – he'd wait for someone else to do that – but still
it illustrates the fact that Randall wasn't in a very good mood this
Sunday afternoon. For one thing, though he'd worked that morning
and was scheduled to have the afternoon off, he'd had to refuse
McKibben's last-minute request that he stay on through the day,
which refusal would not normally have vexed Randall, but he'd
recently negotiated a price of $450 for an ancient disused service
truck of McKibben's, a sum Randall had been determinedly saving
toward. And for another thing, an indeterminate number of hours
– three or four, minimum – in close quarters with an old woman,
even one as nice as the widow, whose bodily smells, Randall had
now discovered, grew fustier as the day wore on and the lavender
water (he'd seen the bottle while snooping in her bathroom when
she was off playing bridge) wore off, was nothing to shout about,
or, more to the point, to miss an afternoon's work for.

'North,' Lucy Witt said, and directed him through a sequence of
turns and straightaways that eventually led to timbered highlands
and leafy canyons that, to Randall's eye, looked like the first place
to come with firearms during pheasant season, which was upcoming.
(He was only partly right – the stubbled cornfields to the south were
harboring greater numbers of the birds.) There were fewer farms up
here; only the occasional field had been carved from the forest and
planted to winter wheat or some other crop, with what looked like
sparse results. Up here the dirt roads became narrower and rockier –
more than once Randall felt the dispiriting thunk of boulder-nose to

crankcase metal – and Lucy Witt's directions became more intricate. It was a dazzling day, the sun high and sturdy, the ruddled and yellowing leaves glimmering in the slim breeze, not that Randall was in any mood for a field trip. 'Ash,' Lucy Witt would say, pointing, and then a half-minute later, 'Box elder,' and then, 'Ash again,' until Randall didn't bother even to make a muffled little 'hmmmp' of polite acknowledgement.

'Here,' she said finally at the slightest widening of the faint track to which she'd routed them. With a heave and a low oofing sound she pushed her unwieldy body upright and stepped out into the autumn sun and silence. Randall got out, too, and walked around the big black car, already filmed with dust. (It occurred to him, since the widow was staring off the other way, to write a quick word on the trunk, *Bear!*, maybe, or *Ax-man!*, or maybe just *Yikes!*)

'Pretty, isn't it?' Lucy Witt said in a near whisper, steadying herself against the car and gazing fixedly down the slope. Randall rose at once to the promise of wildlife, something trophy-sized or exotic (already he'd heard the unsubstantiated rumors of elk) and so had to readjust his focus to a scene almost completely floral in nature. Within a stand of yellow, shimmer-leafed oaks there lay a small brown clearing, and within the clearing stood (or partially stood: one set of legs had collapsed) a roughhewn log table. An upended log bench lay beside it.

'Somebody's old picnic set,' Randall said, which for some reason brought a chortle from the widow. 'Yes,' she said. 'That's what it is.' Then, 'Why don't you go down and take a look at it?'

The table's method of construction was crude but useful. Two logs had been halved lengthwise – how exactly, Randall had no idea – then three of the four splits had been strapped by nailed branches on the rough side and set over two pairs of cross-braced legs of more or less the same length. The final split half had been cradled into two stumpier logs to make the bench, though its long edge, tipped into the earth who knew how many years before, was now honeycombed with decay. When Randall tried to raise and brace the broken-down end of the table, something too much like a snake (and definitely, he thought, of the reptile nation) went slithering away. He quickly let the table end drop back to earth. There were, he saw now, some letters carved into the corner of the table-top, rough, straight-line, Davy Crockett-style letters, *R* something and something something, followed by *193*something.

The initials were more legible on the next table in the next clearing, which they reached by car twenty minutes later. Again the widow waited as Randall scuffled down to surveille. This table lay stomached on the ground – Randall had to kick away leaves, squirrel scat and nutshells (while making a mental note to tell the widow that this particular table was still providing service as both eating surface and shithouse). The initials were again carved in a discreet corner, stacked vertically on three lines.

RW

LW

Oct. 11 1951

Almost forty years before. Without particular luck, Randall stood trying to imagine how long ago that was, and on what kind of day and in what kind of body the widow might've appeared in this clearing. Then he gave up and just stood. He liked it here. There was a nearby creek he could hear but couldn't see, and there were the solitary cries of jays, and the low Coke-bottle whistle of wind through tall trees. It made him wish he could've come to some place like this with Anna Belknap. And yet, and yet – it seemed impossible – but when Randall stood with his back to the widow and closed his eyes, *he couldn't make Anna Belknap's face appear to him*. The image that *did* materialize, in fact, was of another girl. Randall opened his eyes quickly to dismiss it.

'R.W. and L.W.,' Randall said when he'd scrambled back up to the car. 'Guess the L.W. would be you.'

The widow Lucy Witt nodded. Her face expressed neither pride nor embarrassment, so Randall had to recalculate a little bit. It had occurred to him that besides building tables, L.W. and R.W. might have put their backwoods privacy to use of a spicier nature. The widow had always referred to her husband as Dick, but Randall knew that through some particularly weird logic Dick could be squeezed from Richard. 'And R.W. was your husband?' he said.

She nodded again, smiling a fond smile. 'When he was signing for posterity he always went by Richard.'

A moment passed and Randall said, 'Well, forty-something years later the squirrels are still throwing fancy dinners on your table.' (He'd decided that mentioning its doubling as a shithouse might not tickle the widow's funny bone.)

Lucy Witt stared down the draw toward the clearing. 'We'd been married eleven years by then and it seemed clear that we weren't going to have any children, not that, as Dick always liked to say, we didn't have fun trying. But without children we could often make a Sunday for ourselves, and autumn was Dick's favorite time of year.' She stopped and Randall had just decided the story was mysteriously over when she started up again. 'Besides the bank,' she said, 'Dick owned two mills up here, so one Sunday every October he'd pile some split logs in a trailer and we'd drive around until we found a spot for a table and then we'd stop and put it together.' She'd by now directed her gaze some place very far off. 'I'd've gotten braunschwauger from Judah Frmka and we'd have beer on chipped ice and eat braunschwauger-and-pickle sandwiches.'

That afternoon Randall and Lucy Witt found four more of the tables, and at each site the widow would stand in an overview position near the car while Randall went off to scout around, though with less and less curiosity for the furniture itself. What he did do, however, was file away for future reference the exact location of these secluded hideaways. For what and who with, he would not have said. But he knew. Resisted, but knew.

How had Marcy Marlene Lockhardt imprinted herself on Randall's imagination? As easily and guilelessly as, at one time or other, she'd imprinted herself on the imagination of nearly every Goodnight male, fourteen years and over. In Randall's case, the particulars were these. The boys' locker room of Goodnight high was situated in the school's poured-concrete basement and was joined to the football field by a tunnel leading beneath the concrete, home-team bleachers. This tunnel also divided the boys' locker room from the girls' locker room, which was much smaller than the boys', and doubled as the band room. A week or so earlier, Randall was walking by this room as the Goodnight cheerleaders clustered at its door. They were wearing the new uniforms that had been expected since August. Randall heard one of the girls observing how short the new skirts were and then saying to the others, 'Good thing I'm not shy.' He knew who she was. Her name was everywhere. When she had smiled past her cheerleading chums *toward him*, he had glared back in lightning-quick loyalty not so much to Anna Belknap as to the sweet misbegotten dreams about her he'd harbored and wanted to harbor still. No, he thought, fixing his glare on Marcy Lockhardt. You might be hot shit here in Sludgeville, but you are no Anna Belknap. (This was not strictly true: Marcy Lockhardt, to use Randall's term, would've qualified as hot shit almost anywhere.)

'Feeling nappish?' Lucy Witt said as she opened the passengerside door and maneuvered herself into the Buick after visiting the last picnic site. This particular table had been close by and on level ground. Randall, allowing the widow to inspect it alone, had stayed behind and grown drowsy.

'A little,' Randall said, surfacing from half sleep. Outside the car, to his surprise, the sunlight seemed softer, with a longer slant to it. He sat up and leaned more forward than was necessary to turn the ignition key. He wasn't sure exactly what he'd been dreaming, but whatever it was had gotten the member into what Randall thought of as its Miles Standish mode. Randall followed visual obstruction with diversion. 'What's that?' he said, nodding toward the tall bouquet of spikey purple flowers the widow had somehow acquired from the roadside.

'Blazing star,' Lucy Witt said, holding them up for presentation, 'or gay feather, I'm never sure which.' Then, after arranging herself in her seat, she said, 'Just one more stop and after that I want to take you to the Elks in Chadron for a smothered steak. Would that appeal to you?'

'I am hungry,' Randall said, suddenly realizing how true this was. (It was also true that a smothered steak, whatever it was revealed to be, would likely be something to write Louise about.)

The last stop designated by the widow was the old section of the Goodnight cemetery, where, wildflowers in hand, Lucy Witt stepped out into the dusky half-light and in her cumbersome hobble moved toward a headstone. Randall watched her negotiate the uneven terrain with an interest strangely detached from the generosity she faithfully extended to him – she in fact now reminded him of one of those slow, paddle-footed, wind-up toys that work best on hard flat surfaces. When eventually she got to the weedy plot, the widow did something that Randall would've just as soon never seen. She heavily lowered herself to her knees and, after poking the stems of the spiky bouquet into some ground-level receptacle that Randall couldn't see, and still kneeling but with her back childishly erect, she put her hands together in prayer.

To avert his eyes, Randall began a slow, careful study of the cemetery's newer headstones, and when finally he turned back to the old section, Randall for one long disorienting moment mistook the widow for a monument. She was on all fours struggling to get up. Randall, trying to make sense of this sight, stood and stared for three, four or five seconds, for a longer time in any case than he was later happy to remember. When at last he got to the widow, she wouldn't meet his eyes. 'Good Lord,' was all she said, in soft self-disgust. Randall slipped his arms beneath hers and, as he lifted, felt the soft flab flatten against bone. She was heavier than he could've ever imagined; he staggered to get her upright and in so doing felt more of her old body than he cared to. As they eased back toward the car, though Randall couldn't in good conscience completely let go of her, he held her arm with the loosest grip possible.

'Are you still hungry?' she asked in a dull voice once he'd gotten her resettled in the car.

'Not that much,' Randall said, 'unless you are.'

Lucy Witt didn't say anything. When Randall looked over at her, her wrinkles seemed to be gathering and deepening, as if she might break into tears. Randall quickly started the car and, keeping his eyes narrowly ahead, drove her straight home.

V

BY THE FIRST WEEK OF NOVEMBER, GOODNIGHT'S EIGHT-MAN FOOTBALL team had played seven games and lost six. During this course of events Coach Dee's motivational approach had evolved from harebrained esteem therapy ('Come Friday, Gentlemen, when you kick Hemingford's asses six ways to Christmas, you may surprise

yourselves, but you won't surprise me!') to Bo Schembechlerlike
intensity ('Tonight, Gents,' he said, throwing a neat pre-game
chokehold on poor, happy-go-lucky Meteor Frmka, the team's
back-up center and ineffectual nose guard, 'it's time to make
the other team *hurt* –' and here Coach Dee twisted poor Frmka
around so he could with clenched teeth smile at the boy's swollen
and enpurpled puss – 'if you know what I mean by *hurt*.') to finally
the kind of smug derision that allowed Coach Dee in the season's
waning weeks to transmit to his charges the clear message that
this team's year-long all-around sorry-ass performance was their
exclusive responsibility, not his ('Well, Fellas,' he announced the
Monday afternoon following their sixth defeat, 'you've now lost to
everybody you should've lost to and six more besides'). Though he
could never admit it aloud, Randall was no longer just indifferent to
the losses, he'd begun to enjoy them, and to look forward to Coach
Dee's post-game sputterings. Randall, it had to be said, did his job
well and reliably, game in and game out. On defense, he played left
end, as assigned (rather than linebacker or free safety, positions that
Randall believed were better suited to his talents). Still, in spite of his
perceived misemployment, Randall from his defensive end position
contained all sweeps directed his way and, when stirred from his
desultory reserve by pain or anger, could bring pressure to bear on
a pass-minded quarterback. On offense (along with three or four
other of the team's better athletes, Randall played both ways) he
filled the wide receiver slot, remembering his blocking assignments,
and catching everything thrown close to him, though little was. So
that when Coach Dee went through the post-game dissection, relying
heavily on sarcasm and slow-motion videotape, Randall (the coach
called him 'Ocho,' on the basis of finger count) was rarely singled
out for negligence, and almost as rarely singled out for exceptional
play. He did his job and if the other twenty guys on the roster
had done theirs, they might have won a few games, was Randall's
considered opinion.

On the Wednesday night prior to the season's final game, a young,
long-boned man a few years older than Randall drove into the Mobil
station in his late model Blazer. There was another man in the car, too,
but he slouched in the shadows and hardly moved. The driver got out

of the Blazer and stepped into the light. He had milky skin, almost
blueish, the tint of some babies. He chewed on a plastic soda straw
and kept his hands in his pockets as he watched Randall pumping
the gas. After paying his bill, he slid a business card from his wallet.
'I'm Leo Underwood. You might've heard of me. I run the Eleventh
Man Bar and Grill on Main Street, but I don't own it. My uncle does.
Come on in and I'll serve you if nobody's around.'

Randall stared at the card. 'The Eleventh Man,' he said.

'My uncle dreamed that up. Actually *dreamed* it, while he slept.
A voice said, "You will serve the eleventh man." On that basis some
would've started a church. My uncle bought a bar.' Leo Underwood
grinned around his straw.

'Who's your buddy?' Randall asked, nodding toward the dark
figure in the Blazer.

'That's Frank Mears. He's kind of an asshole. He wants me to tell
you that he'd like it a lot if your little football team would come
within ten against Crawford. He says it would mean a lot to him.'

Randall exhaled and watched his breath disperse. It was cold, the
kind of clear-sky cold that seemed to make brittle everything that
wasn't moving. 'Well, you tell your kind-of-an-asshole buddy that
we'll be doing our doggondest, just like always.'

But the next afternoon Randall went to Coach Dee with a
suggestion. How about if for the final game and just to shake things
up, he played free safety on defense and halfback on offense?

Whatever his other limitations, Coach Dee was canny enough
to know that an underachiever's moribund spirits could sometimes
best – or only – be revived by a change of his own devising. 'Go on,'
Coach Dee said amiably. 'Tell me why I would want to do that?'

'Well,' Randall said, thinking as he went, 'if it worked out, it would
give us something to build on for next year. Besides, I think those
positions are better suited to my –' he didn't know quite what to
say and so he said, 'nature.'

Crawford was in second place in the Panhandle Conference, having
lost only to Rushville. Goodnight was in seventh place, having beaten
only Harrison. Coach Dee half-granted Randall's request. He kept
him at wide receiver but switched him to free safety on defense,
where Randall played that Friday night with a ferocity no one had

previously guessed he possessed. No Crawford receiver got beyond him deep and Randall clamped down on runs like a linebacker. Twice he stuck the Crawford halfback so violently that the ball popped free. On three different passing downs, he rogue-blitzed the Crawford quarterback and slammed him to the ground before he could even look for his receivers. For a time, Randall's wildness infected not only the Goodnight partisans in the visitors' bleachers, but also his own teammates. They felt suddenly and wonderfully thuggish. They couldn't wait for the next play. They relished their next chance to do their opponents real harm. Early in the fourth quarter, however, the team's overinflated spirits were punctured by the ignominious collision of Goodnight's own two linebackers from opposite directions. (Ross Ray, a sturdy farmboy, sitting post-play with legs splayed, held onto his broken nose, but couldn't keep himself from crying.) Still, when the final gun sounded, Crawford had won by only three points.

Without quite knowing why, Randall was annoyed that most of the Goodnight squad were cheered by the narrowness of defeat so when, in a quieter moment of the merriment, Meteor Frmka beamingly clapped Randall on the back and said, '*Helluva* contest, Zacker,' Randall swung around and fixed him with a glare. 'It was anything but,' he said and then, sensing the rest of the team turning toward him, he said what he at that moment thought to say and, worse, said it with impatience, as if repeating the most basic axiom to the most basic imbecile (which he privately thought Frmka was). 'When you lose a game,' Randall pronounced slowly, 'you are a *loser*. The score doesn't make you a better or worse loser. You are still just a *loser*.'

The locker room was suddenly cast into stiff silence and, to make matters worse, Coach Dee began to laugh in what seemed like not just smirking agreement but smug gratification, as if everything this particular Friday night, from inspired play to narrow defeat, from broken noses to post-game dissension, had been exactly what he expected.

Two days later, on Sunday, Leo Underwood's Blazer crunched through an inch of frozen snow and pulled up to the unleaded pump at McKibben's Mobil. As he stepped out into the cold, the car's interior light came on. No one else sat inside. Frank Mears asks, Randall thought, but doesn't thank.

Leo Underwood, in dress shoes, picked his way close to the pumps. 'Played good the other night,' he said to Randall. 'I was impressed. Hell, we *all* were.' He gestured expansively, though no one else was in sight.

Randall nodded somberly to indicate his skepticism. (He'd also noticed, while the waving was going on, that Leo Underwood wore a wedding ring, a surprise, because nothing about Leo Underwood *seemed* married.)

When his tank was filled, Leo pulled out his wallet and gave Randall twenty for the gas and twenty more for what he said was a tip. Randall handed the twenty back along with his change. 'Don't take tips,' he said.

Leo Underwood looked up from the money with mock surprise, but didn't refuse it. 'Well, that's between you and your parole board.'

Randall decided against saying that he didn't have a parole board and that it wouldn't have had anything to do with a parole board even if he had one.

Leo, having pocketed his wallet, extended his hand. 'Well, thanks, then.'

Randall looked at the hand without taking it. 'For what?'

'For playing like a maniac. It was kind of fun to watch. And of course for taking your betting fans' concerns as your own.'

It was again cold, brittly cold. Randall took coordinates of the middle of Leo Underwood's grinning milkwhite face then turned away and glowered off, working his jaw and privately massaging the happy notion of ending a wheeling roundhouse in the middle of Leo's nose.

But Leo, who had wiles of his own, said, 'Look, you want to meet a tough guy, come by the bar some night and meet Frank Mears.'

Randall turned around and was surprised to see that from somewhere Leo had produced a plastic straw and was now chewing it with elaborate casualness. Randall said, 'Why would meeting your-kind-of-an-asshole friend be of interest to me?'

Leo Underwood smiled. 'Well, you kind of remind me of him in your own kind-of-an-asshole way,' he said. 'Mears when he played was smaller than you and slower than you, but –' here Leo made a toothsome, straw-pinching grin – 'he was lots meaner.'

'I'm happy to hear it,' Randall said. The impulse to roundhouse Leo was receding, which, besides being in itself disappointing, left Randall unsure of quite what to feel.

Leo waited a few seconds to let things readjust themselves. 'Come by the bar some night. When the season's over, if you'd feel better about it. In the meantime I'll put a little credit on your account.'

Randall meant to decline this outright, but for some reason didn't. 'I'll think about it,' he said.

A week later Randall came home late from work one night to find a note from the widow on his bedroom desk. *I am getting addled!* it said. *I meant to tell you over supper that you're invited to join me at my nephew's next week for turkey and all the trimmings. I sincerely hope you'll come. Lucy.* Well, Randall thought, I sincerely doubt I will. If there was a spookier thought than a formal sit-down dinner with Coach Dee, Randall couldn't think of it, and so the next morning, before school, he swung by McKibben's and arranged to work Thanksgiving, seven in the morning to nine at night. (McKibben didn't protest – it meant after all that his family could eat as one rather than in shifts, as was their importunate Thanksgiving custom.)

Randall received two letters in November from Louise. The first said nothing much – *found a job that pays shit, and as a bonus illustrates why so many otherwise upright individuals turn to crime* – a sentiment that, coming from Louise, couldn't be thought of as news, but the second letter, posted the Friday after Thanksgiving, pulled no punches. *I have as I more than once took pleasure in saying of others a muffin in the oven. I've finished what is called the first trimester. Lenny's of course the father a role he's incapable of playing except in the carnal docking-the-spermboat sense. I'll break all these happy tidings to Mom someday when I'm really bored and needing some fun. Meantime, other than feeling putrid, I want the baby. If it arrives with the little male attachment maybe I'll name him Randallkins.*

VI

DECEMBER RANDALL, TO HIS OWN SURPRISE, AND ALONE AMONG HIS GOOD-night teammates, was elected by the league's coaches (although quite possibly without Coach Dee's supporting vote) to the All-League defensive team, an honor that, for his teammates anyhow, was nicely counterbalanced by the fact that Randall, again alone among his Goodnight teammates, garnered not one of the many assorted certificates and tiny trophies passed out at the Goodnight High School annual football awards banquet. (Meteor Frmka, as a joke, was voted Most Inspirational by his teammates, *probably*, wrote Randall to Louise, *for surviving Coach Dee's chokehold without farting*.)

Otherwise, Randall:

Helped, at McKibben's request and expense, the volunteer fire department span Main Street with twenty-something strings of lights. ('Goodnight's bullish on Christmas,' McKibben noted wryly when Randall returned from this work.)

Managed, in the week before Christmas break, Cs in two finals, and felt himself slipping.

Puttered, while working at the filling station days *and* nights during the school holiday, on his newly acquired '57 Ford service truck (still painted a dirty white, with a faded red flying horse faintly visible on each door).

Pumped gas for Marcy Lockhardt's mother (who, Randall noted, was herself well preserved, a good portent for the daughter, if he'd been looking for portents, which he wanted to believe he was not) while Marcy sat sidesaddle in the front seat ignoring Randall while messing with the radio (she was wearing a short skirt *and*, when he squeegeed her side of the windshield, was slow in bringing her knees together, *but* was wearing dark tights so suggestion exceeded show); accepted with a nod and without question Marcy's mother's personal check (credit cards, while expected from touring New Yorkers, say, or Californians, were often viewed by locals as an indicator of fiscal and possibly moral weakness); and, while standing aside in the frigid air to let Mrs Lockhart's car pass in exit, unreasonably hoped for some departing word from Marcy (*Merry Christmas, Randall!* would've done fine) even though he himself avoided all eye contact (as did she, sitting toasty-warm behind her raised window).

Worked Christmas Day from 8 a.m. opening to 9 p.m. closing time ('The highway,' McKibben liked to say, 'don't close on Christmas,' and, Presbyterian affiliation notwithstanding, his was a highway business); came home to find on the desk in his room a red-ribboned box containing an expensive pair of lined leather gloves from the widow, a fine surprise; and hastily made a card within a card that said, *This deluxe coupon titles Mrs Lucy Witt to five free washes of Buick Electra* and laid it on the kitchen table, where the widow found it in the morning, seemed pleased by its prospects, and said, 'When, of course, the weather improves.'

Received, on December 27th, a Christmas card from Louise that said only, *Mission aborted*.

Worked New Year's Eve until midnight, left alone to enforce McKibben's humanitarian decision to cut off Mini-Mart liquor sales at dusk (free coffee till midnight being small solace); heard in passing from Whistler Simpson (intoxicated) and Jim Six (more so) that among those attending the barn party at Brett Heiting's place were Bobby Parmalee and his girlfriend, Marcy Lockhardt; and felt, for the first time since Utah, the terrible, tender nibble of jealousy.

And so, in the frigid absolute stillness of exactly midnight, as one year in a stroke became suddenly another, Randall Hunsacker locked up McKibben's Mobil and Mini-Mart and, taking exactly the route he had taken on the day of his arrival in Goodnight, headed toward home.

VII

JANUARY. NEBRASKA COLD, RANDALL HAD COME TO FEEL, WAS DIRER THAN Utah cold. By the time he finished the night shift at McKibben's he could stare at his feet without quite feeling them. He'd gotten the old pick-up running, but not its heater, and, as he wrote Louise, *freezing your ass off takes most of the fun out of aimless wintertime driving*. (To this and the other three letters he wrote Louise in January, he received no reply.) The widow kept her house at a throbbing 80 degrees, which meant that almost as soon as Randall returned home and restored circulation, he began to swelter. So Randall, against better judgment, began spending time at the Eleventh Man, detouring there after 9 p.m. lock-up at McKibben's, and whenever else he had a few hours free. (Not that there was anything technically wrong with this – minors were legally allowed within the Eleventh Man to buy food and soda, and to play video games and pool.)

In the bar's warm blue light, pallid Leo Underwood seemed almost ghostly – all the men and women did – but Randall felt strangely at home there, sitting either at the bar listening to Leo's chatter or, more often, over at the table under the illuminated Oly sign, sitting with Leo's hard-edged friends, unmarried railroad boys and truckers and cowboys without wives or work or rodeos to go to. Nearly always, Frank Mears was among them. Mears, it turned out, was a thin sinewy man with a long sloping forehead, deeply set eyes, and concave cheeks, all of which suggested a kind of wolfishness to Randall and, at the same time, made him wonder if women wouldn't find Frank Mears attractive (initially they sometimes did; later, not so much). Unlike the rest of the group, Mears reliably carried money, accrued from a string of three laundromats he'd incrementally acquired (the down payment for the first coming from a round sum he'd won betting against one of Goodnight's best basketball teams, whose center, after eating a pastrami sandwich one Thursday night at the Eleventh Man, had come down with food poisoning). Frank Mears fascinated Randall in the way that a live snake in a clear jar might. He was strangely drawn to watching him, but tried to do it peripherally and, where possible, unobserved. He liked to sit to the side, but not next to, Frank Mears. The one place at the table where Randall learned never to sit was directly opposite this man, because by merely locking you with his eyes, Frank Mears from that vantage point could unsettle you, change for the worse the way you saw yourself, even scare you a little.

ALTHOUGH IT WAS AN OFFICIAL STATE HOLIDAY, MARTIN LUTHER KING'S birthday was not widely observed in Goodnight, with only the schools and post office closing their doors while everyone else, including the bank, conducted business as usual. 'A shadowy kind of holiday, isn't it?' Leo Underwood said, trying to make his racism sly. Nonetheless, Leo was pleased that most of his raggedy cronies could at least embrace the day as a legitimate reason for spending the afternoon drinking.

It was a glary bright day. At 2 p.m., according to the bank's digital time and temperature sign, the temperature stood at an unseasonably warm 52 degrees, balmy enough to lift the spirits. When at about this time Randall had joined Leo's friends at their customary table in the Eleventh Man, they were already pretty far into their drinking and not long thereafter a young girl came into the bar in search, it turned out, of her older brother, who was in the back shooting pool. The girl was only thirteen or fourteen, Randall guessed, but she wore tight faded denims and – what was she thinking? – a thin, too-small sweater, with no bra. Leo's friends fell silent, and the girl's nipples seemed to harden as she passed before their transfixed stares.

'Ee-*yow*,' Jim Six said under his breath, and Frank Mears, slouching a little and tenderly cupping a hand over his crotch, said in a brutal, unmuffled voice, 'Old enough to bleed is old enough to butcher.'

A quiet half-second followed before everyone at the table began to laugh, except Randall, who found himself staring mutely into Frank Mears's sidelong grinning gaze and then, in the next moment, to his own shame, Randall was laughing, too, loud, louder than the rest. At that moment, mid-laughter, he saw a man swiveling to look at him, a tall coarse-boned farmer with a horsey face, who'd come in for a hamburger and what looked like a glass of water and was now staring with what even in this darkness and from this distance Randall could recognize as utter contempt. Eventually the others noticed him, too, and fell silent. Only then did the farmer turn back around.

'Lewis Lockhardt,' one of Leo's friends explained and somebody else said, 'One more tightassed Nebraskan.' And Frank Mears, leaning forward and with a cold knowingness, said low, to the side, to *Randall*, 'Who has a daughter who'll walk your eyes around a room.'

It felt as if, in an instant, Randall had slipped into a nightmare, one in which he'd awakened from deep sleep to find himself in a tiny, shrinking, slime-walled room, and that the only way out was to stand up and step away from this table, to sit or go someplace else and silently announce to Marcy Lockhardt's father and to that young girl, whoever she was, that he wasn't part of this group, that he wanted nothing to do with them and had in fact nothing in common with them, that his laughing at Mears's crudeness was just some weird and surprising mistake. But Randall was like a man who, awakening from drugged sleep, can't make a fist. He felt leaden, lumpish, unable to move, sitting, just sitting, heavy-lidded (but smiling! – idiotically smiling!) until for reasons he would never in the world understand, perhaps just to disrupt the terrible agonizing silence he felt stretching in front of him, he piped up with a question to which he already knew the answer. 'What's her name?' he said. So that this episode, instead of ending, would turn even worse.

BACK IN EARLY DECEMBER, LEWIS LOCKHARDT HAD DRIVEN TO CHADRON TO SEE his tax man, Walter Edwards, in order to dope out his end-of-the-year income tax strategy (he'd had, it turned out, an even poorer year than expected, so there was no need to offset income through prepayment of the following year's seed and fertilizer). Walter Edwards had concluded the meeting with the suggestion that Lewis come by sometime early in the year to go over some new developments in estate planning. Because of his bland, almost passive politeness, Walter Edwards often reminded Lewis of Leo G. Carroll, especially as that actor played his role in the old Topper movies. ('I'm going to see Topper,' Lewis would tell his wife, Dorothy, whenever he had an appointment with Walter Edwards. Dorothy would look blankly at Lewis; the Topper movies were before her time.) It was Walter Edwards's bland, almost passive politeness that made it nearly impossible for Lewis to decline his suggestions, though he did in this case have sense enough to hesitate until Walter Edwards added, 'No charge for an old client, of course,' and Lewis, only half-joking, had said, 'No, Walter, not till you start drawing something up.'

Walter had flipped open his day book. 'Let's say 1 p.m., January 15th.' The tiniest smile played at his lips. 'Martin Luther King's birthday.' He looked up and with wondrously safe ambiguity – was it polite respect or gentle sarcasm? – said, 'We'll celebrate the good doctor's birthday by planning for your future.' Lewis Lockhardt had nodded, but, already sensing his own ambivalence for this project, added, 'God willing and barring bad weather.'

When the day arrived, such were Lewis Lockhardt's misgivings about his appointment that he would've welcomed almost any excuse to stay home, but the weather held, and at 12.30 p.m., after a truncated dinner with his wife (soup and toast – she'd put in a chow mein casserole, but it wasn't quite done) he drove off (as he said) to see Topper. 'Hi-dee-ho,' Lewis said, hoping for the best upon entering the accountant's office, but it wasn't to be a pleasant session. All of Walter Edwards's complicated and wide-ranging discussions of revocable and irrevocable trusts were based on financial assumptions that had been true of Lewis's circumstances the year before, but no longer were, and Lewis, instead of correcting these false assumptions, instead of explaining how much more money he had borrowed and from what sources, said nothing, turned in fact uncustomarily inward, thereby inducing a headache of rampant proportions. (At the heart of Lewis's dilemma was the fact that, when this past year he'd gone to the Bank of Goodnight for a second mortgage on his entire operation, he hadn't revealed the fact that he'd recently received a sizeable, unsecured, 'handshake' loan from a neighbor, and, vice versa, hadn't subsequently told the neighbor about this hefty new second, and so Lewis wasn't especially anxious for these coexisting – and yet, ethically speaking, mutually exclusive – loans to become common knowledge.) When at last Lewis bolted Walter Edwards's office, he felt not only headachy but slightly all-overish.

As he drove east from Chadron on this cold bright afternoon, his head aching and his mind swarming with numbers that, no matter how he maneuvered them, only computed to negative sums, Lewis Lockhardt had a sudden and comforting thought. A cheeseburger. Maybe even a double cheeseburger. He was hungry. Maybe what he had here was a hunger headache. So at the intersection of Highways 20 and 87, instead of turning south toward the flats, Lewis proceeded into Goodnight and pulled his truck diagonally alongside a row of several other pickups already parked in front of the Eleventh Man.

Stepping from the bright sidewalk into the dim smoky interior of the bar, Lewis sensed he'd made a mistake. Though he'd been in this place on a number of occasions, it was always on a Saturday afternoon, and always with his wife or daughter, and always to sit with others like themselves at the family end of the counter. Lewis couldn't yet tell who all was in the bar this Monday afternoon, but there were certainly no families. Still, he was here. He eased his way to the counter, where (another bad sign) Leo Underwood was in charge not, as on Saturdays,

Joanie Baxter (who would give you double cheese at no extra charge).

Lewis ordered the regular cheeseburger and Leo clinked a frozen patty onto the grill. An aromatic sizzle soon followed. Now that his eyes had adjusted to the dimness, Lewis swung a quarter-turn on his stool to see who else was in the room, which, if any, farmers were sitting on their rear ends in a dark bar instead of out doing something useful. There were no farmers, though, just a couple of ex-farmers, and the usual scattered assortment of odds and ends eating and drinking. The only noise came from a table against the far wall, where the town punks had collected, tough boys who never seemed to grow up. Most of them were in their early twenties, but one of them, though his face was dark-stubbled, was younger than the others, possibly still in high school. The others drank beer; he seemed to be sipping a Coke. While Lewis stared at the young men, they abruptly broke into big laughter at something or other, possibly him.

Lewis swiveled back around. 'Got a couple aspirin somewhere, Leo?'

The ache had gotten away from him, had migrated to the deep, tender parts of the eyes. His stomach felt a little rocky. It occurred to Lewis that if he weren't careful, he could wind up sick in public. He began taking his cheeseburger in small bites, washing it down with water.

When the front door opened, a startling wedge of sunlight pierced the room. It was the Plowright girl, coming to fetch her brother. She was perhaps thirteen, her face blotchy with acne, but she was one of those girls whose body, it seemed to Lewis, had burst so quickly into womanhood that it appeared to have caught her by surprise, and she had no mother or sister for direction. She wore a too-small sweater over her budding chest.

In the mirror behind the bar, Lewis watched her pass in front of the table of punks. One of them said something, Lewis wasn't sure what, and then another said something he could understand, something so vulgar that Lewis turned sharply to stare at the young men. To his surprise, they fell silent. He couldn't tell who had spoken the vile words, but the one who'd been laughing the hardest, laughing as if at his own joke, was the dark-stubbled kid.

'Who's the new kid?' Lewis said once the Plowright girl and her brother had departed and he'd turned back around. 'Is that the punk Coach Dee recruited?'

Leo replied congenially. 'Oh, I wouldn't call him a punk. When he feels like it he can flat play football. And McKibben says he makes a pretty fair mechanic, for an eight-fingered fella.'

From behind, Lewis heard his own name spoken in a mumble, followed by more words in a low tone and then harsh laughter. Tiny needles shot into his eyes. Pain clamped his head.

'*Marcy.*' '*What's her name?*' '*Marcy Marlene Lockhardt.*'

Those were the words Lewis heard and in the same moment without thinking he had risen full from his stool and was walking toward the table of young men. They were quiet by the time he got there. He leaned on the table – it tipped slightly and his hand abruptly slipped, which prompted a round of tittering. He stood straight up, unsupported, and felt a terrible needling pain behind the eyes. A sudden qualm of nausea worked his stomach. He stared at the new kid. 'Do I know you?'

The boy's face seemed to stiffen. 'I don't know,' the boy said, a little weakly, and then one of his buddies – it was Marlen Coates – jumped in.

'Mr Lockhardt, Mr Hunsacker. Mr Hunsacker, Mr Lockhardt.'

This drew approving grins from the table.

Lewis's stomach clutched and he swallowed back the first raw taste of bile. 'I think I heard one of you mention my daughter's name.' He tried to scan the group slowly – besides Marlen Coates there was Jim Six, Whistler Simpson, Frank Mears – but all the while he could feel the blood seeping away from his own face. He needed to sit down.

'If we did, it wouldn't've been with disrespect,' one of the men said with exaggerated politeness and, while Lewis was weighing that, another of them said, 'Why would we be bringing up your daughter's name anyway? Your daughter's a nice girl, we all know that, and since we have no interest whatsoever in nice girls, why would we be bringing her up?'

The table of grinning faces waited for a response, but Lewis couldn't speak. His stomach had clutched fiercely. He swallowed back sour bile, hurried for the front door, but was overtaken by the last violent commotion of his stomach. The upheaval was insuppressible and copious. While Lewis on wobbly legs stood over the mess, someone from behind whooped, 'Spill on aisle ten, Leo!'

Lewis, without another word, stepped into the cold glare of Main Street.

THAT NIGHT, OVER SUPPER (CHOW MEIN CASSEROLE, REHEATED), LEWIS reported the episode to his wife and daughter. He didn't repeat the words he'd heard directed at the Plowright girl by, he believed, the new boy from Utah, but, choosing his words, said they were of 'the crudest sexual nature.' (Which was in itself shocking enough language for the Lockhardt supper table.) Lewis recounted with satisfaction how he'd stared the table of town punks into silence and, with far less satisfaction, how, after hearing Marcy's name issued from their punkish lips, he'd walked over to confront the table but, before he'd gotten anywhere, was dropped by nausea. 'Some kind of one-day flu, I guess,' he said, still feeling sheepish about upchucking in a bar. 'I feel better now though,' he said. (He could only imagine what strange shapes such a story would take as it traveled about town.)

'What about this boy?' Dorothy Lockhardt said, turning to Marcy.

Marcy shrugged. 'His name's Randall Hunsacker.' She paused. 'I think he works at McKibben's and lives with Lucy Witt.'

There was a silence at the table, except for Lewis mashing the last of his water chestnuts with the backside of his fork. 'That all?' Dorothy said.

'It's all I know,' Marcy said. 'He kind of keeps to himself around school.' She was thinking of how, in English class, he sat over by the radiators and stared out the windows in a way that could actually make her sad. 'If he's gotten into any trouble here, I never heard about it.'

Marcy fell quiet then and nursed her own thoughts. The truth was, Marcy was a little excited that her name had been spoken at a table of rough men in the Eleventh Man. It caused within her a faint bodily stirring.

Meanwhile, Lewis had cleaned the last food particles from his plate with increasing agitation, and now he set his fork down.

'This new boy we were talking about,' he said in his low, sturdy voice. 'He's not a normal boy. He's disfigured, but on the inside, so you don't see.' An intensity had come into Lewis Lockhardt's voice. He paused. When he resumed speaking he seemed calmer. 'He's a freak of nature, only worse, because he don't look like one.' Lewis fixed his eyes on Marcy, a soft gaze, she could feel its softness, which made the words he then spoke more chilling. 'Watch now and you'll see. Some girl's father may have to shoot that boy.'

VIII

WHEN LEO UNDERWOOD SPIED THE FEBRUARY *PLAYBOY* ON THE RACK AT Lloyds Friendly Pharmacy (but neatly sealed in browser-proof plastic), he fished three dollars from his wallet and made the purchase. 'Matter of local pride, is why,' he said to the clerk and winked. (Privately he thought he'd nick his uncle for the expense, since the magazine would be a nice little short-term incentive for walk-in traffic at the bar.) After his own perusal, he presented the magazine to his friends sitting and drinking at their table under the illuminated Oly sign. 'Page 137,' he said, grinning and teething his soda straw. The Furman girl was among two dozen or so others featured in something titled, 'The Girls of the Big Ten.' She was wearing Levis and a (purple-and-gold) Wisconsin cardigan, draped open to her inarguably prodigious breasts. (Whistler Simpson, who could very occasionally be droll, emitted a soft whistle and said, 'Why, those are Tetonic.')

On Valentine's night, when Bobby Parmalee took a look at this photograph, he said to Marcy Lockhardt (who'd acquired the magazine from a girlfriend who'd filched it from her older brother), 'Well, I'll bet Tina Furman doesn't come back to the Nebraska panhandle anytime soon,' and Marcy Lockhardt, trying to make it sound like a joke, though it wasn't, not entirely, said, 'Maybe that was her objective.'

Without really knowing why, Marcy had gone overboard for

Bobby's Valentine's Day. With her mother's help she'd made a two-layer German chocolate cake, which she'd stacked and carved into the shape of a heart. She'd also bought a fancy, mail-order photo album and filled it with pictures she and Bobby had snapped of themselves over the past year, complete with funny, handwritten notations. (*What sheep shearer gave you* this *haircut?!!* for example.) These were the gifts her mother knew about. The others were the Furman *Playboy* and a pair of white boxer shorts (white with winged red hearts, which she'd found one day in Pine Bluff while shopping with Julie Thies, and had at once, without knowing why, said, 'Oooh!' as she might've over a porcelain doll or a favorite dessert). Bobby had done his part in return. He'd gone to Ahren's in Chadron and picked out a friendship ring. When he saw how much Marcy seemed to like it, he said, 'It was funny, and I know we're too young, but even though I went in there for a friendship ring I kept wanting to buy one of those small diamond rings.'

'I wish you had,' Marcy replied, not because she really did – he was right, they *were* too young – but because she wished she did.

This conversation was reported casually by Marcy to Bernita Landreth and Julie Thies, and spread freely from there, gaining wide circulation and undergoing important reconfiguration, until, by the time it reached Randall Hunsacker, Marcy Lockhardt and Bobby Parmalee were all but engaged.

IX

ON THE MORNING OF MARCH 17TH, WHEN THE POSTMAN TAPPED AT LUCY WITT'S front door, she was in the thick of a game of Napoleon solitaire, and faring pretty well, having already completed four foundation piles, not that anyone, as she often observed, ever won the game more than once in a Chinese epoch.

'Lucy,' the postman said in low-voiced greeting once she'd opened the door.

'Hello, Ed,' Lucy Witt said, and took in hand the bulky manila envelope that, along with her other mail, he was holding out for her. The big envelope was addressed to Randall in what looked like a feminine hand.

'Came that way,' the postman said, nodding at the ragged tear along the flap, subsequently taped.

Behind closed doors, Lucy Witt turned the envelope back over. The postmark was from Morgantown, WVA. There was no return address. She considered – but quickly rejected – the notion of carefully peeling back the tape, taking a look inside, then retaping the flap. On the one hand, nobody in the world would know; on the other hand, it would be terribly wrong. She went back to her solitaire, but abstractedly (she flubbed a critical chance to rid herself of a nuisance king). The envelope kept coming to mind, so much so that she finally got up and walked the packet back to Randall's room, where she left it on his desk, out of harm's way.

It was a calm and warm enough day that, by 3 p.m., when Randall came home to change clothes before heading to McKibben's, Lucy Witt was sitting in a sunny patch of the front porch reading (rereading actually) an Agatha Christie mystery (she owned all of Agatha Christie's books and shelved them in the parlor in alphabetical order, then read them systematically, left to right, so that, by the time she finished the last book, she could no longer remember the specifics of the first). 'Something arrived for you,' she called to Randall in a cheerful voice as he mounted the stairs.

He stopped and peered at her with friendly suspicion. 'What?'

'A package from a woman in Morgantown, West Virginia,' Lucy Witt announced, some instinct pushing her toward shaping the news in this way, knowing somehow that it would please him, and it did. Immediately a broad, uncomplicated grin broke across Randall's face.

'That'd be from my mom or my sister,' he said. 'It's my birthday.'

'Your birthday?' Lucy Witt said in bewilderment, wanting to backtrack, wondering how something so important might've slipped past her. 'Today?'

'Where is it?' Randall was saying.

In a small voice – already she was wondering what she had done – she said, 'On your desk,' and he was off, heading for his room, to open his packet. He stayed in there quite a long time, and when he finally came out, dressed in his work clothes, he seemed stiffened by some unexpected disappointment. He stopped only briefly before setting off to work. 'I should've told you sooner,' he said, 'but Mr McKibben needs me to work straight through tonight, so I can't be home for supper,' and then he was walking away.

Before she could stop herself, and more loudly than she meant to, Lucy Witt said, 'What came for you in the mail?'

Randall stopped halfway down the sidewalk. For a moment, before he turned around, he seemed poised to move on without answering. But he did turn; he turned and looked up at her. There were times, and this was one of them, when Lucy Witt thought Randall's face could grow soberer than a boy's face should. 'Just some old letters,' he said. 'They came back from West Virginia. The post office sent them.'

Then he was gone.

OH, LORD! AND THEN SHE THOUGHT IT AGAIN. LORD!

Lucy Witt looked around. It wasn't late. The roads were clear. She put on her coat and gloves, drove at once to Householder's, in town, and finding nothing suitable there, drove on to Chadron, where, within Anderson's, Inc., she found two shirts she thought would look good on Randall, one short-sleeved and blue, the other long-sleeved and yellow, both with pearly snap-buttons. Blue was a better color for him, she'd noticed, but short sleeves emphasized the hairiness of his arms. Foo, she thought, and bought them both, and a complementary charcoal-gray sweater besides, and had them all wrapped in festive paper.

It was dark by the time Lucy Witt returned to the house. She turned on lights and set the cheerful package on the dining room table where she could see it while she made herself some Earl Grey and cinnamon toast. Then, finished, refreshed, pretending she had no remoter motive, she decided to set the package on the desk in Randall's room, where it would make him a pleasant and private surprise when he returned from work.

Lucy Witt walked in her heavy half-hobble along the wainscoted passageway, opened Randall's door, and switched on the light. The large manila envelope had been torn open and now lay flatly empty on the desk. Something both irresistible and unwholesome pulled Lucy Witt toward it. Lying in a scatter beneath the envelope was a batch of white, letter-sized envelopes, all identically addressed in

Randall's coarse hand to a Louise Hunsacker, c/o General Delivery, Morgantown WVA 26507. Each, in purplish black ink, had been officially stamped UNCLAIMED. All had been opened. This, the widow considered, was probably what Randall had been doing in here all that time – reading the letters his sister had never read. But, if so, it had not disrupted his neatening instincts. He'd returned them all to their unsealed envelopes.

Lucy Witt cleared a space on the desk so she could set down Randall's present. She slid her hand over the white envelopes, fanning them as she might cards. She picked one up and then another, examining the postmarks. They began in late September and ended in mid-January. She arranged them chronologically and in so doing, in completing just that little obsessive task, her relationship to them shifted. They now felt more like her own. Almost before she knew it, she'd turned over the first envelope, plucked out the sheet of blue-lined yellow paper it contained, and, her massive old heart beating fervently, began to read. *Greetings from the bumpkin patch*, it began. *School's in session and what a hoot and a half.* Her eyes skipped here and there. *You got questions Weasel we got answers. What other than school work food football town state life sucks swampwater? (answer – nothing.) How do you know farmboys are crawling across the highway at night (answer some of them don't make it.)* The second letter started *Greetings from Sludgeville* and covered things in general (*worse – surprise surprise*), the most recent football game (*lost – surprise surprise*), and his lessons in English class (*studying metaphores as in 'if a wart was a town you'd call it Goodnight'*).

Oh, it was ghastly, all of it! She tucked the second letter safely back into its jacket. She knew she should leave now, should retire to the parlor, to restore calm, to let things settle, to apply perspective, but she also knew she couldn't. She'd felt, on behalf of her town, the deep sting of insult. She opened the third letter and read as follows:

Oct 11

Greetings from Smudgeville,
 Boy howdy! did yer brother have a Sunday yesterday! The Widow yanked me from work so I could be her unpaid driver

for tour all around looking at the leaves changing color, box
elder, ash, pukewood, elm, she could name them all. Dick was
the dead husband's name. Dick used to just adore these places,
the widow says. Dick must've been a real nature lover, I say
playing along. (I've seen pictures of Dick – he was a big boy too
though not as big as the widow.) The topper is yet to come. Last
stop, we drive out to the graveyard and the widow walks off to
put some flowers in Dick's cup and as you can imagine seeing
her kneel to pray and tipping herself right over and unable to
get up was one of my vacation's real highlights!! I'll write when
more hilarity erupts.

> *Randall*

Lucy Witt read the letter twice because, after reading it once,
she couldn't quite believe what she'd read. Then, without returning it to its envelope, she laid the letter down and left the
room.

IT WAS MIDNIGHT WHEN SHE HEARD RANDALL UNLOCK THE BACK ENTRY
door. Lucy Witt lay in her bed in the dark. She knew he would
think something was wrong. He would find the parlor lights
on, the kitchen lights on, his bedroom light on, each lighted
room more irregular than the last. She heard his bedroom door
open and close. A stillness commenced then, a chilling uncertain
stillness, during which time, she understood, important things
were making themselves known, and were provoking responses.
Randall could turn off the lights and go to bed. Or he could
come into her room and strangle her with one of Dick's old
ties. Those were the two extremes. In between lay the limitless
possibilities.

There.

His door had opened. He was going somewhere. Out. To the
bathroom. No, he was coming down the hallway. To her doorway
and stopping. She held her breath. She realized she was holding
her breath.

'Mrs Witt?'

She said nothing, wondered if she could've answered had she wanted.

'Mrs Witt?'

She waited and – more than that she saw it, more than that she heard it – she *felt* the doorknob turning. A wide rectangle of light had formed, against which Randall stood. 'Mrs Witt?'

She closed her eyes. She didn't stir or speak or, it seemed, breathe.

He stepped forward until, she could feel it, he stood over her.

'I'm sorry,' he said. 'You shouldn't've looked at my mail but still I'm sorry I ever wrote a letter like that.' There was deep silence. Lucy Witt began to breathe again, but kept her eyes closed. At least he's not going to kill me, she thought. He said, 'What's funny is it isn't even the way I ever really felt, so I don't know why I wrote it down that way.' His voice got a little firmer then. 'But I did. And you looked at it, which you shouldn't've done. And now all I can be is sorry about it.'

She could feel him receding. She could feel him walking away. As if that was all there was to it. 'As if that's all there is to it,' she suddenly said aloud and at once heard her voice going wobbly, 'as if you can treat people . . .' He had stopped to listen, but she couldn't go on. 'No more dinners . . .' She felt a sob, a bubbly, childish sob, rise up from within. Oh! Oh, if she were a man! Oh, if she had a club or she had a gun! But all she had was wet whimpering speech. 'Shame on you,' she said. 'Shame on you, Randall Hunsacker.'

X

ON A CLEAN APRIL DAY THAT HAD STARTED COOL AND THEN TURNED pleasantly warm, Marcy Lockhardt had begun to feel restless. During lunch she went into the restroom and took off her tights, then, at the sixth-period bell, instead of going to geometry, she sneaked up to a corner of the concrete bleachers, where, feeling like she'd just received a little gift, she stretched her legs into the sun and began reading an old *People* magazine.

Voices. Out on the football field, short-legged Meteor Frmka had emerged from the door that led beneath the bleachers to the locker rooms. Brett Heiting, the team quarterback, followed, along with a group of several other boys, all in street clothes, that included Randall Hunsacker.

Randall alone sat down and took off his shoes. Barefoot, he streaked this way and that across the grass, catching up to long arcing passes that initially seemed beyond his reach. He wore his black half-glove, but if having two less fingers than everybody else affected his ability to catch a football, it didn't show. He ran and then he caught, again and again, swiftly, easily, as if without any expenditure of effort at all. Before this occasion, whenever Marcy had seen Randall sitting slouched in class or walking unhurriedly around town, he seemed invisibly cooped up or constrained (like everyone else, Marcy thought, only more so). Even now, down on the field, Randall Hunsacker never whooped like the other boys, or even smiled, but when he ran – and this was the surprise – there was a freedom and pure joy in his movement that Marcy associated with antelope or deer and immediately envied.

A week or so later, Marcy found herself behind him in the cafeteria line. Up close, he looked almost mannish. His neck was thicker than she'd noticed from a distance, and the stubble on his face coarser. He looked like he needed to shave about three times a day. The hair on his arms was long enough to comb and, as always, the two nubbed fingers of his right hand were holstered in a custom-fit leather apparatus. He took food mechanically, without speaking, without looking around.

Once, a long, long time ago, Marcy's father had spelled out a single word for her mother in the morning dew in the yard of his farmhouse and now, in the cafeteria line, without thinking it through, Marcy pulled out a pink slip of paper from her purse and wrote down a similar word. She folded the paper. She reached forward and slid it onto Randall Hunsacker's tray.

He seemed to freeze just an instant, then move on. He sat down at a vacant table and before long other boys began sitting there, too. Marcy seated herself a few tables away, next to Bobby Parmalee, who was in the midst of cross-table conversation with Arlene Sipp, something about somebody in the money in mixed-team roping. She stopped listening. She felt her heart gaining speed until, because she couldn't keep herself from doing otherwise, she risked a glance at Randall Hunsacker. He was at that moment *opening the note.*

You, it said. That was it. *You.* She wasn't even sure she knew what she meant by it. Neither, evidently, did Randall Hunsacker. He stared at it, and turned to Marcy, who gave him the long, slow-lidded blink she'd used on lots of boys (only on this occasion, directly afterwards, she felt her skin pinkening brightly). Still, she couldn't turn away and, while the boys around Randall were diverted with some kind of silly dessert-swapping hi-jinks, he did a mysterious and thrilling thing. He slipped the note into his mouth, chewed slowly, and swallowed it.

XI

HOW EXACTLY IT HAD HAPPENED THAT RANDALL HUNSACKER'S NAME HAD arisen at the May meeting of the Goodnight PEO, Dorothy Lockhardt could not afterwards remember. Months earlier the women had sounded out Lucy Witt on the subject of the new boy, and so they believed they knew how she felt (yes, she'd heard he'd acquired some rough friends, but, no, he didn't bring them home with him, and, more to the point, Randall Hunsacker was quiet and clean, he went to school and he went to work, and otherwise it was her policy to presume the best). But today, after most of the PEO women had left and Lucy Witt was amiably hovering while Dorothy Lockhardt and three other of the younger women were tidying up, Coach Dee's name had surfaced, and then somehow, Randall Hunsacker's, and, to the general astonishment of the lingering women, Lucy Witt in a quiet but oddly determined voice said, 'I recently learned something disappointing about our Randall Hunsacker.'

The widow's story held the younger women in a thrall of accumulating indignation. Lucy Witt gave examples of the letters' unfunny salutations ('Greetings from the bumpkin patch,' 'Greetings from Sludgeville'), recited the if-a-wart-were-a-town line, and assured the other women that if she were willing to repeat darker vulgarity there would be much more to tell. The widow's story, when subsequently joined by Dorothy Lockhardt's recounting of her husband's first-hand confrontation with what she called the new boy's 'big city crudeness,' evoked a predictable response from the women. Scorn. These were not ungenerous women. Scorn was a tool they preferred not to use.

But in this case – who could argue otherwise? – it seemed exactly what he was asking for. He was contemptuous? Fine. They would find him contemptible.

Lewis Lockhardt listened with evident satisfaction as his wife related Lucy Witt's story over the supper table that night. 'Somebody may have to shoot him,' he said through a mouthful of carrots and peas. 'Just watch and see.'

If Marcy had spoken, she would've said, 'Well, maybe for some weird reason we don't understand, he was just trying to be funny for his sister's sake and didn't really mean anything by it,' or in some similarly well-intentioned but unpersuasive way tried to give Randall Hunsacker the benefit of the doubt, which would've tipped her hand in a manner she already sensed she shouldn't, so she said nothing at all, in fact seemed with her passive, unperturbed silence to be indicating that, to the small degree she gave it any thought, she couldn't agree more. A moment or two later, when the timing seemed right, she said, 'What's for dessert?'

TWO DAYS LATER, ON WEDNESDAY NIGHT ('CHURCH NIGHT,' IT WAS CALLED locally), Marcy drove her mother's car into town for Bible study at St Columbkille. The lesson was on Proverbs: 'Who can find a virtuous woman, for her price is far above rubies?' And, 'She considereth a field, and buyeth it.' Marcy doodled with a pencil in the margins of her bible, hearts, mostly, with huge arrows exploding through.

From the church, Marcy drove directly to McKibben's Mobil. 'Greetings!' she said in a playful voice to Randall Hunsacker as he emerged from the garage slowly wiping his hands on a red shop rag.

He looked at her blankly, without a visible flicker of recognition. 'Fill 'er up?'

Marcy laughed nervously, as if something funny had been said. 'Yep. Fill 'er right up.'

McKibben's Mobil had the old-fashioned pumps. You had to listen for the gurgle that preceded overflow. Randall clicked it off after less than four gallons, then fed the tank a sip more gas to be sure. It was full. 'Didn't need much,' he said.

Marcy felt her skin tingle and pinken. 'Problem is, the gas gauge doesn't work right. You can never tell what you've got.'

Randall continued to stare at the car. 'Might just be the float,' he said. He leaned in, flicked the ignition, watched the gauge move steadily left to right. He had a dieselly smell, an adult-man smell that Marcy could feel moving through her. When the needle pinned past full he leaned back out. 'Looks like we got it working again.'

Suddenly she heard herself say, 'I'm Marcy Lockhardt. I'm the one who gave you that note.' (Later she would think, If I could've thought of something just a little stupider to say, I would've said that instead.)

Randall stood away and let his gaze settle somewhere just above her head. 'I didn't tell anybody about it, if that's what you're worried about.'

Heat flashed across Marcy's skin. 'No, I wasn't worried about that. I guess I *should*'ve been, because of Bobby, my boyfriend Bobby, but I wasn't.'

Randall didn't say anything, but the way he ran his rag over a grease smudge he'd made on the rooftop suggested not only knowledge of Marcy's boyfriend but also something she took for experience and extreme patience, and suddenly all of Marcy's nervousness drained away. She felt her face soften, her body loosen. 'I saw you out in McKibben's old service truck,' she said. 'That yours now?'

A flicker of pride seemed to register in Randall's dark eyes before he nodded.

'Isn't it ancient? I thought McKibben had junked it.'

'It's old,' Randall said, 'but I've got it running pretty good.'

She waited for him to say something more. When he didn't, she said, 'Well, if you'd keep it a secret, I'd go for a ride in that old truck if you asked me to.'

XII

IF ON A CLEAR JUNE NIGHT UNDER A FULL MOON YOU DROVE SOUTH ON Highway 87 to Jack's Beans, then turned east and drove the straight country road 8.3 miles to its endpoint, you would see glimmering to your right a broad shallow sweep of the Niobrara River and, to your left, a cattleguard at the head of a long curving dirt drive that led to the Lockhardt place. Marcy's room was on the second story, separated from her parents' room by the bathroom. To go out at night unnoticed, she slipped through her bedroom window onto the porch roof, then climbed down the cast-iron sewer pipe. She met Randall out by the cattleguard.

'This is fine for June,' she told him one night after coming out of the wild lilac where she'd been waiting, 'but when winter comes, we'll have to come up with something else.'

Part of what Randall liked about Marcy's conversation was the occasional reference to a future that included him. 'Where to?' he said as they pulled onto Highway 87.

'Wherever. Someplace we've never been.'

They rarely drove to any particular destination. They just drove through the night, talking when they felt like it and otherwise listening to late-night, high-wattage radio (KOMA from Oklahoma City was their favorite). The faster and further Randall drove, the better Marcy liked it. She liked running her hand up and down his hairy arm, feeling it stir her nerves, hoping it stirred his. One night she pulled his right hand from the steering wheel, unsnapped and slid off the leather holster that covered the place where his fingers had been. She turned on the overhead cab light and stared at the pinkish scarred nub. She touched it. She rubbed her finger along its surprisingly smooth surface. 'You feel that?' she said, and he said, 'Sure. It feels good.'

They drove through little towns that Marcy had often seen before, but never so late at night. Now, with nothing open and nothing moving on the streets but stray dogs, they seemed like foreign places. They drove through violent thunderstorms, Marcy turning in her seat for those moments when the lightning flash-lit Randall's face as he squinted into the night. 'What?' he said when he noticed her staring.

'It's like a movie shot or something,' Marcy said. 'It makes you look like Al Pacino in Nebraska.' She laughed. 'Either that or a sniper in a bell tower.'

Randall ignored this last part. It was too much like people really did think of him. 'Who's Al Pacino?' he asked.

'God! In Utah you can't drink, fornicate *or* go to the movies?'

'You can do all those things,' Randall said mildly and, still hunched over the steering wheel, still squinting into the driving rain, he reached over to turn up the radio. It was Dwight Yokum. He had gotten so he liked Dwight Yokum. It was one of the funny things that happen. You get to like a place at just exactly the same time its people, on account of the way you *used* to feel about their town, decide that you're a regal asshole.

'*Did* you though?'

'Did I what though?'

'Drink, fornicate and go to the movies?'

This was something tricky. He liked to tell Marcy the truth. That was his operating principle. Yet he'd learned that Marcy *liked* the idea that he was, to use her word, *experienced*, and he wasn't sure he wanted to correct her. 'No,' he said, 'not anyhow in that particular order.'

INITIALLY MARCY WAS GLAD RANDALL DIDN'T TEAR INTO HER WITH SLOBBERY kisses. He didn't tear into her with kisses of any kind. He would let his hand graze her arm, his arm graze her breast, as if to hint at something beyond her experience that he was too knowing to mention, and totally patient about getting to. But Marcy finally decided she'd waited long enough. One night as they drove, she leaned close, slipped a hand inside his shirt and said, 'You ever going to kiss me?'

Randall took his foot off the gas, cut the lights, pulled the truck into a field of alfalfa. There was a skinny moon. He looked at her, then got out and walked around the car to her door. Marcy closed her eyes. In the quiet, she could hear the crunch of his boots on the rough dirt. He opened her door. Marcy slid from the cab and stood on the running board. Randall stepped forward and wrapped himself around her. 'You,' he said. His low voice moved into her and tugged straight a line she never knew existed, a line that ran directly from her breasts to her private parts. This new current of feeling Marcy felt obliged to identify as some form of love.

'How many times have you . . . you *know?*' Marcy said as they were driving home. Standing on the running board, they had kissed and caressed and carried on for most on an hour. When Randall had fingered the buttons to her pants, she hadn't wanted to stop him, but she had.

Randall, composed with fresh happiness and the prospects of more, was sitting loosely behind the wheel. He tilted his head slightly. 'What?'

Marcy said, 'How many times have you, you know –' she searched for the right term: *fooled around with? had sex with? diddled?* – 'made love with a girl?'

They drove through the black night. Bruce Springsteen was doing 'Blinded by the Light.'

'Never,' Randall said finally. 'I never have.'

And suddenly and all at once Marcy realized she was happy to hear it. 'Never even came close?'

'No, not really.' He remembered how, once, after a trailer set-up job in St George, Lenny had driven him in his Mack truck up to Las Vegas and pulled up in front of a place where other big rigs were parked and men were coming and going. This a whorehouse? Randall had asked and Lenny had grinned. It's better than a whorehouse, he said. It's a *colored* whorehouse. Then he'd said, Happy Birthday, though it wasn't Randall's birthday, wasn't even close. 'I didn't go in,' he told Marcy now. 'It was because, I don't know, even though my sister was kind of wild and even my mother was kind of wild, I never really was, and I just wanted not to do it until it was with somebody that meant something.'

Randall slowed down at Jack's Beans and made the turn east toward the Lockhardt place. Marcy yawned contentedly. 'So did your stepdad say anything when you didn't go in?' she asked.

'Oh yeah.' Randall grinned. 'He said I must be a fruitcake.'

And so Marcy Lockhardt and Randall Hunsacker had from their separate backgrounds and expectations begun moving toward an unmarked danger point. For a long time, and with increasing zeal, Randall Hunsacker had craved sexual relations with Marcy Lockhardt and now, secretly, but self-admittedly, Marcy wanted to have sex with Randall. For each of them, however, the implications of this act could not have been less alike.

For Marcy, it was a gift perfectly customized to her personality. It provided multiple thrills. It meant not only that she was going to have her first sexual experience with someone whom she liked and desired and even *loved*, in some form or other, but also with someone she *felt a little sorry for*. This gift, presented to her by her personal gods, would allow her simultaneously to have sex *and* commit a charitable act. And though Marcy acknowledged that she already loved Randall, in some form or other, she saw further that she *could*, if she allowed it, love Randall Hunsacker utterly, without question or qualification or reserve, but she wasn't about to allow it. She knew what was in store for Randall. He'd told her himself. Keep working for McKibben, he'd said, maybe save up for a shop of his own. He'd heard they were short of good mechanics in Chadron. Marcy knew Chadron and she knew the lot of mechanics' wives and neither fit into her future. Her grades were good. Her test scores were high. She was going to college. She was going to graduate school. Then she was going somewhere else, anywhere else, as long as it was not even close to Nebraska.

And Randall, of course, understood none of this. For him, to have sex with Marcy was, along with all its other happy working parts, a way of accepting her tendered trust, of holding it close and carefully, of putting it into safekeeping. It was, in short, the single act that would become his inviolate pledge to marry Marcy Lockhardt.

As for the actual occasion, he wouldn't ask and she wouldn't rush. She savored the seriousness the subject aroused in Randall, the unspecified significance he attached to it. Marcy had heard about other girls' drunken, disappointing, regretted first nights, and she was determined that hers, with Randall, would be different, better, more self-respecting. She knew that she was in charge of the timetable and yet she didn't know what the timetable was. Sometime this summer, she'd decided. When it felt right. And when she couldn't get pregnant.

XIII

'HOW DOES THIS ALL WORK?' RANDALL ASKED MARCY THE FIRST THURSDAY night in July as they drove through the town of Pine Bluff, far south of Goodnight. 'You go out with friends every Friday night, and maybe another night or two besides, and then you sneak off two or three nights with me.'

Marcy laughed and said, 'That's how it works. The way you just described it.'

He drove on, but dourly. He was patient. He'd accepted that if her parents couldn't know about them, then nobody could know about them, not in a town this small. He'd accepted even that her going out with her girlfriends and keeping on friendly terms with Bobby Parmalee was a good way of throwing everyone off their scent. But this had been going on over a month now. This weekend was the 4th of July, and the rodeo, and the Friendly Festival.

'It's just that it makes me feel queasy,' Randall said. 'It's like lying, except not using words.' This was true in his case, though he knew Marcy did a good deal of more conventional lying whenever, as it now and then occurred, she was going to see Randall at any time other than the dead of night.

Marcy moved close to him in the cab of the truck, threw her arms around his neck, gave him a big friendly kiss. 'You're my late date,' she said. 'You're my back door man.' (She'd learned both terms from songs on the radio.)

'And what's Bobby Parmalee?' This was another thing, as far as Randall was concerned. If Bobby was in love with Marcy, and being strung along by her, well, he felt kind of sorry for him. But if Bobby was in love with Marcy, and was getting halfway as far along with her as Randall himself was, well then Randall would like to kill him.

'Bobby's a friend,' Marcy said. 'I like him and he likes me. But you're the one I love. I don't know if that's good or if it's bad, but it's a fact. I've never made love with Bobby and I've never told him I love him. I like him and he likes me. That's the definition of friends.'

'That how Bobby defines it?' Randall wanted to know.

'That's how *I* define it,' Marcy said seriously, which was exactly the right tone to take because if it was Marcy's adventurous side that Randall loved, it was her serious side that he respected, and he wasn't interested in one feeling without the other.

And so Randall extended his hours at the filling station during the Friendly Festival, and would not let his eyes stray toward Main Street and the park where the parade and turkey chase and pig roast all went on. He ate his meals at the Eleventh Man, where many of the patrons, including Leo's cronies, hoped they might be insulated from the family-flavored fun that ensued without, but weren't. (Leo himself attended the pig roast with his wife and, on behalf of his uncle, who'd footed the bill, was thanked by Bud Drabbel, Goodnight's honorary mayor, for provision of the five, 4-H project pigs, parts of which were, at that very moment, being masticated by many in attendance.) During the festival, Frank Mears was absent from his table under the Oly sign. 'Off with his squaw,' Whistler Simpson said and Marlen Coates explained, 'He's got an injun girlfriend. He says she hates these all-American holidays as much as he does, so they shack up and get shellacked till it's over.'

And finally, though it seemed the Friendly Festival would never be over, it was over, and midnight Monday came, and Randall was with Marcy driving down Highway 87, the windows down, her hand and warm air within his shirt, breathing again, thawed out of hellish, hibernative half-aliveness.

Between songs on the radio, Randall lowered the volume. 'One week from today,' he said, 'I'll have been here one year.' Then before turning up 'Achy Breaky Heart,' which always got Marcy seat-dancing, he said, 'Seems longer than that to me.'

The miles and minutes went by. Further down the road, while idly kneading his neck, Marcy said, 'So do you know any jokes?'

'Nope,' Randall said. Then, 'Well, one. It's *sort of* a joke.'

Randall proceeded to tell the supernormalist joke. 'A supernormalist was out walking one night with another guy,' he began, and when he got to the punchline – the supernormalist saying, 'Well, what if I got halfway up to the moon and you turned off the flashlight?' – Marcy didn't laugh. She turned away and looked out at the night. The joke reminded her of a night a long time before when Bobby Parmalee had looked at the moon and said it was so low you could just about rope it, and she had said, 'Not without some help from NASA,' or something similarly snotty and then felt so bad she'd begun to kiss him.

'Not that funny, huh?' Randall said now, of his joke. She said she guessed it was a pretty good joke, but not a very funny one. They were by then in the town of Hyannis. Randall pulled over to the curb in front of the Dodge agency, got out and began walking around the dark lot. It was 2 a.m. on a Monday night. It was quiet. Marcy watched Randall moving car to car, peering into each interior. That joke he'd told, Marcy decided, was about what people in love do. They climb out on this imaginary light beam, a miracle all by itself, and then they have to hope like anything the other person doesn't switch off the light. But of course, she thought, the other person sooner or later would. Marcy suddenly leaned forward, tapped on the horn, and waved Randall back.

AND SO A YEAR HAD PASSED. IT WAS ONCE AGAIN A SATURDAY AFTERNOON IN July, and within the repair bay of McKibben's Mobil, Jim McKibben was greasing a Chrysler LeBaron while Randall Hunsacker repacked the bearings on Orval Weyers's Chevy pickup; within the community room of the Sleepy Hollow Trailer Court, the jigsaw women were doing a Thomas Hart Benton (difficulty: moderate) and talking not so much about Gary P. Corcoran, the new Methodist minister, as of his wife, a short, rotund woman ('Why, she's five by five!' Flossie Boyles said) who'd shown up for her husband's first service wearing a muu-muu and flipflops); within the Eleventh Man, Leo Underwood laid a square of pre-sliced Swiss on a burger he was frying for Marlen Coates, looked up to the TV just in time to see Ben Crenshaw hit an eleven-foot birdie putt at Turnberry, and uttered a soft 'Damn' (Leo again had money on Norman); and within her Greek Revival home along tree-shaded Ash Street, the widow Lucy Witt had been shuffling a double deck of cards to lay into another hand of Napoleon solitaire when she thought to look at the time. 1.45! And she hadn't eaten a thing! Where in the world had the morning gone? She shuffled again, slowly. 'The morning came and went, as the mornings do,' she said aloud, to herself. She'd had a parrot once, or, rather, Dick had. He'd installed it in the breakfast nook and let his wife name it (Bellavoce, later shortened to Bella), but nonetheless Lucy Witt couldn't stand the bird. It never spoke, not even hello. Instead it screeched like a monkey, all through the day, and there was, in addition, the horrid smell, the scattered seed, the molting feathers, and, of course, the poop. Still, it was Lucy, not her husband, who noticed how much the bird hated snow. When snow fell, Bella stared out the breakfast nook window, grew sulky, wouldn't eat, ceased even to screech. Good, Lucy Witt had thought at the time, but, later, after Dick's death, it was she who would pull up a chair in the kitchen nook on snowy days and read softly to the old bird, page after page, from one Agatha Christie or another.

Chapter Four

VILLAS IN ITALY

BEFORE MARRYING LEWIS LOCKHARDT, DOROTHY LOCKHARDT HAD BEEN A *Rasmussen, one of the four Rasmussen girls, all known for their soprano voices and liquid dark eyes. Dorothy, the youngest, doted on her father, and vice versa (he called her variously Dot, Doe, Dodie, and Piglet). Dorothy followed him everywhere, and though she was otherwise often obstreperous, she fell peaceful in her father's presence. Dorothy's mother, who had her hands full with the other three girls, acceded to Dorothy's inclination to the other parent, and she would smile to watch her husband followed about the place by her daughter, much as she might smile at a man followed about by a pet duck. Until she was six, Dorothy could only fall asleep curled in the lap of her father, who would then carry her back to the bedroom she shared with her sisters. When she was seven, Dorothy slept for several nights on the dusty floor beneath the bed her father shared with her mother, until Dorothy's coughing betrayed her.*

Of the four Rasmussen sisters, Dorothy had been perhaps the prettiest, but believed a small fleshy mole on her left cheek dominated her face and spoiled her looks. It was just her portion, she believed, and she never mentioned the mole aloud (though during her teenaged years she did pray for its miraculous expungement). Dorothy's three sisters were genial, gregarious, and handy. They made friends of everyone, and they made clever gifts – appleface dolls, tatted doilies, ornamented leather wallets – for all their friends, and particularly for Lewis Lockhardt, who lived on the flats with

*his widowed father, and who came Sundays for dinner with the
Rasmussens, sitting always to Dorothy's father's right in a stiff,
ladder-backed chair that stayed at the table even on those other
six days when Lewis Lockhardt wasn't expected.*

*Lewis Lockhardt was not a handsome young man, perhaps because
so many of his parts were too big. His hands were huge and reddish,
and so were his ears. His teeth were large, and there seemed to be
too many of them for his mouth (several had twisted and turned in
order to fit in). He had stiff, short-cropped straw-colored hair that he
habitually (but ineffectually) tried to neaten with water before meals.
It was no surprise then that Dorothy's sisters laughed at Lewis behind
his back ('I almost burst when you said you had an idea for a picnic
and he said he was all ears!') and yet they couldn't really make up
their minds about him. There was something about Lewis Lockhardt
that anyone who knew him sensed and respected and perhaps even
envied, which was his innate competence in the collection and
assembly of the parts of his life. He was only twenty-three years
of age, but he'd established himself as a farmer who could, in Mr
Rasmussen's words, bring in a crop and consolidate his gains. (In
the past six years Lewis Lockhardt and his father had doubled the
number of irrigation units they owned on the flats.) And Lewis had
been a late-born son – he wouldn't have to wait into middle age
to farm for himself. (None of this was lost on Mr Rasmussen, who
discreetly talked up Lewis's eligibility whenever he could.)*

*But there was something else besides decent prospects to compen-
sate for Lewis Lockhardt's plain looks. Somewhere along the line he
had learned to dance. He didn't just know the steps, he had the
feel of them. Music moved through him to his partner, who – it
was dreamlike – seemed transformed into some essential part of
this song, this dance floor and Elks Hall, this town and county.
Often, when one of these partners turned to thank Lewis at the
conclusion of a dance, she would be suddenly struck with the idea
that Lewis Lockhardt, standing there grinning toothily, was, at this
suspended moment and in this particular light, almost handsome.
And so one night, when she was ten years old, Lewis in fun had
swung Dorothy out onto the floor of an Elks Club dance, and she
had felt what older girls had felt, and when later that night, lying in*

*bed, she was too excited to sleep, eight-year-old Dorothy Rasmussen
had gotten up and crept to her dresser drawer, removed two small
red ribbons she'd been saving, and stole down the hallway to the
dining room, where, visiting first her father's chair and then Lewis
Lockhardt's, she tied to the leg of each a small red bow.*

*But as the years passed, Dorothy had changed form and changed
form again. At age thirteen she was no longer allowed to sit in
her father's lap (she sulked; she didn't see why not), but she
still shadowed him, though in less obvious ways (she took as her
own, for example, his opinions on everything, from movie stars
to politicians). She'd forgotten the dance and the red ribbons,
but, if only because of her father's fondness for their neighboring
bachelor farmer, Dorothy, too, was still fond of Lewis Lockhardt
(now twenty-six and still unmarried.) 'Maybe you'll be the lucky
one to marry him, Piglet,' her father said to Dorothy, but he would
also say, 'Get yourself a profession that pays, Dot, in case you wind
up marrying a drunk.'*

*Dorothy's father owned a small sugar beet operation northwest
of the home place, and though he himself didn't run it day to day,
he went out regularly to check on things and, whenever she could,
Dorothy would go along. One day, when she was fourteen and they
were off together on this customarily pleasant mission, her father
abruptly slowed the car as they approached the sugar beet farm
– there were men gathered; something was going on – and her
father at once told Dorothy to lie down on the floor of the car
and keep her head down and not look up. His voice was so urgent
and forceful that she instantly and completely obeyed. Her father
stopped the car and got out. Perhaps twenty minutes passed, but
Dorothy did not look up. Finally her father returned to the car, but
as they drove away she still wasn't allowed to look up or look back. He
never would explain, but Dorothy's sisters were happy to. An Indian
who worked for Dorothy's father had discovered – 'or maybe only
thought he discovered' – that his wife had been running around
on him. He had tied her to a car and dragged her around until she
was dead. When Dorothy and her father had arrived, the woman
was still tied to the bumper of the car. 'Papa himself cut her free,'
Geraldine said. In Dorothy's imagination the skin of the woman at*

rest was the moist, glistening yet gritty reddish-pink of a just-skinned rabbit inadvertently dropped into the dirt, which she'd once seen (her mother had skinned it; Dorothy herself had dropped it), and the next time someone asked Dorothy what she meant to be when she grew up, she said matter-of-factly that she was going to be a nurse. Then she added, 'In France, or maybe Italy,' and while her questioner and other listeners laughed, Dorothy did not.

Dorothy did well in school, and though conspicuously attractive, mole notwithstanding, she was not gregarious. She would turn down dates in order to sit in the front room quilting or working on one of her scrapbooks ('Villas in Italy,' or 'Nurses – Four Corners of the Globe') while her parents sat in their worn wing chairs at opposite ends of the room and read. The truth was, by age seventeen, Dorothy Rasmussen preferred to live in her imagination. She quilted and dreamily washed dishes and stole away on walks by herself. Her mind hardly ever rested. Winter nights, she would burrow into her quilts and, before falling to sleep, she would rework minutely varying versions of the arrival in Goodnight of an exotic-looking foreigner who would spot her walking along a country road or reading on a shady bank of Walgren Lake and would, in that instant, fall madly in love with her. Always this man would be older and foreign, dark-haired and handsomely dressed. Though he spoke French or Italian (and Dorothy did not), she would understand him perfectly. He would wait only moments before asking Dorothy to become mistress of his villa and – she liked her suitor to pause tremblingly here – his life.

Chapter Five

MRS LEWIS LOCKHARDT

I

AUGUST, THE LOCKHARDT PLACE, ON THE FLATS SOUTH OF GOODNIGHT. THE sky in its heat was almost white, and there was everywhere the low, electric-sounding buzz of insects. For the past two hours, while Dorothy listened off and on, her husband had been on the telephone to farm implement companies, asking for a part (Dorothy by now knew the words by heart: 'a shifting fork rail for an Allis Chalmers 1090'), and when an outfit in Hyannis said they had one in stock, Lewis was off like a shot. 'What about supper?' Dorothy called from the stoop and Lewis Lockhardt, poking his big head out the truck window, stretching a grin over his protuberant teeth, said what she hoped he'd say: He said he'd manage.

Dust rose behind the pickup as it moved down the dry, dirt lane. What happened then to Dorothy was what happened almost every time a car drove away these days, whether it contained a visitor or her husband or even her own daughter – a feeling like a fist opening into a hand gently unfolded inside her.

DOROTHY BELIEVED THERE WERE THINGS WRONG WITH HER LIFE, OR MISSING from it, but she couldn't figure out what these things were exactly, or even if they were big enough to worry about. She'd always believed Lewis was a good man. As a husband, he had always provided for her and Marcy, had never struck them or even said a bad swear word to them, had never made Dorothy do anything, sexually speaking, that she didn't want to do. Everybody liked Lewis, and why not? He generally saw the sunny side of things. He paid people compliments and kept his problems to himself. He was thrifty and hard-working, the kind of sturdy, thick-necked, big-boned man who could be happy with farming and lean into its hardships. She couldn't say she felt unloved or underappreciated. He was never too tired for the niceties. His face always brightened when he saw hers, and he always praised her cooking, her quilting, her ways of dressing. And always, last thing every night, he would in his low rough voice say, 'Until tomorrow,' and would with his toothsome mouth kiss her on the back of the neck (and would've kissed her mouth if she'd turned to him, which she would've liked to have done, and believed she should've done, but the baking soda he brushed with never quite suppressed the sourness of his breath, and, besides, it was not a kiss anymore, it was a clash of teeth).

TODAY, WHILE LEWIS WAS OFF IN HYANISS, DOROTHY DECIDED TO MOW the wide, weedy lawn that encircled the house. She ran an orange extension cord out the kitchen window and plugged it into the Craftsman rear-bagger. She set a pitcher of iced tea at the top of the porch steps. A gaunt black cat appeared and unsteadily positioned itself nearby.

'Nadine?' Dorothy said and gave the cat a long look. 'You feeling any good today, Sweetie?'

The old cat, staring off, seemed only barely there.

Dorothy switched on the mower, worked the throttle. She didn't own recreational clothes so, except for the shoes, she was wearing her daughter Marcy's things, a green Goodnight Titan baseball cap, a pair of khaki shorts, and an old white dress shirt, the tails of which she tied into a rabbit-eared knot just below her chest. For a minute or two, it made her feel too unclothed, but then – she was alone, after all – it didn't. She began to feel good. She sweated, and a slow-sweeping breeze felt cool to the skin.

Dorothy moved slowly up and down the west side, in and out of the shade thrown by the cottonwoods, settling into an even, easy pace. 'Did you ever hear a whippoorwill?' she sang in her fine, thin voice. At the end of each mown row, she had to raise the cord with one hand and duck under it, then reverse the mower. Dorothy had just finished such a reversal when the music in her head suddenly stopped.

Over by the yardgate, standing there as if trying to figure out what to do with himself, was Marcy's boyfriend, Bobby Parmalee.

Dorothy shut off the mower and untied the rabbit-eared knot as she walked over. 'Hello, Mr Parmalee,' she said.

Bobby Parmalee dipped his head and touched his DeKalb seedcap, a method of acknowledgment that had always struck Dorothy as endearingly courtly.

'Marcy's not here,' she said. 'She's still off at that camp.' A cheerleaders camp held up at Chadron State, thirty miles away.

Dorothy glanced around for Bobby Parmalee's car – a Plymouth Fury

the color of a cornstarch box – but it wasn't there.

'Where'd you come from?' she said. It came out a little sharp.

'Football practice.'

'No, I mean where's your car?'

'Oh. Over by the barn.' He swung his gaze off in that direction. 'Thought from a distance you were Marcy.' He turned back toward Dorothy, who had folded her arms. 'I was going to sneak up on her. It was you wearing her clothes that fooled me.'

'Even so,' Dorothy said, but Bobby Parmalee had sunken, watery blue eyes that gave to his face a look of perpetual apology that made being angry with him hard to sustain. 'Stay put,' she said, 'and I'll bring out cookies.'

Once inside the house, Dorothy detoured to the bathroom. She retied the shirt the way she'd had it, and looked into the mirror. She hadn't looked so bad. Not seventeen again, but okay.

Outside, the whir of the mower.

Dorothy went to the window. Bobby Parmalee had decided to do some mowing while he waited. Long strides, quick reverses, and the swath of cut grass steadily widened. When he was done, Bobby washed up out back and plopped down on the steps, where Dorothy had set out a platter of cookies alongside the beaded pitcher of tea. He smelled pleasantly of soap. Dorothy sat to his left, the mole side away. He drained one glass of iced tea and while Dorothy poured him another he began on the cookies and glanced off toward the road, where dust would cloud if someone were coming. 'Marcy say what time she'd be home by?'

'Five,' Dorothy said. It was after six. A silence developed, and Dorothy turned the talk to football. 'I hear through the grapevine that the new boy's playing like he means it this year.'

Bobby nodded. 'Yeah. Coach Dee switched him to free safety on defense and he's like a different guy all of a sudden. From another planet, it's like. An animal from another planet.' Bobby grinned at this, then glanced again toward the road. 'Zacker-man tackles you, you stay tackled,' he said distractedly.

Slowly Nadine stood and moved across the porch toward Dorothy, but Bobby intercepted the cat and raised her overhead so that all four legs hung useless. 'A featherweight,' he said.

'Really?' Dorothy said. 'Lighter now than before?'

'Never picked her up before,' he said, and put the cat back down. 'I'm a dog man myself.'

Dorothy took up the cat, tested her heft. She *was* lighter – she seemed in fact all but hollow.

'Well, Lewis is a stockman,' Dorothy said. 'Animals as pets is an idea he just doesn't go for.' She nodded down at the cat, which had curled neatly into her arms. 'He'll abide a dog if it stays out of the way, but cats get his goat. One day a little while back, Nadine got underfoot and Lewis stepped on her, lost his balance and went right down. But instead of saying a few of the words he normally reserves for such moments, his face got purple and he stood up and heaved the cat into the middle of next week.'

The Parmalee boy let out a laugh, as Dorothy had known he would. She told it as a joke, though at the time it had seemed anything but. It had all happened fast, one horrible moment tumbling up after another. The cat, after landing roughly, with a sickening plumping sound, had in terror shot under the house and when Lewis, as if caught at something, had turned to Dorothy, the contorted look on his face seemed both ugly and eerily familiar, as if in dreams she'd seen this ugliness before.

Suddenly Bobby Parmalee perked up and peered beyond Dorothy, where Marcy at last was walking up the dirt lane, at ease, as always, with her own good looks. She carried her cheerleading bag in one hand; the other swung free.

'Greetings, Earthlings!' she called and Bobby Parmalee was up, hurrying to greet her. His back was to Dorothy, but she didn't have to see his face to know that a foolish grin that was pasted across it.

'Hiya, Marcy,' she heard him say. If he was wondering where she'd been and why she was late, he didn't say so.

Marcy lifted Bobby's seedcap from his head and ran her free hand across his football buzz cut. 'Knobby Bobby was a bear,' she said merrily, hauling Bobby into her own high spirits. 'Knobby Bobby has no hair!'

There was an excited flush to Marcy's face, but from what exactly, Dorothy didn't know. This wasn't new, this private area Marcy had staked out for herself, but it was new enough that it still perplexed Dorothy.

'How come you were walking?' she said.

Marcy without a blink said, 'Wasn't. It's just that Merna was running late so she dropped me at the boxes.' The mailboxes. At the end of the driveway. Beyond the shelter belt. Out of sight.

'Ah,' Dorothy said, and gave her a gray look to let her know how leaky it sounded to her.

To which Marcy responded by hooking a finger through one of Bobby's beltloops and organizing a quick departure. She'd already had a cheeseburger with Merna, she said, and Mrs Wilcox had their practice pom-poms waiting, so they ought to get in that big old Plymouth Fury of Bobby's and drive away from here *post haste*.

As the car rolled off, Marcy leaned out the window and shouted, 'Bye, Momster!' Beyond her, in the driver's seat, Bobby Parmalee was grinning happily.

The car receded, the *thip thip* of the sprinklers seemed suddenly louder, and the smell of just-cut grass hung in the air. Once, when Dorothy was eighteen, she had stood with Lewis on this very lawn. It was September and she was due the next week to start school full-time at Chadron State, where she'd already taken classes that summer so she'd have a head start on her nursing course. After eleven years as a widower, Lewis Lockhardt's father had followed his wife to what he called 'the great world of light,' so that Lewis, now aged thirty-one, was farming and living alone on the Lockhardt place. His farming didn't suffer, and he did his best with the house, but still it showed the effects of long years of manly inattention. Often during that summer Dorothy or her sister, Darlene (the second youngest of the Rasmussen girls; the older two had married and moved away) would stop by with a casserole or sometimes even stay to cook Lewis a real meal. Once a week or so, they would come in and tidy up, and in exchange Lewis would take them both out to supper (the Food Bowl in Gordon was his favorite) or sometimes, on a Saturday night, to the drive-in movies in Chadron, where, within the cab of Lewis's pickup truck, Dorothy sat in the middle, presumably as insulation between Lewis and Darlene. At the Friendly Festival dance, Lewis took the floor in equal number with each of them (Darlene was the one who counted and pointed it out to Dorothy), and he danced with a couple of other women more his own age besides. And then in early September Lewis had dropped by the Rasmussen place to tell Dorothy and Darlene that he was driving to Denver and back the following day to deliver a horse, and was hoping one or both of them would be willing to keep him company. 'I'll take you to Cabella's on the way back and get you new gloves,' he said, by way of incentive. Darlene wanted to go, but couldn't (she gave piano lessons and had one of the Sipp girls plus the whole Duncanson brood coming the next day). Dorothy was free to go, but didn't really want to. 'I need to study,' she said and when an awkward silence then developed, she capitulated. 'I guess I could bring my book and study in the car,' she said. Darlene, regretting this missed opportunity, and with the twin objectives of saving Lewis from going several miles out of his way as well as impressing him with her generous and anticipatory nature, volunteered to drive Dorothy to the Lockhardt place early the next morning. Darlene rose at four, washed her hair, and slipped on a white top she'd ironed specially the night before. Dorothy rose at 4.45, peed, brushed her teeth, ran a comb through her hair and sleepily declared herself ready. It had been a cool night, cool enough for flannel pajamas, and all in the world she wanted as she and Darlene bumped along the county road that morning was to fall back to sleep. Whereas Lewis, she noted when they turned the last curve of the Lockhardt driveway, was at 5.15 in the morning already going full tilt, briskly shuttling supplies to the truck. Dorothy leaned mutely against the horse trailer, making plans to sleep as they drove, while Darlene worked hard at conversation even as Lewis was loading the horse. 'Wish I was coming,' she said and Lewis, distractedly – the horse was balky – said he wished she was, too. He'd seemed in a hurry to get going, but – a strange thing – once Darlene had driven off, Lewis seemed suddenly to slow down. He didn't jump right into the truck, as Dorothy had expected him to do. He lingered. He looked around. Finally, moving as deftly as he did on the dance floor, he circled the truck and took Dorothy's hand (his felt, as it always did on those rare occasions when he took her hand in his, absolutely huge). He led her to the yardgate, and stationed her just inside. The sun hadn't yet fully risen; there was dewfrost on the grass. Lewis stepped onto the lawn but before going further turned abruptly around. 'You like this place, don't you?' he said, and she shrugged and in her sleepy voice said, 'Sure, it's a pretty farm. I've always thought it was.' Then, right there in the yard, leaning forward with his big hands clasped behind his back (later – impossibly – she would imagine him during these moments as a figure skater), Lewis Lockhardt, in large script, with his boot in the dewfrost, wrote out the word *Yours*. He turned and grinned a big, toothy, serious grin. 'I've been thinking about it,' he said, 'and that's what I've decided.'

Dorothy was a little alarmed. '*What's* what you've decided?'

'That this house and place and life should be yours –' he grinned – 'as long as you don't mind including me in the package.'

She wasn't sure. She wasn't a bit sure. His words surprised her, but that was all she felt, just surprise. 'What about Darlene?' she said.

'No,' he said, and suddenly – it was shocking, really – his big eyes and his sturdy, vehement voice took hold of her. 'It's always been you. Even when you were just little, I never really thought it out, but I guess I just always knew. You were the quiet one, the quiet and the smart and the dreamy one, and . . . I guess I don't know beyond that, except that you're the most beautiful girl I ever saw.' His voice, to her surprise, had cracked just a little. He stopped and looked away for a second before fixing her again with his eyes. He studied her, and Dorothy somehow sensed that he read in her expression something other than love, but – she knew this all at once – he was wrong. 'You can say no,' he said. 'I hope you won't, but maybe you will. It doesn't matter though. It won't change how I feel. You'll always be the only girl in the world I will ever want to marry.'

Not once during that long pleasant summer had eighteen-year-old Dorothy Rasmussen given one serious thought to marrying thirty-one-year-old Lewis Lockhardt with the ham hands and big teeth, yet when he'd narrowed his sights on her and spoken those words it had sent through her a sensation that seemed both wonderful and dangerous. And now, years later, standing at the same iron yardgate, Dorothy wished that sensation might somehow come fresh again, but it wouldn't. All that was left was a memory of a sensation, which, instead of making you feel different, merely reminded you of how you ought to feel but don't.

DOROTHY HAD ONE SECRET. CAREFULLY HIDDEN IN THE SATIN LINING OF her Chinese sewing basket was quite a lot of money. Some of it had accrued through the sale of baby quilts at the St Columbkille Christmas bazaar, some had accrued through grocery checks written at Frmka's Suprette for $10 over, some had accrued, in Lewis's absence, through the occasional cash sale of a yearling heifer to a man named Joe White Magpie, but most of it had come through an inheritance that neither Lewis nor Marcy knew about. Initially Dorothy had planned to use the money to send Marcy off to college or on a cruise down the Nile or in some similar way to show Marcy what, besides farm life, the world had to offer. But one day, when she was at the Chadron State library looking up articles on sunflower farming for Lewis, Dorothy had idly browsed through an *International World-Herald* and found, on its back pages, a small advertisement concerning a Miss Luel Stevenson's Equestrian School for Young Women near London, England. Dorothy sent for information and by return mail received a brochure printed on beautiful cream-colored paper as thick, nearly, as cardboard. Miss Luel Stevenson's was, it turned out, much more than just a horse school. The brochure noted field trips to Stonehenge, the Old Globe Theatre, the actual Old Curiosity Shop, plus a variety of London museums. There were lessons in ballroom dance, in voice and piano, in the culinary arts, in hostessing social gatherings appropriate to the season and time of day. Fees for the nine-month program, discreetly detailed on a separate insert, were eye-popping, in Dorothy's opinion, but she kept imagining what kind of world Miss Stevenson might open up to Marcy, and she had tucked the brochure into the sewing basket along with the money.

II

WHEN THE OLD CAT STOPPED EATING AND HER FUR, AS IF ELECTRIFIED, WOULD not lie flat, Dorothy knew not only that the cat was dying but that she ought to let her die. Nadine was fifteen, a long life for a cat born in a barn. Dorothy, out walking Marcy, had come upon the ribby young cat nesting in the seat stuffing of a rusted-out DeSoto they'd abandoned years before. There must've been a mother and siblings, of course, but they were evidently dead. Dorothy brought the kitten foodscraps. When the cat began following her and Marcy on their walks into the fields, Dorothy gave her a name. The cat in return brought dead things to the door to present to Dorothy – barn mice, lizards and, once, a small snake. Before long, Dorothy let the cat in. As she kept house, the cat followed along. She lay by the stove as Dorothy cooked, sat on the wicker clothes hamper while Dorothy bathed Marcy, hopped onto the bed and curled against Dorothy's legs as she slept. As a child, Marcy did things to Nadine that would make other cats peevish – Christmas bows taped to her fur, tinker-toys tied to her tail – but Nadine merely waited for Dorothy to intervene. The cat never stopped bringing gifts, though in later years the objects laid at Dorothy's feet were more and more just thefts from the trash – a rubber band, a withered mushroom button, a crumpled piece of breadwrapper. Yet these last gifts affected Dorothy more than the others because, looking down at Nadine's dully expectant eyes, she could almost feel the pleasure it brought the old cat to give them.

Taking Nadine to Bobby Parmalee's father, the only vet in Goodnight, was out of the question – word would get back to Lewis that money had been spent on a cat – so Dorothy took $40 from the Chinese sewing basket, eased the old cat into a box with a blanket on the bottom, and drove to a Dr Hansen's office in Pine Bluff, where Dorothy wasn't known.

Dr Hansen was a peppy little man with happy eyes and thick, sandy-red hair and eyebrows. What Dorothy liked best about him was that he seemed to think that treating a barncat was not laughable. He said he'd keep Nadine for an hour or two, work up some blood tests, then they'd see where they were.

After some shopping, Dorothy went into Woolworth's for a green salad and iced tea. 'I'm just waiting for our cat at the vet's,' Dorothy found herself saying to the waitress, 'a barncat my husband adopted, if you can imagine it.' This was a curious lie, to which she added, 'We only have a large-animal vet in Goodnight, was why he sent me all the way here.'

Only two other customers were eating at the counter, and Dorothy sat far from both. She'd bought the new *Redbook* and closely looked over each page before turning another. She was doing this and eating her salad with melba toast when a man sat down beside her to the right. Dorothy was glad he was on the moleless side, but she was suspicious of his closeness. She moved her parcels onto the counter and set her purse at the base of her stool, where she could feel it against her foot. Then, in the mirror behind the counter, she sneaked a look. He was a trim, compact man with a solid jaw and black, neatly barbered hair. He wore a freshly laundered blue shirt and burgundy tie. His complexion was either olive or . . . what was that other word for people looking Greek or Italian? – she couldn't think of it.

The man ordered quickly, without the menu. Pastrami on rye, plenty of mustard. Fries. Couple of dills. Double slice of lemon meringue. Coffee, plenty of cream.

Dorothy stared at her magazine, but the words printed there kept slipping away from her.

'Borrow your salt?' the man said after his food had been served. He wasn't looking at her. He was looking at the glass salt and pepper shakers that were settled within chrome sleeves attached to the napkin rack situated directly in front of Dorothy. 'Oh,' she said, and pushed the salt shaker toward him.

'Love the pastrami here,' the man said, smiling, glancing now toward Dorothy. 'Best in the state for my money.'

A disquieting fear flooded through Dorothy. She turned her fleshy mole away from the man. She stared down at a magazine ad for

Dial soap. Nothing, she told herself. To this man say absolutely nothing.

Dorothy had had a friend in high school named Faye Nichols, who told her everything. After she'd married, Faye moved with her husband, Ned, to Tampa, Florida and began writing letters to Dorothy that were more like diary entries than letters, long detailed accounts of arguments with Ned, and of shopping excursions, and of wanting to bear children. After a year or two she wrote about men, gorgeous men who, if they said something clever or did the slightest nice thing, made Faye want to take them off to bed. Whether in fact she did take them off to bed was in the letters left unsaid, but it was a situation Dorothy found demeaning, a married woman thinking in those terms, and she'd written shorter and shorter return letters until the friendship was finally reduced to an annual exchange of Christmas cards.

The man to Dorothy's right ate quietly and fast. Finished, he pushed his plate forward and said, 'Mind if I smoke?'

He began to peel the cellophane wrapper from a cigar – the sweet smell of fresh unburnt tobacco blossomed into the air – and all at once Dorothy was standing, grabbing her packages, fleeing.

'Hey!' the man said. 'Is there –'

Dorothy was out of his range, past lingerie, past notions, out and around the building, across the parking lot to her car, where she stopped short. Her purse. She turned back and there the man stood, smiling, offering her purse in his outstretched hand, letting it hang by its strap from two extended fingers.

'Left it there by your stool,' he said. While he waited for her response a mild grin came to his lips. 'Not so easy, is it, thanking somebody you're pretty sure you don't much care for?' He kept his grin. 'Kind of hard to strike just the right note.'

'Yes,' Dorothy said in a thin voice. 'That's it exactly. But thank you just the same.' She began searching through the purse for her keys.

'See the green-and-white Towne Car?' the man said, pointing off.

It was a massive Lincoln, peculiarly painted in the kind of two-tone Dorothy remembered from the fifties. It looked like something that had occurred on a St. Patrick's Day after somebody'd had a few, and

Dorothy might've said so if she hadn't worried it would somehow encourage this man.

But Dorothy's silence didn't deter him. 'I won that beauty two years ago, for top Rainco rep in the tri-state region,' he said. 'And it'll be parked right here one week from today. Pine Bluff and environs are part of my route. My name's Gerald Woodley, I make my living selling center-pivot irrigation systems, and I'm inviting you to lunch, right here at Woolworth's, one week from today, at twelve noon.'

Dorothy stared evenly at the man and said, 'Are you crazy?'

Gerald Woodley appeared slightly abashed by this response. 'No,' he said with less sureness than before, 'I really meant it.'

Dorothy, feeling something start to give way inside her, pulled closed her door and started the car. At the parking-lot exit, when she glanced into the rearview mirror, Gerald Woodley stood motionless, watching her drive away.

NADINE CROUCHED TREMBLINGLY IN THE CARDBOARD BOX WHILE DR HANSEN explained to Dorothy the nature of renal failure. Sometimes the kidneys last a few weeks, he said, sometimes a year, but when they crash, they crash. Age was the usual cause but sometimes it was toxic insult – some cats love antifreeze, for example – or even physical insult.

'Physical insult?' Dorothy asked. She was thinking back.

Dr Hansen shrugged. 'Getting caught in a door, say.' He suggested a slurry of broth and baby food for a week, then checking back.

At the desk, when the receptionist said, 'A week from today okay?' Dorothy said it was.

AN EVENING OR TWO LATER, LEWIS WENT UPSTAIRS TO TAKE MEASUREMENTS of the sewing room that adjoined Marcy's bedroom. He was going to put in cabinets and shelves, convert it to a closet as a present promised Marcy since Christmas. James Thompson, the town carpenter, would normally have been called in for a job like this, but for some reason Lewis had wanted to do it himself, which meant, in Dorothy's opinion, that it would be built crudely and finished who knew when. Dorothy watched Lewis a minute or two, then said, 'Something bad's happened between Marcy and Bobby Parmalee.'

Lewis took the flat carpenter's pencil from his mouth and jotted down a dimension. 'This wouldn't be the first time your observations ran toward the dire,' he said with evident self-amusement and followed the remark with a series of soft snorts that put Dorothy in mind of a horse.

'No,' she said. 'There's truly something wrong.'

Lewis pushed a button on his measuring tape and it snappily retracted. She knew what he was thinking. That from the beginning she'd encouraged Marcy's match with Bobby Parmalee, nursed it along, and that worrying about its little trials was just part of the job. 'What makes you so sure something's wrong?' Lewis said.

This of course was the hard part. She wasn't really sure. It was just that Marcy seemed so distracted nowadays. So many ups and downs. 'She sleeps so late,' Dorothy said. 'And then she'll take another nap in the afternoon.' This wasn't convincing and she knew it. Marcy had always been a sleeper. 'I don't know, it's just that I think she's –' she wanted to say *depressed*, but knew Lewis had no patience for either the word or the self-inflicted mopishness it suggested – 'languishing.'

Lewis gave her a look: *languishing*.

'Wait and see,' Dorothy said. 'Something's wrong there.' Then, 'Bobby's good for Marcy. He's a nice boy, a smart boy. He's going to vet school.' (Unsaid but understood was the fact that, in addition to the aforementioned qualities, Bobby Parmalee's father had money. Plus, according to Marcy – who had undeniably been intrigued by the prospect – Bobby wanted to get married and vet in South America for a while before settling down in the Pacific northwest, preferably Washington or Oregon, in either case a long way from Nebraska winters.)

Some seconds passed before Lewis said, 'Don Sutton – the guy who does the Braves on that Atlanta superstation – he says the beauty of baseball is that every pitch makes somebody happy.'

Dorothy, suddenly in a bad humor, asked what that was supposed to mean.

'Well, if Marcy and her boyfriend have lost interest, why then the chances of her getting into sexual doings with him just went way, way down.' He turned to Dorothy and stretched so taut a grin that she could see his protruding teeth defined behind it.

AFTER LEWIS LEFT THE HOUSE EACH MORNING AND BEFORE MARCY ROSE from bed, Dorothy mixed up baby food and chicken broth in a blender, drew it into a large plastic syringe, and for the next ten minutes squeezed small doses deep into the old cat's throat. 'It's all right, Sweetie,' she crooned, 'it's okay.' Dorothy did this three times a day. The cat hated the process, but her creatinine level was nearly normal when Dorothy returned her to Dr Hansen the next week. This relieved Dorothy so considerably she bought makings for Marcy's favorite meal (lasagna) and Lewis's favorite dessert (pineapple upside-down cake). Leaving town, she went nowhere near Woolworth's, and was home unpacking groceries when the telephone rang.

The man on the line said, 'I waited three hours. Not that I don't understand. I just wanted you to know how much I was hoping you'd change your mind.' Dorothy was still trying to make sense of this when he said, 'Any chance for next Wednesday?'

'How'd you get my number?' Dorothy said.

'Memorized your plate that day when you drove away,' he said.

She hung up. The phone didn't ring again. But a half hour later, when there was a knock on the door, it gave Dorothy a turn. She peeked out. It was Bobby, with something in hand.

'Mr Parmalee,' Dorothy said, opening up.

Bobby Parmalee ducked his head and said hello.

'Marcy's not home. I'm not just sure when she will be.'

But Bobby seemed not to have expected her home. 'Wanted to leave this for her,' he said and held out a small box. It was from Ahren's Jewelry in Chadron, and was the right size for earrings, or a ring. 'It's something she said she wanted a while back though now I don't know.' He looked up at Dorothy with his watery blue eyes, then turned away. Dorothy watched him go. Waiting. Boys waiting. Men waiting. In this at least, it seemed to her, they were no different from women.

But still, that night, watching Lewis brush his teeth with baking soda while telling him about poor Bobby Parmalee, Dorothy's pity was wrapped around the small, stony pleasure of having been right. Lewis, in nodding, was admitting as much. From behind, regarding Lewis's stubbly face, she saw that his beard, if he let it grow, would be gray now, which, in turn and unfortunately, reminded her that, below his ample belly, some of Lewis's pubic hair had already gone gray and would next, she supposed, go white. She was thinking that in one moment, and then – fantastically; what leap had she made? – was in the next moment deciding that, when the opportunity presented itself, she'd better have a look around Marcy's room.

THE FOLLOWING DAY, DOROTHY SAT DOWN TO QUILT, SOMETHING SHE hadn't done in some little while. Her frame sat in the front room and, with the cat asleep in her lap, recuperating, Dorothy felt almost content. She had, to her own surprise, slept deeply and awakened refreshed. Midmorning, when Marcy had gone off to cheerleading practice, Dorothy had tidied up her room. She'd put a few things away. She'd noticed that Bobby's photograph still stood on her maple dresser. In the bottom drawer of that dresser, she'd found the box from Ahren's and it *did* contain a ring, just as she'd guessed, a tiny but tasteful little diamond. What this meant – that Marcy had evidently decided neither to wear the ring nor return it – Dorothy didn't know, but she found it strangely encouraging. (Today, for no good reason, she found almost everything encouraging.)

   As Dorothy quilted she pricked her left index finger repeatedly, which she didn't mind – in a few days a callus would form. Sometimes, to keep the stitches small, she tried to get seven or eight stitches on a single pull of the needle. When she succeeded, the punctured cloth was laced with minute, perfectly spaced hyphens of white thread. The stitched rows were deeply satisfying, a satisfaction Dorothy guessed was similar to what Lewis might feel when a day of cultivating a rolling field produced contours of ridges and shadows in the dark soil. (*Lewis,* she thought in a strangely detached way, as if he were somebody else's cautious and provident husband, a man who, whatever else might be said of him, *did* love his work and his farm and his life!) Dorothy finished the star-of-Bethlehem crib quilt she'd had on the frame, set it aside to bind in the evenings, and started cutting a queen-sized quilt in a bearpaw pattern she loved. She worked furiously, almost excitedly, piecing most of the weekend and on Monday running out of the red background fabric, a home-dyed henna red she'd bought in Pine Bluff.

She thought she'd go for more on Tuesday, but little things came up.

Wednesday morning, Dorothy fed Nadine, fixed a crockpot dinner for Lewis, and then was off, windows down, driving a little over the limit. She bought the red fabric and some other sewing supplies, browsed at Offerman's for a while, bought Marcy some pretty floral pajamas, and then, at twelve noon, realized how hungry she was. She was starving. She could eat a horse.

The goofy green-and-white Lincoln was not in the Woolworth's parking lot. Dorothy knew she ought to feel relieved, and so made herself believe that relief was what she felt. She ordered her customary salad, but then, as the waitress stepped away, she said, 'And a pastrami sandwich. People are always saying how good your pastrami is.'

And it was good. She was on the last bite when she heard advancing footsteps on the store's wooden floor. She glanced up into the mirror behind the counter, saw Gerald Woodley's reflection, and lowered her eyes.

'You're here!' he said, sweet licorice breath washing past her. 'Two weeks late, but you're here.'

Dorothy felt her cheeks pinken and then, realizing this was observable, she colored further. 'I came in to buy lunch and toffee.' She tried to calm herself down. 'My husband likes Woolworth's toffee.'

Today Gerald Woodley was wearing a starched pale pink shirt, gray pleated pants, dark blue tie, mahogany-colored belt and shoes, clothes that would make anyone look handsome, even Lewis, only Lewis would never wear clothes like these.

He nodded at her packages. 'So what did you get for yourself?'

Dorothy didn't answer.

'Nothing,' Gerald Woodley said. 'That's what I bet.'

'Fabric,' she blurted, 'for a quilt I'm making for nobody but me.'

Color rose again in Dorothy's cheeks. Not only did her words sound cross, but they weren't exactly true. She meant the quilt for her bed, yes, but her bed was Lewis's, too.

The waitress appeared for Gerald Woodley's order. When he finished his double portion of pie, Dorothy, to her own surprise, was still there. Gerald Woodley turned up his sleeves and said, 'Know what? Every now and then I try to do something I've never done before, ever, and now I want to ask you to do something I've never done before.'

His complexion – the word suddenly came to her – was swarthy. The hair on his arms was dark and luxuriant and silky. 'No,' she said abruptly. 'Whatever it is, the answer is no.'

'Pee-Wee golf,' Gerald Woodley said. 'Let's go play some actual pee-wee golf.'

Dorothy was flummoxed. 'You've never played pee-wee golf?'

Gerald Woodley let his eyes fall fully on Dorothy. 'Nope, I never have.'

TO DOROTHY'S RELIEF, THE FUNNY FARM MINIATURE GOLF COURSE AND arcade sat well back from the road and, on this weekday afternoon, had drawn only a few clusters of children through its old-fashioned turnstile. Gerald and Dorothy were the only paying adults. They talked as they played. Mostly Dorothy talked. Gerald listened and putted and asked lazy questions. It surprised Dorothy that she had so many definite opinions, and that this man found them interesting. She grew so lightheaded that out of sheer guilt she began talking about Lewis and Marcy and her life in Goodnight, careful to make it all sound as cheery as could be.

At the eleventh hole, Gerald pulled out his wallet and showed her a picture of his only child. 'Charlie, his name is.'

'Cute,' Dorothy said though in fact his head seemed overlarge.

'He's retarded, and 98 per cent blind, but he's a treasure. I know you might doubt it, but he is. See the dog there? Her name's Rosebud. Charlie calls her Rosebug.'

Dorothy flipped the plastic jacket. There was one more photograph. It was of a woman's dark blocky unsmiling face staring fiercely into the camera out of a short, helmet-like hairdo.

'Ruth. My wife. On not one of her happier days.'

Dorothy said, 'She looks like she could breathe fire.'

Gerald seemed on the brink of chuckling, but didn't. 'Well, Ruthie drinks,' he said. 'If it weren't for that we'd be fine.' He tapped his ball through a scarecrow with long windmilling arms. 'Drank during the pregnancy, I'm afraid,' Dorothy thought she heard him say.

At the fiftieth hole, Dorothy noticed the time. 'Yikes,' she said and handed Gerald her putter. She could feel his eyes on her as she walked away, which should have made her feel self-conscious, but didn't. From the car, in an almost singing voice, she called out, 'So now you've played pee-wee golf!' As she pulled away, he stood smiling, a pee-wee putter slung over each shoulder.

III

AS A GIRL, DOROTHY'S FAMILY HAD OWNED A DOG NAMED TEDDY, A black, thoughtful-seeming dog whose remarkable peculiarity was his delayed response to commands. When Dorothy or one of her sisters would say, 'Teddy, go sit on the piano bench,' he would lie exactly as he had been lying, then, perhaps five minutes later, as if suddenly aware of the command, he would leap up and sit smartly on the piano bench, where he would stay perhaps another five minutes after being told to get down. Dorothy was afraid that Gerald's requests of her – and she was certain requests would come – would lodge with her in a similarly delayed way, that she would at first seem to ignore them even as they were at work within her. So she told Gerald she couldn't talk to him when he called (he called repeatedly) and she steered clear of Pine Bluff.

A month passed. Then one morning, while Lewis was on the phone in the den and while Dorothy stood at the kitchen sink washing apples, Gerald's shiny, green-and-white Lincoln appeared in front of the house.

Dorothy stared in disbelief. Hide, she thought. Take off the apron. Change. Fix your hair. Hide.

A knock, then Lewis's heavy step as he crossed the wood floor.

'What can I do for you?' Lewis said, putting into his voice the chesty huskiness that kept a cushion between himself and strangers.

'Well, what say we talk about what Rainco Piping could do for *you*,' Gerald said and at once turned the talk to the sad state of the Lockhardt irrigation system. Dorothy couldn't bear it. She turned the tap water back on. She washed apples, peeled them one after another until finally Lewis came in. He snapped Gerald's green-and-white business card down on the zinc kitchen counter.

'Hear that guy?'

'Some of it.'

Outside, the motor of Gerald's car cranked over. Dorothy kept peeling, the green skin spooling neatly down.

'What did you think of him?' Lewis said.

Dorothy said he was all right, she guessed, for a salesman.

'Exactly. For a salesman.' Lewis ate a whole apple thinking about it. Then – a habit with him – he gave the dripping hot-water tap a quick twist before heading off. 'If Wagner calls, tell him he can find me in the alfalfa.' He adjusted his cap and gave Dorothy a broad wink from the door. 'Any chance of pork chops to go with that apple sauce?'

Dorothy listened to him drive off on the Allis Chalmers.

A few minutes passed before she heard the massive Lincoln return. She peered through the window, but didn't go to the door. She listened to Gerald open it, listened to his footsteps, lighter than Lewis's. She stood at the sink with the water off, her heart beating like a schoolgirl's. When she turned, they stood for a moment there in the kitchen, his mouth smelling first of licorice and then, beyond that, of liquor.

'Where can we go?' he said in a whisper.

Dorothy just stared. Go? They couldn't *go* anywhere.

'Upstairs,' he said, already leading.

Dorothy stayed back, listening to his movements overhead. There were only two upstairs bedrooms, hers – Dorothy's and Lewis's – and Marcy's. She heard Gerald stop in Marcy's room. It was fantastic, nightmarish. Dorothy eased up the stairs, her heart hammering out a wild, dangerous beat. When she peered into Marcy's room, he stood by the window – *in plain view* – staring out.

'Get away from there!' Dorothy said and when he turned, smiling, she said, 'This isn't right at all.'

Gerald sat down on Marcy's maple dressing chair and thoughtfully lighted a cigar. Smoke curled into the air. In a careful voice, he said, 'If there was one mythical person you could tell the absolute truth to without varnishing the smallest fact, how would you describe your life up to now?'

She looked away and considered a few different answers, but mostly she was listening for Wagner's van in the driveway or for the heavy chug of Lewis's Allis Chalmers, all the while mindful of the incriminatory smoke-smell thickening in this room before spilling into the next. 'It's been fine,' she said, 'good, even.' Then, turning toward Gerald, 'I guess maybe you aren't that one mythical person.'

He nodded toward Marcy's bed. 'Couldn't you sit?'

Yes, downstairs, she thought to say, but what difference would that really make? He had no business being here, upstairs or down.

Dorothy moved deliberately to the side of the bed and just stood there. Everything felt eerily dreamlike, this man slipping into Lewis's house and sitting here in Marcy's chair. It was strangely quiet. The white cotton curtains hung straight in the still heat. Without a sound, the old cat appeared in the doorway, blinked, crossed the room and curled at this stranger's feet, and Gerald Woodley, like some demon in charge of this dream, smiled amiably. A small cloud of smoke floated on his parted lips. Dorothy closed her eyes. In a moment she heard his voice saying, 'When I was little, the part I liked about Christmas almost more than my present was the night before, when my uncle came to visit.'

Dorothy without opening her eyes turned away from Gerald Woodley's voice, toward the window, in the direction from which Lewis, would probably come. But Gerald continued to talk. 'My uncle,' he was saying, 'would have all us kids go up to the girls' room – which this room reminds me of – and write down the one question about our future lives that was most important to us. The custom was to say the question to my oldest sister, Annie, who would write it down. Things like, Will I ever get a gray pony? Or, How many years exactly will I live and where will I die? Annie wrote each one on a separate sheet of paper and handed it back to us. Then she'd say what her own question was – it was always something about the babies she would have – how many and what color of hair and would any of them be deformed – and she'd write that down, too. Then we'd each take our question and fold it into the tiniest thickest square and march downstairs and stand in line to hand them one by one to my uncle. He was a banker, a small formal man with pale green eyes who always wore a bright red bow-tie at Christmas. He was slow and serious. He did not unfold the paper we handed him. He closed his eyes, took a folded question into his hands, cradled it, held it to his ear, shook it, swayed his head just a little, then opened his eyes and answered it. "You'll live to be eighty-three, Gerry, and die a respected man on the 4th of July in Duluth, Minnesota," he'd tell me. Or, "Annie, you're going to have all red-haired, healthy children, except one boy, who will have a small physical peculiarity, which he will overcome beautifully." '

Dorothy opened her eyes and, staring out the window, asked what the trick was, even while hoping there wasn't one.

She heard Gerald Woodley drawing at his cigar, then, after a long moment, the leisurely exhalation. 'He listened. He went to the kitchen heater vent, which was connected to the upstairs bedroom. And you know what? – figuring out my uncle's game was a lot worse than finding out St Nick was a figment.'

Dorothy stood stock-still. She hated herself, was sick with the fact that she wanted right now to walk over, lean close and be kissed by this man who thought she was worth chasing after and taking crazy risks for. Who wore nice clothes and who as a boy believed in his uncle's happy prophecies and who had the taste of licorice and liquor and smoke on his mouth. Who was all things Lewis was not.

Behind her, she could feel Gerald Woodley slowly rising from the chair, moving close. A mild shock moved through her as something grazed her fleshy mole. It was his fingertip. Instinctively, she cupped her hand over the small brown growth.

'I like it,' he said. 'I know you don't, but I do. It's your beauty mark.'

Once, when she was sixteen, a boy named Bob Messerschmidt had touched the protuberance and said he bet it was what her nipple felt like when erect. She'd wanted to slap Bob Messerschmidt, but hadn't. She told Gerald this. He chortled and asked what she wanted to do to him. Her face softened. 'Ask you to leave. But not because of the remark. It's just that everything about this is wrong.'

She let him take her hand and after a long moment he raised it to his heart. 'Feel,' he said.

It was true, his heart was pounding.

Somewhere beyond the window an unseen tractor droned.

'You have to go,' she said.

He left. He nodded, bent to run his hand along Nadine's back, and left. Dorothy didn't follow him downstairs. She listened to him go, then watched from Marcy's window as he maneuvered the big Towne Car around and slowly drove away. Dorothy stood at the edge of Marcy's bed. She closed her eyes. As a child, when there had been a good snow, she and her sisters would make snow angels in the yard by going stiff and letting their bodies with outstretched arms fall back into the snow. Dorothy always did it with her eyes closed, and suddenly she replicated the movement now, falling back into Marcy's bed. Upon impact, there was a clacking sound – something loosened from the bedsprings falling to the wooden floor – and Dorothy sat up. Nadine, focused on something, slid across the room and under the bed. Stand up, Dorothy told herself. Get going. Do something.

She rose and fanned the door to dispel the cigar smoke, but then sat down again, this time at the head of the wooden stairs. She felt sullied, as sullied as if she'd let herself go. So maybe I should've, she thought. I couldn't feel any worse.

The cat, suddenly beside her, made the throaty, stretched-out cry that meant she'd brought something. Dorothy glanced down and for an instant recoiled from the object before it came into focus. But it was not, as she first feared, rubbery flesh. It was flesh-colored rubber.

A diaphragm.

Dorothy went back to Marcy's room, got down on her knees and peered under the bed. There, lying open and empty, was the square, pink, plastic case that had been loosened from its hiding place under the bedsprings.

Dorothy sat on the floor with her back against the bed. She held the diaphragm toward the window, saw tiny dots of light shine through Nadine's toothmarks, then set the diaphragm on the floor. It was a device she knew something about. After Marcy's birth she'd used one for years (not trusting Lewis's use of condoms – Lewis who

wanted six kids). To put the diaphragm in, a woman had to squat
or lie down with legs bent. Dorothy hadn't seen Marcy naked for
a long time and now, when she imagined her in these positions, it
was like imagining someone else, not her daughter.

From the open window came the soft hoo-hooing of a single
dove. The cat settled herself into Dorothy's lap. Finally, to no one,
not even to Nadine, she said, 'My name is Dorothy Lockhardt and
I don't think I am the same as when I got up this morning.'

'LET'S RENT A LITTLE PLACE IN PINE BLUFF,' GERALD SAID OVER THE TELEPHONE
a few days later. 'I'm hanging up now,' Dorothy said but before she
did he said, 'Something small but nice. Something with hardwood
floors and fresh paint.'

ONE DAY, NOT LONG AFTER LEWIS HAD FINISHED MARCY'S NEW CLOSET,
Dorothy helped her organize it, though Lewis had pretty much done
that for them. There were, for example, tilted shallow shelves with
narrow stops at the base that were meant strictly for shoes. Nadine sat
nearby with her tail curled loosely around her feet, swaying slightly,
but otherwise unmoving.

'Haven't seen much of Bobby Parmalee lately,' Dorothy said,
letting the subject float, but Marcy didn't bite, merely announced
her decision, after studying the shoe rack, to put the dress shoes
at the top after all because they looked better there even if you did
need to get at them less often.

Dorothy said, 'I always thought he was pretty dedicated to you.'
And, Dorothy knew, still was. Twice in the past week she'd spied
Bobby standing off in the cottonwoods, watching the house.

Marcy rolled her eyes. 'He was getting totally weird. He gave me
an engagement ring, did you know that? And right then I knew it
was all too much too fast.' She slipped a green pump over her hand
and stared at it. 'I couldn't act one way and feel another, could I?'

Dorothy thought a while about that. 'So what did you tell
Bobby?'

'I said let's take a little time out. I said, "You go out with Arlene
Sipp who's so hot for your bod and I'll go out with whatever I can
drum up and then in a couple of months we'll see what's what." '

The differences between Marcy and Bobby Parmalee, Dorothy knew, went back well before the night Bobby came with the ring. 'So he's been going out with Arlene Sipp?'

'Not that I know of,' Marcy said. She reached out to wave the green pump in front of Nadine's unblinking eyes. The old cat stared stonily ahead. 'Some live-wire cat you got here, Mom.'

'And you've been going out with who then?' Dorothy said. She hadn't seen anyone pick Marcy up or drop her off. No one.

'Anybody with prospects who asks, Mom.'

'No, Polkadot, I'm really asking who.'

Marcy stiffened. 'Mom, look, I get good grades. I don't drink or smoke. Wasn't that the deal? – I do my part and I get left alone?'

A few more shoes went up in silence, then Dorothy reached into her shirt pocket and laid the diaphragm onto one of the bare shelves. Marcy stared at it without speaking.

'Aren't you going to ask what that is?' Dorothy said.

'I know what it is. I just don't know how you got it.'

'Nadine brought it to me.'

Marcy laughed derisively. 'That sounds really probable.'

Dorothy showed her the toothmarks.

'Well, *some*body bit into it, all right,' Marcy said.

Dorothy let that pass. She controlled her voice. 'Marcy, you're my daughter. I need to know what's going on here.'

Marcy lined up the green pumps on the top shelf. When finally she spoke, her voice had softened. 'This isn't going to make you any happier, but there's nothing really important going on. It's somebody I like, but I won't marry him. Next year if I get in and we can afford it, I'm going to Lincoln.' She stared off. 'I don't know where he'll go, but it won't be to college.'

'What's the boy's name, Marcy?'

Marcy lowered her voice. 'You don't know him.'

'I know everybody,' Dorothy said. 'Goodnight's not that big a town.'

Marcy didn't answer. In profile, unsmiling, she looked older than Dorothy wanted her to look.

'And you're not telling me because I wouldn't approve?' Dorothy said.

Marcy's face tightened – first one tear then another came squeezing out.

Without wanting to, Dorothy found herself thinking of Frank
Mears, who was famous for his cruel relations with women. 'Is it
Frank Mears?' she said.

Marcy shook her head vehemently.

'Is it a married man?'

'No!' Marcy managed to snuffle and look incredulous at the same
time. 'It's somebody who's not from around here is why you don't
know him. But you can stop asking questions, because I'm not saying
anything more.' With two fingers she stretched taut the cuff of her
sleeve and used it to wipe her face. When she'd done this as a little
girl, it had struck Dorothy as endearingly grown-up. Now it seemed
endearingly childlike. She wanted to pull Marcy snug into her arms,
but she didn't.

'Are you going to tell Dad about the diaphragm?' Marcy asked in
a small voice.

Dorothy knew she should and knew she wouldn't. 'Marcy, I have
this idea.' She tried to assemble her thoughts. 'There's a horse school
outside of London, only it's more than just that. You go to museums
and plays and all sorts of wing-dings. Anyhow,' she said, reshaping
the truth a little, 'I wrote away and, with your grades, there's a
chance you could go there a year on part scholarship and it would
be a chance for you to be somewhere else and see other things.'
She stopped, startled at how odd the idea sounded when spoken
out loud.

'London, England?' Marcy said.

Dorothy nodded.

'*Me*? In England riding horses and going to *wing-dings* at
some kind of finishing school?' There was real alarm in her
voice. Then a thought: 'Is this what I have to do so you won't
tell Dad?'

'Oh, Marcy, Sweetie,' Dorothy said, her voice and the idea trailing
away together. She couldn't think when she'd felt so tired.

Downstairs the screen door swung open and banged shut.

'*Hi-dee-ho*,' Dorothy said in a soft dead voice.

'Hi-dee-ho!' Lewis sang out from the kitchen.

Dorothy could hear him at the refrigerator. He'd be pouring iced tea. Four teaspoons of sugar. The wet spoon dropped carelessly back into the sugar bowl.

'Up here!' Dorothy called out. 'I'll be right down.'

IV

THE GARAGE-TOP APARTMENT GERALD RENTED AND REPAINTED WITH TWO coats of white semi-gloss came with a faded blue corduroy sofa, an ancient, overstuffed armchair and an iron double bed, which Dorothy covered with the bearpaw quilt she'd been working on for weeks. Overhead, too large for the room, there hung a purple-and-clear-glass chandelier that Dorothy liked to lie in bed and look at. The other view she liked was from a rear window that overlooked a neighborhood Conoco. She liked to stand a little back from the window, unseen, and watch people in different colored cars and clothes come and go. Once – an unpleasant shock – she saw Edwin Littlefield pull up, Edwin whom she'd known since grade school, who with his wife, Esther, and daughter, Merna, had often been into her house for Sunday meals. Dorothy, to her surprise, stepped a little forward, into the light of the window and, staring down at Edwin Littlefield, dared him to stare back up. He would have to look past the bare wood fence enclosing the gas station, over three one-story houses, between two ashes in full leaf. He didn't, for a long time he didn't. Then, after paying in cash, after folding his change carefully into his wallet, he glanced behind him, and to the left and right, as if her stare had been faintly received, but he would never look up. He would never look through the window. An Edwin Littlefield wouldn't. A Lewis Lockhardt wouldn't. But a Gerald Woodley might. He might abandon his car right there, might walk right up the driveway, mount the stairs and pound on the locked door until the whole building shook. Thinking about things like this was why on Wednesdays Dorothy liked to get to the apartment first. She liked to get the windows open and the air a little cool, then drink a cream soda in the window and wait. Not just for Gerald. But also for herself to relax and to feel for a few minutes the prospects of lives she hadn't chosen.

*   *   *

DOROTHY TALKED TO NADINE ABOUT THE WEDNESDAYS WITH GERALD. SHE shot slurry down the cat's throat and while Nadine was gulping, Dorothy said, 'It's not anything. But it's not nothing either. It's just something to look forward to, and then to look back on.' She liked sex with Gerald, the closeness and energy of it, the funny way Gerald said 'Whew!' after the activity died down.

'So how about we cut out the wearisome part?' Gerald said one day.

Dorothy, afraid this was a sex matter, asked what wearisome part.

'The part where you live in Goodnight. The servant part.'

'And do what?'

'Get a divorce. Marry me.' He looked at her evenly. 'This has been nice, but the times between seeing you seem longer and longer.'

Dorothy tried to consider it.

He said, 'We could go to Hawaii. Or California. Or Australia. You want finally to go to nursing school? – we'll live near a nursing school. You can dip into that sewing basket of yours for tuition fees.'

Dorothy had always kept the matter of the Chinese sewing basket, and the money hidden within it, to herself, but one day, lying in the apartment with Gerald, the subject had turned to secrets and only when the Chinese sewing basket had come instantly and easily to her lips did Dorothy realize that she had been yearning to part with the secret for a long time, but had never had anyone safe to tell it to. Gerald had laughed and said she was as mysterious as her Chinese sewing basket and a lot more kissable. Dorothy hadn't said exactly how much money the basket contained and Gerald didn't ask, though from time to time he would raise the general subject, as he had just now, so that Dorothy might provide further specifics if she cared to, but Dorothy never cared to. Gerald pushed on with his theme of relocation. 'I see adventures ahead, troubles behind,' he said. 'We could go anywhere. Everybody who's got something to sell needs a good salesman.' A few moments passed. 'Hawaii's my first choice, though. Hawaii's green twelve months a year.'

A white bungalow, an ocean breeze, a goat in the green yard. A thin white uniform, white thick-soled shoes. It was surprisingly easy to imagine. She said, 'Gerald, Sweetie, it's nice of you to say, but I don't suppose living with you in Hawaii is very likely to happen.'

Gerald stretched out long on the bed. 'Wanna bet?'

'Yep. Two bits.' She was grinning, but just beyond it was a fear that this kind of talk would affect her, and it would.

For nineteen years Lewis had come in for supper at five sharp, day in and day out, but a few days later, on an ordinary Monday, Lewis didn't appear at five. At 5.15, Dorothy sat down and watched the clock. Lewis did not appear until nearly 6.15. His truck had broken down. It was nothing. But, by 5.30, before she knew it was nothing, there had developed in Dorothy a feeling that she knew at once was horrible. The feeling wasn't worry. It was hope.

In bed that night Lewis slowly awakened squinting and in a thick voice said, 'How come the light's on?'

Dorothy was sitting up. 'Oh, Lewis, I'm worried about us.'

Lewis lay back down, closed his eyes against the glare. 'Don't be. It won't do any good.' He was quiet a moment. 'Besides I'm the one supposed to do the worrying around here.' He dozed another few seconds, awakened himself with a snore. 'All farms go through these little bad patches,' he said. She turned off the light, but he was awake now. 'I didn't even know you knew,' he said and then, after sucking a long breath between his teeth, he said, 'I'm selling 160 of the school section.'

'The school section?' They'd bought these 640 acres at auction from the county early in their marriage, scrimped and borrowed and made good on it. It had been a risky but good decision, one that they had savored and neighbors had respected. And selling. Lewis believed in buying land, not selling it.

'Just the northwest quarter of it,' Lewis said in the dark. 'To Larson. More efficient for him, just like he's been telling me for years. He'll pay a fair price. And we need the money.'

'But the school section.' She imagined the sewing basket, where there was perhaps money enough to fend off this sale, but something – she believed it was the disappointment she would feel if Marcy didn't go to college if not to England – kept her from speaking.

Lewis broke the silence. 'After losing a big game, a ballplayer, I forget who it was, but he said to a reporter, "Well it ain't my life and it ain't my wife." ' Lewis settled himself into his pillow. 'That's more or less what I say. It's a quarter of the school section, is all. We didn't want to lose it, but we did, and we will all survive.'

NORMALLY GERALD LIKED IT WHEN DOROTHY BROUGHT NADINE TO THE garage-top apartment. More like a home with a cat around, he said. But, on this particular Wednesday, he had ignored the cat and – Dorothy had noticed this more than once recently – had seemed only to be going through the lovemaking motions. Now he stood rubbing his neck and staring out the window towards the Conoco. The record on the turntable ended and he still stood there.

'You know that day I stopped in at your place?' he said. 'It was almost by accident. I'd already turned into the drive when I saw the name on the mailbox.'

Dorothy was lying in bed, smoking a cigarette, which Lewis had never in his life seen her do. Sometimes it occurred to her that if Lewis walked in and stared at her lying naked in bed in this strange room, he would not recognize her. 'Could've turned around I guess,' she said.

'Yeah.' Gerald stared off a while longer. 'Funny thing was I liked him. Kind of no-nonsense, but he just seemed so ... decent.'

The word hung there. Overhead, purplish light refracted from the chandelier. 'Never said he wasn't,' Dorothy said. Then, 'Lots of decent people don't make the people they're married to especially happy.'

Gerald without turning said he knew that, too.

Dorothy smoothed her hand over the sleeping cat. 'It would be nice if you told me what was the matter.'

Gerald stood perfectly still with his back to her. Even the hand that had been rubbing his neck stopped moving.

'Is it Lewis? Is Lewis's being decent a problem all of a sudden?'

'Well, it should be,' Gerald said, 'but it's not.'

Sudden and severe apprehension took hold of Dorothy. With forced calm she said, 'Then what is?'

He said a word.

'What?'

'*Charlie*,' he said, overloud. Then, softer, 'It's Charlie.'

His son. The retarded and mostly blind one. Dorothy – she hated to admit it – was relieved. 'Is he all right?'

Oh, he was fine, Gerald said. But there was a new procedure that might restore his sight, or most of it, and a doctor at the VA in Rapid City had approved Charlie as a candidate, but it was experimental, his insurance wouldn't cover it. 'I've borrowed from my brothers, my parents, from everybody but the milkman. Two churches in town are taking up collections. We sold what jewelry of Ruthie's had value.'

Dorothy began to consider this as she had learned from Lewis to begin, by turning the proposition slowly, exposing all of its facets to cold light, but suddenly she stopped herself. By now she knew she might well be in love with Gerald, and very probably was, and there were provisions you made for the people you loved. 'How much are you short?' she said.

When Gerald turned to face her, he looked different: wholesome, vulnerable, just-scrubbed. He seemed genuinely surprised not just at the kindness of her words, but of this world. 'No,' he said. 'I guess I should've known you'd ask, but no.'

He meant it. He wouldn't say.

The following Wednesday, Dorothy handed him an envelope containing $9,200 in bills, everything that had been hidden in the lining of her Chinese sewing basket.

V

THAT NIGHT, DOROTHY FELT LIKE A GUEST AT HER OWN SUPPER TABLE. Marcy ended one long silence by saying, 'So, did I mention to anyone that I landed the role of Miss Claythorne in the autumn play? Mr Bennett said there was no lead, but I counted the lines and I've got the most.'

'How fun,' Dorothy said distractedly and Lewis, with a mouth full of food, nodded in agreement. His straw-brittle hair, wet-combed before supper, was drying now according to its own designs.

'It's *And Then There Were None*, by Agatha Christie,' Marcy said and, trying out her accent, added, 'A dark drama of 'idden secrets.' When no-one spoke, Marcy said what she always said when she wanted both to diffuse tension and get information. 'So what's wrong with this picture?' she said.

Lewis, who'd been making a point of eating heartily, said in a joking voice, 'Well, I think your mother's peevish because I requested macaroni and cheese.'

Dorothy took in this information and wondered by what strange and haphazard route she'd reached this particular time and place. 'We're on a budget, is all,' she said in a rigid voice. 'Your father doesn't want you to know it, but we are.'

When Lewis went out to check stock and Marcy took her plate to the kitchen, she said to her mother in a low voice, 'Then why spend all the money on an old barncat?' and Dorothy, stung, turned on Marcy and said through clenched teeth, 'Because he kicked her, that's why. Because your father with his size thirteen boot kicked her and when that wasn't enough, he picked her up and gave her a heave.'

The vehemence in her own voice surprised Dorothy and seemed to confuse Marcy, who backed toward the door. 'So, we're eating macaroni to save money and, according to everybody and his uncle at school, we're selling some of our best land to Mr Larson, which of course nobody clued me in on, but at the same time we're spending money to keep alive an old barncat because Dad got mad and kicked her.'

Dorothy straightened herself. 'That's right.'

'And where is this money for the vet bill coming from exactly? – the same place as the money for sending me to finishing school in England?'

'Where it is coming from,' Dorothy said, squeezing anger into every word, 'is not even close to being any of your business, Miss, not unless you've begun to see the contents of that pink, plastic case as business of your father's.'

Marcy said nothing more. She didn't have to. She'd been caught acting undaughterlike, but had in turn caught her mother acting unmotherlike, so that they now stood on each side of some strange new border dispute, one in which each had for her own reasons edged into equal and opposite frontiers, and established outposts that neither intended to abandon.

WHEN THEY NEXT MET, GERALD GAVE DOROTHY A SIGNED, TYPEWRITTEN note for $9,200, with provisions for interest.

'It's just to formalize that the money's a loan not a gift,' Gerald said. 'I'll start paying interest only, but by February I could start paying down on principal.' He said that Charlie's eye operation was ten days away; everything was all set. 'When Charlie can see, first thing we'll do – you and me and Charlie – is go up to Mount Rushmore. Charlie's always wanted in the worst way to see Mount Rushmore.'

Dorothy thought of the last time she was there. It was early winter, a long time ago, before Marcy was born. She'd handed Lewis salted cucumber slices to eat as they'd driven along in their pale green DeSoto. What she remembered most were the crows. There were crows on the snowy fields below the badlands; feeding on sandwich crusts in the overlook parking lot; up there on the rock sculpture, sitting on sunny, sloping foreheads and gliding sleekly in and out of the presidents' eyes. Lewis had laughed when she said they scared her.

'They could be an omen,' she said.

Lewis had laughed, and kept laughing until he noticed annoyance clamping tight Dorothy's face. 'Okay, then,' he said. 'Omen of what?'

Dorothy said she guessed he didn't really care to know.

Lewis stared seriously up at the big faces for a time. 'Okay,' he said, 'you believe in your omens and I'll believe in what I believe in and we'll see who's right.'

'What do you believe in?' Dorothy said.

She hadn't expected him to answer, but he had.

'Me,' Lewis had said. 'I believe in me.'

TUESDAY EVENING THE TELEPHONE RANG. LEWIS ANSWERED IN THE OTHER room. 'She's right here,' Dorothy heard him say, but then he said, 'Okay, sure. I'll tell her.' He put the phone down and called into her. 'That was your appointment tomorrow for your hair – the guy has some emergency and has to change it to the same time next week.'

This was a coded message that meant some unavoidable conflict had arisen. Still, that Wednesday, and each of the days of the following week, seemed interminable to Dorothy. When finally the next Wednesday arrived and Dorothy slipped her key into the lock of the apartment, the door wouldn't open. Through the window, the apartment looked the same, except the record player was gone. And – a shock – so was the bearpaw quilt from the iron-framed bed.

'Hello!' It was the landlord, peering up the stairs. 'Mrs Woodley?'

Dorothy didn't correct him. 'I was expecting to find Mr Woodley.'

The landlord shrugged. 'Haven't seen hide nor hair. Rent didn't get in was why I had to change the locks. Is everything all right?'

Dorothy, suddenly too tired for lying, said, 'No. It's probably not.'

The man nodded and, after thinking it over, climbed the stairs sorting through keys. He opened the door. 'If there's anything that's yours, why don't you go ahead and take it.'

'But I couldn't pay you.' She was surprised how much she hated saying this. Three weeks ago, when she'd had money of her own, she could've asked the balance and made it good.

'No, no, it's okay. I figured something like this might happen so I set the rent a little high at the start.'

In a way, Dorothy was glad that the landlord stood there watching so there was no chance at all of her lingering or touching things – Gerald's towel, his white V-necked undershirt, an opened but unsmoked El Producto Blunt. The bearpaw quilt was nowhere to be found. Dorothy looked under the bed, in the linen closet, and, on her way out, fighting a sickening feeling, in the dumpster at the end of the driveway.

From the phone booth at the Conoco, she called the VA in Rapid City. They knew nothing about a Charles or Charlie Woodley, and there were no eye operations scheduled for anyone on the date Gerald had given her. She took out Gerald's business card and called his company. A receptionist passed her to a secretary who said she was not authorized to give out information over the phone regarding employees or ex-employees.

'Ex-employees?' Dorothy said and the secretary, as if affected by some sudden understanding, said in a less officious voice, 'Yes, I'm afraid that's correct.'

Dorothy drove home and found a large parcel sitting at the base of the mailbox post. It was wrapped in brown paper and addressed

to Dorothy in what she knew to be Gerald's hand. Folded within
the box was the bearpaw quilt, along with a note. *Moved*, it said.
*Me and Ruth, Charlie couldn't come. A big change in employment
couldn't turn down. Thank you for everything. You are a wonderful
charitable woman but it is still a loan, I will pay you back.*

Some kind of trapdoor had fallen open and Dorothy felt all at once
drained of everything human. She didn't know what she meant to
do. She moved automatically, without thought or will. She got into
the car and drove up the lane. She opened the trunk of her car – it
was filthy – and dropped the quilt inside. She watched the edge of
the quilt soak up motor oil that had seeped from a punctured quart.
She took Gerald Woodley's note and Gerald Woodley's business card
and Gerald Woodley's empty paper box to the burn barrel. She lit
it all with the Bic lighter she'd bought at the Conoco in Pine Bluff
and then she threw the lighter in, too. She walked into the house.
She held onto the banister and walked upstairs. She got into bed
with her clothes on. She slept most of the next two days. She wasn't
sure what she heard and what she dreamed of hearing. The sound
of dishes clattering downstairs. The sound of a tractor, the sound
of a car. A boy's husky voice in the hall, followed by Marcy's giggly
whisper.

On the third day Dorothy took soup when Lewis brought it, and
then tried a fried egg sandwich he'd prepared. 'Good,' Dorothy said,
but felt drowsy before she could finish it. She sorted through the
bedding and without thinking said, 'Where's the quilt?'

'What quilt?'

'Oh. I don't know what I'm thinking. Any quilt, I guess. An old
one even.' Lewis found a suit-quilt and Dorothy was almost asleep
again when another thought floated by. 'The cat,' she murmured.

Lewis was still there. 'Died.'

Dorothy nodded with her eyes closed.

'Found her under the porch. She looked like she'd just gone to
sleep. I knew she meant something to you so I made her a wood
box and buried her out in the shelter belt. Took up a little cedar
and planted it over her.'

Dorothy was so sleepy she wondered if she'd been drugged.
'Where's Marcy?' she said.

'Into town. She's got afternoon play practice.' Then, even gentler, 'It's Saturday, Honey.'

Dorothy slept until late the following afternoon. When she awakened, Lewis was slouched in a chair napping, but when she rose, he came to. He followed her into the bathroom. She sat on the toilet and he said, 'You've been sick.'

She nodded.

'If you feel like getting dressed, we could drive into Chadron for dinner. Go to the Elks and get you a meal.'

In a voice not quite her own, Dorothy said that sounded nice.

When she came downstairs dressed in dark slacks and a light sweater-top, Lewis was on the phone. He covered the mouthpiece and pointed to it. 'Larson,' he whispered. In the kitchen, the radio was on to the farm report – highs and lows in the growing zone. Dorothy wandered outside. It had turned cool. The lawn was dry and needed watering. It mashed underfoot. For a moment, when she saw a pair of boots sitting next to the front porch, she thought it was Nadine. This was a phenomenon that would recur now and then over the next months, that and seeing from a distance men who in build or dress or stride suggested Gerald.

It was thick dusk. Within the lighted house, Lewis still stood talking into the telephone. Out here, in the yard, there was only the low steady buzz of insects. A bat jerked past. Dorothy walked out toward the car she saw parked beyond the shelter belt and, when she got within speaking distance, she called out to the figure slouched down in the car's shadowy interior. 'Bobby?'

Bobby Parmalee stepped out and came forward, quiet and sheepish.

Dorothy leaned against a tree, waiting. When he drew near, she said in a soft voice, 'Bobby, I'm going to tell you something you won't want to hear. Marcy's got a diaphragm and is using it, I don't know who with, except I'm pretty sure it isn't you.'

As the words took hold, the boy had taken a step or two back. Now he just stood there looking bewildered and unprotected.

'I was hoping you could help shed some light,' Dorothy said. 'I was hoping you might have some idea who this other party might be.'

Bobby Parmalee stared at Dorothy as if at a ghost. He shook his head dumbly. Dorothy stepped toward him. She wanted only to give him a hug, but it changed somehow, hardened, with her chest against his, and when she eased out of it, he seemed more confused than ever. He turned and disappeared into the trees and dusk.

Dorothy snugged up her collar and returned to the house. In the yellow light of his office, Lewis was just hanging up the phone. Before he came out, he would go to the little bathroom to wet and comb his hair. He'd go room to room turning off lights and closing windows to keep the warmth in. He'd check to make sure the leaky hot-water tap in the kitchen was good and tight. He would not lock the doors – against what? he would say.

Chapter Six

WHAT LETTY HOBBS SAW

NO-ONE KNEW. THAT WAS WHAT DOROTHY LOCKHARDT BELIEVED. BUT A *month or so earlier, Letty Hobbs, who lived four doors down from Lucy Witt, had driven all the way to Pine Bluff to treat her cousin Alberta to an early-bird dinner in celebration of Alberta's sixty-third birthday. Only Alberta wasn't at home when Letty Hobbs knocked on her door.*

This, Letty Hobbs thought, was par for the course.

Alberta knew she was coming, and Alberta knew Letty always arrived a few minutes early, so Alberta really might've had the kindness and respect to plan on it. What if they missed the early-bird prices? What if she had to drive home after dark? What if something terrible happened on the highway? How would Alberta feel about being responsible for that? These were the kinds of thoughts Letty Hobbs used to sustain herself while she waited for her cousin to come home.

Letty had positioned her car in the deep shade of a street tree and push-buttoned open all the windows. It seemed like just another September's day. A low sun threw long shadows. A bird shrilled from the tree. A child rolled noisily along the sidewalk on a plastic tricycle equipped with enormous plastic wheels. Through a screened window came the bass throb of some kind of unpleasantly modern music that sounded to Letty like a huge and agitated heart.

Presently a car approached from the opposite end of the street. Letty Hobbs regarded it, in hopes it was Alberta, and glanced at her watch so she could tell her exactly how long she'd been waiting. It wasn't Alberta, however. It was Dorothy Lockhardt, wearing big sunglasses, leaning into her own rearview mirror, patting her hair into place.

Letty Hobbs had nearly honked and waved (here they were, after all, on the same quiet back street, seventy miles from home; it was the kind of coincidence that often made hometown acquaintances act suddenly friendly), but something kept her from it. Letty Hobbs had sat quiet and watched.

Chapter Seven

FOOTBALL WEATHER

I

THE RATTLE OF DRY CORN, THE SUDDEN COOL OF DUSK, THE SMELL OF woodsmoke. Leaves were raked, wood was split. Storm windows set. By Friday, for the farmers, workmen, and shopkeepers of Goodnight, the pull toward the football field behind the high school was almost gravitational.

In a farmhouse on Mirage Flats south of town, Lewis Lockhardt was stirring cocoa at the kitchen stove. He was going to the game and he was hoping his wife was, too. She'd been sick, some little mystery flu, was what he told people, but it'd scared her somehow, and she was having a hard time getting back on her feet. Football game would do her good, he thought. See people, say hello. Get out of the house.

The opponent was Rushville. Rushville, like Goodnight, was a small town, but less small. It was big enough for its own doctor and its own cable television system and its own Ford agency, none of which Goodnight was big enough for. And Rushville's eight-man football team was drawn from a student body over twice the size of Goodnight's. Rushville's team made beating up on Goodnight an annual festivity. Last year's score was 52-6.

Lewis poured cocoa from pan to thermos, then went to the foot of the stairs and listened. He heard no movement overhead. 'Hi-dee-ho!' he called out and listened again. 'You about ready, Dot?'

Dorothy Lockhardt, still in her housedress, sat immobile on the side of the bed. She'd brushed her teeth, daubed some perfume on her wrist and low on her throat, then – was it the smell? – she suddenly felt too tired to continue. She heard Lewis's heavy footsteps on the stairs, but still she didn't move.

'How you doing?' Lewis asked from the door.

Dorothy made a pale smile. For her own private reasons she felt as if she ought to go, but still, she had no stomach for it. 'I was thinking of staying put,' she said.

It took Lewis about five minutes to get her moving again. He laid out clothes, pulled her gently to her feet. 'Like that smell,' he said of the gardenia scent. 'Something new?'

'Not so new. I bought it a while back.' This was a lie. A man named Gerald Woodley had given it to her. He was gone now. He'd run off. She'd lent him money and he'd run off.

'Perfume or cologne?' Lewis said, hanging up the housedress Dorothy had stepped out of.

'Cologne,' Dorothy knew to say. Perfume was expensive. Lewis knew that much.

ON A DESERTED ROAD IN THE TIMBERED HIGHLANDS NORTH AND EAST OF Goodnight, Marcy Lockhardt sat in an old McKibben's Mobil service truck eating a cheeseburger with Randall Hunsacker, who ate intently, without talking. He'd shaved that morning, but by now his chin and jaw were stubbled in a way Marcy liked.

'What're you thinking about?' Marcy asked.

It took him a moment. 'The game,' he said.

'Specifics?' she said. Marcy was already in her cheerleader's outfit – green sweater, yellow pleated skirt – and she'd turned toward Randall so that there was plenty of leg to consider if he cared to.

Randall Hunsacker grinned. 'I was thinking about knocking somebody's head off.' Randall liked causing fumbles, but what he liked best was separating an opponent from his helmet. He'd done it twice and afterwards, on the films, it seemed for a split second that it was the opponent's head that was flying off. Randall was glad it wasn't, he guessed, but he liked the effect.

Marcy slipped a finger through his beltloop. 'That's it? That's all you got on your mind?'

He relaxed his eyes. 'All I'm willing to talk about right now.'

Marcy laid her half-eaten hamburger on the dash and slid her hand under his shirt. 'Well, I got an idea,' she said in a whisper.

He laughed, shook his head and set her hand away. 'How about afterwards,' he said, turning his eyes fully on hers. 'Provided we win.'

'Do you even *know* how many straight times we've lost to Rushville?' she said.

Randall nodded amiably. 'Eleven.'

'But the twelfth time is a charm?'

'Maybe.' He slowly inhaled the cool, piney air. He liked it up here where nobody else went, overlooking one of the old picnic tables Dick and Lucy Witt had constructed long ago. Other than the old Rawhouser place, he guessed it was his favorite place to do it.

Marcy, fighting the impulse to sulk, ran a finger up his stubbly cheek. 'It'll be *freezing* afterwards,' she said.

Randall leaned away smiling. 'We'll turn up the heater,' he said, then, nodding toward her cheeseburger, he said, 'You going to eat that?'

EAST OF GOODNIGHT, THE RUSHVILLE TEAM WAS SITTING UP IN THEIR LOCKER room before the bus ride west. They had plenty of time – twenty minutes before boarding. At one end of the lockers a group of three or four players stood in partial dress, talking above a James Brown tape that played low on a boom-box.

Charles Tausen glanced at this group with disfavor when he walked into the locker room, and he continued to stare at them as he undressed. Being stared at by Charles Tausen was unnerving. His eyes took divergent paths. His right eye fixed on its object of attention, while the left eye floated skyward. As Rushville's quarterback, he used this to confounding effect. Bent over center, barking signals, he seemed to be looking everywhere, and all at once.

Tonight Charles was in a sour mood. His stomach wasn't right. He had a bad feeling about this game. Goodnight had a team, but nobody fucking believed it so they'd been playing grabass all week in practice like this was a fucking bye week or something. He'd told the coach that his uncle had scouted Goodnight and they had

a quarterback and a kicker and they'd shifted that Utah kid to free
safety where he was playing like a madman or some fucking thing.
The coach had smiled and all but said, yeah, yeah, yeah.

Tausen, naked, felt a tumbling of the bowels. He strode off, sat on
the toilet, managed nothing but voluminous gas. But while he sat he
heard the music go up with voices singing out. *Whoa! I feel good!*

Jesus fucking Christ.

Tausen walked calmly past his locker toward the group. 'The
donkster,' he heard somebody say, which he didn't mind. It derived
from donkey dong, an exaggeration, but not much of one. It was one
reason he liked walking around the locker room naked. It made these
little assholes understand life's important distinctions. The group
loosened as Tausen approached, did nothing as he reached for the
boom-box, ejected the tape and with a violent heave shattered the
plastic cassette against the cinderblock wall. Then he turned to the
other players. 'We got a game,' he said in his thick voice, 'and you're
standing around listening to nigger music.'

A tight silence ensued. Then, in a low voice, his eyes on his bare
feet, one of the boys said, 'That's *African-American*, Charles. And
we could use a couple in our backfield.'

Normally this would've gotten a laugh. Nobody laughed.

Charles turned one eye toward the boy, the other toward the
ceiling. There was a long still moment and then he broke a menacing
grin. 'Goodnight's got a team. You frivolous assholes better digest
that fact or you'll come home a busload of losers.'

UP IN THE LAST ROW OF THE CONCRETE STANDS, WHERE THEY COULD LEAN
against the concrete restraining wall, Dorothy Lockhardt sat listening
to the Goodnight band's pre-game performance while Lewis sipped
cocoa and thumbed through the *World-Herald* sports page he'd
brought along to fill the empty spaces. Old Ed Whiting, who
farmed just west of the Lockhardt place and was now climbing
the steps of the aisle, was caught in an awkward moment. Ed
was a gregarious man. He was looking for friendly faces to sit
with, but as he scanned the crowd his eyes met Dorothy's. There
was something uncertain or incomplete about his smile and nod.
Dorothy sensed he was about to turn down another aisle when

Lewis looked up. 'Room here if you're looking for a landing site, Ed.'

Ed Whiting, looking a little sheepish, turned back toward them. He seated himself next to Dorothy, but spoke across her to Lewis. He'd had sauerkraut with dinner. Dorothy could smell it.

'Who you bettin' on, Lewis?'

Lewis stretched a grin over his protruding teeth. 'If I can't bet on the home team, I don't bet.'

Ed Whiting bumped his knee against Dorothy's in a friendly way. 'And how's the missus feeling?'

'Better,' Dorothy said, trying not to breathe in the sauerkraut smell.

'Much better,' Lewis put in.

Dorothy trained Lewis's field glasses on Marcy, standing along the sidelines with her hands stuffed into her pom-poms for warmth, talking to one of the other cheerleaders, her back a little arched, knowing she was being watched by half the men in the stands. A dullness, almost a numbness, took hold of Dorothy. Marcy. Her own daughter Marcy. Her own smart, beautiful Marcy, the one with real prospects, the one who'd always been such a good girl, never sassy and never sulky, was having doings with a boy. Dorothy knew that much. With which boy was the question.

'*Damn*,' Ed Whiting said appreciatively when the small company of student musicians out on the field struck up a melody. 'That sounds a lot like a band.'

'Yep,' Lewis said and felt compelled to name the tune. 'Raindrops Keep Falling on My Head.'

This is my town, Dorothy thought. This is my portion. Without dropping the field glasses she said, 'Only since Mr Vincent.'

Mr Vincent, the Goodnight music and math teacher, was a source of subdued pleasure to Dorothy. He'd been hired on the basis of his résumé, which contained no photograph, and a telephone interview between him and Ronald Hiles, the superintendent of schools. Mr Vincent hadn't sounded black on the phone, but he was black in person, not dark black, but definitely ancestrally black. Harvey Brandt had pulled his daughter from day one of band class and three or four others followed suit. But then the town had heard the band play at the first football game that year, and they'd been stopped short. The band sounded good. Better than anybody ever remembered. And when Mr Vincent himself stepped forward and played a saxophone solo of 'I'll be Seeing You', it was so beautiful that, afterwards, it took a moment for people to collect themselves enough to applaud. After that, a rumor began to circulate that Mr Vincent might be part Negro, but was in fact mostly Hawaiian, a notion that quickly strengthened into accepted truth.

During the pre-game introductions, Dorothy kept the glasses on Marcy. If the phantom lover were a boy on the team, how she leaped and yelled for a particular name might give the secret away. It didn't, however. For every name announced, Marcy, to Dorothy's eye, carried on like something released from the wilds. Her hair, limbs, and skirt flew every which way. After Bobby Parmalee's name was announced, Marcy perhaps gave a more emphatic skyward thrust of her pom-poms, but then again, Dorothy thought, perhaps not.

Something peculiar then occurred. As Marcy and the other cheerleaders paraded behind the bench knuckling the helmets of every player for luck, Marcy dropped a slip of paper into the cupped hand of number 87. The hand fisted and didn't open until the Boy Scout color guard marched onto the field. Then number 87 opened his hand, looked quickly at the bit of pink paper, and did a strange thing: he folded the paper into his mouth like a stick of gum and began to chew. His other hand, the right hand, Dorothy saw now, was partially sheathed in black leather. This, she realized suddenly, was the boy with eight fingers.

Dorothy lowered the glasses and picked up her program.

Number 87. Randall Hunsacker.

The boy who'd stolen a car in Utah, the boy with the hateful reputation, the boy who'd been horrid to Lucy Witt and crude in front of Lewis. This was the boy having doings with her daughter. *Old enough to bleed*. Dorothy felt suddenly dizzy. She closed her eyes, and felt as if she were swaying in her seat.

'You okay, Dot?' Lewis said in his soft voice.

She opened her eyes, then closed them again.

'What's the matter, Hon?'

Lewis had the kind of decisive, instinctive intelligence that, it seemed to Dorothy, good farmers had and good hunters, too. If she told him what she'd just deduced, he would do something vengeful. He would have to.

'Nothing,' Dorothy said. 'Just a little woozy, is all.'

Everyone in the bleachers had now risen for the anthem and would remain standing for the kickoff. Finally a whistle would blow, the kicked ball would arc tumblingly through the air and the two teams, rushing willy-nilly from opposite ends of the field, would meet in a spate of bone-crunching collisions. Once the return man was tackled, Goodnight's fans could reseat themselves and, without saying so, wait for the worst to transpire.

Dorothy leaned into Lewis, willed herself to put her head on his shoulder, willed herself to keep her eyes closed through all the frantic cheering and whistling and yelling.

'Missing a good game here,' Lewis said to her in a low voice after a little while. 'Our boys're playing some pretty decent football.' But still she kept her eyes closed, so that, hidden from the crowd, her mind could wander whereever it pleased. It went to Gerald, of course, and then for no reason she understood to Ronald Holloway, a man who'd run a successful feedlot for years, then retired, ostensibly to train cutting horses, but more visibly visiting bars instead, and one night in front of their little stump-legged corgi he shot and killed his wife and then himself and Lewis after hearing the specifics had said that Holloway just had too much time on his hands, was all, and then she began to think of her own father and how on the very day he died he'd sent her mother into town for a pint of pineapple sherbet and eaten a whole bowlful and said how much he liked it just an hour or two before he stopped breathing.

Dorothy held her breath and when she finally exhaled, a song came to mind, a song she'd sung as a child in the chicken coop because her father had told her it would make the chickens lay better.

> *Chick chick chick chick chickee,*
> *Won't you lay an egg for me?*
> *I haven't had one since Eastertime*
> *and now it's half-past three.*

Lewis nudged her softly, and Dorothy, unsure whether she'd been singing or humming or maybe neither one, let her mind wander somewhere else.

AS EXPECTED, RUSHVILLE DOMINATED THE FIRST HALF STATISTICS, BUT, through a series of missed opportunities, their dominance was not reflected in the halftime score. Rushville led, but by only three points, 10–7.

During the halftime intermission, a little wind had begun to stir from the north, making gentle undulations in the winter wheat that lay beyond the playing field, though few of Goodnight's farmers or townsmen noticed. Many of them stood in clusters near the pep club concession stand, warming their hands with coffee in styrofoam cups and leaning forward in attitudes of hope and possibility. The local spread had been Rushville by fourteen points. Leo Underwood, Marlen Coates, and Jim Six, all betting types, were telling jokes – and laughing at them – more loudly than was usual, and while Frank Mears wouldn't allow himself to laugh, he couldn't suppress a wolfish grin.

Many of the men didn't go back to their wives in the stands at the second half kickoff. They stood along the fence, close to the field of play, and growled encouragement to their team. Goodnight couldn't move the ball, but their defense was fired up. They stacked up the runs and on passing downs blitzed either a linebacker or free safety, so that Charles Tausen had to rush his passes. Twice the Hunsacker kid shot up from his safety position and nailed Tausen even before he'd set up to throw. On each of these occasions, Randall Hunsacker leaped to his feet and while standing over the fallen quarterback pounded the earholes of his helmet seven times. This was something new this year, and it had caught on: simultaneously the Goodnight student body went *ding ding ding ding ding ding ding*.

Nearing the end of the third quarter, while Tausen bent over the center and, gazing everywhere, tried to anticipate the source of the next blitz, the center, to Tausen's surprise, prematurely snapped the ball. It squirted out of Tausen's hands and was lost in a swarm of bodies. Tausen, fuming, watched as the officials untangled the bodies and when finally Meteor Frmka popped out holding the ball overhead in gleeful triumph, Tausen snatched it away and in one quick motion sped it toward the Frmka boy's nose. The ball bounced crazily off Frmka's facemask and caused no real harm, but it drew Rushville a fifteen-yard unsportsmanlike.

So Goodnight, still down only three points, owned the ball on the Rushville twenty-six. Coach Dee sent in a succession of plays so timid they baffled both crowds. Goodnight swept right for a two-yard loss, took their time, tried the middle for a yard, took more time, and, after a short-gainer off tackle, let the clock run out on the third quarter. Then, after the teams switched ends, Goodnight lined up for a field goal instead of going into punt formation.

Disbelief worked among the men at the fence. They were giving up field position. It was a forty-three goddamn yarder. It'd been years since they'd hit one outside twenty! And what if it was blocked, how about that? What in *hell* was Coach Dee thinking about anyway?

It was a Mirage Flats farmer named Orval Weyers who pointed to the flag. It was snapping now, stretching south, the direction of the kick. 'Maybe Coach Dee has got this worked out,' he said and someone else said, 'Well, it'd be the first time,' but as the Goodnight side grew quiet, the ball was snapped, the hold was steady, and the kick was true. The ball, under the influence of the tailing wind, floated neatly over the crossbar.

10–10. A tie. The men at the fence exchanged wide-eyed grins and were behind their coach 100 percent.

ED WHITING HAD GONE DOWN TO THE CONCESSION STAND AT HALFTIME, FOUND other friends among the men at the fenceline, and never returned. Dorothy saw him down there at this moment, shoulder-punching Orval Weyers after the field goal. She and Lewis sat alone now and every once in a while Dorothy thought she caught someone or other glancing back at them to digest or even savor that fact. How come nobody sits near us? she thought and an answer immediately formed. Because they know about Gerald Woodley.

But it couldn't be that. Who could know about Gerald? Nobody, that's who. Nobody. She hadn't told and nobody had seen.

And yet.

Dorothy's nose was running. She felt, inexplicably, like crying. She fished a tissue from her purse and, wiping her nose, took in the gardenia scent on her wrist. It seemed suddenly to deprive her of oxygen. She closed her eyes and craved sleep. During her whole married life Dorothy had never really been sick, except once, with food poisoning, and, as bad as that had seemed at the time, she'd afterwards come to think of it as an almost amusing postcard view of death, a safe glimpse from behind a restraining rail. But this recent sickness was different. This sickness was the safe dark room she'd looked for and found, and it had become a hard room to leave.

Ding ding ding ding ding ding ding.

Dorothy opened her eyes. Something had happened down on the field, she didn't know what, except it involved number 87. From up in the crow's nest, an amplified voice said, 'Loss of seven. Tackle by Hunsacker. Third and thirteen.'

Old enough to bleed is old enough to butcher. Lewis hadn't repeated these words at the supper table in front of Marcy; he'd told Dorothy later while they were in bed. But maybe Lewis should've told Marcy, so that she'd have known what kind of boy – *Old enough to bleed.* Every time the words came upon Dorothy, she experienced the sudden sickening sensation of a puncture wound. For a moment this sensation could make her feel actually faint. All at once, while staring dazedly down at the field, Dorothy felt someone's sideways eyes on her and, glancing round, saw Letty Hobbs and Flossie Boyles, the town gossips, turn quickly away.

Then Dorothy said to Lewis in a quiet voice, 'They're having doings.'

Lewis, peering down at the field, said, 'What?'

'Marcy and that Hunsacker boy. They're having doings.'

Dorothy watched Lewis's face go out of shape for a long moment, stretch flat and wide, then come back together. 'The Hunsacker boy?'

Dorothy nodded.

Lewis stood up and left in the direction of the truck. Dorothy blinked a long slow blink, and another, then kept her eyes closed altogether. She began trying to think up a good reason for having told Lewis, some reason better than just feeling cornered. So many things had leaked away. She wanted back the scruples that, while she'd been with Gerald Woodley, had seemed silly and useless.

She wanted back the prospects she'd given up when she'd married Lewis, the defection from her nursing course, the idea of living in New Orleans or San Diego. She wanted them back for her daughter if not for herself. Why couldn't Marcy just wait for somebody with prospects, sweet Bobby Parmalee, say, who had plans for vet school, or Tully Coates, who always paid Marcy attention and whose father owned two irrigation units on the flats. Dorothy kept her eyes closed through these considerations, and only opened them when she felt Lewis's body again settle beside hers. 'Where did you go?' she asked.

'Truck.'

Lewis kept a little pistol under the seat of the truck, little enough it could fit into the interior pocket of his quilted vest without much bulge. 'What did you go to the truck for?' she asked.

He didn't answer and she didn't ask again. It was beyond her now. She closed her eyes. So this was how those terrible, impossible-seeming things you read about in the paper begin to happen. As simple as this.

THROUGH MUCH OF THE FOURTH QUARTER THE TEAMS TRADED POSSESSIONS, but Rushville's team went nowhere more bumblingly than Goodnight's did. They lost their footing, jumped offside, dropped passes. They began hearing scattered boos from their own bleachers. For Goodnight partisans, the belief took hold that a tie might be more than good enough for bragging rights. Their cheers had the bluster of victory in them.

The clock kept moving. With three minutes to play, third and three on their own fifteen, Charles Tausen called time out. He talked to his coach, who called a play Tausen didn't care for. He went back to the huddle. His eyes gazed contemptuously out at different parts of Goodnight's team. He checked the flag – it had gone limp. He regarded Goodnight's hotshot free safety, standing tense and poised and looking like a bull waiting for something to light out after. Tausen covered one nostril and shot mucus out of the other. He put on his helmet. He sketched out his own play, schoolyard stuff, a double reverse with a flip back to him. The split end would lame-duck and go long. 'Okay, assholes. On two.'

Tausen felt good for the first time all game. He bent over center, took the snap, fed the ball to his back, who handed it to the reversing left end, who pitched it back to Tausen. It was working. The linebackers froze and the smoke-snorting free safety bit on the fake reverse. Rushville's split end brush-blocked, drifted to the sideline and streaked long. He was open. He was wide, wide open.

Charles Tausen, with ample time, set, stepped forward and threw the football so majestically that it seemed launched from the imagination. Time turned elastic; stretched out; slowed down. Along the sidelines, Marcy Lockhardt clutched her pom-poms to her chest and actually gasped. She tried to close her eyes, but couldn't. On both sides of the field, fans rose and watched in dumb wonderment while the ball in a flawless soundless spiral described a long slow arc, as if spanning a dream.

II

IT WAS MARCY WHO, BACK IN JULY, HAD SURREPTITIOUSLY MEASURED THE size of Randall's truck bed. Marcy who'd gone to Foam City in Pine Bluff. Marcy who one Sunday afternoon had tossed the rolled foam in the back of the truck and directed Randall to the old Rawhouser place out in the sandhills. They pulled back a wire gate and drove through the prairie. Randall, staring out, couldn't find a single tire track. He couldn't see a single building. 'Thataway,' Marcy said, pointing east. 'Deep into the sandhills.'

They bounced easily along. Marcy shrugged her arms inside her blouse and, after some hidden and Houdinilike contortions, slipped out of her bra. 'If you cannot be free, be as free as you can,' she said, laughing. Then she said, 'For a trip to Rio on your birthday, who spake thus?'

Randall smiled and said he had no idea who spake thus.

Marcy leaned close – he could feel her breasts plumpening against his arm – and kissed him. 'You gotta at least guess,' she said. 'I'll give you three guesses.'

After each of his answers – John Lennon, Mahatma Gandhi ('*Mahatma*, I say *Mahatma* Gandhi!' Randall had said) and Dolly

Parton – Marcy made a loud buzzing noise to indicate complete and total wrongness.

'Damn,' Randall said genially after his third wrong guess.

'Burt Lancaster is the one who said it,' Marcy said, 'except I think he might've been quoting someone else.'

Randall said he didn't know all the ins and outs of the who-spake-thus game, but quoting somebody you could remember, who was quoting someone you couldn't, didn't seem to him exactly kosher.

'Kosher-schmosher,' Marcy said.

In front of the truck, a breeze moved the grass in waves. A pleasant feeling about this day had been expanding within Randall, boiling up in a pleasant and affecting effervescence. Geography aside, he had some inkling as to where they were headed.

'See that red stuff?' Marcy said suddenly, pointing right. 'That's how I found this place. It's wild buckwheat. Merna's aunt from Colorado thought you could sell that stuff to florists for dried arrangements or something. There! That stuff!' Marcy reached for the steering wheel, tugged it toward the red patch, and had Randall pull up. She jumped out and bending over in the bare heat snapped off a handful of stalks. 'Whattayou think?' she asked, fanning them for display. 'Look like a cash crop to you?'

Randall said he wouldn't've thought so, no.

They kept driving through the summer heat. In the distance an antelope raised its head and flicked its ears their way. A cluster of magpies rose from a small carcass not old enough to have shed its stench. Marcy, seeing a landmark in an unexpected place, said, 'Oops,' and pointed Randall a new course. 'You've been misguided,' Marcy said, then, trying for fun, 'Probably for many years now.'

Thirty minutes later, Marcy spied the chimney and barn of the abandoned Rawhouser place. The house had burned, but the barn had not, and as Randall eased his old truck inside the ramshackle structure, a few alarmed swallows swooped out. While Randall was taking it all in – the bleached wood, the oily dirt, the partial shade from the partial roof – Marcy pulled him close and began to kiss him. They had kissed many times, but this was a different kind of kissing, hard kissing, serious, urgent, tooth-to-tooth kissing. To Marcy, it was kissing that had been saved up every day since puberty, kissing that peeled back worries, threats, and admonitions, kissing that benumbed the brain and quickened the blood. But she wanted things just so, wanted to savor it and stretch it out, and so she broke off the kiss. 'Want to look around?' she asked.

They walked out, looked at the charred remains of the burned house, the rough rocks of the foundation, the charred stone fireplace and chimney. The red stone reminded Randall of Utah. 'That's nice rock,' he said.

'Probably came from up around Rapid,' Marcy said. 'They've got whole buildings made from it up there.'

A hot breeze worked into their clothes. Randall thought he knew what they were up to out in this gritty and solitary place, and he thought that what had stopped Marcy a minute ago was what he considered her legitimate need to get some assurance that he was committed to her, that he wouldn't ever desert her. In a careful voice, Randall said that if he and Marcy ever built a house of their own, he'd come and get this rock for their own fireplace.

But Marcy, already distracted by something else, said, 'Yeah, it'd probably be good for fireplaces.'

He wandered one direction. She wandered another. When he got back within the cool shade of the barn, she'd hung the spray of rusty-red buckwheat from a wood rung on the wall, rolled the foam pad out in the truck bed, and covered it with a clean white sheet. She sat there, barefooted but dressed, with her back against the rear window of the cab. Her whole body had the attitude of a lazy smile. 'This is as close to heaven as you can get in Nebraska,' she said. 'Want to take a nap with me?'

She looked cool, serene, almost angelic. He would later wonder whether he'd made the right decision, climbing into that truck bed with Marcy, but he would be framing the question unfairly. The pull of her sex was primitive, and irrefusable. His imagination was loping ahead, and the rest of him was already following behind.

What Marcy and Randall chiefly felt when the act was over was relief that they'd done so well. They lay back sweating and in a little bit Randall made Marcy laugh by saying maybe they ought to do it again so they wouldn't forget how. And then, after that, Marcy curled into him and closed her eyes. Randall lay staring up at the concentration of dust motes floating in the slants of sunlight. He heard the little whisking sounds of a browsing rodent. He said something to Marcy in a gentle voice.

Marcy jerked awake. 'What?'

This time, his voice was sharper, a little defensive. 'We need to get married.'

'Why?' Marcy said. 'We're not going to get pregnant or anything. I began spotting yesterday. There's no flow yet, but technically, if you go by the book, I'm having my period.'

Randall let his gaze slide away. This was more than he wanted to know of the subject.

'And there's a clinic in Pine Bluff where I can get a diaphragm,' Marcy said, 'so there won't be any problem from now on.' (This would not be strictly true, as it turned out. Marcy's mother *would* discover the diaphragm, and it would be a problem.)

'I didn't mean because you might get pregnant,' Randall said. He shifted his eyes to the dark corners of the hayloft. She'd been a virgin. He'd been, too. He had known from the beginning that to have sex with Marcy was the same as agreeing to marrying her. Otherwise – Otherwise, it would be something not right. He knew that many people, most even, would think this was lame and puny thinking, but he also knew it was what he felt and thought, and he'd figured Marcy felt and thought the same way, too.

'Look, Randall,' Marcy began, but trailed off. A few minutes earlier she'd felt wonderful. She loved the feeling of her slick, sweaty body against his, and loved knowing in her bones how much he loved it, and loved the closeness and the secretness and even the sneakiness of what they were doing. It was better than anything in her life up to then. And she loved Randall. In a certain way, she *did* love him. But she didn't want to be a mechanic's wife. She smoothed a finger along Randall's stomach. 'We're only still in high school, Randall. I like the idea of getting married to you, I really do, but not before we're older and further along. Then we'd have something, you know, to build on.'

It sounded to Randall a lot like an adult who was saying something he thought you might be willing to hear instead of what was actually true. But Randall also sensed that forcing the issue wasn't going to work to his advantage. 'Well, I'm not saying I couldn't wait a while,' he said finally.

And so on that day back in July, Marcy had curled close to him. 'Sure,' she'd said sleepily. 'It can be like a secret engagement. Like they have in old movies and books.' She didn't mind this idea. It might even push the fun into a smaller space and make it more intense. She'd eased her cheek into the cove of Randall's neck and, listening to his beating heart, had fallen deeply asleep.

III

WHEN RANDALL, SUCKED IN BY THE FAKE REVERSE, SAW THE FOOTBALL FLIPPED back to Charles Tausen, he took off running toward the wide-open receiver. He figured the pass would be completed, but, with the right angle, he might cut the guy off before he scored. Randall took his own coordinates, where the ball and receiver would meet. He fixed on the spot and streaked in a direct line, across open field, unencumbered. As he ran, something changed. It seemed at first like he was moving faster, and he was, but it wasn't completely that. The Rushville wide receiver was slowing. The ball was slowing. Hanging there. Waiting. Randall took two more strides, leaped, sailed through the air, formed a pocket with his two outstretched hands, his eight outstretched fingers, and felt the ball slide snugly into it.

He had it.

Randall crashed into the Rushville receiver, staggered, righted himself and looked up. There was a faraway trumpeting roar from the Goodnight side of the field. The Rushville end was rolling backwards out of bounds. Bobby Parmalee, who'd been instinctively following Tausen's pass downfield, quickly reversed direction and neatly blindsided the nearest Rushville tackler. Randall had some room. He tucked the ball under his arm. He began to run.

All Randall heard was the air rushing through the earholes of his headgear, all he saw was the sudden convergence of red-and-black jerseys. They were everywhere. But he lagged for an instant, shifted weight and scooted by the first tackler, sliced behind the next. Two red-and-blacks bore down from the left. Randall planted hard, pushed off right, poured himself into a move so nimble and surprising he knew it would never come back to him again.

A strange elation began to swell in Randall. Something was going on, he could feel it. He cut and swerved and as if by magic found himself inside a passageway only he could see, narrow and winding and changing shape, but always there, this path through which Randall twisted, faked, popped, and swiveled until, suddenly, he was out the other end with what seemed like miles of open field in front of him.

Randall, thinking he was home free, eased up and looked back for flags. For a clip, say. But there were no flags. There was nothing but wide bland faces staring at him, and at something else, too, off to the side. Randall had just begun to follow their gaze when a blur of black and red flew into view.

It was Charles Tausen hurtling helmet-first toward Randall's chest.

ALONG THE FENCELINE, NEAR THE PEP CLUB CONCESSION STAND, THE MEN from Goodnight had been mesmerized by Tausen's pass. They knew what it meant. They could already sense the unfair diminishment in self-respect that was on its way. In their farmers' bones, in their shopkeepers' bones, they had expected it. It was what living on small farms and in a small town taught them to expect. They would lose. They would walk away, muttering or maybe working up a joke, beginning to pretend it didn't matter. But it did. Not in any way they could adequately define or defend, but still, it did. It mattered.

So when this new kid, this Hunsacker kid came full-tilt out of nowhere and stole, *stole*, the ball from the Rushville receiver, the men from Goodnight could hardly believe it. Convulsive joyous spasms shot through their bodies. Whoops of shocking intensity issued from their lungs. They grabbed their hats off their heads. Balding men, rickety men, hard-ridden men, they climbed the fence to see a little better.

UP IN THE STANDS, DOROTHY HAD GAZED AT TAUSEN'S PASS, HAD MARVELED at its beauty, and had been disappointed when the Hunsacker boy stole the ball from the Rushville player. The crowd bellowed. Dorothy stood, couldn't see, climbed up on her seat. The Hunsacker boy had the ball under his arm and was streaking up the field with it. To

Dorothy, he was a thief with the goods under his arm trying to get away, and she rooted against him on that basis. *Get him*, she thought. *Get him*. But they didn't. They slid off of him, they stumbled, they missed. He got lost in the crowd, finally squirted out again and Dorothy, sensing that Randall Hunsacker, the hateful boy with eight fingers, was about to become the game's hero, looked away, but as she did, the crowd almost as one issued an abrupt *oooh*, and fell silent.

Dorothy turned quickly round. The Hunsacker boy was down. *Ha!* That was Dorothy's first thought. But then in the next instant it seemed to her that the boy's body was in some sickening way compressing back into itself, and then was not moving at all. For one fearful instant, before she told herself that her husband was standing next to her with his hands in his pockets, Dorothy wondered whether Lewis had shot the boy.

Someone in a somber voice said, 'Jesus Christ, what a hit.'

One of the Goodnight players was looking down at the Hunsacker boy and then waving wildly to Coach Dee. 'Not breathing! He's not breathing!'

Murmurs worked through the stands. Coach Dee was running onto the field. Marcy was running onto the field. Lewis without a word began to move, became in moments like a man in a fire-flight, pushing furiously through the crowd, yelling and elbowing his way down the stairs. Dorothy followed in his wake, she didn't know why, but she moved numbly behind him across the field until Lewis reached Marcy, who was standing outside the circle of people surrounding the boy. Lewis put his red, weathered hands on his daughter, surrounded her with his gangly arms. Marcy, in the hold of her father, looked out at her mother with wild desperate eyes.

'We're engaged,' she said, something wet and gurgly in her voice.

Dorothy glanced around. From within his dark helmet, Bobby Parmalee's eyes stared fixedly at Marcy. Dorothy turned back to her daughter. 'Who?' she said.

'Randall,' Marcy said. She'd begun to cry. 'Randall and me.'

A second passed. Dorothy hesitated only a long second. Then she found a seam in the circle of people surrounding the boy and stepped inside. Charles Tausen stood with his helmet off, his head back, his eyes on different points in the night sky. Nobody in the circle moved or spoke. The coach was working on Randall Hunsacker, but not right, Dorothy could see that much. 'Pray,' she heard somebody say. A few moments later, Coach Dee stood up, looking stricken, and at the exact instant he said 'Dead,' everybody seemed to lean a little back except Dorothy, who fell to her knees beside the boy.

He was already blue at the lips. His skin felt doughy. There was no pulse. She made a fist and popped it into his lower breastbone. Nothing. She pointed his chin up and pinched his nose and breathed into his mouth. When she took her mouth away the first time, she yelled for Lewis – how did she know he would come? – how could she be so certain? – and in an instant he was there. She had him start pressing on the boy's chest, once per second, counting out every five. They worked up a rhythm, they kept at it, but nothing happened. The boy just lay there. There was a point, Dorothy knew, when it was no good, no matter what. That the brain –

Close by, Marcy was weeping and slurping. She took the boy's hand and was saying in soft sobs, 'C'mon, Randall, oh, please, Randall.'

'*C'mon*,' Lewis said in a sudden sharp voice through clenched teeth. He was talking to the boy. 'C'mon, you little punk, you little asshole,' he grunted, the words squeezing out between compressions, words Lewis Lockhardt never used, words that nobody would've guessed ever came into Lewis Lockhardt's mind. 'C'mon, you little punk, you little asshole, get up.' Dorothy could feel people slowly moving away, the circle widening, staring at her and Lewis and Marcy like they were zoo monkeys doing something sickening. 'C'mon, you little mutant, you little chickenshit –'

In another minute (although the citizens of Goodnight afterwards agreed that it seemed much longer), Lewis Lockhardt in desperation or anger or perhaps complete if passing lunacy, knitted his fingers into a double-fist, raised it overhead, and, swearing still, slammed the double-fist into the boy's diaphragm, furiously, as he might a sledgehammer to a splitting wedge, and almost at once Randall Hunsacker droolingly expelled mustardy-yellow bile, and coughed, and began to draw into his lungs the cool autumn air.

Chapter Eight

THE PARMALEES' DOG

THE PARMALEES' THREE-LEGGED DOG WAS A TERRIER MIX THAT A STRANGER *had brought in from the highway twelve years before, when Bobby Parmalee was almost six. The stranger hadn't hit the dog, he told Dr Parmalee, but he'd seen it hit and stopped when the dog seemed still to be alive. He said he'd pay to have it tended to, but he couldn't stay, he was on his way back home to California. He'd wrapped the dog in an army blanket and nested him on the passengerside floorboard. Dr Parmalee had told the man he was a horse-and-cow vet, but he could probably save the dog by amputating one leg or – and this was his more practical recommendation – he could put the dog down. 'How much for amputation?' the man had asked and Dr Parmalee knew right then that it must've been his car that hit the dog. Dr Parmalee told him a fair price. 'And you could find a home for the dog?' the man asked. Dr Parmalee had given that more thought, and finally answered yes. The man paid and drove away. Six years later he drove back. He said a few words to Dr Parmalee and Bobby, petted the dog, and chuckled when they told him they'd named the animal Foolish. 'After him or me?' the man asked, and Dr Parmalee had said, 'Oh, after all of us, I suppose.' The man went to the trunk of his sedan and brought out a thirty-pound bag of nuts, which he'd grown in California. 'Hope you like pistachios,' he said to Bobby, who, eleven at the time, said he hoped he did, too, even though he didn't know what they were. They all shook hands, even Bobby, and after the man left, Dr Parmalee had said, 'He's a nice man, but he thinks there's an unpaid bill.'*

Though Bobby Parmalee's father had operated a successful veterinary practice for many years, there had been a bad dark period of time that Bobby would later remember only vaguely: memories of late-night travels with his father driving hunched forward over the wheel toward a distant hospital while his mother talked as if neither he nor his father were in the car with her. Something terrible was wrong with his mother, but Bobby didn't know what. Looking back, he wasn't sure what he actually remembered or what had been suggested later by overheard conversations. He knew that his mother had begun turning things on without ever turning anything off. Lights, ovens, stoves, fans, car engines. Water taps were her favorite. Bobby could remember – or had constructed images for the story he'd heard repeated – his father coming home one afternoon and finding him sitting on the linoleum floor of the bathroom while water gushed from the bath tap, sheeted over the tub, covered the floor and slid through the hallway to the living room. Another time a UPS delivery man came to the door and, when no one would answer, looked through the front window. Bobby was sitting on the coffee table playing with tiny toy cars while his mother stood stark naked in the middle of the room talking and gesturing with her eyes fixed at a point just below the ceiling. At school, an older boy said Bobby's mother should be in the nuthouse and someone else said that they should take Bobby's mother to a nudist colony. In the end, they took her to a psychiatric hospital in Lincoln. The last time Bobby visited her, she'd called him Henry. He had tried to tell her about their new three-legged dog and she'd said, 'That's you to a tee, Henry. Always a weakness for the injured creatures.' 'She thinks you're her brother,' Dr Parmalee explained to Bobby as they were driving away. 'Henry was always your mother's favorite brother.' Before long, Bobby's mother had ceased to recognize anyone, ever. Bobby and his father continued living in Goodnight, though they moved to a different house. Bobby took care of the three-legged dog, his father paid the nursing home bill that came from Lincoln every month, and his mother never got better.

Chapter Nine

THE CROOKED BRIDGE

I

THE NIGHT BEFORE MARCY LOCKHARDT'S WEDDING TO RANDALL HUNSACKER, Bobby Parmalee couldn't sleep. He'd tried reading, he'd tried to imagine himself lying in a flat boat on a calm pond, and finally he just lay in bed staring at the ceiling. He felt the whole house tremble as the 3.20 freight train passed by. He heard a dog stop barking.

Bobby had been among the players gathered around Randall that night on the football field, but with his attention directed as much toward Marcy as Randall, he was among the first to see the words *we're engaged* form within the wild contortion of Marcy's face. He saw the words clearly though he would never remember hearing them. In the weeks and months prior to that Friday night, Bobby had patiently nurtured his fading hopes for Marcy and himself, and fading hopes, he would later see, were nothing if not pliant, so that even as Marcy was tearfully declaring her intention to marry somebody else, Bobby for several seconds had stood unmoving in the midst of the general alarm and disconcertment, had stood quiet and invisible, watching Marcy and waiting for a sign to indicate that what she was really meaning to say was that she was engaged to him, himself, Bobby Parmalee.

Except for a slim moon, the sky was still black when Bobby rose and went to his second-story window. Across the street, a dim light shone from Walkinshaw's Barber Shop and, two doors east, the

Mellons had left a porch light burning, a mistake, Bobby knew, because the Mellons were tight. Off beyond the rooftops and fields, a pair of headlights cut through the dark plains. To the west, the pale moon hung so low it looked as if a cowboy up on Crow Butte might just rope it. It was not the first time this notion had occurred to Bobby; he'd once amused Marcy with it. She'd replied something cheeky – he couldn't remember what – and then begun a line of nibbling kisses that started at his collar and climbed to his earlobe. That was a long time ago. Still, since they'd parted company, it had become a source of faint solace to Bobby that, at any given moment on any given night, he and Marcy, from their divergent points, might be staring up at the same moon.

Bobby pulled on some clothes and combed his hair. He tiptoed downstairs carrying his shoes. He coasted his car out the driveway, jump-started the engine on the roll and in the pre-dawn darkness headed south, toward the crooked bridge.

THE PRIOR NIGHT, BOBBY HAD WALKED OVER TO THE ELEVENTH MAN BAR and Grill for no other reason than that he'd told himself he would. Leo Underwood was giving the bachelor party and there was a bunch of his crowd drinking clamorously at the center of the turbulence. Jim Six was there, and Whistler Simpson and Marlen Coates, all of them whooping it up. Frank Mears was doing boilermakers with beer chasers. The groom alone wasn't drinking much – Randall Hunsacker seemed to Bobby like a stone holding against fast-moving water. Bobby went over and shook Randall's partially sheathed hand and said in a sturdy voice the words he'd come to say. He wished them every happiness. Randall nodded seriously, but also, behind the seriousness a wonderment bordering on suspicion seemed to hover. When their hands unclasped, Bobby began to slip away. 'Before the entertainment?' Frank Mears said in a sly mean voice. 'We got ourselves a generous portion coming.' Somebody else, one of the happier drunks, crowed, 'Wyona Apple!' Leo Underwood grinned at Bobby and chewed on a soda straw. '*Ample* is the exotic dancer's actual name. Wyona *Ample*.' As Bobby made his way out to the cool night air, someone from within yelled, 'Generous portions!'

Bobby was walking home when a Buickful of girls slowed

alongside him on 2nd Street, Bernita Landreth and Julie Thies and he couldn't tell who else. He nodded and kept walking. But the car stopped, a rear door swung open and out stepped Marcy. The Buick pulled ahead, parked and cut its lights.

'Greetings, Earthling,' Marcy said when she got close to Bobby, an old familiar salutation, but sad-seeming now.

'Hey.'

They were standing under a redbud tree that flickered with the breeze and, backed by a yardlight from the Finkey place, threw moving shadows. Bobby was trying to see Marcy's eyes when she said, 'Pretty night, wouldn't you say?'

'Yeah. Yeah, it is.'

'You been up to the bar?'

Bobby ducked his head in a way he knew she'd know meant yes.

For the first time she put a little fun in her voice. 'To see the striptease artist?'

Bobby shook his head. 'Just wanted to congratulate Randall, is all. Then I left.'

'Before the striptease artist appeared?' Bobby knew she was having fun with the term, like there was something secretly witty about it that she was willing to share.

'I left before the entertainment,' Bobby said, and then let himself be drawn into Marcy's sphere of influence. He made a small grin. 'Leo says her *actual* stage name is Wyona Ample.'

Marcy's laugh floated off into the night. They both listened to it go. Then Marcy said, 'So are you coming tomorrow?'

Bobby poked a finger in his ear and looked away. He did mean to go, as a matter of fact, but for some reason he didn't feel like saying so.

'I wish you would,' Marcy said. 'I mean, if you thought you wanted to.'

In a mild voice Bobby asked why he would want to.

'So I'd know you aren't mad at me.'

Bobby in the same mild voice said, 'I'm not mad at anybody.'

Somebody tapped the horn of Bernita Landreth's Buick. Marcy turned, yelled, 'Okay!' then turned back to Bobby. She waited a second or two. 'I was thinking that at exactly dawn tomorrow I'd go skinny-dipping at the crooked bridge.'

This was a strange idea, in Bobby's opinion. Two summers ago, at this very pool, while wearing a full swimming suit, a leech had stuck itself into Marcy's pierced ear and he'd had to remove it. 'Why would you want to go skinny-dipping there?'

Marcy shrugged. 'A way of ending one part of my life and starting another.'

Bobby tried to make out her features in the skittery shadowy light. 'So how come you're telling me?'

The question seemed to take Marcy by surprise. 'Not sure,' she said. 'Guess I just wanted to.' And then she was walking away, sliding into the back seat of Bernita Landreth's Buick, glancing over her shoulder through the back window as they drove away.

IT WAS STILL DARK WHEN BOBBY PULLED UP TO THE CROOKED BRIDGE. MARCY'S car wasn't there. He turned off his engine and lights and sat waiting and wondering just how much more foolish he could get. What in the world was he doing here? What could he say that wouldn't make everybody, including himself, just feel worse? That Marcy was motivated not by love and sound thinking but by a blubbery, as-he-lay-dying engagement announcement one Friday night on a smalltown football field? That if she had any doubts about Randall or this marriage she should take a big step back and think things through? That nobody in the world could love her like he, Bobby Parmalee, did? No, not one word of that. Besides, it was Marcy's folks who should've somehow stopped this wedding, but – he wasn't sure how or why – their stepping in to save Randall Hunsacker's life that night on the football field and then being honored for it, not officially, but in the unspoken yet keenly felt way that honor and shame are transmitted and received in a town like Goodnight, had made them rubbery in their disapproval of Randall, and had left them arguing not so much against early marriage to Randall as against early marriage at all, which, as a strategy, was of course doomed to fail.

Bobby rolled down his window and from the darkness heard nothing but the suck of water rushing past the bridge piles. But what *could* Marcy's folks have done, really? Randall had nearly died playing football for good old Goodnight, and those people who had always been quick to point out Randall's faults had now fallen silent. Word of Marcy's teary announcement had spread quickly, and the shock and sheer romance of it had created among Marcy's friends – and a good many others who should've known better – a rising wave of sentiment that was giving Marcy the ride of her life. It had carried her through winter and it had carried her through spring. It probably felt to Marcy like it would carry her forever. Bobby leaned forward and clicked in an old Doors tape and played it loud enough that he couldn't think.

When the sky began to lighten, he switched off the music and, in the sudden silence, thought he heard a twig snap somewhere. He looked around, but saw nothing. He walked out to the crooked bridge, as it was called, though it was actually bowed, the effect of an ice floe. The planking was rough, warped, and loose. Nobody was there. 'Hello?' Bobby said in a soft voice. It was quiet except for what sounded like a small animal lapping up water somewhere. 'Marcy?'

No-one answered. The darkness was stretching thin, giving way. Bobby closed his eyes and stood stock-still until he could feel the first long lines of sun behind his eyelids. He opened his eyes and slowly looked around.

Nothing, nobody.

He sat on the edge of the bridge and took off most of his clothes. Then he took them all off. He stood and considered whether to jump or dive. A phrase came to him, from Spanish class. *Que profundidad tiene el agua aquí?* How deep is the water here? Somewhere in the distance, a tractor cranked and fired and began to chug. Bobby jumped, one leg straight, the other bent and braced by locked hands. The cold water swallowed him whole, spun him around, sent him back up gasping sharply for air. He liked it, though. For a moment or two, he felt better instead of worse. He picked his way through the rocks and brush, dried himself with his undershirt and was pulling on his boxer shorts when he heard something from the dense brush where the stream fed the pool. 'Marcy?'

Behind the brush, there was the slightest movement, then muffled laughter.

'Who's there?' Bobby said.

'Just us chickens.' It was a girl's voice, but not Marcy's, followed by another girl's laughter.

Bobby, white-faced, walked woodenly toward the voices. 'This isn't funny,' he said, more satisfied with the serious way he said the words than with the words themselves. 'This isn't funny at all.'

Two girls rose from behind the woody brush, first Bernita Landreth and then Julie Thies, which stopped Bobby short. He liked Bernita and Julie and though they'd been laughing they were at least trying now to keep a straight face. 'Since when was this kind of joke your idea of fun?' he asked.

Bernita answered first. 'Isn't,' she said. 'And we weren't playing a joke. We just told Marcy we'd meet her here and of course she didn't show, but then you showed up as kind of a surprise guest.'

Bobby had begun to relax and he saw that reflected in their faces. A few seconds passed. Then Julie said, 'For 5.30 Saturday morning, this was pretty good entertainment.' She was trying to suppress a laugh. 'Definitely beats cartoons,' she said and, her face giving way, she broke into gleeful laughter. Bernita did, too.

Bobby walked back to the rest of his clothes. When Julie and Bernita finally composed themselves, he looked up from buttoning his shirt. 'You think you could do me a favor?' he asked, but then, looking at their flushed grinning faces, he decided they couldn't. He made to go.

'Wanna go to Chadron and buy us breakfast?' Julie asked.

'I don't think,' Bobby said. He didn't want to and besides he couldn't. He was helping his father with some steers this morning. Bobby was almost to his car when he had a thought and turned back. 'Where'd you park at, Bernita?'

She pointed further up the road. 'Up by those trees. In plain sight if you'd come that way.' Bobby was looking off in that direction when Bernita said, 'What favor were you going to ask?'

She seemed serious. Bobby said, 'I was kind of hoping you wouldn't mention my showing up here to Marcy.'

Bernita thought it over. 'Okay.'

'Okay what?'

'Okay I won't,' Bernita said and after a second or two Julie said, 'Me neither,' but Bobby knew they probably would.

II

GINNY WALKINSHAW HAD A CRUSH ON BOBBY PARMALEE. SHE HAD WRITTEN that very thing down on a sheet of paper. *Ginny Walkinshaw has a big orange crush on Bobby Parmalee.* Then she'd wadded it up and thrown it away so none of her nosy brothers would ever see it. Ginny would be thirteen in three weeks and six days. She'd be a teenager then. She rolled over in bed and lifted the curtain to see out, squinting because already the morning light was harsh and glary. Across the street, Dr Joe was driving away in the red pickup that said, DR JOSEPH PARMALEE, DVM on the side. Bobby Parmalee followed behind in his Plymouth Fury, just like normal. He lowered his window, shot his arm out and gripped the hood, just like normal. He was wearing a long-sleeved work shirt. That was just like normal, too.

Ginny padded down the hallway to the bathroom door and beat on it. 'Who's in there?' she yelled and when one of her brothers identified himself, Ginny said, 'Well, hustle it up, Deirdre.' She'd read the name Deirdre in a library book and decided it was the weirdest name ever. Using it on one of her brothers never failed to please her.

After breakfast Ginny put on her hightops, picked some strawberries, including two very fat ones, and set out for the Mendenhall place, where, she knew, Bobby was helping his dad fix some steers. She went by way of White Creek, crossing and crisscrossing, looking at this and that. Raccoon tracks, edible mushrooms, blowflies swarming off a fresh dead calf. She put rocks in the crotches of trees so that the next time she walked this way, she'd see them and be reminded of walking along the creek on Marcy Lockhardt's wedding day.

Ginny couldn't figure out how she felt about Marcy Lockhardt's wedding. She felt bad for Bobby, because she knew he'd expected to marry Marcy. Boys liked the Marcy type – Ginny's own brothers were always coming to the window to spy google-eyed whenever Marcy was over at Bobby's – but Ginny didn't think Marcy was all that great. You couldn't count on her at all. She was always bouncing here and there and hardly ever showing up where she was supposed to. Bobby was serious. He wanted to be a vet like his father except do all animals not just big ones. He needed somebody who went in a straight line –

About a mile along White Creek, Ginny Walkinshaw would cut west, but before she left the creekbank she sat down and turned back her cuffs to expose her white socks. There were some brown ticks there, not as many as she expected, but a few. She dropped one of them in the middle of her scalp and held perfectly still, not breathing, trying to feel it take hold. She thought she felt it, but wasn't sure. She touched the place where she put it – it was there, all right – then took the rest of the ticks and put them in a little hollow of the rock and crushed them with another rock, one at a time. 'Adios, Deirdre,' she said to each one.

When she got to the Mendenhall place, Ginny didn't make herself known. Dr Joe's truck was out near the pen, where the men and cattle were, but Bobby's car was parked over by some abandoned outbuildings under a cottonwood tree. There was a tire hanging from a limb and somebody had set a wooden picnic table under the tree. Ginny sat in the tire and ate all but the two biggest strawberries, then climbed the tree and sat on a limb watching Bobby.

Gordy Hughson was hot-prodding steers through a chute that funneled to a restraining rig. Bobby dropped a bar over the animal's neck and cinched the rig so the steer couldn't bolt or kick, then he held the tail, which more or less looked like fun to Ginny, plus you got paid for it, but Bobby didn't seem to be having much fun. Dr Joe carried the scalpel in his mouth and a crimping tool in one hand while he lifted the sacs with the other. The balls when they came popping out were the size of small peaches and Dr Joe dropped them into a tub of water that Ginny knew from past events to be the color of red Easter-egg dye. Then Dr Joe would crimp the sac. It was at this moment of pressure that a steer would want to let fly. Dr Joe could step back from most of it but not all. When he got it good, Gordy Hughson and the other cowboys would hoot and laugh like anything, and normally Bobby would've joined in, but not today. Today he just looked at his father's splattered arms

and then at the cowboys and then he released the rig and kicked
at the confused steer to move him on.

There were only a dozen or so steers left in the holding pen
and when the last of them were moved through the chutes and
cut and tagged and turned out, all the men except Bobby stood
around talking. Bobby went over to a stand of ash, peed, and then,
buttoning up, said something to the men before heading off toward
his car.

'Fran'll have dinner,' Ed Mendenhall yelled after him, but Bobby
kept walking with his head down.

Ginny got right down from the tree and curled up on top of the
picnic table and acted like she was asleep. If Bobby was leaving,
he'd come right upon her and wake her up and see how sleepy
she was and then he'd lift her in his arms and carry her over to
the car. The plan was so perfect she had to work not to laugh. But
something went wrong. Suddenly Bobby's car was revving up.

'Hey!' Ginny yelled and went running over.

Bobby, turning, looked surprised. 'What're you doing here?'

'Came out to watch you work and then I got bored and went to
sleep right on that table thinking you'd wake me up when you went
to leave.'

Bobby swung his gaze around to the table. 'You were sleeping
right there?' he asked.

Ginny was pretty disappointed in his behavior. 'You got to be
more aware, don't you think?'

She came around the car and climbed in. They drove for a time
without talking, and Bobby didn't turn on the radio, the way he usually
did. 'What're you doing this afternoon?' Ginny asked and when he
didn't answer she said she was waiting for her Aunt Tudie who had
this big Dodge pickup with duallies and a huge camper on the back
with complete kitchen and complete bathroom and everything. She
was going to take Ginny on an overnight down to Walgren Lake.

Ginny kept talking the rest of the way. She knew Bobby wasn't
interested, but she couldn't help herself. It was stupefying how boring
and dopey you could be at the same time. 'I always liked the idea of
being a vet, but now I might decide to become a cowboy instead.'
She was thinking about who got splattered with hot cow manure

and who got to laugh about it. The next thing she said was, 'Don't you think Marcy was kind of too bouncy for you anyhow?'

Bobby turned, surprised. 'Bouncy?'

'Yeah. I think she was too *bouncy* for you. What do you think?' Ginny's father, as the town barber, had taught her and her brothers that it was usually better to give no opinion at all, but if you did, it was always important to let the customer have the last word.

Bobby returned to his private thoughts, but after a while he said, 'In my opinion, Marcy's more like this pool you dive into because it looks real inviting and real deep, only it isn't, it's just two feet of water with a rocky bottom.'

Ginny liked this way of looking at it. 'Yeah!' she said, 'and it's like there are warning signs all over the place, but if you're dumb enough you dive in anyway!'

Bobby made a chuckle that didn't sound very happy.

Once they'd turned off the highway, Ginny knew there were two routes home. The first went by St Columbkille, the church where Marcy's wedding was going to be in about two hours, and the second route, a little slower, took you up Main. Bobby took Main. When they pulled into the carport to the side of the Parmalee house, Ginny said, 'Uh-oh.'

'What?' Bobby said.

Ginny was holding a finger to the top of her head and trying to look scared. 'Tick.'

Bobby pulled her over and tried to look. He smelled of cow, which Ginny liked. 'Can't see,' he said. 'Let's get into the light.'

Out in the heat of the yard, Bobby gently parted her hair and with his thumb and index finger plucked the tick from her scalp, then crushed it under his boot on the concrete. 'You were somebody's blood meal,' he said with a half-laugh. He turned and moved toward the house.

'Shouldn't you wash my hair with some special anti-tick soap or something?' Ginny asked. She'd seen a movie where Robert Redford washed his girlfriend's hair out in the middle of Africa and it had looked pretty romantic. But through an open window Jaye Ball, who cooked for Bobby and Dr Joe and took Dr Joe's phone calls and who always seemed just around the corner whenever Ginny was over, said in her falsely friendly voice, 'If you're going to do anything, you should shave the spot and put on merchrochrome.'

Ginny didn't like Jaye Ball. The only time she was at all interesting was when she was out in the back cleaning up the kennels and thought nobody was around. Ginny had heard Jaye Ball say *shit* any number of times and *Goddamn-it* twice. Once she'd said *fuck-a-duck*. 'I guess my head'll be all right without shaving it and coloring it orange,' Ginny said.

The Parmalees' ancient three-legged dog came limping over for a scratch, which Ginny provided, near the base of the tail, where he liked it. 'There, Foolish? Or right ... *there?*' When Ginny looked up, Bobby was heading inside. 'Hey, you coming back out?' she asked.

'Not till later on,' Bobby said without turning.

'Want to see Daisy's puppies?' Ginny asked. Daisy was the Walkinshaws' yellow Lab.

Bobby said he'd like to see them, but not right now.

'Hey!'

He turned. 'Hey what?'

Ginny didn't know what to say, so she said, 'Want these?' and pulled her two prize stawberries from her shirt pocket and held them out.

Bobby eyed them dubiously.

'They're kind of mooshed now,' Ginny said, 'but they were the best of all I picked.'

Bobby nodded and smiled. He took each berry by its stem and, one at a time, neatly clipped them free with his teeth. He chewed slowly, then closed his eyes and swallowed. He kept his eyes closed a while. When finally he opened them, they fell on Ginny. '*Yummmmmm,*' he said, stretching it into a mild comic effect. Then he went inside.

III

ASH STREET WAS ONE OF ONLY SEVEN PAVED STREETS IN GOODNIGHT, AND along the westernmost of its three blocks there were a number of shops and offices attached to modest homes, a congenial arrangement that allowed small businesspeople to wake up in their place of employment. The offices of Larsen's State Farm

Insurance, No Peer Lock & Key, and Walkinshaw's Barber Shop, for example, were all connected to the homes of their proprietors. So was Joseph Parmalee's veterinary office.

Dr Parmalee's two-story brick house and one-story office fanned out over two lots, with the cinderblock kennels and Jaye Ball's cottage situated behind the main structure. Adjoining the back porch was a sunken utility room that Dr Parmalee had always called the inside backroom, but which Bobby in his boyhood had transmuted to the inside-out room, because the temperature there always seemed inside out. The room, set into a five-foot excavation, was cooler than the rest of the house in the summer, and warmer in winter.

When he came inside today, Bobby went upstairs, showered, and carried a wrinkled dress shirt down to the inside backroom, where he folded down the ironing board. He plugged in the iron and while waiting for it to heat went to the high window that was just above yard level. The sun was high and bright. The boarded dogs slept unseen in their covered runs. A rotary sprinkler whirled. Otherwise, nothing moved until old Foolish got up and resettled himself in deeper shade.

Bobby's ironing was self-taught. He smoothed out his white dress shirt on the board, sprinkled water on the cuffs and started there. He could never avoid creasing the underside of the sleeves, so he hardly even tried.

Bouncy. What did Ginny mean by bouncy? Too much air, too much elastic, not enough solid? But her – An image of Marcy's bare breasts presented itself. Bobby blinked. He looked up from his ironing and pinched his nose. He clicked his teeth. He was trying to make himself think of something else. But he couldn't.

One May afternoon over a year ago, during their fourth or fifth month of dating, Marcy had passed Bobby a pink note in the hallway between class. *Meet me 3.15 at football field*, it said. *Bring 30 feet good rope.*

Bobby had shown up with a coil of towing rope. He followed Marcy to the base of the fifty-yard-line light tower. Attached to this tower, 110 feet up in the air, was what the school board, in order to get government money to build it, had called an elevated media booth. The rest of the town called it a crow's nest. It was a high, fenced platform equipped with microphone jacks and speaker connections, from which the public address announcer (normally Frenchy Olson, the shop teacher) could describe the on-field goings-on. The lower section of the ladder leading to the crow's nest was removable to prevent unauthorized access.

Bobby tied his rope to a stick and, after a few tries, lobbed the stick and rope through the lower rung of the permanent ladder, then tied the rope off. Marcy kicked off her shoes. 'Me first,' she said.

Marcy was a farmgirl. She'd climbed trees. She'd hung from the railroad bridge while a train passed. She took hold of the rope and, putting her bare feet flat against the metal light pillar and grabbing the rope hand over hand, slowly walked her way up. She was wearing a cotton skirt that swung out as she climbed. Beneath the skirt she was wearing lacy white briefs. When Marcy glanced down at Bobby, he didn't even try to pretend he hadn't been staring.

'What're you waiting for?' she called down.

Bobby began to follow.

Once they'd reached the permanent ladder, they climbed easily up the metal rungs, but entry to the platform was through a trapdoor, and the door was locked.

'Damn,' Bobby said in a way that meant, Well that settles that. Let's head back. But Marcy, leaning out and stretching up, grabbed hold of the platform's outer edge and without a moment's hesitation swung free. 'Boost,' she grunted and Bobby, reaching back, not looking down, strained to set his hand to her foot so that she could push up just enough to reach the next crossrail on the platform's restraining fence. She pulled herself to a foothold, pushed herself up and over, and then, from within the crow's nest, let out a little whoop.

Bobby looked down – it was a dizzying height. At the base of the pillar, jagged fragments of concrete reached upward.

'What's keeping you?' Marcy was leaning over the rail, staring down. Bobby looked at her as if across a vast ocean. 'C'mon,' Marcy said, bending far over the rail, stretching her body long and thin, extending her hand.

But Bobby wouldn't take her hand. He took one more look at Marcy's happy flushed face and without thinking grabbed hold of the platform and swung out. He gasped and couldn't breathe again.

All that held him were his fingers and his fingers had no feeling. He grabbed for the rail and missed, caught himself and against his will looked down. He was going to cry. He was going to cry and then he would fall.

'Here,' Marcy said in a happy, exhilarated voice.

Bobby glanced up at her extended hand and in inexplicable anger snapped at it, as a trapped animal would, but, to his surprise and relief, she had his wrist and he had hers. He grunted, hoisted himself up, swung a leg over the rail, and spilled into the booth.

Marcy laughed and swarmed over him, and he began to laugh, too, basking in the sun and pure pleasure of unpunished recklessness. He began to kiss her and she let him. He began to unbutton her shirt and she let him. He slid the bra straps from her shoulders and she not only let him but crossed her arms to plumpen the view. But when he'd begun to work his hand fumblingly up her leg, Marcy had stiffened. 'Sorry,' she'd said in a cooing voice that Bobby hadn't yet associated with deception. 'I shouldn't've let us get started, because once you start kissing me, I get too carried away.'

Now, on Marcy Lockhardt's wedding day, Bobby stretched tight his dress shirt and began nosing the iron around the buttons. Bring good rope. She'd led him this way and that and then one day without a word she'd just let go of the leash. Only without knowing it or wanting it, he was still dragging it around.

Down the hall the telephone rang twice, followed by Jaye Ball's voice, high and cheery and false. *Dr Parmalee's office.* A few minutes later she came to the door. Bobby didn't look up, but he could feel her studying the situation.

'If it's somewhere important you're wearing that shirt, I could finish it up for you,' she said finally.

Bobby said nothing. She knew where he'd be wearing it. He was going to wear it to Marcy's wedding. He was going to go a little late, sign the book, sit in the back row, then come home. Or, if he felt like it, go over to the reception, stand in line, kiss her and tell her he wished her every happiness, then come home. Jaye Ball probably guessed that, more or less, but Bobby wasn't going to confirm it. Finally Jaye Ball said, 'That was your father on the phone. He's about done with Schmitz's pigs and then he'll be here for dinner.'

Bobby ironed a hairline wrinkle into the left cuff of his dress shirt. 'Okay, thanks,' he said. Jaye Ball waited a few seconds. 'This afternoon he's going up to Scenic to see to a horse.'

Bobby could feel her not going away, standing still at the door watching him iron the shirt that she knew he'd be wearing to his ex-girlfriend's wedding. 'He said you were welcome to ride along,' Jaye Ball said in a soft voice.

Bobby looked up for the first time. 'Can't,' he said. 'I've got plans.'

THE PARMALEES' WINDOWLESS DINING ROOM WAS ALWAYS DIM. THE SQUARE table, which could be expanded but never was, stood in the middle of the room. Bobby's father sat on one side. Bobby always sat to his left and Jaye Ball always sat opposite the doctor. Nobody ever sat to the doctor's right. That was Dr Parmalee's bad ear. Today, as was usual, dinner was eaten in general silence. The clock on the mantel in the front room gently chimed the quarter-hour. The old dog lying at Dr Parmalee's feet whimpered then snored. When the propeller of the old black fan in the kitchen chinked against its protective cage, Dr Parmalee said, 'Bobby might fix that for you, Mrs Ball.'

After the main dishes were consumed, Dr Parmalee took coffee and Bobby took ice cream. Normally the doctor would carry his coffee to his office, where for the duration of the dinner hour he would read the *World-Herald* and perhaps nap, but today he remained seated, saying nothing, just sitting. From the kitchen came the sound of running water: Jaye Ball was doing the dishes.

Beneath the table, the old dog shifted his weight and made a little mumphing sound. Bobby began to whip his caramel-swirl ice cream into a liquid. His father's staying put made Bobby nervous. He was used to eating his dessert alone and in peace. What if his father had some lecture in mind? – some kind of long, leisurely reprimand or, even worse, one of his weird, wooden talks on some dusty subject he'd suddenly decided Bobby needed to know much more about.

But Dr Parmalee wasn't talking. He merely held his coffee cup in both hands and let his gaze float. Bobby dipped his spoon into the soupy ice cream. He was halfway through the bowl, trying not to slurp, when his father, still staring off, said in a low voice, 'You remember your mother, I guess.'

'A little,' Bobby said, and his father nodded, more to himself than to Bobby. He still didn't speak. He just sat.

From the front room the clock chimed the half-hour. From the kitchen a sudden bang of pans. Dr Parmalee sat perfectly still in the dim room. Finally he set his cup down and, without looking at it, turned it in a slow circle in front of him. 'We met in a funny way, your mother and me. Did I ever tell you about it?' He didn't look at Bobby when he said this.

'Not that I remember,' Bobby said.

Bobby's father kept staring into the dimness. From within his narrow chest, he expelled a great sigh. 'We were both students at Lincoln and your mother began to follow me around. A fraternity brother noticed it before I did. One day I ducked around a corner and into a doorway and then stepped out after she passed me by. She stopped and looked around. I told her I didn't like being followed. I said it none too nicely, I'm afraid. She looked absolutely terrified, like a snared wild animal. I asked her what she wanted from me. 'Nothing,' she said and then all at once she began to cry. We walked to a coffee shop and she drank hot chocolate. Once she'd gotten calmed down she said something fantastic. She said she'd dreamed of me – my actual face and my actual name – *before* she'd moved to Lincoln and then one day while looking out the library window she'd seen me and whispered out loud, "Joseph Parmalee," and when her girlfriend said, "What?" she explained and then they'd found out that it was in fact my name and she said then she couldn't help it, she'd begun to follow me.'

Bobby's father breathed in and breathed out. Foolish had resettled himself and begun again to snore. Someone next door had started up a lawnmower. There were no sounds coming from the kitchen.

'Your mother was a beautiful girl, but, more than that, there was something persuasive about her. I became persuaded of everything. Of the depth of her beauty. Of my great good luck. Of our shared fate being foreordained.' Bobby's father kept his eyes forward. 'That night I borrowed a car and we went driving. Your mother was strictly chaste, absolutely chaste.' He narrowed his gaze as if trying to find his way in the dimness. 'And yet there was something ungovernable and almost savage in her kissing. My ear,' he said and cocked his head slightly to indicate the ear he meant. 'She broke the eardrum one night with one of her kisses, clamped her mouth over my ear and formed a suction cup that actually perforated the drum. I yelled and she pulled free and began to cry and hug my face to her chest.' Dr Parmalee made a melancholy smile. 'The pain subsided of course and everything would've been fine except infection developed. Another night, I awakened in my room in the frat house and there your mother was, sitting in a chair drawn close to my bed, just leaning forward and staring at me, waiting, she said, for me to awaken. I was nineteen years old. She called me Joseph. She believed we had slipped into some rare chamber where love is eternalized. Egyptian love, your mother called it. She was chaste and I wanted to be honorable. We married. She worked while I went to veterinary school. She didn't mind supporting us. What she minded was our being apart. Every night, every morning and, very soon, every time we talked she told me she loved me.'

For the first time, Bobby's father turned his eyes toward Bobby. 'It felt as if a great stone had sealed the chamber.' Dr Parmalee blinked slowly and turned away. 'I began finding reasons for going to school early and staying late, always good reasons, but more and more of them, and then, later on, I did the same thing with work.'

A silence developed that Bobby finally broke into. 'Is that what? –' he said and stopped. *Is that what made her crazy?* was the complete question.

But Bobby's father didn't need the complete question. He seemed to understand. He sat for a few moments and then he said quietly, almost to himself, 'I don't know.'

After a long empty silence, Bobby heard a water tap open in the kitchen, and dishes began again to clink, sounds that from their newness indicated that Jaye Ball had been standing quietly out of view, listening. Dr Parmalee scraped his chair back from the table, rose, and, taking his coffee cup in hand, walked to his office, the old dog following behind.

*   *   *

BOBBY WENT TO THE INSIDE BACKROOM, LAY DOWN ON THE COOL CONCRETE floor and tried to think. His father wasn't an impulsive man. He didn't tell a story without thinking it through. So why had he picked this particular time to shine this new light on Bobby's mother? Bobby curled his arm and set his head into it. He closed his eyes and then opened them again.

Welcome to the club. That was what his father had been trying to say. It was a huge club, humungous, full of people who walk around and eat meals and answer telephones and go to work and who keep tucked away inside them the sad secret stories that got them into the club.

This thought was a sedative to Bobby. His whole body seemed to loosen. He yawned and stretched. He thought of people's colors. Of Ginny a sunflower yellow. His father a brownish wooly color. Marcy a freckled apricot, bright and blurry. Himself a gray, a light gray before but maybe a darker gray now. Foolish a bleached bonish white and Marcy's mother . . .

When Bobby awakened, the air in the room had changed completely. It was darker now, and cooler. There was a pillow under his head. For just an instant – he couldn't help himself – he hoped Marcy might somehow have put it there, which was of course impossible. Jaye Ball, probably, or maybe even his father, though that seemed doubtful. Bobby checked the clock. 5.45. The wedding was over. The reception was in full swing. A band. Dancing.

Bobby pressed a finger to the temple of his clamped achy head. He felt tied down inside his stiff body. He got up, went to the kitchen pantry, opened a jar of the green Spanish olives his father always kept on hand. He walked back to the inside backroom and stood at the window eating them one at a time. Across the street, parked in front of the Walkinshaws' house, was the big Dodge pickup and camper that evidently belonged to Ginny's Aunt Tudie. Out in the yard Ginny played with her puppies. She was lying on the grass in the middle of a makeshift wood-and-chicken-wire pen. Fat yellow puppies were climbing up her legs and spilling over her stomach, buffoonishly slipping and tumbling and climbing up again, while Ginny laughed and chided. But something was not right. Bobby cocked his head slightly. From somewhere the gurgly cooing of pigeons carried, and the quick shuffle of wings. Suddenly, almost indiscernibly, the world shifted. He actually felt it shift. Its new light was soft, calm, buttery warm – it lighted the world from the inside. It streamed out everywhere. It slipped through windows and open doors, through cracks, keyholes, and weak seams, through flaws, truths, and misgivings. Bobby, staring as if at a dream, afraid he'd lose this vision even while trying to memorize it, stilled his body, held an unbroken green olive between his teeth, and tried not to breathe.

IV

WITHIN THE BANQUET ROOM OF THE VFW, MOST OF THE OLDER OF NON-dancing guests had departed, stiffly seen off by Marcy's parents, who themselves seemed anxious to withdraw. It was late afternoon. The music was getting louder, the dancing and talking more exuberant. A few of the pink-and-white crêpe-paper streamers overhead had torn and were left dangling. Julie Thies, who'd caught Marcy's garter, was dancing with anyone who asked, and asking anyone she pleased. In the men's restroom, Leo Underwood was taping clear plastic over one of the urinals so that the poor man too intoxicated to notice would suffer from backsplash. It was by now understood that this was a party certain to be judged a success.

'Bride's father wants last waltz, bride's father gets last waltz!' pronounced the DJ's amplified voice. 'Why? Because bride's father is writing my check!'

Marcy's father stepped up to Marcy and said, 'Last dance?' and before Marcy knew it she was on the floor, the walls and faces twirling around her. This would be their second and final dance of the afternoon. The first had passed quickly, mostly in surprise at not only the fact that her father was willing to dance at a wedding to which he'd never officially given his blessing, but also at the ease with which this big goofy-seeming man could manage her on the dance floor. This time she relaxed and put her head on his shoulder and simply glided along.

'Happy?'

Marcy, who'd shut her eyes, opened them. 'What?'

'Are you happy?' her father said again in the low-lying voice he always used when Marcy's marriage to Randall was the subject.

Marcy laughed uneasily. 'I think so, yeah.'

'Well, okay then. Because that's all a father's after, is giving his children a good crack at happiness.'

Neither spoke for a time, then her father said, 'Fascination.'

'What?'

'That's what this song is. It's called "Fascination." Your mother and I used to dance to it.'

And they kept dancing, it seemed forever, and when finally it was over, her father and mother went from young person to young person, awkwardly paying respects, saying goodbye. After they left, Leo Underwood was standing next to Marcy, talking, but she barely listened. She was looking around the room. Randall stood among his football and bar buddies, handsome and glowing, not talking, knowing he didn't have to. When he caught her staring, he grinned and silently mouthed two words: *hot chaw!* While Leo Underwood hooted and kibitzed, Whistler Simpson waltzed with Leo's wife. Julie Thies was dancing with her little brother. Bobby Parmalee hadn't shown.

Bernita Landreth passed by with a glass of pink punch in each hand. 'Those contain your secret ingredient?' Marcy asked.

Bernita made a wide smile and extended one to Marcy.

The DJ switched to 'Achy-Breaky Heart' and Leo drifted away. Marcy drank her punch faster than she expected. 'Thirsty,' she said.

Bernita sipped from her plastic cup and gazed out at the dance floor. 'We went to the crooked bridge this morning, Julie and I.'

A laugh burst from Marcy. 'You did! Did you skinny-dip, you nasty things?'

Bernita grinned. 'No, but we thought about it.'

Marcy laughed again, and watched Julie spin by on the dance floor. 'Nobody else was at the bridge, was there?'

Bernita acted surprised. 'Like who?'

Marcy turned up a hand in a who-knows gesture. She set her glass down, picked up a paper matchbook that said, MARCY & RANDALL. 'Bobby didn't come to the wedding,' she said. She looked at Bernita. 'I don't know why, but I thought he would.'

A minute or so later, an electrical cord somewhere loosened and the music abruptly stopped mid-song. The room glided to a stop. For a long moment, everyone was still. The day's last long yellow light slanted through the high line of transoms. It ran to the furthest corner, began to fill the hall with dense honeyed light that caught and held the revelers where they stood. It was as if the whole room were holding its breath. Everywhere she looked, familiar friends looked to Marcy like bland familiar-friend impersonators.

'What?' Bernita asked, looking at her with alarm, but just then the music resumed.

> *Mary's got a big idea*
> *Charley's got a chance*
> *Lucinda's got em all beat*
> *Lucinda's gotta dance*

It was a song that had always jumped inside of Marcy and sent her rocketing onto the dance floor, but now it seemed suddenly like someone else's song instead of her own. That was what she thought while at the same time knowing it was no way to think.

> *Suzy's got a new tattoo*
> *Raymond's got romance*
> *Lucinda's got em all beat*
> *Lucinda's gotta dance*

Marcy let out a long, raucous whoop she hoped would sound happy. Across the floor, Randall Hunsacker glanced up with a wary grin. Marcy turned to Bernita. 'Wanna two-step?' she asked, and then they did.

Chapter Ten

FRMKA'S MARKET

DURING THE DEPRESSION, LUCY WITT'S FATHER-IN-LAW HAD BEEN GOODNIGHT'S banker. His name was Ernest. At that time there were two small markets in town, one owned by Carl Thompson and one owned and established by Meteor Frmka's great-grandfather, whose name was Judah, but whom everyone simply called Frmka or, sometimes, Jew Frmka. Both of these markets banked with Ernest Witt, but the Witt family, without ever knowing why, traded exclusively with Carl Thompson. When Ernest Witt's bank closed down like the rest of the banks, he went home and started digging a garden in his front and back yards. He had a big family, a lot of mouths to feed. He worked the garden every lighted hour of the day. One day his son, Dick, the boy who would become Lucy Witt's husband, came home bloodied from a fight with two boys at the high school. The other boys had said everyone knew Ernest Witt had stolen all the town's money and buried it in his garden. Ernest Witt told his son that of course this wasn't true and everyone who mattered knew it, but he began to notice how few of Goodnight's citizens were talking to him anymore. One night he awakened to find a party of men with lanterns digging up his garden. They dug up every inch and every plant, and when they didn't find anything, they threw rocks through the Witts' windows. Threats came in the mail. Every time Ernest Witt tried to lay out his garden again, someone would come in the night and tear it up. One day Judah Frmka came to Ernest Witt's door. The savings Frmka had lost at Ernest Witt's bank were equal to anyone's. 'Hello, Mr Frmka,' Ernest Witt said. 'If you've come for money, I haven't got any.' 'No, no, no,' Judah Frmka said. 'I am here for one reason. I want you to know I think you are an honest man and if you ever need goods for your family, your credit is always good at Frmka's market.'

Over fifty years later Lucy Witt told this story to Dorothy and Marcy Lockhardt while they sat in her parlor sipping tea. Marcy was eleven. Her mother had just joined a club called PEO; Lucy Witt, as its president, had invited Dorothy and Marcy for a visit. She'd served tea with cream and sugar, and delicious little sandwiches with the crusts cut off. When she went off to the kitchen for more, Dorothy's mother smiled like she was in a dream state. 'That Frmka story was an interesting story,' Marcy said, but her mother just murmured and held her empty white teacup to the bright light of the window – it was so delicate that light passed through it. From the kitchen, in a musical voice, Lucy Witt said, 'So that's why I've always shopped exclusively at Frmka's.'

There was a sugary syrup at the bottom of Marcy's teacup that she collected and sucked from her spoon. She thought the Frmka story might be like most peculiar and interesting things you heard, that it would slip away or be replaced by new peculiar things, but she was wrong. Even as the years passed by, she thought of it every time she drove by Frmka's Suprette and glanced into its dim interior. She thought of it every time she saw Mrs Frmka with her head in a scarf out sweeping the sidewalk. She thought of it every time she saw Meteor Frmka out in the family delivery truck, grinning like an idiot.

Chapter Eleven

TELL ME SOMETHING

I

FIVE YEARS HAD PASSED. MARCY MARLENE HUNSACKER WAS NOT TWENTY-three, and her life had turned tricky. One moment she'd been the high school cheerleader, honor student, and senior class president, then, in what seemed like the next moment, she was a married woman trying to figure out how aspects of her husband's personality that seemed less than minor before the wedding could enlarge and harden so unlikeably afterward.

Randall had always liked a routine – seeing Marcy certain nights at certain times, doing the same certain things – and, prenuptially, Marcy had liked the way these routines lent steadiness and shape to days and weeks that were otherwise dull and loose-seeming. But, once married, Randall used his rituals and routines to harness their life, to keep it moving slowly up and down the same rows. He liked things ordered, invariable, undeviating. He was content (he said so all the time) and pursued nothing so much as unastonishment. Marcy had heard bits and pieces from Randall about his mother and sister and the horrible man named Lenny. She supposed that the unexpected turns in Randall's former life had been so ghastly that he'd come to look upon even the smallest surprise as unwelcome. Still, this didn't make his rigidness any less trying. When, for example, Marcy would try an unusual recipe, Randall made no attempt to hide his impatience. 'What's this?' he would say, raking a fork through a rice-like dish slowly and with suspicion.

'It's curried couscous,' Marcy said. 'I found it in *Bon Appetite*.'

'What's that?'

Marcy chose her words. 'A magazine for people who prefer dining to bolting and burping.'

Randall was unimpressed. He ate his serving without a word, laid down his fork and said, 'I wouldn't call that a repeat.'

Marcy let a few weeks pass before trying paella. Randall ate around the fish ('Nebraska's not the best place for seafood,' he remarked), then spent a half-hour composing a list of his seven favorite meals, which he then presented to Marcy. Each meal was written under a day of the week. He saved his favorite – meat loaf, mashed potatoes, and gravy, and cherry Jell-O with nothing in it – for Saturday nights.

Marcy was stung by this suggestion, but the next day, looking over the list, she decided she didn't *totally* hate the food he was suggesting and, besides, it would be a whole lot easier to prepare than the recipes in those fancy magazines, especially since Frmka's Suprette didn't carry a lot of the called-for ingredients – fennel bulb, for example, and saffron – so she'd had to make all sorts of hopeful substitutions, which even she had to admit hadn't always turned out so well. So, she told herself, why not make meat loaf and be happy your husband has simple tastes and comes home every night for supper? But accommodation, Marcy's guiding principle in the first year of the marriage, would find its limits.

Marcy and Randall lived in a fourteen-wide trailer-home located in the Sleepy Hollow Trailer Court, on the south edge of town. Entry into the home was through the living room, which gave onto the kitchen-dining-room combination and a wider, all-purpose room that the park manager, when she'd shown Randall and Marcy the home, had referred to as a 'pop-out.' A narrow passage led past the bathroom into the single bedroom. Marcy had heard a lot of remarks about trailer life, but, initially at least, she herself didn't mind it. It was cozy in the winter and nobody said you had to stay inside in the summer.

And yet, while the trailer-home had at first seemed ingeniously designed and surprisingly spacious, in their second year of tenancy the home began to feel smaller and smaller. This was an effect,

Marcy came to believe, of displacement – the home was filling up with Randall's peculiarities, which, instead of breaking down over time, seemed instead to expand. When he slept (he went to bed at exactly 10 p.m. and rose at exactly five), he wanted everything absolutely quiet; when he was awake he played his country-western tapes (Billy Joe Shaver, Earl Thomas Conley, Robert Earl Keem Jr.) at top volume. At the same hour of every morning of every week, he ate microwaved oatmeal from the same bowl (the white one with vertical sides and a single spoon-shaped handle). He wore the same clothes. He said the same things.

Randall accepted variation only in the matter of sex, but by the third year Marcy found herself less interested in the subject, and allowed its practice to become perfunctory and, as much as possible, timed to effect pregnancy. Randall seemed indifferent to the pull of fatherhood, and Marcy craved a baby not so much from maternal instincts as from her need for some – *any* – kind of change in their lives. Marcy was not insuppressibly restless, but she *was* a *little* restless, and she sensed how much that bothered Randall, and pushed him further into his reassuring routines. It was like the man who speaks softer because his wife speaks loudly, and the wife who responds to his lowered voice by speaking louder yet. Marcy was aware of the lives she wasn't living – she often wondered to what more interesting cities and circumstances a college degree or a professional career or a marriage to Bobby Parmalee or someone like him might've pushed her – and yet she also knew that choosing one life, whichever one it was, meant discarding the others, for better or for worse.

Nonetheless, it surprised Marcy that she found herself kindling an argument whenever the opportunity arose. Marcy was nimbler than Randall, and with a few clean-cutting strokes she could leave him feeling slow-witted, then hurt, hunting for something tangy to say before storming out of the house and heading for The Eleventh Man, where he could quietly nurture his resentments.

In their fourth year of marriage, Randall began to miss work at McKibben's Mobil. He missed work for the opening of pheasant season and then he missed work for the opening of deer season. He missed work to overhaul his truck. Shortly after learning

Marcy was pregnant, he took up golf, and missed work to drink beer with his buddies while whacking the ball around Goodnight's dirt-and-packed-sand golf course. Randall's behavior was mysterious. Marcy had read in a magazine how foster children who finally found themselves in a stable home with people who really loved them would begin testing that love with extreme behavior, and for a while she told herself that Randall was exhibiting some weird variation of this pattern. In the late summer of that year, he'd come home on a Friday night after one of his rounds of golf and wondered aloud why Marcy hadn't prepared steak and fries, since it was Friday night and Friday night was supposed to be steak and fries. And if money was the reason, *as she claimed*, where had all the money he'd made gone exactly? And if there wasn't enough money, *as she claimed*, then why couldn't she work at the drugstore or laundromat or something and help out?

Marcy said that, number one, if she went to work, it wouldn't be at the drugstore or laundromat and, number two, he seemed to be forgetting that she was pregnant.

That was another thing, as far as Randall was concerned. He wondered if they weren't kind of rushing this whole baby deal.

When Randall, without a prior word to anyone, sneaked out one Friday morning in September and drove off to Lincoln with Leo Underwood and Frank Mears to take in the Nebraska-Kansas State game, Mr McKibben telephoned Marcy. He told her he was sorry, but he was going to have to let Randall go. 'When he's here, he works real good, I mean *real* good, which is why I strung along with him for so long, but I need somebody I can count on.' Marcy sympathized with Mr McKibben. She said she understood completely, and she did. It was funny, in a way. Before marriage, before Randall, *she* had been the one who skated around obligations, who showed up late, stood people up, let people down, and – everybody's pal or pet – somehow got away with it.

A month later, after Randall lost his second job, this one with the railroad in Alliance, he said he believed he'd just take a little time off from work and maybe collect his thoughts. Marcy said, Well, she would do right by the baby, no matter what Randall did, but as for connubial duties, she'd resume those when he had a paycheck again.

Randall asked what that was supposed to mean, *connubial duties*. She waited for him to figure it out, and, when he did, he looked hurt. 'There are girls everywhere, Marzikins,' he said. 'Actual temptations.'

Marcy didn't take this threat seriously, but it annoyed her all the same. She had planned that very evening to hand Randall a vocation-school brochure given her by Ed Wetteland, a grading and excavation contractor in town, but she now saw that tonight definitely wasn't going to be the right moment, so she said, 'Well, I guess I could count the *actual temptations* in Goodnight on about two fingers.'

Randall squeezed his eyes into slits and worked his jaws. She could tell he was searching for something worth saying, and knew also that the best way to preempt that possibility was to goad him further. 'Yes?' she said. 'You got a big idea you'd like to impart?'

Randall got out a guttural 'you' – but stopped.

'Say it,' Marcy said. 'Say what little you have to say. I'm always anxious to hear the comments of the chronically unemployed.'

Randall's face screwed even tighter, but all he could think of to say was, 'You've changed, Marcy,' to which she replied in a mild voice, 'That could be for a variety of reasons. My husband whiling away his days on the golf links would be just one.'

Randall stalked out of the house, leaving the front door swinging open behind him. As Marcy pulled the door closed against the cold, Randall gunned his truck out of the driveway, the spinning tires spitting gravel against the metal siding of the house-trailer.

Two days later, with Randall and Leo and Whistler camped in the living room drinking beer and talking up some harebrained scheme involving construction of a hunting lodge on Leo's cousin's property up in the timberland, Marcy peevishly grabbed a sackful of trash in each arm, set out to the burn barrel, and slipped on the icy unsalted stoop.

Marcy felt almost nothing, just a slight cramping pain, a dribble of blood, and nothing much else except a strange stillness within.

The bleeding continued and worsened and, eight hours later, the doctor in Chadron confirmed what Marcy already knew, that she had miscarried. When she turned blankly to Randall, he began rubbing his stubbly chin to cover the relief spreading over his face. It was a look Marcy wouldn't forget. Until that moment, she hadn't known two things. How much she'd counted on this baby was one. The other was the possibility that Randall, the boy she'd loved and the boy she'd married, had become a man almost wholly foreign to her.

When they got home from the doctor's office, Marcy handed Randall the brochure she'd gotten from Ed Wetteland:

CALIFORNIA EARTHMOVER'S SCHOOL
COMPLETE TRAINING IN THE OPERATION
OF LOADERS, BACKHOES & GRADERS
COALINGA, CALIFORNIA

Randall was still staring at it when Marcy said, 'Take that course and Ed Wetteland'll guarantee you a job at nine dollars an hour.'

Randall looked up from the brochure and, as if sensing his shifting position, said in an almost tender voice, 'I'd be gone three and a half months, Marcy.' When she didn't speak he said, 'Look, Marzikins, I've got some other ideas,' and just like that Marcy heard herself say, 'Well, Hun, unless they involve a steady wage, they won't include me.'

Hun, from Hunsacker, had always been a marital term of endearment, but spoken in this new voice, it had a sharp jab to it. Randall said nothing before he walked out, but – a surprise to Marcy, and one she would not forget – his long fingers had rolled into tight fists. The right one – the three-fingered one – was simply a smaller version of the left.

When Randall came back two days later, smelling of horse and beer and sweat, he walked to the kitchen. He fixed and ate three hot-dog sandwiches, which he washed down with a quart of milk drunk straight from the carton. Then he looked at Marcy and in a dull voice said, 'Okay, so where's this Coalinga you're sending me off to?'

Randall had not been gone three and a half months. He'd been gone four. He'd missed the end of winter and all of spring and summer. October had come. Today, as Marcy sat waiting in the gravelled parking lot of the train station, the air was cold and still. It wasn't winter yet, but it almost seemed like it. In the sky there was a pale white unfelt sun.

The train on which Randall was returning from Coalinga, California was late. Marcy fidgeted for a while with the radio, then closed her eyes and dozed – did she doze? – until she thought she felt a trembling beneath her, as if the train were coming, but when she opened her eyes there was nothing, nothing but the same graveled lot and the same metal tracks and the same brown flat treeless plain.

Marcy hunched a little forward in the cold closed cab of Randall's truck and, between her knees, she gently tapped the knuckles of one fisted hand against the knuckles of the other, a practice that had in the past few years become so habitual Marcy hardly knew she was doing it.

WHEN THE TRAIN ARRIVED, IT TOOK A MOMENT FOR MARCY TO REALIZE THAT the startlingly unattractive man who stepped out of the first car was her husband. He was dark-chinned from not shaving, he wore a hideous pair of fluorescent green sunglasses and, beneath his untucked shirt, he carried a small, but noticeable paunch.

'Get you, in the sunglasses,' she said after he'd slung his bag into the bed of the pickup. Marcy hoped he'd take the glasses off so she could see him in a normal way, see what he was thinking, but he didn't, so she kissed him to find out. His mouth was soft but stayed closed. There was a beery smell on his breath.

When she leaned away, she said, 'Those sunglasses are really something.'

'Got my good ones busted,' he said. 'These are some they give away free with hamburgers at one of the chains out there.' They turned west onto Highway 20 and Randall slid out a grin. 'So, Marzikins, Sugar, tell me something significant that happened while I was gone.'

Marcy went through what came to mind – babies, crops, sicknesses, deaths – and finally couldn't think of anything else. She might've talked about her job at KDUH-TV (a small station located on a knoll a mile south of Goodnight and where, after all, Marcy was doing the weekend newscasts) or about that guy who shot his family down in Pine Bluff, but decided against it. The cab slowly filled up with silence.

At first, Randall and Marcy had talked every other day or so after he'd left, but then there'd been the phone bill, and they'd settled on

Sundays only, though after a while he'd begun to miss even those. When she called she could only leave messages because he was living in a motel without phones in the rooms.

A few more miles passed before Randall slowed to peer into the dry corn on the Coates place. 'Got a card from Leo saying he walked that field last week and counted a hundred pheasant, then stopped counting.'

Marcy looked out at the field and tried to see it as Randall and his friend Leo did, a field where certain cash crops grew and certain shootable animals lived. What Marcy saw were colors. Some of the fields were dark and fallow, some showed the bright greens of winter wheat, some were the light, dry brown of stubbled corn, a pretty color, Marcy thought, that was only really shown off when the ground was white with snow. Suddenly Marcy was ready for winter, ready to wear leggings with dresses and make corn chowder and at night slip under a comforter with Randall.

'Glad you're home,' she said and let out a soft laugh almost of relief. Then she said, 'At the train station? – I almost didn't recognize you, it's been so long. It was the sunglasses, I guess.'

The pleasantness that had taken hold of Marcy lasted only until a truck approached from the opposite side of the highway, white and tall, a bread truck, Marcy hoped, but it wasn't. It was the Frmka Suprette truck all right, with roundfaced Meteor Frmka driving standing up, then slowing slightly, it seemed to Marcy, when he recognized the pickup. Marcy had the sudden unreasonable urge to duck. Meteor Frmka's hand was half-raised in greeting when he saw Randall behind the wheel and then her sitting beside him.

RANDALL SHAVED AND SHOWERED WHEN THEY GOT BACK TO THEIR TRAILER-house, and Marcy put on an emerald green bustier he'd bought for her in California. It pushed up her breasts and made a presentation of them. She didn't want to wear it, but did anyhow and, once they'd gotten into bed, soon began to like the way she was feeling. Randall outlasted this feeling, however. He just kept going on in his own slow way. He'd told her before that the only thing he wanted, when they were together like this, was for it never to end, and that was the way it sometimes felt to Marcy. She began to think of other things and was a little surprised when finally he was done. They parted and while lying there Marcy thought of saying, *Hope that one's a baby*, which was the truth, but she was afraid it wouldn't sound like it, so she stretched and made lazy sounds instead. Randall closed his eyes, but didn't fall into the noisy breathing he slept with.

Marcy grabbed a handful of her long hair and pulled it across her mouth, an absent habit she had when thinking. 'You hear about that man in Pine Bluff who shot his family?' she asked.

Randall without opening his eyes said no he hadn't.

'Well, this man down in Pine Bluff called his wife and five sons all under twelve into the living room and shot off his own foot while they watched, then shot and killed his wife, then shot and killed four of the sons while they scrambled for it, then shot himself in the head but didn't die and is in fact in the hospital doing fine.'

Randall lay with his arms to himself. 'Why didn't he shoot the fifth boy?'

'That's what they asked him. He said he guessed in all the commotion he just lost count.'

'He lost count.'

'That's what he said.'

Outside, in the field beyond their backyard, a tractor clanked by. After it passed, Randall said, 'Somebody should go at night to that man's hospital bed, wake him up, and shoot him dead.'

'Oh, I guess that would help a lot,' Marcy said. She gazed at Randall's closed eyelids and, without wanting to, imagined him in final rest, handsome and serene. 'Which would you rather be,' she said, 'the fifth boy or one of the four?'

Randall didn't answer. Probably he thought it was a silly question. Marcy herself believed she'd rather be the fifth boy. He at least had a fighting chance, might even, if he could manage it, somehow turn the horror to his advantage. He was the boy who survived everybody's worst nightmare. Maybe people would want to help him, hire him, pull him ahead. She said, 'How do you think that kind of thing came about anyhow? I mean, how did it get to the point where a man's got a gun in his hand and is calling his family into the living room?'

Randall said he'd bet it was easier than you'd think. A few moments passed. Marcy with extreme casualness said, 'I was just thinking of it because Mr Rawley wants me to go down there to Pine Bluff tomorrow to do a remote broadcast, a one-month-after deal.'

'Who's Mr Rawley?' Randall asked, his eyes still closed.

'The station manager at KDUH. But it's okay if I don't. I told him you were just coming home after being gone for four months.'

Marcy listened as the clanking tractor came and went again. It was probably Strotheide, who was normally worth taking a look at, or his boy, who wasn't, plowing under potatoes. Randall's eyes blinked suddenly open.

'Smells like something in here.'

Dogs. It smelled like dogs, but Marcy had used Lemon Pledge, Lysol, and jasmine incense to cover it. 'Like what?' she asked and after a few sniffs more Randall said, 'Guess I don't know yet.'

II

BECAUSE SLEEPY HOLLOW TRAILER COURT SAT CLOSE TO PIONERR MANOR, THE town's only rest home, it had become an informal waystation for retirees, but the older people took to the younger ones if they were of the right sort, which, from the beginning, they'd decided Marcy was. Marcy was grateful for their thoughtfulness while Randall was gone, the deliveries of squash and tomatoes, the invitations to bingo and bunko (whatever that was), and to puzzle days, which was where she met Mr Rawley.

Marcy had been helping three older women with a giant jigsaw of Cadmus sowing the dragon's teeth when the door to the rec hall bumped open and a wooden-faced woman in a wheelchair was pushed into the room by a man in starched white shirt and black suspenders. The woman looked hardly alive, but was smoking a cigarette, no-hands. The man parked her wheelchair near the women. 'Hello, you two,' one puzzler said without looking up and another in an abstracted voice said to the smoking woman, 'Ivy, we're doing the darnedest puzzle.' Not a thing seemed to move in the smoking woman's face – it was as if a cigarette had been stuck into a stone mask and was made by some hidden mechanism to let out smoke.

The man went to the kitchen nook and poured himself a cup of coffee. A lot of the older men in Sleepy Hollow didn't keep themselves tidy, but this one looked the way Marcy hoped her own

father would look in advanced age, a large hand wrapped around a
coffee cup, shirt turned up at the wrists, pants held just so by smart
suspenders, and something in his eyes suggesting a readiness to be
amused at whatever might come next. He brought his coffee near
and watched the women fingering pieces, trying them here and
there. Finally he leaned forward, selected a piece, and snapped it
into the unvarying black sky Marcy had been consigned to. 'There!'
he said and chuckled as if a small joke had been made. Then he said,
'Well, I'd stay, but Ivy's bored,' and wheeled the petrified smoking
woman out of the room.

For Marcy's benefit, Flossie Boyles, a large florid woman who
made everybody's business her own, said, '*That* was Mr Rawley
and his wife, Ivy. He just moved here three years ago and is station
manager at KDUH-TV, not that it's much to manage. His wife is not a
bit well, but smokes like a chimney anyhow. He takes her everywhere
he goes, I'll say that for him, but he has his moments. You should've
seen the puzzle he brought us to do, for example, but who would
do it? *Lady on a Cobalt Couch*. Whew! Can you imagine *that* on
the puzzle wall?'

The other women at the table made noises indicating they
couldn't. The puzzle wall was where the jigsaws were hung
once completed, glued and shellacked. The Sleepy Hollow Trailer
Court also had a little lending library, two tall bookshelves with
a sign that said, BRING A BOOK! TAKE A BOOK! There were Har-
lequins mostly, a few Louis L'Amours and a surprising number
of Hollywood biographies. The afternoon Mr Rawley knocked at
Marcy's trailer, she was reading one of these, was in fact into
Lana Turner's third marriage. Mr Rawley stood on the porch
with a loose grin on his face and a sheet of paper in his
hands. Behind him, parked in the street in her wheelchair, was
his wife, staring blankly, a smoking cigarette in her mouth. 'Read
this,' Mr Rawley said.

Marcy took the paper he handed her and began to read.

'Out loud.'

'Today at Camp David,' she began and after a few more lines Mr.
Rawley said, 'That's what I thought.'

'That's what you thought *what*?' Marcy said.

'I'd overheard you at the post office,' Mr Rawley said. 'Your voice is pleasant and relaxed yet you articulate and project.'

Marcy was mystified by this appraisal, and a little suspicious of it. 'Well, that's news to me,' she said and scratched her nose with her left hand, which was as close to waving her wedding ring in his face as she could come.

But Mr Rawley leaned assuredly forward. 'And I hear you've had coursework in communication.'

'One class,' Marcy said. 'At Chadron State.'

Mr Rawley was leaning close, studying her face. When he said, 'I'm prepared to offer you a position,' she noticed how sweet his breath was.

'For what?' Marcy said.

'Reading the weekend news. For KDUH-TV.' He nodded amiably. "From the Black Hills to the Sandhills". Pay's poor, and the company's not so great either. It's just you, me and the missus. Still, the title is Weekend Anchorman. Woman. Person.'

'That's a laugh,' Marcy said, but she'd felt her skin prickling with the kind of excitement she hadn't felt in she didn't know how long.

TONIGHT MARCY WAS COOKING ONE OF RANDALL'S FAVORITE SUPPERS. Ed Wetteland had, as promised, given Randall a job. Today was Randall's first in the employ of Wetteland Construction, but when he came home he avoided specifics, took a six-pack from the refrigerator and went out back. From the kitchen window Marcy could see him out there working the dogs. One of the reasons Randall was willing to rent this trailer was its situation on a perimeter lot overlooking a field where he could train the dogs. Behind their backs he tossed canvas-covered dummies, took a gulp of beer and then, by whistled commands, directed the dogs to the bags, which they retrieved soft-mouthed, then sat smartly waiting for the next command. Get you, Marcy thought. The dogs' names were Guido and Boo, stout black Labs who were normally confined to their concrete and chain-link run, but at night, with Randall gone, Marcy had begun to hear noises, and the trailer felt suddenly empty and too big, so she'd brought the dogs in. What was interesting was how, after a couple of hours in the trailer, these nervous, overeager dogs went limp with ease. Guido liked snoozing on the rag-rug under the coffee table. Boo preferred the sofa. They were good company. Their tails wagged when she talked to them, or when she talked back to the book she was reading. ('What a glutton,' she said, for example, to Lana Turner when she took up with Johnny Stompanato.) Sometimes, when Meteor Frmka delivered fancy ice cream, Marcy let Guido and Boo take turns licking the serving spoon.

Tonight, when Marcy called Randall in for supper, he didn't remark on the meal. He said nothing at all in fact until he'd served himself seconds of everything. Then out of the blue he said, 'So, Marzikins, tell me something significant that happened while I was gone for four months to California.'

Marcy, hoping it might be her newsreading job that was gnawing on Randall, decided to plunge right in. She gave him the specifics of the routine, told him how ugly and unglamorous the tiny cinderblock TV studio was, how on her first day she had mixed up the hockey and baseball scores but had otherwise done okay, and had been doing more or less okay ever since.

Randall finished the last of his plain cherry Jell-O and pushed away his plate. He took out his wallet. 'I went into a department store out there and had a girl put a couple drops of your perfume on a card. I carried it with me so whenever I wanted I could take it out and smell your smell.' He pushed a smudged and softened business card toward Marcy. In wonderment, she took in its mixed smells of leather and money and her own perfume.

'I guess you like this new job then,' Randall said after a moment.

Marcy laid down the scented card. 'Job's fine,' she said, 'and it was nice not having to take money from my folks.' Then, surprising herself with a lie, she said, 'I've already told Mr Rawley that once you're set with Wetteland I'd be giving it up.' Marcy grinned and hated herself for grinning.

'Well, it'd be hard,' Randall said. 'Me working weeks and you working weekends.'

After dinner, Randall went to the refrigerator and dished himself out some chocolate ice cream and pulled out two beers, all of which he consumed on the living room sofa while remoting between ESPN and a *Rockford Files* rerun. Marcy, who'd hoped they might go to the Eleventh Man or at least the Dairy Queen for a dipped cone, settled nearby with a book on Marlon Brando. During a commercial she said, 'I'll take you to Paris, France for your birthday if you can tell me Marlon Brando's two favorite foods.'

Randall, playing along, said, 'Ice cream and beer.'

Marcy made a loud buzzing noise to register a definite miss. 'What are pomegranates and peanut butter?'

'Adios, Paris, France,' Randall said and went back to ESPN, which was covering women's pocket billiards from Las Vegas, though Marcy doubted this would be the case if either contestant were wearing a bra. When one contestant went for the bridge, Randall bent suddenly forward and sniffed at the sofa. He got down on the floor for a closer whiff. A smile slowly dawned on his face. This was what Marcy would remember – how pleased he was that vague suspicion had turned into unpleasant fact. 'Dogs,' he said. 'That's what I've been smelling down below the cover-up smells. Dogs in the house.' He turned his calm smile toward Marcy. 'I *knew* those dogs were acting a little poodly.'

IT HAD TAKEN A WHILE FOR MARCY TO GET USED TO HOLDING CONVERSATIONS with Mr Rawley while his petrified wife sat so close by. After a newscast, they would all three sit in the little TV studio, Mrs Rawley stonily smoking her cigarettes while Marcy and Mr Rawley drank Cokes and talked about how the show went. Mr Rawley didn't beat around the bush. 'A stiff smile's worse than no smile at all,' he'd say, or, 'Pretend the camera's an uncle you like.' If there wasn't much to praise, he would just say, 'So forget it. There were only about seven people watching anyway.'

At first they went right home after the critiquing, but as time went along Marcy realized she was in no hurry to leave, and neither was Mr Rawley. They would sit and talk about whatever came to mind. One day, after watching him light a cigarette and slip it between his wife's lips, Marcy said, 'So did you used to be happily married?'

'Oh, yeah,' Mr Rawley said, chuckling. 'Were we ever.' He gazed approvingly at his wife. 'I'll tell you, Ivy knew the secrets. She could hold a fellow's interest. Always kept the water just

beyond the witcherstick, didn't you, Ivy-girl? Kept a fellow from
straying.'

Marcy regarded Ivy's stony unhappy face. 'How?' she said, and
when she heard how rude and frank it sounded, she said, 'I mean
how did she go about doing that, not that it's any of my business.'

Mr Rawley, smiling, seemed to be gazing back over time. 'Well, for
one thing, we had separate rooms.' Marcy's face must've registered
surprise because Mr Rawley nodded. 'That's right. At different corners
of the house. Sometimes I'd sneak into her room, sometimes she'd
sneak into mine. And we had our own bathrooms. I'll tell you
something. Until she got sick, I never saw her totally naked with
the lights on.'

Five years before, at Randall's bachelor party at the Eleventh
Man, there had been a stripper named Wyona Ample, who Leo
had hired down from Scenic, South Dakota. Marcy, more than a
little curious, had gotten Joanie Baxter, the waitress, to tip off her
and Bernita and Julie when the entertainment was about to start.
They climbed through the window of the women's restroom and
peered in from the swinging door. Wyona Ample, wearing layers
of clothes and serious black-rimmed glasses, had been lifted onto
a pool table and stood under dim smoky light. The rest of the bar
was totally dark, and swelling with an expectant stillness that was
all by itself of interest to Marcy. When the music started – some
kind of slowly pulsing reggae – Wyona Ample visibly relaxed. She
smiled and slipped off her glasses. She started with her hair up
and her several layers of clothes and, a long time later, ended in
a G-string with her hair down. When it was over, Marcy and Bernita
and Julie had clambered back out the bathroom window, laughing
like maniacs, but the truth was, Marcy had been impressed. Wyona
Ample was not much different than Bernita or Julie or herself. She
was a slightly above-average dancer with a slightly above-average
body. What separated her from them was the fact that she was an
actual striptease artist whose fascination derived from secrets hinted
at but either not quite or only fleetingly revealed. Back then, full of
prenuptial hope and ardor, Marcy had resolved to put this lesson
to good use, but of course she couldn't. Within a marriage, when it
came to the body, the secrets ran out in a hurry; there weren't any

illusions left to conjure up. It was just you and your everyday body standing in the glare of the fluorescent bathroom lights, a body that, as much as for sex, was evolved for the purposes of procreation, digestion, and elimination. Sweat, Marcy thought, blood, urine, shit. No wonder people lost interest.

Mr Rawley had turned his smile from his wife to Marcy. 'Now you, Marcy, you seem like the naturally faithful type, am I right?'

'You're right,' she said quickly. 'I am.'

'Ah,' Mr Rawley said, shifting in his seat and seeming to put the subject aside. 'So how about this hubby of yours? How'd he get his hooks into you?'

Marcy laughed. 'Well, my mother thought he was useless and my father wanted to kill him, so that helped.' She thought about it. She explained to Mr Rawley how Randall had nearly died in a football game and how her parents, who'd despised him, had been the ones to save his life. 'You can't believe how happy I was,' she said and grinned at Mr Rawley. 'This was a few years before you came here, but it was a big local story. They had some terrible fuzzy videotape – you couldn't see anything – but they kept playing it on K-DUH.' (She pronounced it kay-duh, as the locals often did.)

Mr Rawley was nodding. 'So now all of a sudden your folks had invested in the dread boyfriend?'

'Yeah, more or less. From that point on, they just kind of stepped aside.'

Mr Rawley's face broadened with a grin. 'And you rushed through the breach?'

Marcy nodded. 'I guess so, yeah.'

'Without any reservations?'

Marcy laughed. 'Oh, I wouldn't go that far.'

After an easy silence, Mr Rawley said, 'And at what exact point did you know you were falling for the hubby-to-be?'

She'd just started watching him in school, she said, how in class before the bell rang he always stood alone by the radiator looking out the window. And she'd seen him once sitting alone in the back of the church. And then one spring day she'd seen him running barefooted on the football field and that was it. 'You know what? That was honestly the first time in my life I ever wanted to see

a boy naked. The way he was running was so graceful and free
I just wanted to see all of him.' A little chuckle rose from deep
within her. She felt suddenly able to be honest, as if to a stranger
she would never see again. 'I even wanted to see his, you know,
deal flopping around as he ran.' She laughed again and returned to
herself. 'Anyhow, pretty soon thereafter I got him to ask me out.'

'Lucky him,' Mr Rawley said. A moment of perfect stillness
followed, then he leaned forward and thoughtfully undid the
first two buttons of her top. On the newscast that day, there
had been a clip of a Yugoslavian basketball player just drafted
by an American team. Mr Rawley, sitting back, regarding Marcy's
slightly unfastened self, mimicked the player's words. 'Is good,' he
said. 'Is sensational.'

Marcy felt her skin go prickly. 'I don't think so,' she said and
while re-buttoning glanced toward Mrs Rawley, who – when had
she turned this way? – stared back with the unmoving eyes of a
corpse.

III

DAYS PASSED. MARCY HAD QUIT HER JOB. MR RAWLEY TOLD MARCY THAT HER
replacement couldn't carry Marcy's bags, but the pleasure of the
sentiment was only temporary. Marcy's replacement, it turned out,
was a Chadron State coed with one of those sassy short haircuts
that women lawyers were going in for, and Marcy noticed that
Mr Rawley occasionally pulled the camera back ever so slightly
to give the viewer just the barest glimpse of wholesome coed
cleavage. If Randall was home, Marcy wouldn't watch the new
girl, but if he was gone she couldn't help herself. She'd eat
chips and drink one of Randall's beers and talk back to the new
girl, whose name was given as C.J. Henry. 'Sez you, C.J.,' Marcy
would say aloud to the TV. Or, 'Oh, C.J., if you are not just the
chipperest.'

Everything everywhere began to seem boring to Marcy. There
were the same songs on the radio, the same cars on the streets, the
same people in the cars. She saw Meteor Frmka everywhere – he
was like a nagging tune she couldn't quite dispel. He was driving
the Suprette truck out of Sleepy Hollow, he was slurping up a malt

at the Dairy Queen, he was standing on Main studying the sticker price on somebody's new Blazer.

Randall went to work every morning for Wetteland Construction, initially to a site close by and then, a few weeks later, further south to Pine Bluff. He went to work day after day. He went to work the first day of turkey and deer season both. 'It's fine,' he said when Marcy asked about the work, but he didn't give details. The job was part of a routine that, to Marcy, had a strangely makeshift feel to it, as if what it was built on was brittle and thin.

'Tell me something significant, Marzikins, that happened in my absence.'

This was another part of the routine. Nearly every night Randall asked this question and listened to that night's answer. It was like a test question that would be repeated until she got it right. 'There aren't that many things to tell, Randall,' she said, but she began to tell him more and more, in hopes of putting a truer face on stories he might've heard elsewhere.

One night over chicken-fried steak, she told him how Bobby Parmalee had stopped by and they'd sat out on lawn chairs drinking iced tea and talking, mostly about him. He'd graduated from Creighton and was going to vet school in Davis, California, she said.

Randall had fixed his attention on Marcy when she began to tell him about Bobby Parmalee, and he kept his eyes fixed on her for a time after she'd finished. Then he broke off a piece of white bread and began sopping up the last of the gravy from his plate. 'What else?' he said.

'Nothing else!' she said, but then she thought to tell him about Julie Thies's cousin, Lynnette, who Marcy helped show around during a visit here. She worked in television in Los Angeles, but during something called summer hiatus was in Nebraska looking for locations for a movie Robert Redford was making. On Saturday night, Marcy and Julie and Lynnette went to a barn dance, 'where all we did was dance with each other and watch the farmboys get shellacked,' she said, and the next day they drove out to look at possible movie locations on the White River, though in short order they gave it up and went swimming near the Sanders place, skinny-dipping actually, though Marcy didn't say so. Afterwards, they'd lounged on the rocks dipping their feet in the water and drinking Coors splits from a cooler. 'If I had that particular body,' Lynnette said to Marcy, 'I'd marry a rich producer and hire many, many maids.' 'And houseboys!' said Julie Thies, who was a little drunk. Marcy said she'd be happy just living in Hollywood and doing something small and behind the scenes in TV. A week later, Marcy received a card from Lynnette thanking her for what she called a 'splendid time' and inviting her to visit if she ever made it to California.

Randall listened to Marcy's abridged version of this without comment, then headed for the refrigerator, the bottom shelf of which he'd filled with a twelve-pack of malt liquor.

Marcy said what she'd been telling herself to say. 'Randall, I don't know what you're thinking I did while you were gone, but whatever it is, it's way off base.'

Suddenly, as if from his darkest center, Randall opened on her a look of utter contempt. He set his can of malt liquor on the table. He sat calmly down, folded his hands together and, after staring at them a long while, said, 'Do I look stupid, Marcy? Do I look particularly stupid to you?'

There was a long silence that seemed to swallow them. The room began to darken. Marcy wanted to turn on a light, but it was like waiting for a rabid dog to stagger by and she didn't want to move. Finally, in a low, hollow voice, Randall said, 'I was just now trying to think of the last time I felt normal and almost happy and you know when it was? – it was way last summer when Leo and me spent the afternoon in Leo's basement drinking cherry vodka and shooting potato bugs off the wall.' He peered toward her in the dimness. 'Pretty fucking pathetic, huh?' He flipped on the lights, gathered up his canvas-covered dummies. He was going out to work the dogs, but at the door, in the gentlest voice she'd heard him use in a long time, he said, 'I got to tell you, Marcy, I've got a bad feeling that I'm doing no good at getting rid of.'

SUNDAY MORNING. RANDALL WAS SLOUCHING ON THE SOFA WATCHING A football game. Marcy said, 'Remember how when we first met we'd sneak off on long rides to no place in particular?'

Randall flicked a glance her way.

Marcy said, 'So why don't we get in the truck and start driving?'

Randall kept his eyes on the television. Finally, when the wrong team scored and went up by twenty, he said, 'Okay, then. Let's go.'

As they pulled up to Highway 20, Randall said, 'Which way?'

Marcy was beginning to feel good. She shrugged and smiled. 'You decide.'

West on 20, south on 87, a loud Dwight Yokum tape, fields with long fingers of snow sliding by – Marcy felt the sullenness shaking out of her and wondered why they hadn't thought of doing this a long time ago.

'Grissom's?' she said between songs as they neared Pine Bluff. Grissom's was their favorite spot for hamburgers.

They picked up cheeseburgers, but, instead of eating them there in the parking lot, Randall said, wait, he knew a place where they could park and eat. He drove over the tracks, and picked his way through neglected neighborhoods. It was becoming familiar to Marcy, but in an elusive way. It wasn't until he'd pulled up in front of a dingy white clapboard house that she understood where she was.

'This is where that man shot his family,' she said.

Randall, staring at the house, nodded. 'James Elliot. Wife, Doreen. Dead sons, Edward, Thomas, Melvin and Gaylord. Fifth boy's name is Harold.'

Marcy stared at him.

Randall said, 'Guy at work knew the family personally.' He looked toward the house. 'I come here pretty often to eat my lunch. Park right here and eat. Nobody ever bothers me.'

'But why would you want to?'

Randall peeled back his hamburger wrapper and studied its contents. 'At first it was that question you asked, whether you'd rather be one of the four boys who died or the fifth one who didn't.' He bit into the hamburger. 'I finally decided it all depends.'

On what, Marcy wanted to know.

'On whether the fifth boy cared about his father or not. Whether he loved him. Because if someone you loved wanted you dead, then, personally, if it was me, I'd just as soon be dead.' He stopped chewing for a long moment, then started again.

After a few seconds Marcy said, 'This place is giving me the creeps.'

'As soon as we've eaten we'll go,' Randall said quietly.

Halfway through her hamburger, Marcy said, 'You said at first you came here because of the question. What about later?'

This question seemed to confuse Randall. He slowed his chewing until finally he'd stopped. 'I don't know. I get in the truck and about half the time this is where I just end up.' He stared at the house. 'It's sort of interesting to me. I heard the fifth boy was sent off to his grandparents in Idaho, but I guarantee when he's old enough he'll drive back and park right here and stare at that house.' He waited. 'When I was living outside of Salt Lake, a kid up the hill from us raised racing pigeons, a whole bunch of them, and then one day he just decided he was tired of it and starting shooting them. He killed about 75 percent right off. What was weird was that the rest would circle around and eventually come back because it was the only place they could think of as home.'

Marcy hated the way he was making her feel. She turned away from the house and Randall both. She wanted to go home. 'I don't know, Randall. It's like all you're interested in anymore is people's weak spots,' she said and when, a moment later, she looked up at him, he was staring at her with what looked like surprised wonderment. 'Yeah,' he said, 'you might be right.' Then he said, 'But you know, in the end, the weak spot is what we all boil down to.'

A WEEK OR SO LATER, SHORTLY AFTER DAWN, MARCY DREAMED OF DOGS barking, dreamed of smoke and fire and stretched-out voices, dreamed even of the town siren, but didn't wake until the fire engine screamed along the single street that wound through Sleepy Hollow Trailer Court. Marcy felt for Randall – he was already gone to work – pulled on her robe, and joined the crowd collected on the street behind the fire truck. Mr Rawley's double-wide trailer home was still burning, the heat ferocious even out to the street. Inside the ambulance, to Marcy's horror, Mr Rawley's head craned up wall-eyed and panicky while a nurse tried to keep him down.

'Where's Ivy?' Marcy said and one of the old men in the crowd gave a grim nod toward the burning trailer-home.

After the ambulance and fire truck left, after the old people went back into their homes, a sharp chill took hold of the trailer court and a film of ash settled on windows, flowers, and cars. Marcy felt like talking to someone. She walked down to the cafe, which was deserted, and while drinking hot chocolate spied Meteor Frmka across the way, standing on the sidewalk in front of the Coast-to-Coast talking to Merna Littlefield. Their faces were widened with what looked like the same big, happy, and stupid grin. Marcy thought of going over there and breaking up their little party by asking him for a lift out to her folks' place – it seemed the least he could do – but then she thought better of it and set off on foot instead. Often, in the course of this half-mile walk, someone Marcy knew would stop on the highway to give her a ride, but today there were nothing but trucks, each rumbling by and churning an updraft of gritty, freezing air.

Marcy's mother was in the backyard, bundled up, wearing gloves with clipped fingertips, painting storm windows an overbright shade of blue. Marcy sat on the porch steps nearby and daubed a tissue at her runny nose. 'Guess you heard about the fire.'

Her mother nodded and kept working a fine edge of paint along the window frame. Her mother had always been pretty, not in just the ordinary, not-homely sense, but in the real, response-tightening way (Marcy had seen even high school boys sneak looks at her mother), but now she seemed somehow faded, and shrunken, and not just from age; it was as if she were living in a basement and not getting quite enough food or light. She'd had the mole removed from her cheek, but it seemed to Marcy more noticeable in its absence – what remained was a small, flat, bleached-seeming circle, like a knot in otherwise perfect wood.

Her mother turned and caught Marcy staring. 'We called to find out if you were okay but you'd already left. The manager told us that nobody else was hurt though.'

'No,' Marcy said. 'Nobody else was.'

Marcy was looking around her parents' farm as if at some new place. The fields seemed grayer, the outbuildings grainier.

It reminded her of a pretty but sad black-and-white photograph. She said, 'Mr Rawley's invalid wife was sitting in the front room watching TV and smoking while Mr Rawley was still sleeping in the back. Her cigarette got into the chair and smoldered and caught.' Marcy tried to imagine it. What did she think, poor Ivy, in that moment when she started swallowing smoke? Was it just mute panic or did she still have some safe place in her mind to go to? 'That poor woman,' Marcy said.

Her mother said nothing for a while. Marcy supposed it was because of her personal aversion to smokers as a group, but then her mother said, 'People say you're a pretty good friend of the husband's.'

Marcy felt slapped. At first, she couldn't speak and then, when she could, she decided not to. Finally her mother in a softened voice said, 'I was just passing it on, Marcy.'

'Pretty terrible thing to pass on.'

A silence fell. Her mother finished one window, set it aside, and propped the next one against a sawhorse. 'So how're you kids doing?'

'Fine. Better anyhow. Randall seems to like his job okay.'

Her mother studied her as she said this, then gazed down the row of already-painted windows. 'I didn't pick this color, I just want you to know. Your father brought home this color.'

'I kinda guessed,' Marcy said.

Her mother carefully dipped her brush into the paint. 'I hear Randall stays down there some nights.'

'About once a week. Driving gets him down, he says, and besides he was putting too many miles on the truck.'

A silence stretched out between Marcy and her mother. Finally Marcy gave in and said, 'Sometimes when I try to look at my life now it reminds me of how as a kid sneaking around outside at night I would peep through the window of our house and for a split-second think that my own furniture and my own family seemed like somebody else's.'

Her mother in a soft voice said, 'Polkadot, sometime or other everybody thinks something like that about even the best of lives.'

Marcy supposed that was so. But what she believed was that it would be okay, or at least tolerable, if she just had something to be interested in. A baby, for example. 'I guess I shouldn't've given up my newsreading job,' she said.

Her mother kept painting. 'I was never a big fan of your Randall,' she said, 'but he did go off to that school and now he goes off to work every day, so it seems like he's trying. Does he bring his paycheck home with him?'

'Every Friday night. Sets it under the salt shaker on the kitchen table. Not that we're going to be rich any time soon.'

She wished at once she hadn't used the word *rich*. She didn't expect to be rich. She didn't even expect to be happy. She just wanted to feel whole again. *Entire* was a word stockmen used to describe an uncastrated horse. That was what Marcy wanted. She wanted to feel entire.

'You know, your father and I went to see Randall at that construction site in Pine Bluff.'

Marcy, whose gaze had drifted off, turned sharply back. 'What?'

Her mother nodded. 'We'd run down there on an errand and Lewis said we were in the vicinity of Wetteland's jobsite, so we drove by, only we were cut off from it by an unbridged canyon. We parked in the dirt and looked across at all the work going on. Lewis thought he saw Randall driving one of the big graders, but when he got his binoculars out of the trunk it turned out he was wrong.'

Marcy waited. There was something about the way her mother was telling this story, and about how she'd waited to tell it, that made her afraid.

'We found Randall finally. He was doing hand-shoveling. Moving along a ditch shading dirt over some kind of just-laid pipe. It was freezing cold and I wanted to go, but Lewis wouldn't leave. He just kept watching Randall work through the binoculars. There was another laborer on the other side of the ditch who stopped all the time to look around, but Randall never stopped. He just kept shoveling.'

Marcy felt like she was being strangled by something invisible. 'Why're you telling me this?'

Her mother looked up surprised from her painting. 'Well, it kind of won Lewis over. On the way home he was saying maybe he could teach Randall farming, turn the place over to him when the time came.' She dipped her brush and studiously kept her eyes on the window she painted. 'You and Randall could move out here with us.' She turned then and looked at Marcy.

'Sure,' Marcy said. 'That might be a good thing to do.' She let her gaze drift, thought of those pigeons from Randall's boyhood circling in the sky before automatically descending. 'It's definitely worth considering,' she said, and tried to make it sound like she meant it.

Two nights later, when Randall next asked Marcy to tell him something, she told him about Meteor Frmka.

ONE MORNING ABOUT SIX WEEKS AFTER RANDALL LEFT, WHEN SHE'D RUN out of food for Randall's dogs, Marcy out of some strange petulance had called Frmka's Suprette for home delivery.

Meteor Frmka delivered the dog food. Meteor was compact, roundfaced, and gap-toothed, a miniature version, Marcy always thought, of the main character on the *McHale's Navy* reruns. Meteor also wore an out-of-fashion crew cut that, to Marcy, made him seem from another, more innocent era. To others, the odd looks and non-stop cheeriness made him seem a little off, possibly even deficient. Randall, for example, liked to refer to Frmka as the village idiot.

The bag of kibbles was a fifty-pounder. Meteor insisted on bringing it in, tearing it open, going out to the kennel with filled dishes. From the kitchen window, Marcy watched him lay one dish down and then, as he was laying down the other, suddenly stiffen. He straightened himself slowly, but otherwise didn't move. He seemed stricken somehow.

'Cripes,' Meteor said when Marcy came out. 'It's like *bam!* and something just goes.' He carefully touched a hand to the lower part of his spine.

The nightgown Marcy wore couldn't be seen through and came nearly to the knees, but, still, it wasn't really the right apparel for standing outside chatting with the delivery boy. 'Let's go inside,' Marcy said and, after they did, wondered what to do next. 'Shall I drive you back or call somebody or what?'

Meteor said that this had happened a couple of times before and it helped if he just lay down for a while. He positioned himself stomach-down on the sofa. 'A couple of times it helped when my mother just sort of rubbed on it,' he said.

Marcy had knelt alongside the sofa, pushed up his Frmka's-Suprette T-shirt and begun to rub his back, which was alarmingly hairy. 'There?' she'd said, kneading the heel of her hand into his blubbery white flesh. 'Here?' After a while Meteor made little soughing sounds to indicate when her hands were doing something especially helpful. For a long time he'd had his eyes closed, but when she next glanced up, he had his head turned to his left and his eyes opened. Marcy had followed his gaze to her own reflection in the full-length door mirror. 'He was getting a pretty good view of my backside,' Marcy said and laughed. She hoped Randall would laugh, too, or at least smile, but he just sat. 'So anyhow I stood up and said, "You must be feeling better now," and he eased himself up with this sheepish look and said, yes, he thought he was.'

'You were the village idiot's peep show,' Randall said flat-voiced.

'Not intentionally,' Marcy said. 'And, besides, I wasn't anybody's *peep show*.' She thought about it for a second or two. 'All he possibly saw was the very edge of my underwear.'

In the silence, the ticking of the oven clock carried all the way from the kitchen. Finally Randall said, 'So that's it?'

'Yep. He stopped by a few times with what he said were day-old donuts or expired-date Haagen-Dazs ice cream, stuff he said was perfectly good, but he didn't get past the front door. I'd say, "How's that bad back?" and he'd look sheepish and say, "Much better, thanks," and then he'd leave.' She made another laugh.

Randall considered it. 'You took the donuts and stuff he offered?'

Yes, but without ever letting him in. That was the correct answer. 'No,' she said, and waited.

'And that's it?' Randall asked.

Marcy said it was. Then, collecting herself: 'And it's important you believe me. Because although I guess you could love someone you didn't trust, I think it would be like living in the darkest pit of hell.'

Randall, sitting in his own strange calmness, smiled. 'I'll tell you what I think, Marcy. I think you believe what you're telling me is the truth.'

IV

MARCY DIDN'T SEE MR RAWLEY, BUT SHE HEARD BITS AND PIECES. HE WAS spending a few weeks with a brother in Oregon. Through his insurance, there was to be a new double-wide mobile home on the lot, with all new furniture inside and a brand-new Ford under the carport awning. One weekday he telephoned Marcy while Randall was at work. The burns weren't so bad as they'd thought, he told her. He'd soon be good as new – he laughed – or possibly better.

Randall began spending most nights in Pine Bluff. He always called and told Marcy when he'd be home so she'd have supper waiting. After the Meteor Frmka story, he'd stopped asking the tell-me question, but there was still a lifelessness at the table that was hard, bony, and sad. Marcy tried not to admit it to herself, but the days were worse when she knew Randall would be home that night.

One morning, Flossie Boyles dropped by with a Nebraska-Oklahoma pool, two dollars a number, and the talk turned to Mr Rawley. 'Have you seen him?' Flossie Boyles asked and without waiting for an answer said, 'He's back and then some. Driving all around town in his brand-new, red Thunderbird from the insurance money.'

'He's back?' Marcy said.

'And then some. I say he hit the jackpot fair and square, but there are some here who now say he may have started that fire himself.'

Marcy said that told her more about the lunatics who lived in this trailer park than about Mr Rawley, and then, immediately after Flossie Boyles's departure, she dialed Mr Rawley's number. 'You're home,' she said when he answered.

'Marcy?'

'How long have you been back?'

'Since Sunday night.' Two days. A silence, and then he said, 'I wanted to call, but I've been running errands like a madman. I stand surrounded by unopened boxes even as we speak.'

Marcy said she thought he might just have called to let her know he'd come back, was all.

Another silence, but shorter. 'Well, I'm running into Chadron this afternoon. Could I talk you into riding along?'

When, an hour later, he came to the door, Marcy was amazed. He looked like a new man. His burned-out hair and eyebrows had grown back in. He was fashionably dressed in pleated wool pants. As they rode along, the pleasant new-car smell mixed with a men's cologne she'd never before noticed him using. 'So when are you coming back to work?' he said to her as they pulled west out of Goodnight.

'Who said I was?' Marcy said.

Mr Rawley let a mile or so pass. 'What if I were to tell you there was an opening for weeknights?'

Marcy considered the process. If she said yes to Mr Rawley, then she had to pitch it to Randall, who would hate the idea. 'Randall and I're trying to get pregnant,' she said. 'In fact, I might already be.'

This was a complete lie, but it put the subject behind them. They drove along in easy silence. Marcy, gazing out, wished they could just keep driving on and on and on. She turned to Mr Rawley and said, 'I *like* this new red car.'

Mr Rawley smiled. 'Well, it's red all right. Naples Red, the Ford people call it.' Pastureland passed quietly by. Almost to himself, Mr Rawley said, 'I always wanted a red car, all my life, but Ivy always wanted white.'

A jagged sensation of surprise ripped through Marcy. She stared at the flat straight road in front of them. She suddenly knew in her bones that Mr Rawley *had* started the fire, yet what she felt was not the pure revulsion that knowledge should trigger. What she felt instead was more like envy.

After a time she said, 'Randall's always trying to get me to tell some terrible secret that doesn't exist. When he's home, he's always watching me and even when he's not, it feels like he is. When he's there, it's like I'm living in the tiniest trailer in the tiniest trailer park in the world.'

'I've known that feeling,' Mr Rawley said in a somber voice.

'It's not like he doesn't love me.'

'No.'

'I know for a fact that he does.'

Mr Rawley nodded.

'The other day, for example, I went out to visit my folks and when I got back Randall was already home. He was sitting with the lights off watching that video you made from clips of me doing the weekend news. I thought he'd have something sarcastic to say, but all he said was, "I don't know about this stuff, Marzikins, but you seem okay at it to me." '

Mr Rawley made a dry, cheerless laugh. 'There's high praise.'

'Well, from Randall.'

The car hummed along.

'Yet he's the reason you're not working anymore.'

Marcy thought of protesting this assessment, but didn't. From Farrell's winter wheat a browsing mule deer turned its head to watch them pass.

'Do you have any money of your own?' Mr Rawley said.

'A little, not much. Why?'

'Because if you could, I'd buy a car, a decent serviceable car, and register it in your own name. Then I'd tuck it away in the RV storage area of Sleepy Hollow Trailer Court.'

'And what good would that do me, a car in an RV storage yard?'

'Oh, I don't know,' Mr Rawley said. 'It might be a comfort.'

V

TODAY, THIS FINAL DAY, RANDALL DIDN'T CALL FROM WORK TO SAY HE'D BE home. He just arrived, late, quietly unlocking the front door. The television was on. Guido slept on the floor next to a splayed-open book on Vivien Leigh. Marcy and Boo slept on the sofa.

'*Out*,' Randall said to the dogs in a low growl.

It was a warped watery scene for Marcy – the dogs in the blueish television light skulking toward the door, their eyes peeling back to Randall, who was standing stiff-faced above her, just staring. 'You bought a car,' he said.

It seemed like a dream. 'I did what?'

'You bought a car. A Mercury Cougar.'

Before she even really knew why, Marcy began to sob. 'What do you want, Randall? What in the world do you want?'

'The truth. Not one thing else.'

'Yes,' she said still sobbing, 'I bought a car, was that a crime?' Her crying went on a while after the impulse for it was spent. During this winding down, Marcy, in a moment of instinctive understanding not just of her needs but of Randall's, too, said, 'There was more to it than what I told you about Meteor Frmka.'

Randall – it was as if his whole body relaxed – said, 'Yes.'

I am Randall Hunsacker's wife, she thought, and I am about to do something I don't know what.

There was, in point of fact, *not* more to it with Frmka, except that he'd withdrawn beamingly from the front room, as if a glimpse of her underwear were all a male could ever want, a notion so childlike that it had endeared him to Marcy and opened up in her a well of generosity that Meteor Frmka hadn't tapped.

'Quite a bit more,' Marcy said evenly.

Randall eased himself into his favorite chair. 'Tell me, Marcy.'

Marcy looked at him in the blue light. For months he had been testing her. That was what she believed. Now she would test him. She would tell him plenty. She would tell him so much that either his fears would collapse under their sheer preposterousness or they would expand to burst point and explode everything. She didn't care which. Either one was better than the hellish state she was now suspended in. Marcy closed and opened her eyes in a slow blink. She sighed so deeply it felt almost like a moment of sleep. She said, 'At first I was just, you know, shocked at Frmka for looking at me in the mirror, but then, while he was lying there with his eyes closed pretending he hadn't been looking, I kind of began to think –'

'Think what?' Randall said in a low, almost reverent voice.

Marcy waited. She wondered if it was too late to turn back.

In his quiet coaxing voice Randall said, 'Think what, Marcy?'

Marcy told him she'd leaned a little forward to give Frmka a better view of things and that, later, when he came on deliveries, she always set him down in the same place and rubbed his back and made sure there was always something for him to see, and when she said she'd even bought lacy black briefs from a catalogue for this particular purpose, she thought Randall might snicker and laugh, so laughably absurd her words when spoken sounded, but Randall didn't laugh. Instead, his body stiffened and his fingers rolled into fists.

'What else?' he said.

'Bobby Parmalee,' Marcy made herself say. 'One morning early he came to the door before I was dressed. He said he had a girlfriend in Omaha, a sorority girl who wanted to have sex with him, but after all this time he'd never actually done it and was afraid he'd seem clumsy, and so he was wondering –' She paused before going on. Once, in a motel room with Randall, she'd turned by mistake to a cable channel showing two big-breasted women pretending to make love and though she'd immediately switched the station she knew she was stuck with that false image for life. She had the same feeling now about the crazy, grotesque images she was setting loose in this room, one after another. When she was finished with Bobby Parmalee, Randall sat slumped, his hands still fisted, but his body completely motionless, as if benumbed.

'What else?' he said.

The air in the trailer was so compressed that Marcy couldn't lift her head. She could barely open her mouth. 'There was also something with Mr Rawley,' she said and sounded to herself like someone on a sickbed. 'At the studio. We put a tablecloth on the desk. With his wife there watching, his petrified wife who couldn't do a thing, or utter a word of what she saw, ever.' She looked up at Randall with dead-alive eyes and to this terrible lie gave her head a little nod.

But Randall, barely audible, said, 'What else?'

What else? Marcy wanted to cry and weep and sob. In a low, wooden voice she said, 'I went to the construction site in Pine Bluff. I parked on the other side of the canyon and through binoculars watched you work and the whole time all I could think of was, That's my husband, a manual laborer.'

Slowly, as if with great difficulty, Randall raised himself up into the blueish watery light and hit her. He hit her one time with his three-fingered hand. Her teeth slammed together, through the tip of her tongue, and, she was not sure why, her left eye seemed suddenly to be floating in its pooled socket. Randall stood with a look of shock, as if awakened too fast from a dream. His fist unfolded into a hand. 'Marcy?' he said and took a step forward, as if to hold her, but she turned away. There was the taste of blood in her mouth and the fierce, pushed-in feel of her eye, but she did not cry out. She was not unhappy. She was more than leaving soon. She was Marcy Marlene Hunsacker and she was already gone.

Chapter Twelve

CARES AND WOES

THE DAY WOULD BREAK CLEAR, BUT AS THE SEVEN HUNTERS DROVE FROM *separate points of origin toward their meeting place near Horse Creek, all but one had some fresh burden with which to trouble themselves.*

The night before, Randall Hunsacker's wife had said a whole stream of things, one worse than the other, on and on, until he did something he never believed he could do.

Jim Six had overdrunk himself square dancing with Janine Hyde at the Elks and believed that while she was driving him home in her old red Volkswagen he'd asked her to marry him. This wasn't so bad. He wanted to marry Janine. What was bad was that he wasn't sure if she'd said yes.

After dropping Jim Six off shortly after midnight, Janine Hyde hadn't gone straight home. She'd driven west to the Coates place and awakened Marlen Coates, who'd come out on the porch in his boxer shorts. 'What're you doing here?' he asked Janine. 'Tonight your friend Jim asked me to marry him,' she said playfully. 'I've come for your advice.' She was wearing a square-dancing dress. It rustled when she cocked a leg over the porch rail. Marlen said, 'Marry him's my advice.' He said, 'Jim is more or less my friend.' He said, 'I'm going hunting with him in six hours.' But Janine Hyde grinned loosely and Marlen felt his darker appetites coming alive. 'G'wan now, git,' he'd said to her in a growl, but she didn't leave.

The prior day, Frank Mears, who ran launderettes in Gordon,

Rushville, and White Clay, had opened twelve coinboxes containing almost as many blanks as quarters, and then profanely accused two Indians lounging near the dryers, in hopes he might draw them into a fight, but both men, probably because they knew he was carrying weapons, just stared at him morosely and walked away.

After Leo Underwood had come home from closing up the Eleventh Man, his wife had declined his advances. By Leo's accounting, this was two full weeks now. 'Not with these thin walls and that boy right in the next room,' Leo's wife had whispered. The boy in the next room was Leo's sister's son and, as far as Leo could tell, he was going to be with them indefinitely.

And in the middle of the night, while idly fingering the fleshy mole behind his left ear, Whistler Simpson had become suddenly apprehensive. Using his thumb and index finger as calipers, he measured and squeezed. The mole had grown, and it was much harder than before. He was sure of it. Positive. By 4 a.m., Whistler had concluded that a pernicious cancer couldn't be ruled out. He'd lain open-eyed in the dark, compressed his lips, and begun softly to whistle, first 'Beautiful Dreamer' and then, repeatedly until dawn, 'Bye Bye Blackbird.'

The seventh hunter, Meteor Frmka, hadn't a care in the world, that he knew of.

Chapter Thirteen

THE HUNTING PARTY

I

METEOR FRMKA WOKE UP HAPPY. IN MOMENTS OF SELF-REFLECTION, FRMKA knew he was too eager for happiness, that he too often rushed willy-nilly toward its faintest outlines, but he couldn't change his ways. For Frmka, hope was a muscle made strong by regular exercise.

This morning he sat up and in the pre-dawn darkness wiggled his toes. All but the big ones were wrapped in Band-Aids. Under the Band-Aids were tattoos, a message to Merna Littlefield that he'd first feared was not only irreversible but weird, but he'd now come to think of the message as his ace in the hole. This as well as other things made him happy. As far as Frmka was concerned, things were going great guns. He'd just got his own car. Merna was kissing him with her mouth open. And he was beginning to make notable friends.

Just last Sunday, for instance, Frank Mears and Leo Underwood, men Frmka hardly knew, came by to look at his car and, before Frmka knew it, they were all three on their way to Scenic, South Dakota. Frmka drove, Leo rode up front with a cooler at his feet, chatting happily and chewing on a soda straw while Mears sat in back never speaking at all except when he was out of beer. Then he would say, 'The jasper in back needs another unit,' which, with each repetition, seemed funnier and funnier to Frmka, and made his spirits soar.

In Scenic, they visited the whorehouse and tattoo parlor both.

Frmka didn't tell Merna that. 'We just made ourselves seen,' he said to her, swelling up, trying to sound like Leo. It was Leo who on the way back from Scenic had turned from staring out at the ceaseless plain and said, 'I meant to tell you, Frmka, four or five of us are shooting birds next Saturday. Me and Mears. Randall Hunsacker, Whistler, Jim Six, maybe Marlen Coates. The whole bunch. So whattaya say, buddy, care to join us?'

Buddy.

Frmka felt as if he'd just received some kind of small but meaningful award. His face glowed. His smile shot ear to ear. He glanced back at Mears, who, while staring out the window, was gently and privately picking his nose. Leo, however, kept smiling chummily. 'Okay,' Meteor Frmka had said. 'You betcha.'

It was still dark this morning as Frmka drove slowly down Main Street toward his father's market. He parked in the back, unlocked the delivery door to Frmka's Suprette, found the flashlight in its place atop the fusebox. He went to the liquor department, unfolded the list Leo had given him, trained the beam of light upon it, and began filling the order. Supplying their liquor wholesale was part of the deal.

Frmka's contentment, as he poked his car down 2nd Street, was almost complete. The order was boxed and safe on the back seat. The darkness was just beginning to lift. Full unbroken leaves lay in the street. It reminded Frmka of that moment when, just before breaking the seal on a new toy, expectation and actual pleasure finally came together.

Frmka turned east onto Highway 20, made note of the prices at Sipps's Gas-for-Less, turned north on the cut-off, and then, at the county road where he was supposed to turn west, Frmka began to hum a melody of his own making and turned blithely east.

THEY STOOD AND MILLED ABOUT IN THE COLD, JUST-BREAKING DAWN, THE six men, a boy (Leo's nephew, an unexpected addition), and five hunting dogs, Randall Hunsacker's two black Labs, Frank Mears's two German shorthairs, and Whistler Simpson's part-poodle. The boy and the dogs were waiting on the men. The men were waiting on Meteor Frmka. Of them, Randall Hunsacker was the most impatient. Finally he said, 'So where's your little delivery boy, Leo?'

Leo Underwood, chewing on a plastic straw and scanning the horizon, didn't answer.

'He still going out with Merna Littlefield?' Jim Six asked, and when no-one replied, he said, 'She's got no tits whatsoever.'

The hunters had collected at a widening in the road beyond Horse Creek, near enough to the Petersen place that the breeze carried the clinking sounds of his pigs rooting creepfeeders. The idea was to shoot Petersen's cornfields, which had a reputation for pheasant. But nobody liked the idea of a liquorless day, and Frmka had the liquor, so they settled into waiting. They sprawled on warm motor hoods or leaned against trees, rubbing their hands and quietly smoking cigarettes and drinking coffee with a little whiskey that Leo had found behind the seat of his cab, though it was almost gone now.

Randall, when he saw that, led away his dogs and squatted alone. He'd been staring at his right hand a while, slowly curling and uncurling its three fingers, when he looked up and discovered Frank Mears regarding him with a self-amused grin. Mears had always had a long, handsome face, and his receding hairline made it seem even longer. 'What's the matter, Zacker?' he asked.

'Not a thing,' Randall said, which was not exactly the truth, but it wasn't the kind of question that warranted the truth. Besides, Randall never knew exactly how he felt about Mears. He was oddly drawn in by him even while not liking him very much. Mears's grin, at least the particular grin he was showing now, seemed to hide within it something cruel.

Mears said, 'Well, Zacker, you look more than normally pissy to me.'

Randall was surprised at how little he felt like fending off this remark, but he did so anyway. 'No,' he said mildly, 'this is how pissy I normally am at this hour.' He went back to flexing his hand.

Mears kept his grin. His German shorthairs sat at his feet. When Mears raised his hand suddenly to flick at something in the air, the dogs, habitually expecting the worst, shied and hunkered down.

There was another dog, too, off to the side, a part-poodle whose coat was a dirty shade of butterscotch, and who scooched its hind end urgently through the dirt while its owner, lank, unshaven Whistler Simpson, used his hand to delicately explore the mole behind his ear.

To Leo Underwood, who stood nearby, Whistler said, 'Isn't a growing mole one of the seven signs of cancer?'

'Sounds right,' Leo said without interest. 'Another one is if one of your extremities turns black and falls off.' He snickered appreciatively at his own wit.

Nearby, Leo's young nephew was eating a candy bar and watching the part-poodle with uncomplicated disgust. The boy hadn't wanted to come hunting – he didn't like getting out of bed so early – but Leo's wife had forced the issue. Leo's wife couldn't stand the idea of being alone in the house with the boy all day long. Though he was only thirteen, he gave Leo's wife the creeps. 'He stares at me,' she said, 'and whenever I happen to look at him he makes a point of scratching his private parts.'

'Dog's name is Rat,' Whistler said when he noticed the boy staring at the animal. The boy just kept looking at the dog dragging itself about, so Whistler, who was fond of the dog, said, 'His manners are kind of bad, but he can work up birds like nobody's business.'

The boy said nothing, but Whistler noticed he kept staring at the dog. 'Something the matter?' Whistler said.

The boy didn't even look at Whistler. He said, 'My real dad said all dogs carry bad germs but red-assed dogs carry the worst.'

There was a tense silence, which seemed to amuse everyone but Whistler. Leo slid his chewing straw from his mouth and said, 'It's true, Whistler. It's awful hard to warm up to a red-assed poodle-dog.' This time Leo laughed so hard Whistler could smell what he had for breakfast, or at least the ham-and-eggs part of it. Whistler took a step away and stared at the boy. He'd never seen him before and already he felt like turning his little asshole inside out. He told himself to count to three. Afterwards, in a controlled voice, he said, 'Here you're insulting my dog and I don't think we've even been introduced.'

'Probably not,' the boy said and didn't give his name. He looked twelve, but his voice sounded older. He broke off another inch of Baby Ruth.

'He's my sister's kid,' Leo explained. 'Only nobody knows at the moment where my sister's at.'

The boy in his sullen voice said, 'She's probably with a Indian or smelly black dude. She likes Indians and smelly black dudes.'

Leo laughed and said, 'I had to bring him because my wife can't stand him around the house.'

This fact seemed to please the boy. 'She says I'm unsettling,' he said.

Whistler, who always went to the standards when he was feeling uneasy, stared at the boy and began whistling 'Stardust.'

Minutes passed. Finally Frank Mears in a low voice said, 'That'll be your errand boy, Leo,' and nodded toward a cloud of dust moving *away* from them on a county road to the east.

Randall, who'd been running a broken twig over the palm of his hand, stopped, and pressed its jagged point until it deeply dimpled the skin. He slid the twig into his pocket and said, 'We going to hunt or sit on our asses all morning waiting for the village idiot to find us?'

'Five minutes,' Leo said.

'Then we go,' Mears said in a low decisive voice. 'Liquor or no.'

Leo, to change the topic, nodded across at Jim Six, who was wearing a new fluorescent pink vest and gazing down the Horse Creek gully. 'Nice vest, Six-Man,' Leo said. 'Would you call it hot pink?'

Jim Six had to laugh. His tightly curled hair had been orangeish-red as a child, but had over time darkened toward auburn, though his wispy mustache was still unquestionably red. His cheeks were so heavily freckled that they suggested the color of over-creamed coffee.

'Janine dress you up in that?' Leo asked.

This reminded Jim of his proposal of marriage and the answer he couldn't recall. They'd been dating for eight months. Janine Hyde's tight clothes had pulled Jim close, at which point her pale blue eyes took over. Jim found himself looking into them whether she was there or not. 'So she bought me a vest,' he said. 'Something wrong with your girlfriend not wanting you shot at by dipshits with guns?'

Scattered laughter came and went.

Fifty feet opposite, Marlen Coates spat into the dirt, rubbed it in with his boot, and didn't look at Jim Six. Surreptitiously, Marlen brought the tips of his fingers to his nose, then quickly took them away. Janine Hyde's smell was still on them.

Leo Underwood, anxious to keep the party's mind off Frmka,

said, 'So did Whistler tell you all he's not hunting today but tagging?'

This was of general interest. Eyes shifted to Whistler.

'What's that mean?' Jim asked.

Whistler took his hand away from his mole so as not to be distracted. He'd borrowed Doc Parmalee's stun gun and tagging kit, he explained, and if he saw an elk he was going to down him and tag him with a tracking device.

Frank Mears turned his sly grin toward Whistler. 'Elk? Hereabouts? I'd have to doubt it.'

Whistler hurriedly cited a university report and then, less confidently, another by the state game commission. These were not, with these men, reliable sources; their interest began to slide away.

Somebody said, 'If I see a rogue elk, I'm not waiting for Whistler's stun gun.'

'Only thing I like better than a big thick college thesis,' Leo proclaimed, 'is a big thick elk steak.'

Appreciative hoots.

'Elk burger,' somebody said.

'Elk salami!'

'Elk pie!'

'Elk cake!'

When they'd settled back down, Leo, eyeing the orange metal case with DR JOS. PARMALEE stencilled on the front, said, 'Heard Bobby Parmalee and Ginny Walkinshaw set a date.'

Randall looked up. From the uninterest of the others, the news was evidently common knowledge. 'Thought I heard he was engaged to some sorority girl off at college,' he said.

Leo said he'd never heard anything like that.

'No,' Whistler said. 'Him and Ginny've been engaged since summer. They knew all along it'd be June but only now picked the day.'

Randall stared blankly at Whistler. 'And he didn't have even a side girlfriend off at college?'

'Maybe. Only that don't sound like Bobby.'

It was true, Randall thought. It didn't. Only why would Marcy lie about something like that?

'One minute left,' Mears said. He began getting his gear together

and others were doing the same when Meteor Frmka's car drew
into view.

'Our delivery boy finally reckoned west,' Leo said, grinning
with evident relief. Hunting sober was not Leo's idea of an
outing.

Frmka, upon arrival, jumped out of his car apologizing.

'No need,' Leo said soothingly. He eyed the bottles in the back
seat of Frmka's car. 'Get everything?'

Frmka grinned and nodded. 'You bet. In pints. As ordered.' He
got out the register tape. 'Came to $43 and –'

'Buddy, buddy, buddy,' Leo said, loosely draping an arm around
Frmka's sloping shoulders. 'The way we –'

'Everything strictly at wholesale,' Frmka said, still beaming, but
already beginning to feel a little out of his element.

'Which is dandy,' Leo said. 'Wholesale is dandy. But the way we
work it is the two with the fewest birds divvy the bill.' Frmka glanced
around. The others were paying him no attention. They were pulling
the pints from his car, sliding them into their pockets and Leo was
saying, 'So you can see why we have to wait for the end of the day
to settle accounts.'

The others were setting out on foot. Frmka began walking
with Leo toward the rear of the group. He was for the first
time wondering why Leo didn't bring the liquor himself. Leo
could get it wholesale, too. Unless maybe Leo had a hard time
collecting from the others, and if Leo had a hard time collecting,
well, where did that leave him? It wasn't at all a happy thought.
They'd gone a little distance in silence before Leo, sliding his straw
to the corner of his mouth, turned to Frmka and said, deadpan,
'You bringing something to shoot with? A firearm, maybe, or a
Kodak?'

Frmka stopped. Leo kept walking. Over his shoulder he said, 'I'll
be up with the others.'

By the time Frmka had gotten his gun and gear, the rest of the
party had disappeared from view. He broke into a dogtrot and,
when finally he caught up with the others, his face was pink and
his skin was wet and a misgiving he couldn't name was throbbing
in his ears.

II

WITHIN THE FIRST OF PETERSEN'S CORNFIELDS, THE PARTY FANNED OUT
along the fenceline and, intending to make pheasants take wing,
began crashing guns-up through the cornstalks, whooping and
whistling. The Labs heeled alongside Randall and the German
shorthairs heeled beside Mears, waiting to retrieve while, out
front, Whistler's part-poodle scooted about trying to rout the birds,
without result.

When they reached the opposite end of the quartersection, Leo
said, 'I am goddamned. "Lousy with birds," Petersen told me. This
very field.' He looked around at broadly dubious grins.

'I am unamazed,' Jim Six said.

'Here's to the Hoochinoo,' Whistler Simpson said and began to
gargle a mouthful of bourbon.

Jim Six did his old Sam-the-Sham routine. *'Uno dos, uno dos tres
fartro!'* he cried and let fly.

Frmka was smiling, not so much because he felt like smiling, but
because he didn't want anyone to see how lost he was feeling. The
party again began to move. Mears shouldered the loop from the
gatepost and let the wired gate fall. The last one through – Leo's
nephew or, more often, Frmka – reset it. Again they fanned out, set
up a racket, headed west.

'When they said you was high-classed,' somebody sang out, 'well
that was just a lie!'

Jim Six, feeling the sun on his face and the bolstering effects of
sloe gin, drew within range of Marlen Coates and said, 'Isn't this
about the best thing you can do with pants on?'

Marlen looked at Jim Six and thought of twisting Jim's girlfriend's
nipples into hard bullets and then without ever kissing her bending her
over like a she-goat. He wondered how long he would have to think
that way, because if it went on very long he'd have to cut Jim loose.

'Square dancing's good too though,' Jim was saying cheerily. 'It
brings out Janine's saucy side.'

In a sullen voice Marlen said, 'I never understood how anybody
under sixty could take up square dancing.'

Jim Six exploded with an overloud laugh. 'I like it,' he said. 'Besides,
Janine claims she could square dance with me till kingdom come!'

Marlen decided this would be a good time to deal with his boot. There was something needling from within. He sat down and was left alone. Jim Six caught up with Leo and shouted something exuberant to him. *Might be getting hitched*. Was that what he said? The din, which was beginning to bother Marlen, moved on, and he was left with a steady little wind shuffling the dry corn. He smelled his right hand. Her smell was still on his fingers. It wasn't his fault, though, not completely. He'd been asleep, in fact. A horn had honked. It was after midnight, he'd turned on the yardlight, and there was Janine Hyde's faded red VW bug, though she wasn't in it. He'd been standing there in his boxer shorts, staring out, when Janine stepped out of the darkness talking and walking very deliberately, as if navigating an obstacle course. 'Tonight your buddy Jim asked me to join him in matrimony,' she'd said. 'And I told him maybe, I told him who knows, which was okay because he was so corned up he could hardly stand, but what should I tell him tomorrow?' Marlen could tell from her sloppy grin that she was pretty far gone herself. He knew it for sure when he put his hand up her dress and she just laughed. He'd said a few false words of discouragement, and then he'd told her to get out of there and go home, and then when she just laughed he did what he'd wanted to do to her for a long time without ever really knowing it. She'd passed out on his bed and when he left this morning in the dark he poked her a few times until she opened her eyes and then he told her that whatever it was that happened last night she sure as shit better not go calling it rape.

Marlen unhooked the laces and pulled off his boots. It was a nail working through, and the heel of his sock was red with blood. He was deciding whether he wanted to do anything about it or not when he heard boots breaking through the brittle cornstalks.

'Marlen?' Jim Six called. 'Where you at?'

Marlen sat still.

'Marlen? You out here?'

Marlen waited a long second and then in a low voice said, 'Over here.'

'Jesus,' Jim said when he'd found him. 'Thought maybe something had happened.'

'Like what?' Marlen said in a surly voice. 'Abduction by Martians?' Which made Jim Six chuckle.

After assessing the boot problem, Jim offered moleskin from one of his fluorescent vest's many pockets. While Marlen was cutting the bandage with a knife, Jim said, 'I think I proposed to Janine last night.'

Marlen didn't speak.

'Funny part is, I don't remember if she accepted.'

Marlen pulled up his sock and while relacing his boots surprised himself by saying, 'I wouldn't go marrying Janine Hyde if I was you.'

Jim Six felt his throat tightening up. Something about the serious way Marlen spoke the words made him not want to know anymore. He knew he ought to say, 'And why's that?' but he couldn't bring himself to say it.

Marlen Coates told him anyway. He stood up and told him all the details and looked evenly at Jim even after Jim had had to look away. Marlen knew he should feel terrible telling him these things, and thought he *would* feel terrible, but he didn't. He wondered even if there weren't some part of it that gave him a kind of grimy male pleasure. 'Janine Hyde might be the right one to fuck,' he said finally, 'but she's the wrong one to marry.'

When Marlen was done, Jim Six's face looked flattened and strangely discolored. He didn't say anything for a time. Finally, as if in dumb amazement, he said, 'Jesus, Marlen, it's not that hard to get laid. Why'd you need –'

He broke off. He didn't wait for an answer. There wasn't any answer to wait for. He turned and crashed off through the dry corn.

FOR NOVEMBER, IT WAS WARM, AND IF THERE WEREN'T BIRDS TO SHOOT, IT was at least a pleasant day for hiking, seeing the sights, and breathing the clean air. These were the sunny sentiments Meteor Frmka had passed on to Leo Underwood, to whom Meteor had attached himself. Leo looked at him blandly and said, 'Hey, buddy, how about us spreading out a little?' Leo grinned, something mean sliding into it. 'In case we get something to shoot at.'

Meteor, stung, moved off. He began to think of Merna in the

Littlefield kitchen putting up pears with her mother. She said she was going to do that today. It was warm enough that the windows would be open, the breeze would be moving the yellow curtains, and maybe she would be wearing a dress. Merna didn't have big breasts or anything, but she had legs that went on forever and she'd sometimes wear short dresses. Meteor wished he were there. Sitting at Merna's kitchen table and eating gingersnaps, telling corny jokes and looking at Merna's legs.

When the party came upon fallow ground, they bunched up and took stock. 'Think the birds're winning,' Leo said.

Most of them nodded. Most of them were uncapping pints. The boy worked on an Abba Zabba. Jim Six, who'd abruptly picked up his drinking pace, slipped an unlighted cigar into his mouth, climbed atop a cottonwood stump and looked around grandly. 'Elk tacos!' he declared around his cigar. 'Elk pancakes!'

Leo stared across at Randall, who'd whistled up his dogs, found a stump to sit on, then taken his twig from his pocket. He was now idly twirling its sharp end into the palm of his hand. 'Zacker, my man,' Leo said, 'you're taking all prizes for sulking. What've you got to sulk over?'

Randall didn't look up at Leo. He felt the stick break suddenly through the skin and needle into the wet flesh. 'The standard shortcomings,' he said.

'Who said anything about dick size?' somebody said and drew laughs.

When Whistler started up on 'Heartbreak Hotel,' Jim Six, from his stump, pantomimed a guitar, gave it a deluxe pelvic thrust and crooned along.

Leo chunked a dirt clod at him which, when Jim Six ducked, flew by and landed six or seven rows deep in the cornfield, and there, with a sudden shuffling of wings, four pheasant screeched and rose and swooped low over the cornstalks, three hens, which were protected, and a brilliantly feathered cock, which was not. The birds had settled again in cover before a gun was shouldered.

'Brer Pheasant safe with this company,' Whistler said amiably.

Frank Mears made a slow blink of disgust. He drank from his

pint, wiped his mouth with his hand and his hand on his pants. He turned to Leo. 'What about the Macy place?'

'Asked. Answer was no-can-do.'

Mears grimaced derisively and Leo, seeing this, turned back to the others and gave his straw a sequence of quick clinches with his teeth, which produced a droll wagging effect. Then he said, 'Though I guess we could just sort of wander off in that direction.'

NORTHWEST. THEY'D FOLLOWED THE COUNTY ROAD THROUGH PASTURELAND and then winter wheat, a brilliant green, when they began to hear faint singing somewhere ahead of them. They followed the sound of it into rolling hills and unfarmed timberland, until eventually it brought them first within sight of a rusty pickup and then into the smell of burning marijuana. The pickup was parked where the dirt road crested. A boom-box sat on the roof. The music could not have been stranger. It was some kind of woman opera singer, her big voice played so loud it seemed to come from everywhere.

'Jim Biddle,' Leo said.

The party drew closer.

'And his faithful injun companion.'

Albert Sharp Fish was slouched to one side of the cab surveying things the sleepy careful way the Oglala do.

When Leo and the others approached the truck, Biddle reached up and turned off the music. He greeted the hunters with a serene smile. Sharp Fish smiled, too. So did Leo, but less naturally. He noticed Biddle was holding a joint in the low space between his knees. 'So what're you two assholes doing way out here?' he said, trying for cheeriness.

'Just sitting here in the ol' Dodge pickup listening to C.C. Bartoli and planning . . .' Biddle's voice trailed off and his face went blank. He looked at Sharp Fish. 'What was it again we were planning?'

'Our next trip to France,' Sharp Fish said straight-faced and Biddle exploded into loud, extended, solitary laughter. Sharp Fish took the joint from Biddle's hand, drew from it, and passed it back. Biddle, composing himself, presented it to Leo.

Leo looked at it. There it was, limp and brownish and slobbery with their different salivas. 'I'll stick to my plastic straw,' he said.

From off to the side, Frank Mears looked at the metal softball bats in Biddle's gun rack, and at the sticker on Biddle's window that said, AS IS, and then at Biddle and Sharp Fish with their skinny little necks sitting there with mocking little grins. Frank Mears spat. He grunted to his dogs. He'd seen enough. He was leaving.

They all were.

As they were going, Sharp Fish in a sleepy voice said, '*Vaya con Dios*,' and when Biddle again burst into a laughter all his own, Mears stopped short. The others did, too. But Whistler in a coaxing voice said, 'Shit, Mears, we got better things to do. Let's just leave'm be.'

Mears scowled at Whistler and walked ahead, his anger not so much diffused as divided, directed half now toward the wimps in the truck and half toward his wimpish friend Whistler.

For a while, the party was silent, just drinking and walking, but Leo finally broke into it. 'God-*damn!*' he said, and raked his hand up his crotch. 'Worst comes to worst, we'll come back and shoot the legs off Biddle's Dodge pickup!'

Most of them nodded or laughed or in some other way agreed, and they began to walk faster, as if somehow their muscles suddenly had more nerve to them, and short-legged Meteor Frmka, to keep up, broke into an occasional trot.

III

MACY SIGNS, PAINTED IN WHITE ON BLACKWALL CAR TIRES, SEEMED TO HANG from every fence post:

NO HUNTING

L. O. MACY

Jim Six let his unlighted cigar poke jauntily from the side of his mouth as he streamed urine at one of Macy's signs, then walked about shaking it dry to what the rest of the party viewed as unmatched comic effect. Jim had decided that alcoholic modification was the best way to deflect images of Marlen's fornication with Janine Hyde, and, more importantly, to convince himself that he'd probably never cared that much for Janine Hyde anyway. The other hunters were nearly as tight as he was and, after Jim had completed his comic urination, hooted loudly for an encore. 'Once is not enough!' Leo yelled, which he and several others found side-splitting.

Mears stood apart, sullenly regarding this merriment until he had to cut it off. 'We need blockers,' he said. 'Least one.'

He looked at Frmka, and the others looked at Frmka, and Frmka looked back at them. When they weren't laughing, their faces were bland from drink. Frmka said, 'Okay, sure. Might be fun.'

Leo said, 'You know what to do, don't you? – just wander down the other end and set up a commotion so they won't go that way.'

'Blow your nose or something,' Jim Six said. Sober, Jim Six had little use for meanness, but when he was drunk, he kept it handy, like a pocketknife.

Frmka and the boy blocked a quartersection, without result, then Frmka alone blocked two more, without result, and after that nobody mentioned it again. The boy hadn't wanted to do any blocking at all. He'd pointed at Frmka and said, 'He'll do something stupid and get me killed.'

Leo had laughed and was ready to let the boy off, but Mears had interceded. 'This party may be too big by one or too big by two,' he said. His eyes shrank to hard seeds and fell on the boy. 'You can either block like you were told or you can take your skinny ass back to your uncle's truck where you belong.'

For a moment the boy had stared as if in disbelief at Mears and then, when the other men's eyes turned and settled on him, he turned away. Only Randall could see his face or guess at his boyish anger and humiliation. But the boy's smooth face, which seemed for a moment about to break apart, firmed and tightened. He swung back around and shot a look at Mears before walking off to take his place with Frmka at the opposite end of the field, where he blocked once and thereafter made himself scarce.

They got off just one shot, and that was Randall's, upon reaching the shelter belt at the west of the second field. Leo had been muttering to Mears about the generally fucked-up state of this hunt when, directly behind Frmka, Whistler's part-poodle barked once and a single cock pheasant suddenly screeched and got up. Frmka froze. Randall snapped his gun to, swung it past Frmka's head, and fired.

The bird swooped safely away.

'Missed,' somebody said after a moment, and somebody else said, 'Which one?'

Nobody could keep from laughing, either out of relief or because of some arousing scent that hung in the air with the smoke from the gun. Even Frmka, who didn't hear the joke for the ringing in his ear, made himself laugh and, when the party began again to move, he made his feet move, too.

Toward the middle of the pack, with his Labs heeling alongside, Randall was lost in thought. All morning, at the sight of Meteor Frmka, Randall had been needling himself with the knowledge that Marcy had let Frmka into the house while he, Randall, was at her request off in California, and that Marcy had worn lacy black briefs and rubbed Frmka's hairy back and positioned herself so that all the while he could get an eyeful. And then Randall was as surprised as anyone else when he'd shot so close to Frmka, but was secretly pleased at how Frmka's face, the second after, had turned brittle with fear. He thought pleasantly of Frmka breaking apart like dropped pottery. And now, tramping along, it came unbidden to Randall that a hunting party was like a football game – in the middle of its chaos you sometimes fall into a calm center where unexpected things can happen and hardly anybody is ever held accountable for it.

THE LINE KEPT TRAVELING WEST, MEARS AND HIS GERMAN SHORTHAIRS in the lead. After a time, Whistler drifted back to Frmka. 'Ear okay?'

'I can still hear,' Frmka said, and nothing more. The fun was out of this day. He kept his eyes straight ahead.

'I always wanted to ask,' Whistler said. 'How'd you get a name like Meteor?'

Frmka said, 'It's just a weird old family name.'

'Yeah,' Whistler said, 'my tribe's got a few of those. We've got three different fellas named Delmore.'

He grunted a laugh and Frmka did, too, grateful that the subject of his name had passed. Sometimes he told people what his father told people: that he was named Meteor because he'd entered the world with great velocity. ('He all but shot out of the womb!' Meteor's father would say in an embarrassingly loud voice.) But the truth was, the name was his mother's crazy idea. They were Jews, non-practicing Jews, but still Jews, Goodnight's sole specimens. Meteor's mother had come from Chicago to marry Meteor's father. She wanted to fit in. She loved the Oglala practice of naming a child after the first noteworthy occurrence following its birth and, two hours after delivering her baby boy, she'd seen a meteor in the summer sky.

From up front, Leo called back, 'Anybody seen my sister's kid?'

Nobody had.

'Probably with Rat,' Whistler said. 'He's also vamoosed.' In a lower voice, almost to himself, he added, 'Though it's not exactly like him.'

Leo, for his part, wasn't worried about the boy. 'Hey, Whistler,' he yelled back, changing the subject altogether. 'While you're conversing with the Meteor, ask him about his talking toes!' Leo grinned at Frmka, whose round face had suddenly pinkened, but Leo left it alone, as if it were something he liked having there to come back to.

'Talking toes?' Whistler said, still friendly.

Frmka felt burned down. 'Ask Leo. Leo brought it up.'

Ask Leo? What kind of answer was *Ask Leo?* Whistler picked up his pace a little, not much, but enough so Frmka caught on, and lagged behind. He looked back south at the squiggles of smoke from leaves burning in Goodnight, and soothed himself by imagining one of them rising from a leafpile in front of the Littlefield place.

The hunters walked and drank and wiped sweat and fell silent under the afternoon sun. Mears in a snarl asked Whistler if he knew anything but death dirges, and Whistler, hardly missing a beat, slid from 'Baltimore Oriole' into a mocking version of 'Zip-A-Dee-Doo-Dah'; Leo Underwood urinated as he walked, indifferent to spattering his boots; and Jim Six, who wasn't used to mixing bourbon, tobacco, and bad news, tossed away his soggy, half-chewed cigar, bent over his knees and vomited copiously.

The hunters stopped securing gates after themselves, and they leaned a little forward as they trudged ahead, but so gradual was the incline they were mounting that none of them took any real note of it. Corn gave way to stubblefield, stubblefield to pasture. Pasture rose to woodlands.

Faraway, a dim yipping, and a squeal.

Whistler stopped and cocked his head. They all stopped. The squealing came again, this time trailed by a small shout – was that what it was? It sounded miles off. 'Rat and the kid,' Whistler said in a whisper, but everyone heard. Without realizing, they'd bunched together as they'd entered the timbered hills, where the land made a difference, where it rolled and gave way under the feet, rose and fell, and seemed, to Meteor Frmka, as he stood listening with the others, to breathe in and breathe out.

IV

THEY SPOTTED THE BOY EATING A CANDY BAR ATOP A GAUNT BOULDER ALONG the creekbottom. When he saw the line of men dipping toward him, the boy jumped down, waded knee-deep into a beaver pond, and pulled something out of the water. He held it up dripping and threw it into the mud on the bank. 'Your rat-dog found himself a coon!' he yelled up at the party.

Whistler began to run. He knelt close to the animal on the bank, but didn't touch it. The rest of the party gathered up behind. It wasn't a raccoon; it was his dog Rat. On the back of the dog's head was a bloody gash shaped like a smile. 'Coon drownded him right here,' the boy said.

'Smart coon'll do that,' Leo said.

Randall put his Labs on a down-and-stay command. He came forward and regarded the dead dog, then the kid. 'You watched?'

The boy looked away. 'From a distance.' He pointed off in a general direction. 'From off that way.'

'And the dog was dead when you got here?' Randall asked.

The boy didn't flinch. 'Whaddaya think? I come down here, found it half-dead, and put it out of its misery?'

Randall didn't know what he thought. He kept looking at the dead animal and thinking how the boy had picked it up and tossed it carelessly into the mud like you might a squirrel or some other vermin but not somebody's dog.

With one hand Whistler lifted the dog's head from the mud, and with the other he covered the bloody gash.

People were milling. 'Goddamn,' Frmka said. From him the oath sounded funny. 'Maybe we oughtta call this one a day.' It was a good idea, more than one of them thought so, but its coming from Frmka made it impossible to admit.

Whistler gently lowered his dog's head back to the mud and stared at him. 'I would've sworn he was smarter than this,' he said in a low voice.

Frank Mears wasn't interested in dead pets. 'Coon went off that way,' he said, nodding at tracks.

'Shoot the coon dead when we find him,' Leo said.

'I'll help dig if you want to bury him,' Randall said to Whistler, but before he could speak, Frank Mears said, 'Dead's dead,' and Leo said, 'Let's just leave him a natural part of the food chain,' and, Whistler, by saying nothing, by just staring at the dead animal, assented.

Mears whistled up his dogs, who had edged close to sniff at the muddy carcass, then began walking. The others followed. Whistler, in the rear, looked back just once.

To the north, clouds began to pack. The air seemed to thicken. The hunters zippered their vests and threw long shadows as they sloped up toward a ridge, not talking, just looking for something moving to shoot at. It had rained here; the ground was soft and the walking was quiet. When they got to the ridge, which overlooked a steep-walled coulee and widened to meadow, Jim Six said, 'Where in holy shit are we?' and looked around at faces full of *Who cares?* 'How come nothing lives here?' he said. 'How come there aren't any sounds? Or crows?' He thought about it. 'Anybody seen a single fucking *crow?*

Silence. Hardly any of them had seen Jim Six get this worked up before. Hardly any of them had seen him this shellacked before. Somebody noticed he was no longer wearing the fluorescent, hot-pink hunting vest Janine Hyde had given him, and thought to ask where it had gone to.

Jim Six grinned lopsidedly and scanned the faces until he got to Marlen's. 'Lost it,' Jim said, directing his strangely unhinged grin at Marlen.

A chill passed through Frmka and, though it wasn't from cold, he turned up his collar.

Frank Mears, attended by his dogs, walked twenty yards off from the rest of the party and in plain view dropped his pants to his ankles, squatted, and shat.

'Well now, that's bohemian,' Whistler said after a moment, trying to make light. If it had been anybody but Mears, the party would've lobbed insults or stones enough to drive him waddling from view, but it wasn't anybody else. It was Mears, and Mears did what he wanted.

'Well,' said Jim Six, returning to his theme, 'I've walked about fifty miles and I'd like at the fucking least to fucking shoot a fucking crow.'

Leo, who'd been chucking rocks at an empty pint bottle he'd set on a log, said, 'Fucking Six-Man's fucking cranky.'

For a moment Jim Six seemed not only speechless but suddenly afraid of speechlessness. He gave his head a quick shake and said, 'What kinda place is it that even fucking crows don't go?'

No-one else said anything. Then, after a while, Whistler did. '*Is* something queer about this place.' He tilted his head. 'You can feel it. It's like something's missing.'

Leo, looking for another rock, said, 'Think it's women.'

Nobody laughed. Nobody was laughing at anything.

It was while this silence deepened that Meteor Frmka made his mistake. He opened his mouth and reminded them of himself. 'An old guy named American Horse told me Crazy Horse is buried up here someplace,' he said. 'On a ridge east of Beaver Creek that nothing grows on. He said he did his vision quest here.' Frmka looked around and knew he was in trouble. Partly it was the way he saw meanness begin to enliven the men's dull sullen faces, partly it came from a lifetime spent keenly attuned to other people's rising resentments. 'That's where you fast till it comes.'

Frmka felt everybody turning toward him with stilled faces. Quickly he said, 'Maybe it wasn't here. I don't know why I thought it was here.'

The others just stared at him. Leo Underwood felt something pleasantly evil coming out inside himself. He waggled his flattened soda straw between his teeth. He worked a finger in his ear and grinned. He said, 'Meteor, buddy, I believe it's time you show us them toes.'

Frmka looked stricken.

It was Randall who with surprising quickness armlocked Frmka from behind and slammed him to the damp ground, where his head made a small crater. He kept him pinned there while Leo tore off Frmka's boots and socks, and lifted Frmka's stubby feet for viewing. The toes were the attraction; all but the big ones were wrapped with bandages. Leo ripped each off slowly.

LETS

was tattooed on the knuckles of the right toes, and tattooed on the left was

USDO

'Whatzit say?'

'Let's us do!' whooped Leo. He let Frmka's feet drop. 'The meteoroid told me *confidentially* that it's how he's going to propose to Merna Littlefield. He's going to whip off his boots and show her them toes!'

Most of the others made a point of a big laugh. Frmka sat on the ground pulling on his boots, his face beginning to collapse around his mouth. He wasn't going to cry, but he wanted to. In a small voice he said, 'Tattoo was your idea, Leo.'

Leo wagged his chewing straw and spread a smirk all around. 'This is what happens,' he said. 'Mears and me are outta gas money so we in our wisdom let the meteoroid drive us to Scenic. He gets fall-down drunk. We visit the whorehouse. He feels remorse. He feels real disloyal to his gal. So when he sees the tattoo parlor, he barges right in. I ask what he has in mind. "Message to Merna in a private location," he says. I think he's talking pecker so I say, "Better make it short." '

More loud, bitter laughter.

When it quieted, Randall, who for the last long minute had been staring at Frmka with real curiosity, spoke up. 'So whad she say when you peeled off your socks and popped the question?'

Frmka lowered his eyes. 'Haven't yet.' When he looked up again, Leo's nephew was staring at him and sucking on a Sugar Daddy at the same time. The boy was staring with the same frank disgust he'd directed at Whistler's dog when it was dragging its hind end throught the dirt. Frmka turned from the boy and didn't look at anybody else. He quietly moved twenty or thirty feet away from the rest of the pack and stared off toward the meadow below.

'Let's us do!' Leo whooped, hoping to keep things going.

Whistler Simpson stared at Frmka standing perfectly still off by himself, staring out, hoping to be left alone, as Whistler himself had done more than once on schoolyards in his youth, and so, when Leo in his needling voice once again said, 'Let's us do,' Whistler Simpson said, 'You know, Leo, you're an asshole for about twelve different reasons.'

Leo turned sharply to Whistler and, in a tight voice that was impressive for all the meanness he was able to squeeze inside it, said, 'Maybe the whistling idiot would like to give me a lesson in etiquette.'

'Screw you, Leo,' Whistler said lamely, and let his eyes slide away.

In mimicking falsetto Leo said, '*Screw you, Leo,*' and, sorry Whistler wouldn't rise to the bait, he shot a menacing look at Frmka, who was still staring off, but fixedly now, as if at something of real interest, as if he thought his moment of danger had passed and he could go on to other things, and Leo suddenly realized the episode with Frmka didn't feel anything like complete. 'See a dime down there?' he asked. 'Or is it a dollar?'

Frmka started, and quickly pulled his gaze free of the sight he'd been holding in view. 'What?' he said, but it came out sounding abrupt and oddly high-pitched.

'*What?*' Leo croaked and, folding his hands into his armpits, began to flap his elbows and croak raucously. '*What! What! What!*' Then, while staring at Frmka, he said to Jim Six, 'Now doesn't that sound like the crow you was looking for, Jim?'

Leo cast a look at Jim Six, who was grinning sloppily, and then at Mears, who was studying Frmka, and trying to follow his gaze to the valley below. 'Whaddaya see?'

Meteor Frmka pretended he didn't hear.

'I asked what you saw,' Frank Mears said in his lowest, edgiest voice, and the boisterousness of the group stilled completely.

All his life Frmka would wonder why he did what he did next. He'd always had the idea that when the time came, when honor was required, he would act decently, maybe even nobly, but when the time came, he couldn't. He motioned Mears over to a place where the view was unobscured. From there he pointed down to a fringe of the meadow far below. Others clustered to look and then all of them were looking.

It was a couple, on a blanket in a square of pale sunlight.

'Lovebirds doing the work of increase,' Whistler Simpson said in an uncertain voice, and Leo said, 'Ain't their asses cold?' and Jim Six, peering down in a squint and presuming they were loking at a man and a woman, said, 'Who's the girl?' For a while then, nobody spoke. The party stared as one, slow-focusing eyes in wide slack faces. Of the couple below, the one on the bottom could hardly be seen. The man on top wore only a denim jacket and the back of his head blocked out his partner's private parts. Finally, Mears said, 'What am I seeing or am I seeing things?' Whistler was tweezing violently at his fleshy mole. When he released his fingers, a small, perfectly formed half-globe of dark blood formed on the head of the mole.

Leo went to one knee, fumbled his field glasses out of their case, looked into them for a few moments, and shrank back. He started to stand, and threw his arms out to steady himself, but sat heavily back down anyway.

'Feeling punk, Uncle Leo?' the boy said in a wide-awake voice.

Leo held the glasses out to Mears. 'That's Sharp Fish and Jim Biddle,' he said.

Everyone looked through the glasses except the boy. Faces changed. Jaws slackened and went tight. They all backed up, below the ridgeline, out of view from below.

Leo in a stiff whisper said to his nephew, 'Scoot now,' and pointed off. 'We'll meet you back at that stand of trees.'

When Leo turned his back on his nephew, the boy didn't move.

Frank Mears regarded the boy and in a tight low voice said to Leo, 'Is your bastard pissant nephew deaf as well as dumb?'

The boy gave Mears a long, closed-up look, then merely withdrew far enough to recede from their notice. Off to the side, Frmka withdrew, too, but kept going. He tried to walk calmly, quietly, though when he'd slipped from view he broke into a downhill dogtrot and just kept going, south, away from the shooting party, toward town, the Littlefield place, shelter from his thoughts.

Behind the ridgeline, out of view from the meadow below, the hunters collected without a word. They squatted in an arc, and Mears, like a quarterback, began glancing around, making his seedlike eyes felt. He liked what he saw. Their faces were flat, blank, waiting for instruction.

Whistler started to say something, but Mears said, 'Another time, buddy,' and flipped open Doc Parmalee's orange metal case and stared in at its contents. 'Maybe we'll tag us an exotic after all,' he said and made his long grin. He put his dogs on a stay command, and so did Randall. They all slipped out of their hunting colors. Frank Mears moved forward in a stoop. They all did, a single file of stooping men, Mears in the lead. The boy hung back but kept coming. Randall followed Mears, who followed a narrow deer path. They began to descend toward the meadow. Nobody spoke. Walls of air pressed in from all sides. Randall didn't like it. He didn't like any of this. It bothered his stomach. He stopped almost experimentally. To his surprise, the others flowed silently around him. It was like he'd been water and now he was rock. They all went by without a word and then, a little time later, the boy silently passed by, too.

Randall stood staring at them. They moved stoopingly along their makeshift path, working their way down the steep-sided canyon, growing smaller, turning in and out of view, but moving always closer to the unmindful couple in the clearing. Randall turned and climbed to the ridgeline and with his dogs headed south, in the direction of home. Almost at once he imagined he heard something rising from the meadow behind him – a whistling of 'Blue Moon' that was soft and slow and seemed already to issue from regret – but when Randall stopped and cocked his head, he heard nothing, nothing at all.

V

IF, IN THE TWILIGHT OF AN AUTUMN DAY, IN A HIGH MEADOW NORTH OF
goodnight and east of Beaver Creek, malice swelled and good sense
fell away and lives jumped course ... other less unlikely things
happened that day, too, before night fell. During the Lutheran
social hour, Eleanor Tyler unveiled her just-completed ceramic
reproductions of the forty-one US presidents; Robert Jackson killed
a badger that had molested his chickens in broad daylight; Carl
Smith made that very morning's *World-Herald* with a photograph
of a double radish shaped like a heart; Randall Hunsacker returned
to his trailer-home and found that his wife Marcy was gone and so
was her car and most of her clothes and all of their cash; Marlen
Coates went into the bedroom where he and Janine Hyde had spent
the night and found a note propped on the pillow that said, wishfully,
This never happened; and Meteor Frmka, without taking off his shoes
or socks, sat in the darkening kitchen of Al and Esther Littlefield and
proposed marriage to their daughter Merna, who, while giving way
to tears, whispered, 'Yes, yes, a thousand times, yes.'

Chapter Fourteen

ASH

AFTERWARDS, RANDALL WOULD BEGIN TO LIVE IN A MOTEL ROOM IN PINE Bluff. When he did finally come back to the trailer for his clothes, it had the irresistible allure of a house where someone had recently died, or been killed. The milk in the refrigerator was bad, but the bread was good. In the bedroom, Randall put some of his clothes in paper sacks but couldn't leave. He opened the drawers of Marcy's dresser. He tried to find her scent on one of her T-shirts, but smelled only soap. The green bustier he'd brought her from California was still in the bottom drawer, but some of her other lingerie, the things Marcy liked best, were gone. Randall found a large cardboard box and stuffed it with all of Marcy's clothes. He took the box out to the carport and set it down. He brought a wheelbarrow around from the metal shed behind the trailer and began a little paper fire within it. He added cardboard, kindling, scrap wood. When the wood was burning hot, Randall fed Marcy's clothes into the fire, one article at a time, beginning with the green bustier.

Chapter Fifteen

WINTER IN LOS ANGELES

MARCY WAS AWAKE, BUT PRETENDING NOT TO BE, WHEN RANDALL HAD RISEN that Saturday before dawn to go pheasant hunting with friends. She lay in bed listening. Randall didn't turn on lights and loud music, as he usually did. No, he was getting ready to go hunting and for once in his life he was being quiet about it. He sounded almost like a prowler, in fact, the slow, cautious way he moved through the dark trailer-home, setting out his coat and gear, wrapping up sandwiches, feeling in the closet for a gun. When he stepped outside, he set the front door softly to behind him. There was a clinking sound as he eased open the metal kennel gate, and the tinkling of collars as the dogs crossed the yard and bounded into the truck. The truck door opened and closed, the engine started and idled.

But the truck door opened again, and then the front door to their trailer. Randall moved slowly along the dark narrow hallway toward their bedroom – under his boots, the trailer trembled slightly on its piers – then stopped at the open door. Marcy was turned from him, but she could feel him there staring in. Finally he came near and touched his hand to her neck. She didn't move. When he spoke, his voice was gentler than usual. 'Guess you know I'm sorry I hit you,' he said. 'I laid there in bed all night trying to figure out how I could've done that. And you were saying so many things.' His voice trailed off. 'Marcy?'

She still didn't move.

His voice was low and serious. 'Well, I just want to say that I love you, no matter what. Even if I wanted to, that's something I couldn't ever change.'

Marcy opened the one good eye and turned over in bed without speaking. She and Randall peered at each other in the darkness, but she could only guess at what was in his face. Looking through just the one eye was strange – it threw off her depth perception and made the distance between them seem uncertain. Some seconds passed before she saw that he'd brought one of his shotguns into the room with him. 'What's that for?' she said. Her voice was sleepier, softer than she wanted it.

'It's the wrong one. I'm putting it back for something else.' He forced a little laugh. 'Shoulda turned on the light, I guess.' She didn't say anything. With three fingers she was delicately exploring the edges of the bad eye. He said, 'If you want, Marcy, I won't go. I'll call Leo and tell him . . .' This was a sticking point for Randall – lying was something he prided himself in not doing. 'I'll tell him we both feel punk and I need to lay low.'

'No,' Marcy said, 'it's nice to offer, but it wouldn't help that much.'

'Truth is, I'd rather stay,' he said and stood waiting. The silence lengthened. In the darkness his face seemed like a sad, ghostly mask of his face. At last he said, 'Okay then, Marcy, Sugar. I'm going now.'

He did. He went, Randall and his dogs.

After he left, Marcy went to the mirror and looked at the one eye. She commanded it to open, but it lifted only slightly and painfully. When, with her forefinger, she delicately retracted the eyelid, she could see only dim light. Marcy closed the eye and left it closed. She dressed, retrieved her car from its parking place in the RV storage yard, and moved in a daze back and forth from the trailer-home to the car, not thinking, just taking what she could and piling it into the trunk and back seat. She kept at it until the sky began to lighten. Not too far off, the sudden sound of somebody's television news moved through the still cold air. Across the street, in another trailer-home, a light went on. Marcy put on her dark glasses. She didn't write a note. She didn't consider what more she ought to take. She got into her old Mercury Cougar and began slowly to drive away from her home and hometown, her parents and her husband.

She drove south out of Goodnight, through Alliance and Pine Bluff, toward Cheyenne, where, beyond her range of acquaintances, she would swing the Mercury west onto I–80, toward California.

Once she settled into the drive, a low-grade melancholy overtook her. Old sights put her in mind of Randall, and old songs, so while she drove she tuned instead to call-in self-help shows, people with terrible-sounding lives talking to announcers who believed they had all the answers even though Marcy personally doubted it. Every now and then Marcy glanced at the radio and said, 'Well, that's one theory.' Her favorite thing to say to a caller was, 'Join the club, Lady.' But, once, when a woman doctor left a caller speechless by saying, 'Listen up, Honey, desires affect decisions and decisions have consequences and you have to take responsibility for those consequences,' Marcy was suddenly overcome with sadness. She could see nothing but the caved-in look of Randall's face when he came home and found her gone. What would he do? What in the world would he do? He would swallow it whole, she knew that. He would tell no-one. Would answer not one question from one friend. He would swallow it whole and bear it alone. He would become one of those thin still men with gray eyes and stubbled beards and stained coats whose insides were not right, whose sadness made a perfect nesting place for cancers. She'd pulled into a rest stop to rest her eye. There was a statue of Lincoln, but it was cold out, and she stayed in the car. So mixed were her impulses that when she looped the Mercury out of the parking lot, she wasn't positive which onramp she would take, the one going west or the one going back. She went west.

It took two days, driving like this, to make the desert. She had her ups and downs. Late the second night, she crested the Cajon pass and dropped into the San Bernardino Valley, a vast blackness dotted with what seemed like a million million shimmering lights. Marcy, in that jangly state of hope that sometimes comes from travel alone across wide open spaces, saw each dot not as a light but as a person, a single person, suddenly come to life and made bright and brand new. That was one moment. In the next, she wished more than anything that Randall were here, too, so they could both start new.

*   *   *

ON HER FIRST MORNING IN LA, MARCY DROVE ALONG SUNSET BOULEVARD,
past places she'd only heard of – Frederick's, Grauman's, the Roxy, the
Whiskey. To her surprise, there were frightening people everywhere.
When a man in black leather pants, no shirt, and lemon yellow hair
glanced at her license plate, stepped out of the crosswalk and,
leaning into her window, drawled, 'Miss Nebraska, I'd like you to
meet Mr Peanut,' Marcy wound up the window and didn't lower it
again until the street turned residential.

Further on, in a normal-seeming commercial section of town,
Marcy went into the first realty she liked the looks of. It was a
big, oddly formal office with thick gray carpet and, on each of the
many white desks, a small vase of bright flowers that Marcy had
never seen in Nebraska. She asked about rentals and got passed
around. The men in the office wore blazers and ties. The women
went for skirt suits, a nice look, Marcy thought, though it was
hard to tell exactly because she didn't want to take off her dark
glasses.

One man in the office seemed to change the way everyone else
acted. He was a stiff, frail-seeming man in wire-rimmed spectacles,
white shirt, and burgundy bow-tie, the man, Marcy realized, who
was the source of the office's formality. A trim secretary followed
behind as he went through the office desk to desk, chatting briefly
with different agents. Each stiffened slightly at his approach. 'A rental,
sir,' the agent helping Marcy told the man and then they passed on,
the frail man, his secretary, and her perfume.

'Whew!' Marcy said in a low voice of the perfume, and in the
same low voice the agent, still clacking away at his computer, said,
'It's not that Mr Realty likes it potent. It's that Mr Realty's got no
sense of smell.'

Marcy laughed. In a funny, happy way this was what, without
ever having put a finger on it, she had wanted from Los Angeles.
This fancy office. The muttering help. The frail, feared executive.
Marcy kept her eye on him. He was talking on the telephone while
filling his briefcase with papers. When he looked her way, Marcy
did something that surprised her. She tilted her head and combed her
fingers through her long hair, a method of flirtation she'd developed
way back in high school but which, here and now, seemed suddenly

klutzy. The man snapped closed his briefcase, handed the phone to his secretary, moved through the office in stiff strides, past Marcy and her agent. But he stopped, turned back.

'Look, Miss,' he said, 'I know of a place that's not listed, a nicely old-fashioned studio. May I ask if you smoke?'

Marcy, looking up at him, knew this was the moment when anyone with an ounce of politeness would take off her sunglasses, but she couldn't. 'No,' she said.

'Pets?'

'Nope.'

'Drugs?'

Marcy stifled a laugh. 'Hardly.'

The man asked a few more questions. His glasses were Coke-bottle thick and, behind them, his eyes were hard to read. Quiet? he asked. Responsible? Employed, or soon will be? Marcy smiled and said yes to each.

For a moment she could almost hear him thinking her over. 'Okay,' he said, 'why don't I just run you up there and show you the place.'

The car they drove away in was white, enormous, and deeply quiet. 'This is like driving in a new refrigerator,' Marcy said, going for a joke, but the man merely responded by turning down the air conditioning. 'Two stops to make,' he said, almost to himself. With one hand he unsnapped the briefcase lying on the leather seat between them and brought out a roll of chocolate toffees. Before partaking himself, he offered one to Marcy, who wanted to accept, but didn't.

The first stop was at a place called Prestige Motors on Melrose Avenue. The man left Marcy in the car while he went inside, where the salesmen treated him a lot like the people in the real estate office had. They smoothed their clothes and worked their faces into smiles. It was funny to watch. Also funny to watch was the way the man walked. He was so stiff that Marcy imagined that someone had just wound him up and pointed him her way. When he got back in, she said, 'That where you bought this car?'

The man stared at the car agency and without evident offense said, 'This car was a little newer than those.'

After he'd accelerated smoothly into traffic, Marcy said, 'You left me and your keys in the car.'

The man said nothing, made a lane change, turned up a narrowing canyon road.

'I could've stolen this big, fancy, newer car of yours,' Marcy said.

The tiniest smile formed on the man's lips. 'It was part of my tenant-screening process.' He gave her a quick sidelong look. 'You seem to have passed.' For the first time, Marcy sensed something playful in the man's formality. And he had the right voice for it. Besides his brains and expensive clothes, it was the voice, Marcy decided, that had gotten this man up in the world. It was a clear, pure voice that went into your ear in a ticklish way. Marcy gave him another look. Forty-two to forty-four, she thought. Marcy would soon turn twenty-four.

Their second stop was at the man's home, perched on a cliff out among tall, slender, smooth-barked trees. Marcy waited in the car. As the realtor approached his house, a male gardener very slightly picked up the pace of his clipping, but a woman in gardening clothes merely pushed back her dark red hair with the heel of her hand and said something before she resumed puttering with the potted flowers along the walk. Marcy picked up the tube of toffees. *Callard & Bowser*, it said on the foiled outer wrap, *Made in Great Britain*. Inside, each toffee was neatly wrapped in waxpaper. She slipped one into her mouth, fiddled with the radio, then the car windows. As they slid quietly down, a pleasant menthol smell wafted in from the outside air. She asked about it when the man returned.

'Lemon eucalyptus.' He pointed to the tall, smooth-barked trees.

The man drove slowly, the road spiraling upward. He started to set the toffees back into his briefcase, but paused to hold the roll out to Marcy. 'Another?' he said and she said, 'Nope, one was fine.'

A turn in the road afforded a sudden, sweeping view of the city. The car slowed just a little. 'That's the way it used to be,' he said. 'You could see Catalina Island almost every day. It was a wide-open world then.' He stole a last look before resuming speed. More tall eucalyptus passed by, more snug bungalows. The man said, 'One day, when I was ten or eleven, I walked into the Sav-On drugstore at

3rd and Fairfax and found myself standing at the candy counter not far from a man who seemed dimly familiar. My eyes were terrible even then, so, without much awareness of doing it, I began edging closer and closer to this man, squinting up at him until I was so close I could smell his heavy tobacco smell. At the exact moment that I realized that he was in fact Bela Lugosi, he curled his lip and let out a hissing sound that scared the pea-wadding out of me.' A small, self-mocking chuckle slipped from the realtor. 'I hastily retired. But as I was climbing onto my bicycle, a clerk caught up to me with a box of Callard & Bowser toffee. There was also a note, which I still possess, that said, "With this gift Mr Bela Lugosi wishes to commemorate the pleasant occasion of your acquaintance." '

The realtor glanced at Marcy. 'This reminds me that we haven't been formally introduced.' He kept his left hand on the wheel, short-armed his right toward her. 'I'm Harmon Martin.'

That was what the sign had said in front of the real estate office. HARMON MARTIN'S MR REALTY. Marcy decided to slip a small one by him. 'Marcy Marlene Lockhardt,' she said, 'but everybody calls me Lena.' This was untrue. Nobody in her lifetime had called her Lena.

Harmon Martin released her hand. 'So where are you from, Lena?'

Marcy considered lying about this, too, but worried that the man might've seen the plate on her car. 'Nebraska.' She expected him maybe to ask what part of Nebraska, but he didn't.

'I think of Nebraska as a kind of English-speaking foreign country,' Harmon Martin said and made a smile so small Marcy wondered if she imagined it. 'All that *swaggering* and *roping* and *branding*.'

'They don't brand so much anymore,' Marcy said. 'Mostly they just tag their ears.'

'Ah,' Harmon Martin said softly.

They fell silent. Marcy leaned out the window, stared up at the slender, smooth white trees, took into her lungs this new, mentholated air.

After a while she said to the man, 'Your wife's pretty.'

Harmon Martin looked at her in surprise. 'Yes, she is.' Then, 'How did you know she was my wife and not, let us say, a fetching, Hollywood Hills gardener?'

Because she wasn't like all the others. She treated Harmon Martin like just another human being. 'I could just tell,' Marcy said, and as they drove along a fact presented itself like a utensil she had no use for, namely that if a woman wanted to get to Harmon Martin, the way to do it was to force him to imagine everything, and allow him to touch nothing.

MARCY LOVED THE STUDIO. IT HAD HARDWOOD FLOORS, WHITE WALLS AND, beyond the parted French doors, an enameled deck with solid siding. 'For total privacy,' Harmon Martin said in an abstracted voice, as if he were saying one thing and thinking another. She asked about rent, and was shocked at how high the figure was. 'You're kidding,' she said.

'I know. It's a very good deal. The owner could get quite a lot more, but won't advertise. She's afraid of the riff-raff.' He gazed down the canyon toward the freeway. 'You'll get a nice view at night.'

She stared out.

'This a Los Angeles address or Hollywood or what?'

'You're in the city of LA, but the mailing address is Hollywood.' He glanced at her. 'Have you by any chance heard of Tom Hulce?'

'*Amadeus.*'

Harmon Martin seemed pleased. 'Yes. A good young actor, I'd say. He lived here nearly two years, until his salaries grew. He has a reputation, but he left the place neat as a pin.'

Marcy knew she shouldn't take the apartment, but said she would. She took out her folded cash, counted out the first two months' rent, and presented it to Harmon Martin, who, moving close as if to take it, instead reached forward and gently slid off Marcy's sunglasses. In the change in his face, she saw what he saw: a swollen eye almost the color of eggplant with a yellowish subsurface. He slid the glasses back and stepped away. 'Who's the party responsible for this?'

Marcy answered quickly, as if there were only one answer. 'A guy.' She looked away. 'My husband actually.'

Harmon Martin stared at her. 'This isn't, I hope, an accepted form of husbandry out there in the hinterlands.'

'No,' Marcy said, pinkening a little, she wasn't sure why. She also wasn't sure what Harmon Martin was up to. He still hadn't taken the money.

'So is this imbecile husband going to be a problem?' Harmon Martin asked.

Marcy felt funny, letting this man call Randall an imbecile, which Randall was not, but she shook her head certainly. 'No,' she said, 'no problem whatsoever.'

MARCY LIKE THE NEIGHBOURHOOD, SMOOTH-PLASTER COTTAGES NESTLED INTO the hillside, as different from Nebraska as different could be. She'd painted the mailbox blue and was nearly finished stencilling L. LOCKHARDT in yellow when a dog arrived, a small, bowlegged Dobermann mix with a frisbee in his mouth. He dropped it at her feet and looked up expectantly. She threw it, it wobbled off, the dog retrieved it. They did this several times. The dog's focus on the frisbee was absolute. Marcy could make him shake or nod his head by either waving the frisbee side to side or up and down. She kneeled down, held the frisbee overhead, and in a low voice said, 'Will I find a job in television?'

The dog nodded a slow yes.

'Will Randall find me?'

No.

'Will I find someone?'

An even more definite yes. Marcy laughed.

'Am I the fairest in the land?'

Yes.

Marcy laughed and tossed the frisbee a few more times, until it got too slobbery to throw. The dog took no offense. He merely picked up his toy and trotted away, looking suprisingly businesslike. He knew what he wanted and how to get it. He visited strangers, dropped this plastic disc at their feet, and gave them the chance to make him happy. It seemed so simple.

A FEW DAYS LATER, MARCY SAT IN THE SUN ON THE PRIVATE DECK HUGGING HER knees. She'd come to LA with the idea of working in television, but the truth was, except for Julie Thies's cousin who was an assistant director on *The New Price is Right*, and who, it turned out, had left yesterday for Berlin, Marcy knew no one in LA She thumbed through a *Variety* with her right eye closed. Something was still wrong with that eye. She could see from it only fuzzily. The shiner had healed, but the eye floated, felt unhinged, drooped to the left. Below the eye, a weepy pink sag had developed.

Marcy put down the paper and didn't know how many minutes had gone by when she realized that, in this space of time, however long it was, all she'd done was look at her feet. There was so much *time* here. In Goodnight, there were tons of ways to keep yourself busy, but here it was like a vacation, except with all the fun drained away because there was no stop to it.

Somewhere a dog barked, but not the frisbee dog, she knew his bark by now. It was 79 degrees, mid-November. Marcy lay back on her towel, closed her eyes and tilted her face to meet the exact angle of the sun. What she wanted was something in the television or movie business, not in acting or anything big. Just something that helped keep things going day to day.

She told Harmon Martin this the next time he telephoned, which he did fairly often. Just checking in on the newest leaseholder, he would say dryly. 'Sure you wouldn't like to shoot a little higher?' he said today.

'Naw. I like to shoot at things I have a chance of hitting,' Marcy said.

Harmon Martin made a little humming sound, then said he'd do some asking around, see what he could turn up.

THANKSGIVING DAY, MARCY CALLED HOME AND WAS SWARMED OVER BY questions. 'Where are you?' her mother asked. 'Are you okay? Do you have enough money? What're you doing? Are you coming home?'

'Not for a while yet,' Marcy said, 'but I'm fine, Mom. I am.'

'But where –'

'Someplace warmer,' Marcy said. 'Has he been asking, do you know?'

'Not that I know of. His friend Leo was asking around for a while, but I don't know if that was on his own or for Randall.'

Marcy didn't know what to say. 'Is Dad okay then?' she asked finally.

'He'll be better now, knowing you're okay. Provided you are.'

'I am, Mom. I really am.'

After a little silence, her mother said, 'We heard he hit you.'

'Where'd you hear that?'

'Flossie Boyles. I guess your neighbor saw your face the morning you left.'

Marcy didn't say anything.

'Why would he want to do that?'

'He had it in his head that I was running around, Mom.'

'But you weren't.'

'Nope. But I couldn't convince him, he had it so much in his head.'

This much was true, but the larger truth was that Marcy had concluded she'd married the wrong man. She didn't want to spend her life in an ingrown town with an ingrown man who wouldn't be happy until she was ingrown, too. Almost without realizing it, Marcy had wanted out. And she needed Randall to give her a good enough reason to go, so she invented and told him a story that she had wanted to believe might puncture Randall's fears, but in fact had been instinctively shaped to feed and animate Randall's anger. She'd poked at his soft spot and hadn't stopped. At the moment Randall struck her, he was more surprised than she was. Marcy knew this. And for this entrapment of Randall's pitiful worst self, Marcy was beginning to believe that she could never be forgiven.

In a soft voice to her mother, Marcy said, 'So do you think Randall's doing okay?'

'I wouldn't know. He doesn't call and they say he hardly speaks when spoken to. He still goes to work, I guess, but he stays mostly now in Pine Bluff. People say he's hardly been at the trailer. It's a mess, they say.'

A silence on the line, then Marcy said, 'I'll call again soon, okay? I love you, and tell Dad I love him, too.'

Later that day, Marcy cooked herself Thanksgiving dinner for one – a cornish game hen, fresh peas, and a yam – then sat looking at it. She took a few bites, wrapped the rest in foil for the frisbee dog and went outside, but he was nowhere to be found. She climbed a winding set of public stairs to the top of a knoll where a small park was maintained, and where the dog lay sleeping. He stretched, then wagged his nubby tail. 'Happy Thanksgiving,' Marcy said as he

greedily bolted the food. Marcy was gazing down at the city when –
a slight shock – she realized that from here there was a narrow line
of downward sight to Harmon Martin's house. She stood looking into
the brightly lighted kitchen where guests were milling. She could
pick out Harmon Martin from among the men – he seemed to be
mixing drinks, measuring things very carefully – but she couldn't
be certain which of the women was his wife. From this distance,
the women seemed to be of a different species. All of them looked
elegant, handsome, and happy.

HARMON MARTIN HAD LINED UP THREE JOB INTERVIEWS FOR MARCY, ALL ON
the same day. 'Trial by fire,' he said. 'But my advice is not to commit
to anything. Say you have another offer pending, that you will tell
them something definite within seventy-two hours.'

'Three days,' Marcy said.

'But you might say hours,' Harmon Marton said and added his
little smile. 'In order to create the impression that your time units
are small, compressed, and important.'

The interviews were a nightmare. Marcy wore a simple beige-and-
black dress that she hoped would seem elegant, but, she realized,
was made to be overlooked in. The men who interviewed her wore
more color than she did. They asked questions like, *What unique
talents can you bring to this job?* Marcy sweated, stammered, and
introduced to the room the kind of awkwardness that infects others.
At the final interview, the man broke a long, horrible silence by
picking up her application and reading through it. 'What's KDUH?'
he said finally.

'Channel 4 in northwest Nebraska.' She daubed at her eye to
keep the liquid in its pink sag from spilling down her cheek.
'For about six months I read the weekend news.' There was an
awkward pause. 'That was before my eye problem.' She waited
another moment, then blundered on. 'That occurred last fall during
a thunderstorm. I was standing at the kitchen window and lightning
hit a cottonwood just two or three feet away. That's what happened
to my eye.'

The man had smiled evenly during this preposterous tale. When
Marcy was done, he again glanced down at her résumé. 'What's the

ENG capacity there at KDUH?' he said and then, when he saw her confusion, 'The electronic newsgathering capacity.'

'Oh. I really don't know. I guess I should, but all I did was read the news.' She pulled out another tissue from her purse.

Later, when Harmon Martin telephoned to find out how the interviews went, Marcy said, 'Not that great.' She thought about it and said, 'Thinking about it makes me kind of tired.'

'You might be wrong. You might be pleasantly surprised. But it doesn't matter. Those fellows are flyweights, very small potatoes. So let's say we keep looking until we find just the right fit.'

The right fit, Marcy thought. Fitting in. When she realized she might begin to cry, she made a quick excuse and said goodbye.

ANOTHER SUNNY DAY. WHERE SHE HAD COME FROM, WEATHER DICTATED activities and affected moods, and Marcy missed the little indicators. The smell of burning leaves, the creak of frozen porch-boards, Randall carrying the fresh smell of winter with him into a warm room. But December in southern California was relentlessly green, leafy, and bright. There was only the changing angle of the sun as it streamed onto the deck, where Marcy spent her afternoons reading and tanning.

Marcy had been offered a job. She could work as a cocktail waitress at a country-western place called the Palomino. Harmon Martin had nothing to do with this. Marcy saw the ad, called up, drove out to the valley. A woman looked her over the way a man would and said, 'The one position's filled. But there's another opening next month if you can you wait that long.'

Marcy said she could, but in truth she wasn't so sure about the job. The money would be good, and she wouldn't mind the get-up, but it seemed so different out here. In Goodnight, she knew how to say no to men because she knew who they were and they knew who she was.

A crow glided past Marcy's deck. Marcy blinked, realized she'd been thinking of Randall. Of the tons of things she knew she shouldn't do, the one she knew she shouldn't do most of all was think about Randall, but she couldn't always help it. Usually she hoped Randall was with somebody, but today, a bad sign, she hoped he wasn't. She sat down and wrote Randall a long rushing letter full of explanation and questions and soft thoughts. Without reading it over, she sealed it and meant to walk it down the canyon to the mailbox before the last pick-up, but when she opened the door, Harmon Martin was standing there about to knock. He hadn't saved her, not in any real sense, but when she awakened the next morning with the letter still in her purse, she would allow herself to think of it in almost that way.

Harmon Martin had come to the door because he had news. 'Something quite remarkable.' He made his little, self-knowing smile. 'A significant interview.'

'Who with?' she said, but he merely winked. He'd brought makings for what he called 'a celebratory gimlet.' He mixed it precisely, savored his first sip. 'Well,' he said, seating himself. 'I put in a word with a colleague. The colleague put in a word for me.' He took his handkerchief from his suit pocket, fogged and cleaned his thick glasses, held them to the light, gave them a finishing touch. He slid them on, looked beamingly at Marcy. 'You have an interview on Tuesday, January 17th, 10 a.m., for the position of assistant to the personal secretary of Mr Steven Spielberg.'

Marcy stood frozen for a moment. 'This isn't some kind of joke?'

'That's correct,' Harmon Martin said. 'It is not.'

Marcy gave him a quick kiss on the cheek before walking about the apartment in a state of agitation. 'You did it,' she said, as much to herself as to him and then, beside herself, she whooped, '*Hot chaw!*' – a phrase that made Harmon Martin actually chuckle, a phrase that Marcy had never used before, a phrase that until now had been exclusively Randall's. She danced up to Harmon Martin, slipped off his glasses, put them on herself, kept dancing. She took his hand and, against his protests, pulled him up to dance. He moved mechanically for a minute or so, then retreated to his chair. It was a surprise, the pleasure Marcy felt in this rich man's boyish embarrassment, and yet it was endearing, too. 'The awful truth is, your Harmon Martin can't dance,' he said. He smiled weakly. 'If I'd thought it was pertinent, I'd have told you sooner.'

ON CHRISTMAS MORNING, MARCY DIALED HER OLD NUMBER IN NEBRASKA, imagined the telephone on the coffee table in the living room of the trailer as it rang and rang. Finally she gave up and tried her parents' number. Her father answered on the second ring. '*Ha!*' he said when she said hello. 'I *knew* it was you. It was the third time it's rung today but this time I said to your mother, "It's her," and, sure enough, here you are.'

They talked amiably for a while, her father relying mostly on local crime stories to avoid touchy subjects. After telling about the stolen tractor discovered hidden in Ray Falon's haymow, he said, 'Okay, okay, I better give the phone to your mother before she turns blue.'

'Hi, Polkadot,' her mother said and, following a rush of questions, she took a breath and said, 'I was hoping you'd be home by now.'

'I think I'm here to stay, Mom. The people are nice to me and I'm beginning to like it.' Then, 'Did you get my presents okay?'

Marcy had sent presents anonymously through a mail-order catalogue, a Swiss chalet in a snow-globe for her mother and for her father a wooden set of six nesting presidents, each slightly smaller than the one in which it was enclosed. (Her father had always taken pride in his ability to tick off all forty-one US presidents in order.) To Randall she'd sent a pair of flannel boxer shorts in a duck-hunting pattern and a plaid electric blanket. She mentioned this and her mother said, 'I don't know that he'll receive those kindly.'

'Why's that?' Marcy said. She could tell her mother was thinking something over. 'What?'

'Oh, a story,' her mother said.

'About him and somebody else?'

'No, but how would you feel about that?'

'Fine. I want him to be happy, is all I want.'

'Well, I don't think he's so happy.'

'What makes you think that?'

Another pause, then, 'Well, according to Flossie Boyles, the story is that Randall took all your clothes out onto the carport by the trailer and heaped them up and burned them. Then he put the ashes into a tupperware container which, the story goes, he consumes a teaspoon at a time by spreading it over his meals.'

Marcy felt actually sickened. 'Mom?'

'What, Polkadot?'

But Marcy caught herself. The story she was about to tell would've just played into her mother's hands. 'I love you,' she said, 'and just tell Dad it's warm here and the people are nice to me and I miss him.'

What she had thought to describe to her mother was the recurring dream she'd been having. In it, she's brought Randall to the edge of a bluff overlooking the beach. They're both younger, in high school, happy, unsteady with laughter, trying to catch with their mouths black jelly beans they lob into the air. From the overhanging bluff face there is a steep, red-dirt channel, made by erosion, that looks like a long chute down to the beach. There is sheer happiness in Randall's face when Marcy brings him to it. He plunges down at once, on the seat of his pants, whooping at first, but the moment he turns a corner, beyond Marcy's view, his voice stops and there are loud sickening thuds as his body bumps its way down the rocky slope. Marcy runs for the stairs, but cannot go down to look.

THE FIRST WEEK OF JANUARY, MARCY BROWSED DEPARTMENT STORES FOR THE right thing to wear to her interview (no luck) and read everything about Steven Spielberg she could lay her hands on (the East Hampton inside-out barn in *Architectural Digest*, the money to Harvard for an extraterrestrial scanner in *Physics Today*, the rumors about Kate Capshaw in *People*). 'Steven's boyish,' said Richard Dreyfuss in *Life*, 'and financially canny, but the word that really nails him is adventurous.' In the background of one photograph, Marcy found his secretary. She was dark-haired, too. Like his first wife. Like Amy Irving. Like Kate Capshaw.

The next morning Marcy spent $75 on tinting her hair. 'That color,' she said to the hairdresser and pointed to a photograph of Kate Capshaw she'd torn out of a magazine.

This was the first of two changes Marcy made. The other was a neoprene eye patch a doctor had fitted for her, at Harmon Martin's expense. It stopped the leaking and it covered the abhorrent bad eye, but Marcy wasn't so sure about it. The first time she wore it outside the house, she turned away when a car neared. She whistled and before long the little bowlegged Dobermann trotted smartly around the corner carrying a new red frisbee. He dropped it at her feet. She picked it up, held it close to her head. 'Shall I wear the eye patch?'

Yes.

No.

She tossed the frisbee into the empty street. It skipped off the pavement and floated over the hillside. The dog leaped out into the air, disappeared over the side. For a moment, time stood still, then the dog reappeared, grinning around his red frisbee.

Whether she'd wear the eye patch, Marcy decided, would depend on the outfit she bought for the interview, but the days went by without her finding the right thing. Finally, the day before the interview, in the dressing room of Bullocks Wilshire, she began to cry. Everything that looked good on the rack looked horrible on her. She took off what she had on, went to the most stylish saleswoman on the floor and said, 'I'm looking for something for a job interview at Universal, something nice, but with a sense of adventure.'

WHEN MARCY ARRIVED FOR THE INTERVIEW, SHE WAS DIRECTED TO A LARGE, tightly quiet room where about a dozen applicants were already waiting. Most of the women were wearing tasteful coat dresses in navy or cream, expensive but not too expensive. Marcy's outfit, she realized, was just foolish. A semi-safari look, the saleswoman had called it. A khaki skirt, a Chinese peasant coat worn open to a tight, stretchy top in an orange color the saleswoman called quince. With suede flats, long, dangly, costume-gold earrings and a brimless red hat, the total was $625, more money than Marcy had, so she'd opened an instant charge account.

'I heard the job was as an aide to Steven Spielberg's private secretary,' Marcy said to the woman closest to her.

Several of the women turned to regard Marcy. One of them, before turning just slightly away, said, 'I hope you're right, Sweet Pea.'

At a little past noon, Marcy was given a brief interview by a man – it went

fine – and then was shown into a round, windowless room where she was left alone. The walls were meant to be funny, Marcy guessed, but they scared her a little. White Roman columns had been painted on every wall and door, with dark vines trailing from one to the other. Walking among the columns was an odd cast of creatures – browsing zebras, penguins with parasols, grim-faced businessmen in bowler hats. The room was furnished with just two black chairs and a white, glass-topped table. Standing on top of the table were a typewriter, a clock, a telephone and a leather-bound appointment book with the letter *M* embossed in one corner. Marcy was staring at the telephone when it began to ring. She answered and a woman's voice said, 'Miss Lockhardt, kindly check Mr. M's appointment book, confirm for Lafcadio's and with Miss Wittenburg at CBS, cancel everything between 1.15 and 3.25, and if Mr Wallace, White, or Wilson calls, advise them that Mr M will be out of the office until tomorrow.'

Marcy did these things, politely and, as far as she knew, correctly.

Shortly thereafter, as if of its own, a door Marcy hadn't seen before swung open, cleanly sweeping out most of a Roman column. A woman rode into the room on a wave of confidence and energy, gave her name as Connie DeVrie, and, after a glance at Marcy's outfit, said, 'What a *dramatic* coat!'

Connie DeVrie was wearing a dark gray, executive-looking skirt-suit.

'First a five-minute typing test,' she said and set the clock.

The text concerned itself with the stress capacities of concrete. Moments after Marcy started typing, the telephone rang. At the instant that Marcy picked it up, Connie DeVrie suspended time on the test. 'Mr M's office,' Marcy said as briskly as she could.

A woman said, 'Mr Wade's office for Mr M please.'

Wade. Marcy, uncertain, said, 'Your name again?' and the woman at the other end hung up without a word. Connie DeVrie started time running again and Marcy tried to concentrate on the typing. There were numbers and fractions everywhere. Marcy's fingers moved unsurely over the top row of the keyboard. Her bad eye watered, her good eye blurred. During the last minute of the test, she tried to think up something she might say to excuse her performance, but couldn't. She fought off the impulse to cry.

There were other tests, too, not quite as horrible, but almost.

When they were all completed, Connie DeVrie disappeared through the swinging door, tests in hand. From the inner sanctum beyond the wall, Marcy could hear rich male laughter, and then laughter from men and women together, until finally the wall swung open again, but not completely. Connie DeVrie used it like a shield, around which only her head appeared. She said she'd call Marcy when all the interviews were completed, then, before Marcy could say a word, Connie DeVrie closed the door that wasn't a door.

WHEN SHE RETURNED TO HER BUNGALOW, THE DOG WAS ASLEEP ON HER STOOP. The door was ajar. Through the window she could see Harmon Martin in shirt sleeves, wearing an apron, standing at the kitchen sink washing spinach leaves one by one. Marcy, stepping inside, asked how he got in.

'Key,' he said, with enough unconcern to annoy Marcy. He didn't look at her. He nodded toward the sinkful of carrot peelings. 'You know if you keep eating nothing but carrots, you'll turn yellow.'

She thought of telling him that the reason Howard Hawks wanted Lauren Bacall for *To Have and Have Not* was her yellow complexion, which looked good on film – it was the kind of story that interested Harmon Martin – but Marcy was too annoyed for small talk. When she said nothing, he turned and was brought up short.

'*Good grief*,' he said.

He'd never before seen the eye patch, the peasant coat, the quince-colored top. Marcy's shoulders dropped. 'I know, I know,' she said.

He laid down the spinach leaves. 'Look, Lena,' he said, 'I knew you were very attractive, but I didn't know you could be so . . . fetching.'

Marcy wondered if he was joking.

'I spoke to my colleague. He said the interview didn't work out so well. I was going to make you dinner as a way of . . . *condoling*, but, just for the record, whoever turned you down ought to have his head examined.'

Marcy stared at him. 'You're not joking, are you?'

'We're going out, Lena. I'm taking you out.' Then, as if slightly alarmed at his own vehemence, he added, 'If you'll kindly allow me.'

They went to a place called Sports. She ordered crab and a flaming dessert. She enjoyed every bite. 'I'll pay my half,' she said while he was sipping coffee. He smiled. Half, rounded off, was $72.

She paid it. She paid it so that after he drove her home, she could say goodnight, give him a quick kiss, and feel virtuous even while experiencing the strange pleasure of watching his appetite grow.

LAST NIGHT MARCY WORKED HER FIRST SHIFT AT THE PALOMINO. JOE ELY played, she made a couple of mistakes on drink orders, but still took home over $90. Except for some unfunny flirtation, it was okay, so this morning, a Saturday, Marcy felt just fine. She'd gone out to sit in the sun on the deck, but as the sky clouded over she put on a T-shirt and, a while later, sweat pants. When she heard Harmon Martin's peculiar knock on the door, she sang out, 'It's unlocked and I'm decent!'

He set a grocery bag on the drainboard, pushed open the French door that gave onto the deck. 'I've been wondering if you got mauled last night,' he said.

She laughed. 'No real bruises.'

Harmon Martin regarded her, then went to the deck rail and looked out.

'Rain,' Marcy said from behind him. 'Or would be if this was Nebraska.'

He stared off. 'It's coming up from the Gulf. It's of the kind that can really open up.'

It was quiet except for the drone of an airplane. For the first time, Marcy wondered where Harmon Martin's wife thought he was.

'Did I mention the hotel project we've begun in St Martin?' he said, still looking off. 'It's quite reckless, 400 rooms, on the Dutch side.' He turned around. 'I have to go over there this week.'

'How nice,' Marcy said. It *did* sound nice, actually.

'Yes, well, I've been thinking,' Harmon Martin said. 'Do you remember the car dealership I went into the day I showed you this place?'

'The place with the old cars.'

'*Vintage* cars, we call them, but yes. I own that agency. We sell pre-68 Rollses, Mercedes, Porsches, Bentleys, and Bugattis that we bring over from Europe. We restore them to mint condition, guarantee them, and sell them as investment-quality classics, which they are.'

Since when, Marcy wondered, did Harmon Martin fill her in on his work? 'That's interesting,' she said.

'There are three salesmen, but one will soon be leaving.'

Marcy didn't say anything.

He said, 'What got me thinking were those clothes you wore the other night, the Asian coat and orange top. Tasteful, but somewhat . . . *sportive.*' He smiled his subdued smile. 'I think you'd be, as they say, a selling fool.' On the freeway below, loose lines of traffic flowed smoothly along. Gently he said, 'Six figures is not out of the question.'

Marcy tried to keep her voice calm. 'I don't know red beans about old cars.'

'Well, it's complicated, and our clientele is discerning. We'd start you in reception then move you to one particular line – Bentleys, say – once you've learned them backward and forward.'

'The backwards-and-forward part,' Marcy said. 'That's the part that concerns me.'

Harmon Martin snugged his glasses to the bridge of his nose. 'This is why I mention St Martin. I'll have meetings, but there will be dead times. We could put them to use going through the different models.'

Marcy felt lightheaded. She needed to say something. 'I never thought I was coming out to Hollywood to sell used cars,' she said.

'*Vintage,*' Harmon Martin said, with his smile.

Then he half-closed his eyes, a few moments passed, and his lids slowly opened. 'Look, Lena,' he said. 'In a way it *is* part of the business. Take the day before yesterday. Alec Baldwin came in and used his American Express for a Porsche roadster, the '58 Super Speedster, $22,000. Last week Randy Quaid purchased a three-wheel Morgan. We sell to anybody, but it's amazing how many of the buyers are recognizable. Julie Newmar bought a '31 Bentley, and before he died Steve McQueen bought his 356 from us.' Harmon Martin spread his hands, looked at them, spread them wider. His voice grew almost melodious. 'Both of John Wayne's sons. Dennis Quaid. Rita Moreno.'

It was a surprise and not a surprise, this new use of his fine pure voice. Faraway a car horn sounded. Harmon Martin slowed his pace. 'Fernando Lamas,' he crooned. 'Whit Bissell . . . Strother Martin . . . John Cassavetes.' Marcy grinned dreamily. 'Sterling Holloway . . . Elizabeth Ashley . . . Lou Diamond Phillips . . .' One after another, the names, the dreamy, beautiful, expensive names, hovered close by, floating, then on the updraft rose overhead.

'We'll need to leave by 4 p.m. Tuesday,' Harmon Martin said. 'You can pack light. We're building on the Dutch side, but staying on the French, where dress is informal, especially on the beach.'

Slowly and with real effort Marcy brought the room back into focus. She had to say no, thanks but no thanks, and she had to say it now. Thanks, but no thanks. Say it.

Harmon Martin was at the door, looking as lightheaded as Marcy felt, and then, before Marcy said a word, he was gone.

THE STORM TOOK HOLD THAT NIGHT AND DIDN'T LET GO. THE WEATHERMAN Marcy watched was called Dr George by the cheery co-anchors. Dr George ran a clip of two women in rain-drenched bikinis rollerskating in Santa Monica, then shoved his face muggingly into the camera and said that what we have here, folks, is a good old-fashioned gullywhumper. Marcy spent the day reading and watching TV, eating popcorn and thinking of spending similar days when snow floated idly down in Nebraska. She put on her swimming suit and stood on a stool to look at herself in the mirror. She tried it with the top off and actually laughed. If Harmon Martin thought she'd go out on a public beach like that, he had another think coming. She wished he would call so she could remember how his voice made her feel while he was saying those names, but he didn't. By Sunday afternoon, whenever she looked at a clock, Marcy converted it to Nebraska time. That evening, for the first time since the storm moved in, she thought of the dog. She opened the front door, whistled into the sheets of slanting rain, but her call was swallowed in the gurgling din of the storm. Through the night she imagined hearing the dog scratching at the door, but when she shined a flashlight out, he wasn't there. There was only the splash of water.

The storm was supposed to let up Tuesday morning, but didn't.

Marcy packed her suitcase in hopes that her feelings would catch up with her actions. She packed perfume, lingerie, diaphragm. But Harmon Martin's knock on the door made her do something unexpected. She slid the packed suitcase under the bed and opened another one on top, empty.

Harmon Martin shook out his umbrella at the door and entered uncertainly. He didn't seem completely surprised when Marcy led him to the empty suitcase. 'I'm not going,' she said. He fretted and coaxed, growing smaller by the minute. Beneath his linen jacket, he wore a pale pink silk shirt that seemed to Marcy unpleasantly showy. While he walked stiffly about the room, he fussed with the pale pink cuffs, tugging them down on his too-thin wrists. When finally he sat down and pleaded, Marcy said, 'No. Once and for all, no.'

Moments later, clouds outside parted to a startling blue and the entire room lightened. Harmon Martin wrote something down. 'This is my home number. I'll be there another hour, in case you change your mind.' He tapped his glasses. 'If my wife answers, just say, "About the leak in the studio on Ione, tell Harmon never mind it's been fixed." '

After he left, Marcy went outside and was surprised that Harmon Martin's car was actually gone. The sun glared down; vapor rose from the wet asphalt. Everywhere on the ground there were worms, and snails, and soaked newspapers. People began popping out of houses. From a distance, a dog barked, *her* dog, his sharp clear anxious barking. Marcy followed the sound down the hillside streets, along Ione, down finally to Cahuenga. In the traffic, the barking was lost, or perhaps it had stopped. Marcy kept walking, further from her studio, further from Harmon Martin's house, taking deep breaths of the new clean air. In Goodnight, after a storm like this, there would've been careful appraisal of crops and stock, but here there was nothing but a general sense of freedom after long constraint. Joggers appeared. Bicycles whizzed by. Music carried from open car windows.

The clearing, however, was a false one. The skies again turned dark, car windows slid up, fat raindrops spattered and the sweep of windshield wipers began again. Marcy, coatless, kept walking, following the flood control channel, watching the water pour by, branches and bottles and plastic containers all rushing along on the fierce current.

It was from a bridge spanning the channel that she saw the dog. He was down below, to the right, in a muddy lot within the fence enclosing the channel, an area used to park orange government trucks, where neither the dog nor the group of boys surrounding him should have been. The boys were bickering over whose turn it was to throw the frisbee next. When finally one of them threw it, the dog seemed to skate above the mud, and to rise out of it for the long moment needed to pluck the frisbee from the air. Marcy could hear the boys' shrill voices. '*Whoa*! Check it out! This canine can *fry!*'

The cars continued to splash past Marcy on the bridge, but the pedestrians and bicyclists had disappeared. The rain turned hard and finally the boys noticed it, too. They hunched their shoulders, looked up at the sky, and moved toward their bikes. One, however, lagged back and, as he saw the others mount their bikes, this last boy picked up the frisbee for one last throw.

What was this like? Like watching one of those TV nature shows and knowing that the snow rabbit or the lame gnu was going to get it and not turning the channel. Marcy wanted to call out to the dog, to retrieve him from danger, but she didn't. She stood mute as the boy turned toward the storm channel and without a moment's hesitation flicked the frisbee toward it. The dog raced after the frisbee, pitched forward when the level ground gave way beneath him, then tumbled and skidded down the concrete bank into the rushing current. His neck stretched up out of the water for a moment before he was swept away.

Marcy felt suddenly boneless. There were so many ways to act cowardly. There were just so many ways to do it. She could've yelled at that boy and saved the dog. She could've done that little bit. And she could've given Harmon Martin, a married man, nothing whatsoever to think about. And she could've told Randall that for reasons she didn't understand and couldn't explain, she had to change her life or go crazy. She could've done that instead of telling him lies and making him hit her, making him feel and look to all of Goodnight like a brute. She could've done these things, if she were only not such a coward, and then besides saving that dog's life and saving Randall and Harmon Martin a lot of trouble, her life would now have more of the decency she always meant it to have. Marcy began to walk. Water streamed from her hair into her face. Her pantlegs and sweater soaked up the rain and pasted themselves to her body. She walked and walked, along Cahuenga, up the canyon toward Ione, past Harmon Martin's house, soaked through, not thinking, just walking in her own watery world.

MARCY WAS AT HER GATE WHEN IT DAWNED ON HER THAT THE ANCIENT WHITE pickup she had just passed seemed familiar. She turned and stared in disbelief. It was Randall's truck. The shadowy form slouched behind the steering wheel must then be Randall. Marcy moved toward him. Scattered on the dashboard were a seedcap, a roadmap, a box of Good & Plentys. Randall didn't move at all, an indication, she guessed, of sullenness or mean satisfaction, and all at once Marcy had no real idea what she was feeling, what she would say. But she didn't have to say anything. Behind the fogged windshield, behind the streaming rivulets of water, Randall was fast asleep.

There were times, in dreams, say, or when drinking, when Marcy felt like you could finally see inside things, how they actually worked. What she saw right now, wet to the bone, staring through the water and glass at her sleeping husband, was that there are some kinds of love, the ones we're all after, that are meant for open air and natural light, but there are other kinds, too, more than we'd like to think, that come out of the dark and drag us away and tear parts from our bodies, kinds of love that work in their own dim rooms, and harbor more sad forms of intimacy and degradation and sustenance than those standing outside those rooms can ever dream of.

With a fingernail Marcy began to tap lightly on the windshield. Listen, she thought. Listen. It's me.

Chapter Sixteen

GRAND-SLAM BREAKFAST

MARCY HAS ASKED RANDALL TO WAIT IN THE TRUCK WHILE SHE CHANGED INTO *dry clothes. She didn't want him to come in. She didn't want him seeing what magazines she'd been reading or what clothes she'd been wearing or what jokes she'd taped to her refrigerator or anything. She decided to change into something semi-businesslike, Levis and a black blazer, but she wasn't sure of the top and it took her a couple of tries on the accessories to get it right. She dried her hair with a blower. She switched from the neoprene eye patch to the leather one with the black leather strap. She re-did her face. It all took time. Only when she took a last look in the mirror did she realize she was giving Randall plenty of opportunity to leave.*

But he was still there, waiting.

She climbed into the cab of the old truck and was surprised at the smell. She'd expected something pretty stale, but it was as if Randall had rolled up the windows in Nebraska and somehow brought along the smell of winter. It smelled like him, too, but she'd always liked his scent, and she liked the mingling smells of oil and boot leather, coffee and flannel. It was still raining; the windshield wipers made the heavy clacking sounds that she'd always liked. This immersion into old sensations was affecting her. In a sudden panic, she cracked the window, then gave the handle another turn. 'Kind of stuffy in here,' she said and Randall, as if embarrassed, cracked his window, too.

They went to a coffee shop, and though there were a number of pretty women and oddball dressers among the customers, Randall never took his eyes off Marcy. 'You look pretty good, Marzikins,' he said. 'Warm winters must suit you.'

'I look okay,' Marcy said. She didn't say anything about warm winters, because the truth was, she'd grown to miss cold ones. She also didn't tell him that he wasn't looking bad himself, though this seemed to her to be true. He'd lost his paunch and his face had a handsome three-day growth. He'd gotten back his sturdy look, or maybe he just seemed sturdier in comparison to what she'd seen locally.

When the waitress came, Randall said he'd go for that grand-slam breakfast deal he'd seen in the window. Marcy, to make a point, ordered decaf cappuccino and a blueberry croissant.

Randall nodded toward Marcy's bad eye. 'That patch permanent?'

Marcy made a laugh. 'Until my next large inheritance.' She explained the condition as best she could. There had been a broken supply of blood to the nerve, which resulted in something called infarction, which in this case meant that the eye could move to the left, but couldn't turn up or in. 'Learning just that much cost $400,' she said. 'For 25,000 more they could make the eye look straight ahead.' She shrugged. 'The patch isn't so bad. My depth perception's lousy, but I got used to it.'

Randall sat silent. He'd removed his hands from the table, the left one, which hadn't hit her that night months ago, and the three-fingered right one, which had. Marcy had the impulse to tell him it wasn't his fault, but that wasn't 100 percent true, and, besides, it might encourage him, which she wasn't yet willing to do. Still, she was fighting the pleasant effects of Randall's presence. 'So where are the dogs?' she said.

'Back at the trailer park, in their kennel. Whistler's feeding 'em.'

The trailer park. The chain-link kennel. Whistler Simpson, who had for years tightened his oversized thrift-shop pants with a recycled Chevrolet seat belt. Marcy was grateful for this tumble of grim images. 'I don't think I'm going back, if that's what you came for,' she said.

Randall trained his eyes on Marcy, who looked down and began to spoon some cream off her cappuccino. 'If you don't want to come back, it's okay,' he said. 'But it's true I came out here to ask.' She didn't say anything, so he went on. 'I found out that everything you told me that night was a lie. I found it all out. At first I was mad, you know, but after a while it dawned on me that you must have felt pretty desperate to resort to something that awful, and I began to feel bad that you were feeling that alone and cornered and all.'

If Marcy had spoken, she would've begun to cry, so she didn't speak.

Randall said, 'I talked to that Mr Rawley guy and he says you can go back to doing the weekend news right away if you want to.'

He said, 'I talked to your dad and he's got me pretty interested in learning how to farm that place.'

He said, 'I guess I don't need to say it, Marcy, but I miss you so much it hurts.'

Chapter Seventeen

YOURS

I

WHEN MARCY AND RANDALL HAD COME BACK FROM CALIFORNIA, THEY'D MADE some changes. They'd given up their rented trailer at Sleepy Hollow and moved in with Marcy's folks down on the flats. Randall had quit Wetteland Construction and begun to learn farming. Marcy had gotten her job back reading the news for KDUH, first on weekends, then weekday mornings and now she'd moved up to the noon and evening news. She wore the eyepatch, she read the news and people liked her. She'd received two telephone calls from other stations, one in Rapid City, one in Fort Collins, feelers, she supposed, but she hardly listened. She told them both she was staying put.

Living at home was odd, Marcy admitted, but the walls of her childhood room and home brought back an ordinariness, an everydayness, a tight artificial wholesomeness that was steadying to live within and fun to sneak away from. She and Randall went for a lot of walks and drives. They had sex in the barn and sex in the car. They had awkward sex standing up behind the corn crib. They had sly actual sex at the Chadron Drive-In. Randall wondered aloud whether any other married folks in Nebraska had this much fun. Once, they found an open window at the high school, climbed through, tiptoed upstairs and had sex on the floor of Mr Hammaker's third-floor classroom. Afterwards Marcy said, 'Well, if that's a baby, it'll be a peppy little thing.' Just as, after muffled sex in their own room next door to her folks's, she would whisper, 'If that's a baby, it'll be a quiet little thing.'

After she came home from reading the evening news, she and Randall would sit with her parents if there was something to keep everyone occupied, a game of Hearts, say, or a video from town. One night, while watching *Giant*, Marcy told Randall that he reminded her just a little of the James Dean character, Jett Rink, and in the next instant her father said, 'Well, you might want to add that your mom and me remind you just a little of Rock Hudson and Liz Taylor,' but even while they all chipped in with a hollow chuckle, Randall was privately probing at the pleasure Marcy's casual comparison to James Dean had created in him.

Marcy herself was surprisingly happy. There had occurred a strange dilation of her attitude so that now she found the quirks and petty complaints of farmers and neighbors and family quasi-comical, endearing even. Perhaps it was because, as the regular noon and evening newscaster, she now moved about Goodnight and surrounding towns in a beam of attentive approval such as she had not felt since her cheerleading days, high-stepping along the chalked sidelines of the football field in a green sweater and pleated skirt.

It wasn't just friends and neighbors who seemed to view her with new respect. Randall did, too, and said so. 'You did good tonight, Marzikins,' he'd say and if her parents weren't within earshot he'd say, 'I looked at you there on the screen and I thought, See those buttons? – A little later on I'll undo every goddamn one of them,' which made Marcy laugh, and open up to him in a way that felt weirdly prenuptial. Some mysterious trick had been played, a hand had reached into her life and pulled the light-side out, and sometimes, after work, driving home from the station on the dead-straight two-lane highway, with only the occasional shelter belt to break the long horizon, Marcy would find herself humming something cheerful and would have to stop herself and wonder how in the world this could've all come about.

'FARMING,' LEWIS LOCKHARDT HAD PROCLAIMED EARLY IN HIS INSTRUCTION of Randall, 'is planning, sweat, and prayer,' and Randall as a little joke had said, 'Well, then, how about if I take care of the machinery?'

Lewis Lockhardt was nothing like Randall's own father, not in any physical aspect, and yet he was as methodical in his planning and execution as Randall's own father had been, and was as patient as Randall's own father might have been in leading Randall through the intricacies of planting, irrigating, fertilizing, cultivating, harvesting, selling, and, finally, if you were still standing, planting again. 'It's good to follow alfalfa, which builds nitrogen, with wheat, which needs it,' Lewis might say and ten seconds later Randall wasn't certain which built and which needed. Farming was a less simple process than it had at first seemed or sounded, but Randall listened and watched and did. He kept a little plastic-covered notepad in his hip pocket and used it to write things down. He learned hour by hour and week by week. He disliked rising from bed in the pre-dawn morning with Marcy still lying warm under the covers, and he disliked going down the hall to the bathroom where Lewis, having used it first, would have left the sulfur smell of burnt matches meant to mask the other odors, but he didn't mind at all walking through the front room into the smell of frying meat that floated from the kitchen, and he didn't mind seeing Marcy's mother standing with her back to him in one of her flowered housedresses in the pale creamy colors of candy-store mints, dresses which, if not buttoned to the throat, could give a disturbing glimpse of things when Marcy's mother leaned near to slide, for example, sausage patties to Randall's plate from her black iron skillet. 'Yessirree,' Randall would say of the sausage in the kind of mumble he thought James Dean might employ and Lewis would say, 'C'mon now, Dot, Randall's got some work to do, give him enough to stick to his ribs,' which she would ignore, either silently or with something like, 'Marcy says she likes Randall *svelte*,' or maybe, if she were especially tired of Lewis's chatter, 'There's no rule that says a man *has* to have a pot belly to make a go of farming.'

Randall made himself chuckle not so much because he thought it was funny as because he wanted it understood that he thought it was meant for a joke, though in fact he thought it wasn't. He liked being around Marcy's mother and he liked being around Lewis but being around them both at the same time drew up all the loose parts into something strained tight. There were differences between them that went way beyond the difference in their ages. She still had her looks and Lewis, judging from his early photographs, never had them to keep. Yet he was the one who seemed happy, and exposure to his cheeriness seemed only to turn his wife sour, a fact that nettled Randall in some vague way.

One day, picking apples with Marcy and her mom, the subject of dogs came up. Marcy's mother was quiet for a time and then said, 'I just tried to remember the names of all the dogs we've had on the place since I've been here and there are so many I can't remember half.'

'Raven was my favorite,' Marcy said. 'And Gypsy.'

Randall asked what happened to them.

'Can't remember,' Marcy said. She set her ladder against a limb clustered with apples.

'Lewis shot Gyp because she killed a lamb,' Marcy's mother said. 'Raven got into coyote bait.' She said these things with an obstinate matter-of-factness. She'd been picking through the windfalls and straightened her back. 'The other day I saw a show on television about whippet dogs. They can run seventy miles an hour in a one-minute sprint, but make them run five minutes and they'll drop dead. I thought: That's just what being happy is like because it can't go on for long either.'

When Marcy didn't speak, Randall said, 'Well, I don't like the sound of that.'

Marcy then jumped in. 'I think happiness keeps changing right along with the body, like they have parallel life cycles or something. As a baby, milk might make you happy, then a rattle, then it goes doll, pony, a new dress, making cheerleading, finding a boyfriend . . .' She stopped short and made a laugh. 'I guess it's the later stages that get tricky.'

As the three of them were lugging the baskets of apples toward the truck, Marcy's mother said in a tired voice, 'Now Lewis is another story. You give him a slice of apple pie with a big slab of Velveeta and he'll be happy.'

It was not so much the words themselves as the nasty brine they seemed soaked in that made Randall's blood rise. He knew he ought to keep still even as he opened his mouth. 'Yeah, it's one of the things you got to hand to Lewis,' he said, his voice tightening a little, 'how he can be at home enough with himself and his life that he can get all the satisfaction he needs out of just the littlest everyday things.'

There was a long still moment before Marcy with exaggerated surprise said, 'Well, well. Randall gives a speech.' She kissed him nibblingly on the neck.

'Wasn't a speech,' Randall mumbled, calming now, coming back into himself. He didn't know whether he was glad he'd spoken up or not. It didn't matter. He'd done it, and now things would be slightly different. The center of gravity had moved a fraction. He'd watched Marcy's mother as he spoke, watched her face harden, and he'd sensed what she was thinking – that he'd gone over to the enemy, that he'd somehow declared himself to be as simple as Lewis.

IT WAS A FULL YEAR AFTER MARCY AND RANDALL HAD MOVED TO THE FLATS, on a fitfully snowy February day, that Dorothy Lockhardt had happened to bump into Dixie Bailey at Frmka's Suprette. Just as she turned into the cereal aisle, Dorothy's cart actually bumped into Dixie's. The joined metal made a quick clank. Dorothy glanced into the other cart – it contained nothing but puny, loose-skinned grapefruits – and then up at Dixie, who looked more than a little amused. Within Dorothy's cart, on top of the flour, potatoes, and other staples, was an opened bag of Chip Ahoy cookies.

'What're you doing so far from home on a day like this?' asked Dixie Bailey, who lived in town.

It was true that the weather was of the bleak chancy kind that kept most farm wives home, but Dorothy hadn't been out of the house in three days. She needed milk, she needed flour. She was going stir-crazy. She'd decided to risk it. 'Shopping, is all,' Dorothy said.

She made ready to move on, but Dixie Bailey didn't then do the expected thing. She didn't smile, nod, and move away. She stood fast and kept smiling at Dorothy, a funny little smile, as if at a private joke she might be willing to share. Then she said, 'This is no accident. I've been meaning to talk to you.'

Dixie Bailey was not Goodnight's most widely respected citizen. She'd come here at age nineteen, after the break-up of her second marriage. Her car had broken down between Rushville and Goodnight and while it was being repaired, she'd found a job and never left. She drank bourbon, smoked unfiltered cigarettes, and had been through a string of boyfriends, a couple of them married. She was thirty-eight. Her good looks, if they were good looks, had a toughness to them. People said she had quite a collection of underwear. Her hair was not naturally red and her voice went with the rest of the package, a deep easy smoker's rasp that Dorothy envied and thought exotic.

'You said you'd been wanting to talk to me,' Dorothy said, once they'd quickstepped across the slushy street and settled themselves with coffee at Sisters Cafe. 'What about?'

'Oh, just about things in general,' Dixie Bailey said in her smoky voice. 'Nothing in particular. You just interest me.'

This was so unlike anything ever spoken to her by another woman, and especially another woman from Goodnight, that Dorothy hardly knew what to do. She laughed. 'Well, that's pretty good,' she said, 'because *I* hardly interest me.'

Dixie Bailey had slipped her liners from her boots and, before lighting a cigarette, offered one to Dorothy, who wished she were somewhere else, some town faraway from here, where she could accept it. There was a table of three men at the far end of the cafe. Otherwise it was empty. Dorothy looked out through the reversed letters of SISTERS CAFE painted in red on the front window. Snow slanted down hard. A single car slowly passed in front of the window without making a sound.

Dixie Bailey said, 'I hear your girl and her husband moved in with you.'

Dorothy smiled. 'At our invitation, but, yes, that's right.'

'What's it like?'

Dorothy did her best. 'The good part is the house feels like it's breathing again. The bad part is, it's somebody else's breath.'

Dixie Bailey nodded and picked a piece of tobacco from the tip of her tongue. 'A friendly occupation,' she said, and Dorothy laughed again, not just because she found it funny, but also because for the first time in ages she felt she was in the company of someone who hailed from the same imaginary hometown she did. When

Judy Treadwell came over with the coffee pot, Dorothy accepted a refill.

She blew lightly on her coffee and studied Dixie Bailey's face. 'So how long have you been in Goodnight now?'

Dixie Bailey wagged her red eyebrows. 'Next year I get my twenty-year pin.' She chortled. 'Still a newcomer.'

Dixie Bailey lived and worked at a home for mentally handicapped kids, 'clients,' they were supposed to be called, though outside the home many in Goodnight, including Dixie Bailey, called them 'retardates,' or 'tardates,' or sometimes just 'tards.' A few years before, Dorothy had gone to the home to donate some of Marcy's old clothes and found Dixie Bailey in charge. She'd insisted on giving Dorothy a little tour of the home. What Dorothy remembered most vividly was that there had been a mock motel room upstairs, where the clients who'd reached working age could learn how to clean the room in preparation for work in the outside world. The day Dorothy visited this mock motel room, a young male client was supposed to be cleaning it, but, as she and Dixie Bailey mounted the stairs, the room seemed strangely quiet. Dorothy drew back, but Dixie Bailey kept ascending. At the head of the stairs, she stood and waited for Dorothy to catch up. Within the room, on the unmade bed, the young man was curled into a near-fetal position, snoring gently, easily, like a large costumed baby. The sweetness of it affected Dorothy, and she wanted to retreat at once, to close the door quietly behind them, to let the boy enjoy the kind of innocent sleep that lay beyond the reach of sound-minded adults. But Dixie Bailey tiptoed toward the bed. Dorothy – what was she doing here? – followed. Dixie Bailey put one hand at the base of the boy's back and the other flat to his chest and, with the slightest pressure, eased him onto his back. She pointed, grinning. Dorothy looked down at the bulge below the belt. He slept with an erection, as any man or young man might. 'Donald,' Dixie Bailey crooned, 'Donald,' and the boy awaked smiling, and pulled his knees into the air, and with his small chubby hands made small chubby fists, which he rubbed for a moment into his eyes before turning to Dixie Bailey and saying, 'I'm thirsty, Dicky.' Dorothy had not fled the home exactly, but she was relieved to walk out the front door. And though she'd never gone back to the center, she was reminded of her visit every time she saw one of the home's female clients walking along the sidewalks of Goodnight in one of Marcy's castaway sweaters or skirts.

Now, drinking coffee with Dixie Bailey in the cafe, Dorothy said, 'Remember how a long time ago you took me up to that fake motel room and we saw that boy sleeping instead of cleaning?'

Dixie Bailey smiled. 'Donald Hardy.' She made a man's leer and lowered her voice. 'Donald Hardy had a hard-on.'

To her surprise, Dorothy laughed, a deep full laugh that leaped up from her diaphragm. It alarmed her. Dixie Bailey alarmed her, even as she found her strangely captivating. In any case, she hoped that none of the men at the far table had heard Dixie Bailey's words.

Dorothy lowered her eyes and her voice. 'I guess we don't tend to think of the mentally retarded as particularly . . .' She let her voice trail off. She didn't want to say *sexual*, out loud, in Sisters Cafe.

'Oh, the tards're randy little characters,' Dixie Bailey said in her same husky voice. 'They're clumsy as bear cubs but not always ineffective. We've had to tie some tardate tubes.' She was smiling and then she was not. 'To tell the truth, there's not much to envy in the tardate world, but I'd be happy to have their clean consciences. They just don't feel guilt, and you couldn't make them, even if you were crazy enough to try.'

The cafe's plate-glass window trembled under a gust of wind. The snow was slanting hard from the north. The sky was white and soon the road and fields would be white. There would be no horizon, no dividing line. 'I better go,' Dorothy said and made herself stand up.

But before Dorothy left, Dixie Bailey pulled a paper from her purse and handed it to Dorothy. At the top of the page it said, *30-Day Grapefruit Diet*. 'Want to try it with me?' Dixie Bailey said.

They compared results every few days. At the end of the month, Dorothy had lost seven pounds, Dixie had lost three, and there was very little Dixie wasn't comfortable revealing to Dorothy on the telephone.

She said, 'My new boyfriend Dale is a serious case. What he likes to do is suck the fingers of my smoking hand. He says he can get a nicotine rush just from my fingers.'

She said, 'Craig Lang – that drooly VW mechanic in Chadron? – he supposedly chained his wife inside a micro-van for three days last week and now she's back with him loving him up instead of sending his sorry ass to jail.'

She said, 'We have a tardate boy now who's legally blind and I don't know why but I asked myself how I would feel about a blind tardate boy sitting in my bedroom when I was undressing and you know what? – the answer I gave was that it'd be just like it was when I was married and one of my husbands was in the room!'

Dixie Bailey had tickled herself with this observation. When she'd stopped laughing, Dorothy said, 'Did you ever have another near-blind boy at the home?'

'Sure. One or two.'

'One named Charlie Woodley?'

'Charlie! Sure. But Charlie died. Life expectancy for these little characters is not so high. I think he had an enlarged heart.'

'Did you meet his parents?'

'Creeps. The father was a drooler. The mother seemed nice, but when they moved out of state they left Charlie and just stopped calling. I wouldn't say it killed him but it didn't help any.' A pause. 'They didn't even come to claim the body.' Then, 'Why? What's your interest?'

The next time they were alone together, Dorothy told her. Dixie's response was surprising. 'Big deal!' she said. 'It was probably worth the money anyhow. Besides, when you fall off a horse . . .' She looked at Dorothy. 'Whaddaya think?'

Dorothy knew what she ought to say, and she said it. 'No, not me, never again.' But Dorothy didn't know what she truly thought. After Gerald Woodley had left she'd tried to tell herself she'd had an escape, that she shouldn't be unhappy with her life, that there was nothing she needed she didn't already have. And yet, for a long time now, for seven or eight years, ever since Gerald's departure, she had lived with a low-grade melancholy that seemed to her both causeless and ceaseless. It was like living in a winter afternoon that wouldn't end. It wore her down, dulled her to her own interests. Her yearnings, though not quite dispelled, had lost all shape.

*   *   *

IN THE AUTUMN OF THEIR SECOND YEAR ON THE LOCKHARDT PLACE, MARCY and Randall had put a down payment on a used double-wide trailer that they pulled out to the farm and installed on a site that Randall had carefully graded-out at the edge of the Niobrara. When Marcy's father objected to their moving from the main house, Marcy had asked her mother to run interference. 'Tell Dad we need a little space of our own so we can start raising a family,' Marcy said and her mother made a faint smile. 'I'll tell him,' she said, 'and he'll probably believe it.' Meaning, Marcy understood, that her mother did not, that she didn't believe the mere proximity of parents could seriously impede the needs of procreation, but then her mother, as if it were a fact she'd just discovered, said, 'It's your father's best feature, isn't it? – how much he trusts the world.'

The lot for the double-wide was only fifty yards or so from the main house, but was afforded privacy from it by the interposing barn and outbuildings. The site itself was set into a wide sweep of the river, so that its easy unending movement could be viewed from three sides of the mobile home. It was all perfectly okay. That was what Marcy said, but before long she'd gotten a library book on deck building and with help from Randall had constructed a full front porch, with a simple white rail and a corrugated metal roof, which pleased them both so much that they soon thereafter built a screened porch off the back of the home, where from June to early September they could fall to sleep under the influence of a low moon and the watery hush of the Niobrara sliding by.

Their third and fourth years on the place slipped past, and as Randall's life took hold in the flats south of Goodnight, he began to feel a part of things, relied upon, respected. Lewis Lockhardt thought Randall was born to farm. The only thing he was weak on was the planning end of things. That's what Marcy told Randall one Sunday afternoon.

'You and your dad were talking about me?'

'Course,' Marcy said. 'What else've we got to talk about?'

'When was this?'

'When he dropped me at the station the other day.'

'But he said I was born to farm?'

'Yeah, but I told him you were born to fornicate,' Marcy said, and laughed at her own joke.

Randall did, too. 'Probably that was something you said in another lifetime in a different town to a different father,' he said.

They were at home, sitting on their screened porch, which dimmed now as a cloud slowly eclipsed the sun. It was early June, but the afternoon had the close, smothering feel of July. Randall wore denim pants, an old snap-buttoned shirt and a yellow and black cap promoting Caterpillar tractors. Marcy wore a dark cotton dress with a long line of buttons down the front.

Randall took off his shirt and stood at the screened window looking off, feeling for a breeze. Overhead, somewhere out of sight, a small airplane droned. Behind him, in the sleeping porch, Randall heard a rustling of clothes and the metallic pinch of bedsprings. Then nothing, until a lilting, 'Hey, Cutie.'

Randall deliberately did not turn.

'Hey, Zackerpoo,' she crooned.

He still didn't turn. As he stared out, he saw Marcy's mother ease her big gray horse down the bank to the river, where it felt its way across before bolting up the opposite bank. She prodded the horse into a smooth gallop and headed off toward the sandhills.

'Where does she go?'

'Who?'

'Your mom. When she goes riding off?'

Marcy seemed to think she knew. 'Oh, she's just getting away. Everybody has their own means. Some people read books or take naps or make up prayers or go to the movies, but they're all just getting away.'

Randall kept staring out. 'How do you do it?'

'I used to always think of going to California, but now, it's funny, it's not like I have to get away because I like it so much being here.'

It occurred to Randall that his own chief means of escape was fooling around with Marcy, if not in the actual act itself then in simply tumbling into long thoughts about what they last did or would next do.

'Hey, Cowboy,' she called, reverting to the low tones of mischief.

Randall turned around. Marcy was lying back, her head cradled in clasped hands, her one good eye fixed on him. She was naked.

'My favorite outfit,' Randall said, sounding mostly like himself, though he'd gone for the small scratchy mumble he associated with Jett Rink.

'C'mon over here,' Marcy said.

Randall kept up his routine. He smiled, took off his cap, scratched the back of his head, looked off and grinned as if at some private joke. Then he turned his eyes again to her. 'Well, I don't know about that, Miss Marcy. I'm not sure I ought.'

'Oh, you ought all right,' Marcy said laughing.

When they were done, and Randall had rolled away, Marcy rocked back to her shoulders and, locking her elbows and bracing her hips with her hands, pointed her toes to the ceiling.

'What's that for?' Randall asked.

'To give your swim team a little help. Let 'em swim downstream instead of up.' These words came out almost in grunts. 'I'm ovulating,' she said.

Randall asked how she happened to know that.

'My little home testing kit.'

Randall stood, went to the screened window and let his gaze float away.

Marcy from her bum-up position said, 'What's the matter anyhow?'

'You buy that kit at Lloyds?' Lloyds Friendly Pharmacy in Goodnight.

'Yeah. So?'

'So that means by now everybody and his uncle knows you're thinking something's wrong with my reproductive system.'

Marcy issued a sigh of exasperation. 'Or maybe they think I'm afraid something's wrong with me. Which *is* what I'm afraid of, by the way.'

Randall didn't speak and for a full few minutes Marcy kept her outstretched legs pointed to the ceiling. Only when she stretched flat again did Randall speak, and in a softer voice. 'Marcy, we got pregnant before without testing kits or calisthenics or anything else, so why don't we just relax and let things take their course?'

'Randall, that miscarriage was ages ago, and according to the books it should've been *simpler* to conceive afterwards, not harder.'

Books? Randall thought. What books?

'Sometimes you got to give mother nature a hand, Randall. That's all I'm doing here.'

Randall felt like putting on his clothes and going out to the barn, where Lewis was puttering in his workshop, fixing something, maintaining something, improving something, checking something off the top of his Do-list, then adding something to the bottom. But Randall knew how much like a desertion this would feel to Marcy, so he lay down alongside her and she settled her head into the crook of his arm and before long they slipped into the distortions of uneasy sleep. It was dusk when Randall awakened to the first widely spaced sounds of fat drops thupping on the tin roof and, far off, the soft heraldic roll of thunder.

'What?' Marcy said, barely awake.

'Weather,' Randall said. 'Nothing. Go back to sleep.'

TWO WEEKS LATER, RANDALL AND LEWIS WERE CAREERING ALONG A DIRT county road in Lewis's black pickup truck. It was the pleasantest kind of weather – a mild, mid-June morning swept clean by a breeze, the distances tinted with the rich browns and greens of a wet spring. Churned gravel chinked idly at the wheelwells.

They were headed toward home for a quick unscheduled stop to pick up Lewis's logbook before heading off to the Friday stock auction in Crawford. Randall slouched on his side of the cab and watched the road as Lewis loosely guided the pickup south while surveying his neighbors' fields and his own. Things looked good, Lewis thought. Things looked just real good. But still. Panky had been a hair fast with his corn and Chubb White a good week late with his beans and Bates's boy, bless his college-boy bones, was still trying soybeans.

The fine weather, combined with the fact that his own beans and corn were doing better than anyone else's on the flats, made Lewis Lockhardt feel more than usually like talking. He leaned back in his seat, rested one big hand near the six o'clock slot on the driver's wheel, just below his ample stomach, and began to give Randall his speech.

Randall had heard the speech. Anyone who'd been around Lewis for any length of time had heard it. What it got down to was this. Lewis believed you shaped a life the same way you shaped a farm. You felled trees and you dug out the big rocks. You graded and you fenced. You planted the seeds, you delivered the water and you killed the pests. You acquired with care and when the bills came due, you paid them.

When he'd finished, Lewis turned his gaze to Randall and held it there. Randall gave Lewis the quickest glance before returning his eyes to the dirt road before them. Randall liked his father-in-law, but his driving was hair-raising. Lewis would slow down and speed up for no reason whatsoever. He would sail through unmarked crossroads without a glance in either direction. He would drift to the center of country roads and stay there, even over blind crests. But none of it was worse than when he paid more mind to you, the passenger, than he did to the road. 'There's a wet patch coming up,' Randall said now to get Lewis's eyes back to his driving.

Lewis, taking no discernible notice, stuck to his message. 'Oh, it don't happen overnight,' he said, casually glimpsing the road before returning his gaze to Randall, 'and you have your setbacks and regrets, but over the years the farm will finally take the shape you mean it to take, and so will your life.'

Randall, his eyes in a narrow forward stare, considered this doubtfully. He was thinking of how you couldn't control the nature of the soil it was your portion to farm, and you couldn't control the weather over it or the water table under it.

'Take yourself,' Lewis said with a broad, inclusive wave of his hand after fishtailing the truck through a slippery turn. 'You came here when you had your peer problems in Utah, you went out and got that big-machinery license, you stuck with that puny job with Wetteland, and when Marcy was gone, you went off and found her and got things straightened out. And then you took up this opportunity here to learn farming with me.' He kept his eyes on Randall and stretched a grin over his protuberant teeth. 'You see what I mean?'

Randall stared ahead and said he guessed so, sure.

'No guesswork about it!' Lewis said with surprising vehemence.

Up ahead, a badger waddled across the road and into the turnrow.

Almost to himself Lewis said, 'What your life finally looks like is what you meant it all along to look like.' Then, again letting his gaze lounge on his passenger, 'I hate palaver, Randall, but this ain't palaver.'

Randall didn't know. It seemed to him all he'd ever done was what he'd felt like doing at any given moment, and the fact that he'd never given the line of his life any more thought than he might give to where he might next fool around with Marcy or first stalk his buck come fall made him feel suddenly deficient.

Lewis pulled up in front of the farmhouse that he'd been born in, that he'd inherited from his parents and remodeled and added to and as a finishing touch painted robin's egg blue. Off toward the barn, under a cottonwood, there was a parked sedan that Randall didn't recognize. Lewis jumped out of the truck, swung open the yardgate, and as he entered the house through the mudporch sang out, 'Hi-dee-ho!'

Randall considered following him inside, maybe seeing what refrigerator snacks were there for the taking, but since this was just the sort of short-term thinking that suddenly seemed his own particular area of expertise, he decided to play against tendency, as Coach Dee used to say. He sat tight and closed his eyes and tried to think up a ten-year plan for himself. It wasn't easy. The problem was, it was hard to think what he might want in ten years that he didn't have now, other than maybe a Dodge Ram V-10. He thought about it some more. Then he scooched over to the driver's seat and sat waiting behind the wheel.

A half-minute later, Lewis banged out of the screen door of the mudporch looking to Randall like a man who'd just swallowed laughing gas, but was afraid to open his mouth for fear the jollity he set loose might prove unstoppable. Randall started the truck and Lewis slid into the passenger side, his face still a contortion of mirth.

'What?' Randall said.

Lewis pointed a finger back toward the house, but couldn't speak. He kept his mouth clamped tight, but little sniggers kept slipping through. It wasn't until they'd turned onto the highway that he'd minimally collected himself.

'What then?' Randall asked.

'Dot and . . .' Lewis said and again had to swallow back laughter. 'Dot and Dixie Bailey. I walk in and there they are, dressed in black leotards laying on the floor elbows down and stomachs up watching Jane Fonda on the TV set and doing *undulatory* exercises that I got to admit put me in mind of an overturned stink bug, though of course I don't say so.'

'No, I suppose not,' Randall said. His mind drifted to Dixie Bailey. Dixie Bailey was a woman men's minds drifted toward.

A minute or two later, Lewis began glancing suddenly around the cab as if at some impressive act of magic. He looked at Randall. 'So how come you're driving and I'm not?'

Randall stared at the road ahead of him. 'While you were in the house I started working on my own ten-year plan. The first thing I decided I wanted one year from today was to still be in the land of the living.' He made a big, self-pleased grin. 'That's why I'm driving.'

After a half-second's pause, Lewis's face brightened. 'There! You see now. That's just how it goes. You make the little adjustments. You bring water to this field and over there you fence it hog-tight. You see the point I'm making?'

Randall did, he said, and before long Lewis began to sing and then whistle the same chords again and again – 'somewhere over the rainbow, way up high' – while distracting himself in rough calculations involving beef cattle, with numbers sliding up and down according to the average weight gain per day that might be attained in each phase of the operation.

Randall, driving a level sixty-five, was lost in his own thoughts and after a while, without really meaning to, he said aloud what went through his mind. 'Wonder what's got into them.'

Lewis left off whistling. 'What's that?'

The question startled Randall slightly. It was more like he'd been talking to himself. 'Mrs Lockhardt and that Dixie Bailey. Wonder what's got into them.' When Lewis looked blank, Randall added, 'All the exercise stuff.'

Lewis snorted out a laugh. 'What's got into 'em is something foolish and notional and better left unknown.'

Randall told himself this was probably true, even if it was a truth he didn't care for.

A mile of straight highway passed before Lewis decided he wanted to refine his position on life's little mysteries. 'Now when it comes to business, reading between the lines is a whole other matter. It's what you build hunches from, and hunches are what allow you sometimes to see around corners and, if you're lucky, meet the future unsurprised.'

Randall glanced past Lewis and thought of something Marcy's mother had said to him one night this past winter while he was running her over to Chadron to pick up Lewis's truck, which had been worked on at the Ford agency. It was January, already black dark at 4.45 in the afternoon. At that point where the road cut through a sudden reach of timber, Mrs Lockhardt had jerked her head abruptly to the right and a long second later said in a low, serious voice, 'Did you see that?'

'See what?' Randall said.

'An elk. A big spike elk standing close to the road staring at us. Just off to the side of our headlights.'

Randall wished he'd seen it, but he hadn't. 'Every now and then you hear of an elk getting this far east,' he said and then he said something he wished he hadn't. 'Usually it just turns out to be a deer though.'

'It was an elk all right,' Marcy's mother said. She swiveled to look behind them into the blackness. 'It just stood there staring.' Then, turning back, she did something surprising. She reached under the passenger seat and pulled out a small greeting-card box. Hidden beneath a short stack of cards were loose cigarettes. She punched in the electric lighter, turned up the heat, lowered slightly her window so that a sudden hiss of cold air shot in. She lit the cigarette, snapped the smoke into her lungs and a few moments later, tilting her chin up and away from Randall, extruded the smoke toward the lowered window.

'Didn't know you smoked,' Randall said.

Marcy's mother kept staring out the window into the darkness. 'Well, now you do.'

Except for the whistle of cold air through the window, it was quiet. Randall felt strangely off-balance. He said, 'Not that I mind somebody's smoking. My father smoked and the smell always reminds me of that.' This was only loosely true. It was cigar smoke that put him in mind of his father.

Marcy's mother, her eyes staring out toward the darkness, hadn't responded. They'd passed the Ferrell place and were nearly to town before she had spoken again. 'I know this much,' she'd said. 'What you see out of the corner of your eye is almost always the most important part.' She'd held the cigarette out the window until it was dead, then pushed it out. She'd pulled a breath mint from her purse. She'd brushed and smoothed her dress. She'd recrossed her legs. In a cool, measured voice, she'd said, 'Let's make the cigarettes our little secret, shall we?'

When, today, Randall and Lewis arrived at the saleyard, it was nearly noon. Already there were long ragged lines of dusty pickup trucks, many with stock trailers, parked in the dirt. Lewis and Randall stepped out into the rich smells of stock and stock byproduct. On their way in, Lewis caught up with Gordon Moore, who dry-farmed wheat and alfalfa just east of Crawford and was known for his expert appraisal of stock. His tips were worth having. Lewis in his most companionable manner said, 'So what're we looking for, Gordy?'

But Gordon Moore was keeping his own counsel. 'Rain,' he said amiably, grinning first at Lewis and then at Randall. 'A little each morning and a little each night.'

Lewis played along with a laugh. 'Well, what we'll more likely get is a lightning fire or freak hail or late freeze,' to which Gordon Moore produced a chuckle of his own before turning the talk to taxes, a subject that simultaneously drew Lewis in and shut Randall out, not that Randall cared. He was already pointing himself in the direction of the Women's Auxiliary foodstand, where there wasn't much to buy except exactly what he wanted – sloppy joes, iced tea, and lemon meringue pie.

II

IT WASN'T A LIGHTNING FIRE OR A FREAK HAIL OR A HARD FREEZE, BUT IT MIGHT as well have been. Today, by the visitation of outside forces, things

would change. Lewis and Randall were, as always at ten minutes
to noon, washing up at the basin in the outside storeroom. Lewis
finished first, bumped open the interior door and tramped into the
dining room singing out, 'Hi-dee-ho!' and then, as always, 'Well,
well. Smell them vittles.'

Dorothy, slicing bread in the kitchen, didn't respond.

This particular day they would be eating a beef stew and
home-baked white bread, which Lewis would use as an appetizer
once it was enriched with thick layers of butter and chokecherry
jelly. Sometimes, before the first bite, he would lift it in his open
hand and say, 'Dorothy's chokecherry jelly – proof positive there's
a God.'

In the kitchen nook, in the recess of the bay window, the portable
television was already tuned mutely to KDUH, to the final few minutes
of *All My Children*, which preceded the noon news. The television
stood in the bay window and partly blocked the view of the lawn
that Dorothy herself mowed and tended. She'd had a sinking feeling
when Lewis had put the television there, its face making a dark hole
in the center of the one view she liked to examine over a cup of
coffee when the house was empty. The bay window had been a gift.
When she and Lewis had first moved into the house, there had been
a metal casement window, its workings rusted shut, and Dorothy had
hardly mentioned how nice it would be to have a big bay window
there before Lewis drove off to Rapid City and came back with this
window, which he'd installed himself, and she'd thought how nice
it was to be married to a man older and more knowledgeable and
thoughtful than the boys her own age. That was many years before.
And when Marcy had begun doing the noon news, Lewis without
consulting Dorothy had gone off to Radio Shack in Chadron and
bought this portable television and put it in the bay window and
run a long brown extension cord over and under and around things
and, once he'd plugged it in, had turned beamingly to Dorothy and
said, 'There!' So what could she say?

Today, before the news came on, Lewis noticed that Dorothy had
set plates for only him and Randall. 'You're not eating, Dot?'

Dorothy, carrying dishes from the table, said she'd eaten earlier.

'Ate what?' Lewis said.

'I had some tuna,' Dorothy said. 'And some tomato.'

'You're your own disappearing act. You'll vanish before our very eyes.' When Dorothy said nothing, Lewis took a moment to regard her. 'You'll get sick again if you don't eat right, Honey,' he said in the lower tones he used when he finally became serious.

'I do eat right,' Dorothy said, almost to herself.

Randall, sensing trouble, turned up the TV volume and focused on an ad for Ford T-250s.

'Ask Randall what he thinks,' Dorothy was saying. 'What do you think, Randall?'

Randall reluctantly muted the sound. 'About what?'

'Whether I look sickly.'

'For Gods' sake, Dot,' Lewis said. 'I didn't say sickly. I said you'd get sick if you didn't eat.'

Randall didn't offer an opinion, though it was true that Marcy's mom looked anything but sickly. She'd kept up her exercises and her arms were brown from riding. And, he supposed, from her afternoons at the Rushville pool with Dixie Bailey and those kids from the home. She wore a bathing suit he'd heard about. Leo and a couple of other guys had driven up to Rushville just to take a look. 'It wasn't like something in the *Sports Illustrated* swimsuit issue or anything,' Leo told Randall one night at the Eleventh Man. 'It's your basic one-piece, but in white. We waited till she went for a dip and got it wet, which was well worth the wait.' Randall felt weirdly defensive, as if Leo's remarks reflected on him, or Marcy, or Lewis. 'It's a volunteer deal she's doing there,' he said. 'For those deficient kids.' Leo had smiled and said, 'I'll tell you what, I wouldn't mind getting in on a little of that charity,' and all at once dots of anger appeared behind Randall's eyes and he'd grabbed up a fistful of Leo's shirt and pulled him forward. Leo looked both stunned and scared. 'No,' was all Randall had managed to say before letting loose of him. 'No.'

When at twelve noon the KDUH news logo appeared on the screen, Lewis would turn up the volume. Marcy would appear on camera, sitting at a small spotless desk, studiously shuffling through the papers in her hand while the stentorian voice of Terry Dishong, a former anchor, declaimed, 'From the Black Hills to the Sandhills, this is KDUH news.' Marcy would then look up and say, 'Today, in northwest Nebraska, Rushville's the place where they're making news . . .'

.(If it wasn't Rushville, it would be Hyannis, Pine Bluff or some other nearby locality where a burglary had occurred or a fire had broken out.) Until the commercial break, no-one at the dinner table would speak a word, and then, after Randall reached forward and muted the commercial, Lewis, of Marcy's performance, would say, 'So, how're we doing?' and after a moment Dorothy might say, 'She's doing fine.'

But today was something different. After the logo and voice-over, Marcy raised her eyes to her audience and in her somberest voice said, 'Today a Goodnight resident has been found dead and mutilated on the Pine Ridge Reservation. According to the Sheridan County Sheriff's Department, Frank Mears, aged thirty-one, a resident of Goodnight, Nebraska, was found in an abandoned house within the town of Pine Ridge. Cause and time of death have not been determined although sources confirm that Mears had been dead for at least seventy-two hours and that unspecific mutilation of the body had occurred. Other details have not been released, but it is known that because the crime was evidently committed on the Pine Ridge Reservation the FBI has been requested to help with the investigation.'

To Randall, it seemed too fantastic, too nightmarish, staring at his wife on the television, listening to her saying these words. *Found dead. Mutilation. Seventy-two hours.* A soft sticky dampness worked out from within, took hold of his body. Marcy kept talking. While she spoke, a camera very slowly scanned a trash-strewn dirt yard and a small, unpainted clapboard house before finally zooming in on a jaggedly broken window, behind which absolutely nothing could be seen.

THAT NIGHT RANDALL ARRANGED TO MEET MARCY AT THE ELEVENTH MAN AFTER she did the evening news. He'd hoped to talk to Leo Underwood, who was tending bar, but Leo was never alone, so Randall drifted to the pool tables at the back of the bar. 'Hubba, hubba, Hunsacker,' a man named Ross Ray said to Randall in a low voice, an old high school greeting that Ross Ray now managed to make sound wry.

Randall played some cutthroat and listened to the talk fly about Frank Mears. He'd been executed, point blank, someone said, in one ear and out the other. His testicles had been slipped from their sacs and stuffed in his mouth. 'Mountain oysters, Indian-style,' one of the pool kibitzers said and somebody else said the county sheriff was already getting up a list of suspects. 'Hope they can keep it under a hundred,' Ross Ray said, chalking up lazily. 'Name me an individual who at one time or another *didn't* want to kill Frank Mears?' This met with quick ragged laughter and then, when there was a quiet moment, a voice from a shadowy place along the wall said, 'What was done to him out there was something no white man would do,' to which a general assenting murmur worked the room. The climate reminded Randall of that day on the ridge watching Frank Mears collecting his group before going down toward that meadow, and it caused in him a tender, unsettling queasiness he wanted loose from. He looked around for a moment, then laid his cue down on the green felt and walked off. 'Hey, Zacker!' Ross Ray called after him. 'You're only behind, Champ. You haven't lost yet.'

Randall was just stepping out of the bar as Marcy walked up. 'Hey, there's my hubby,' she said and then, seeing his stiffened face, 'What's the matter?'

'Nothing.' Randall tossed a glance back toward the bar. 'It's just that I hadn't been in there in a while and didn't realize how little I missed it.' Then he said, seriously, 'It's all that palaver.'

A laugh burst from Marcy. 'In my whole life, up until this very minute, the only other person in the world I ever heard say *palaver* was my father. Next thing, you'll be saying *hi-dee-ho*.'

Randall considered this and then in a deadpan said, '*Hi-dee-ho*.'

They strolled down the wide cracked sidewalk of Goodnight's main street, some businesses closed for the day, more closed for good. 'No wonder everybody either stays home or winds up in the bar,' Marcy said.

Randall scanned the dark street. 'First day I came here, I walked up the other side of this street.'

'And what did you think?'

'Nothing, probably. I think I was too scared to think.' Then he said, 'That was a long time ago.'

They kept walking, turned east on Ash, past Dr Parmalee's office, Walkinshaw's barber shop, and then a line of residences with the sound of television sifting through screened doors and windows. 'Know what Bobby Parmalee told me once?' Marcy said. 'He said when he was little you could ride your bicycle up and down this street on a Saturday night in the summer and you'd never miss a note of the *Lawrence Welk* show because it was playing in almost every house.'

'Yikes,' Randall said mildly.

After a minute or two Marcy said, 'Heard Sheriff Yardley was going out to see some of Frank Mears's friends and that you were on the list.'

'Yeah,' Randall said, and let out a quick laugh. 'He came this afternoon and acted like a man who was late for supper, which he was. He asked two questions: *What do you know* and *what do you think.*'

'And?'

'I told him since I don't know anything, I don't think anything.'

'And that satisfied him?'

Randall smiled. 'He was late for supper, like I said.'

A WEEK OR TWO LATER A MAN APPEARED ONE AFTERNOON AT THE SOUTH end of the number four field, where Randall was working. The man had parked his gray Dodge sedan on the county road and now stood beside it, waiting until Randall, cutting alfalfa, came to him. When Randall drew near in his closed-cab Case, the man pinched the strands of barbed wire and ducked through the fence. Randall cut the motor and climbed down.

'You Randall Hunsacker?' the man said. He was dressed in dark pants, dark shoes, white shirt and dark tie.

Randall grinned and said, 'Thought Mormon missionaries always traveled in twos.'

The man didn't laugh. He presented a card that gave his name as Duncan Simcoe. Above and below that, it said a few different things, but the phrase that jumped out was *Federal Bureau of Investigation*. Randall looked up at the stranger with new eyes.

Duncan Simcoe was slight-seeming, and fair-skinned, as if he spent too much time under artificial light. He regarded Randall with a fixed squint. The quieter Duncan Simcoe was, the less good Randall felt about things. Finally the agent looked around. 'You mind if we walk over into the shade?'

Randall followed him. At the stand of cottonwoods, the man picked his way among fallen leaves and debris until he found a limb suitable for sitting. From an interior pocket he withdrew a little notebook that he began flipping through. Finally he found his place. He read for a while, turned a page, read a while more. At last he looked up.

A strange, surprising thing: Duncan Simcoe blinked slowly and let his eyes fall so fully, so completely, so intimately on Randall that he couldn't look away. If this man had been a woman, Randall would've guessed she was about to say, *Let's go somewhere.* What the man said was, 'Five years ago, on a Saturday in November, you went pheasant hunting with Meteor Frmka, Frank Mears, Leo Underwood, Jim Six, and the man known as Whistler Simpson.'

Randall felt his face and body go wooden. 'That's correct,' he said with a weird formality, as if already he needed to watch himself.

The agent kept his full dark eyes on Randall. 'In as much detail as possible, tell me what went on that day.'

Randall said, 'You make it sound like a test question.'

Duncan Simcoe gave the first part of a patient nod. 'Why don't you start from the moment Meteor Frmka pointed out the two men down in the meadow.'

With Duncan Simcoe occasionally stopping Randall for clarification and moving him forward with gentle prompts, Randall went through the last stages of that day step by step, until he got to the hunters huddling above the rim of the canyon and then heading down a switchback trail toward the meadow where the two men were. 'Frmka had already left and then I decided I would, too.'

'And you did?'

'That's right,' Randall said, putting some spine in his voice. 'I started to go down there and then I just stopped.'

'And the men who went ahead were Frank Mears, Leo Underwood, Jim Six, and the man known as Whistler Simpson?' Duncan Simcoe asked this question without reference to notes.

Randall said, 'Those were the ones still walking when I stopped, yeah.'

'And do you know what they did to the men in the meadow?'

Randall viewed the question with suspicion. 'You probably know more about it than I do,' he said.

In a patient voice, Duncan Simcoe said, 'I'm gathering first-hand accounts, is what I'm doing.'

'I can't give you a first-hand account though, can I? Because I wasn't there.'

'And you don't know what happened that day in the meadow?'

Randall looked down and turned a twig with his boot. 'I heard rumors is all.'

'And what rumors were those?'

Randall didn't want to talk about it now for the same reason he'd never wanted to talk about it, though he'd never been sure what that reason was. Finally he said, 'What I heard third- or fourth-hand was that they wrote something on one of them.'

Duncan Simcoe waited.

Randall said, 'I never knew what they wrote or what they wrote it with.'

'And you never talked about it with Frank Mears, Leo Underwood, Jim Six or the man known as Whistler Simpson?'

'No, I never did.'

'Why was that, Randall?' To his patience, Duncan Simcoe had added something else – something kind, almost sweet.

'Don't know,' Randall said. He *didn't* know. He said, 'I always had a bad feeling about that day, I guess.'

'You feared the worst, is that it? – and you were afraid to have those fears confirmed?'

'*Yeah*,' Randall said, glad to have his feelings put into words for him.

Duncan Simcoe expelled a deep breath and gazed around. It was cool and pleasant within the stand of trees, an airy shady room. Randall was thinking that if he *did* have anything bad to confess, this is where he would do it. The agent brought his eyes back to Randall. 'What were your feelings about Frank Mears?'

Randall didn't think about his answer. 'I didn't like him,' he said. 'Only it took me a while to realize it.'

The agent took this in. 'Any particular reason you didn't like him?'

'No. I just didn't, is all.'

'He rubbed you the wrong way,' Duncan Simcoe said gently.

Randall shrugged. 'Yeah.'

The agent waited just a moment. Then he said, 'Kind of like your stepfather in Salt Lake rubbed you the wrong way?'

Randall felt his face whiten and then color. He made a contorted smile. 'That's a little below the belt, isn't it?'

Duncan Simcoe studied Randall with an absolute calm. Finally he said, 'I don't know yet.'

A breeze rattled the cottonwood.

'Your wife does the news from that little station outside of town, doesn't she?'

Randall nodded.

Duncan Simcoe said, 'She's the nice-looking woman with an eye-patch.'

This was a statement, not a question. Randall felt a prickle of apprehension.

'Why does she wear that eye patch, Randall?'

A second or two went by. Then Randall with his eyes low said, 'I hit her. I got crazy and hit her.' He looked up. 'It's not something I'm proud of, but it was quite a while back.'

Duncan Simcoe kept his eyes calmly on Randall. Finally he said, 'Okay, let's get back to the pheasant hunt.' He turned pages in his little notebook for a minute or two, then said, 'When you were all heading down to the meadow in single file, you just stopped and the other men passed by you. What about Leo Underwood's nephew?'

Randall had forgotten about him. 'He was just a boy,' he said. 'He went down there with them. He lagged behind, but he went. I should've stopped him, I guess.' Then, looking off, 'I never even knew his name, I don't think.'

The agent checked his notes. 'Daniel Underwood. His mother had never married. Thirteen then, eighteen now. Presently living in Elkhorn, Colorado. No criminal record.' He quit summarizing but

continued reading a few seconds. Then he closed his little book
and stood.

Randall stared out at the number four field and suddenly didn't
care about the cutting that wasn't getting done there. He turned to
the man. 'I don't know if you know it or not, but except for my
wife nobody around here has ever heard about that deal with my
stepfather.'

Duncan Simcoe smiled placidly.

Randall said, 'Those court records were supposed to be legally
sealed.'

Duncan Simcoe nodded again. Then he said, 'If you think of
anything that might be relevant to this murder, you definitely ought
to get in touch with me.'

Randall caught the meaning of this. He studied the agent a second
or two and said, 'Look, when you were checking me out, nothing
came up about the rest of my family, did it?'

The agent kept his face expressionless. 'Like what?'

'I don't mean something criminal or anything like that. It's just
that after I came out here I lost touch with my mom and sister.'

The agent considered it. 'All I would remember is something
unusual.'

'Yeah, I guess,' Randall said.

'So I guess they didn't pole-ax anybody,' Duncan Simcoe said with
a small smile. Then, still regarding Randall, he said, 'Either that or
they did and didn't get caught.'

The interview seemed concluded, but Duncan Simcoe, after
standing, didn't move from the shade, as if it were a comfort he
was reluctant to give up.

Randall said, 'So what exactly *did* happen to Biddle and Sharp
Fish that day?'

After considering it, the agent said, 'Well, I have several corroborative accounts.' He fixed Randall with his dark eyes for just
a moment before turning and gazing off across the flat, green
field. 'Of course your buddies might've tailored their stories to shift
blame to Frank Mears, the dead man.' The agent stopped here, as
if there was nothing more to say, and yet he still stood unmoving
in the shade.

After a time, Randall said, 'Well, what *probably* happened down in the meadow?'

Without waiting and without looking at Randall, Duncan Simcoe in a flat voice said, 'When the hunters got down to the meadow, one of the men, possibly Frank Mears, shot Sharp Fish in the neck with a bear-sized dose of muscle relaxant, which subdued him. James Biddle saw the dart in Sharp Fish's neck, panicked and fled. While Sharp Fish was unconscious, one of the men, possibly Frank Mears, used a buck knife to carve the word *quee* into Sharp Fish's stomach.' Duncan Simcoe spelled it out: *q-u-e-e*.

Randall expected the agent would turn his eyes on him then, if only to emphasize the monstrosity of his friends' behavior, but he didn't. Duncan Simcoe just kept staring off.

'They ran out of room for the last letter?' Randall said.

'No,' the agent said. 'They seemed to think it was comical. They had carved an exclamation mark at the end of it.' He made a bitter grin. 'When I interviewed Albert Sharp Fish, I was required to take a photograph of the word, written now in scars.' He turned and looked at Randall with bland impassive eyes. 'So of course, when Mears was murdered, James Biddle and Albert Sharp Fish were suspects.'

For a moment the word *were* hung in the air.

Finally Randall said it. 'Were?'

Duncan Simcoe said, 'James Biddle was killed in a construction accident two years ago in North Dakota, and Albert Sharp Fish didn't kill Frank Mears.'

Randall waited a second. 'How would you know that?'

'Because when I told him about the circumstances of Frank Mears's death, his whole body relaxed with satisfaction and he immediately said what I believe he actually felt. He said, "I'm only sorry I wasn't the one who did it." ' The agent made a wan, pained smile. 'It's also true that Sharp Fish has a half-dozen corroborative witnesses to attest he was nowhere near Pine Ridge within a month of the crime's commission.'

'So –'

'So that's all I can tell you,' Duncan Simcoe said. 'And just for the record, I've told you nothing.' They walked back into the glare, toward the agent's gray sedan. He had started the engine when he poked his head out the window and for the first time eased his smile into something completely ordinary. 'I once *was* a Mormon missionary, by the way.'

IN EARLY SEPTEMBER, WHEN AFTERNOONS FELT LIKE SUMMER AND EVENINGS felt like fall, Lewis Lockhardt's untroubled life collided with two discoveries. The first seemed benign. He'd noticed an abandoned pipe that ran from the yard, under the dirt driveway and over to a rusted valve near the barn and, just for the fun of it, he'd sawed off the riser and begun jamming a length of stiff wire into the pipe. He poked and rammed and finally, to his surprise, felt the wire pop through. He could hardly believe it, but when he went to the yard-end of the pipe, there, sticking out, was the end of the stiff wire.

Ha!

As Lewis stood and stepped round, he saw Dorothy standing in the dining room window staring out, maybe at him, maybe not. Lewis grinned and waved, but at just that moment, or perhaps the moment before, Dorothy had turned away.

Lewis was beginning to enjoy himself. He walked to the barn and found a coil of telephone wire lying next to the old phone on the bench of his reorganized workshop. He began to whistle. *Somewhere over the rainbow, way up high.* For weeks now he'd been trying to figure out how to hook up a telephone extension in the shop without trenching or stringing overhead wires. But now, he thought, the old farmer had found his way. The abandoned water pipe was his new telephone conduit. He took one end of the insulated telephone wire and tied it to the stiffer metal wire he'd pushed through the length of the abandoned pipe. From the barn-end of the pipe, he grabbed hold, tugged it through, and never quit whistling. *Where troubles melt like lemon drops.* He put on his glasses, spliced into the existing line, ran the wire to the jack in the barn. He stripped the insulation, ran red to red, green to green, black to black, and yellow to yellow. He tightened the cover. He found the old rotary phone he'd stored in a corner. He wiped it perfectly clean. He plugged it in. He put the receiver to his ear. He expected to hear a dial tone. Instead he heard a man's easy laughter, which stopped short. A voice followed, hushed, male, oddly accented. 'What is this noise?' the voice asked.

'Nothing,' Dorothy replied, but her voice, too, was hushed and tight. She didn't say another word. Neither did the man. They waited and listened until Lewis couldn't stand it. Something moist and qualmish moved through him. He depressed the button to disconnect. He held it there a few seconds and then released it. He heard a dial tone. He put the receiver down. He unplugged the telephone. He put it back into storage. He stood sweating and swaying. He wished that what he was feeling was anger, but he knew in his bones it was not. It was something else, a sensation new to Lewis Lockhardt. It was fear.

There had been another time in his life when Lewis had worried about Dorothy's feeling restless. Walter Fink, a friend since boyhood, had stopped Lewis one day in town and pulled him aside. 'It's Dorothy,' Walter Fink had said. 'Is everything all right with Dorothy?' and then before Lewis could say that everything was, Walter Fink said, 'Because she seems to be getting around.'

Walter Fink had tried to let those words settle in, but Lewis wouldn't let them. 'Oh, yeah,' he said, 'I've been sending Dot all over the countryside checking out this sunflower deal. I've had her talking to all kinds of people.' And then he'd begun within his thoughts to will her back into place, to will and to wait and to believe nothing else and to think nothing else and then one day she'd come back sick, and gotten better, and they were out the other side, it was behind them, further and further behind them, this unspeakably bleak period that had since been layered over by ten years of reassuring normalness, an old wound that had healed up and haired over and could only by looking with difficulty even be found. Except now, here it was again –

Lewis was lying on the wide-plank floor of the tack room. He hardly remembered walking here from his shop, but he had, and he'd laid himself down on the tack room floor, something he hadn't done since he was a child and had come here to hide after some little humiliation or another. He did now what he'd always done then. He kicked closed the door so that no-one could see him. He lay curled up, brittle and leaflike. He breathed in the straw dust and stared at the motes that hung in the dim light that slanted through the room's single pane of window glass, loose in its stops, unwashed for decades, perhaps unwashed ever in Lewis Lockhardt's lifetime.

TO RANDALL, THE SUMMER SEEMED TO HAVE SNEAKED PAST. THERE WAS Frank Mears's murder and there was work and then suddenly it had been August and weeds were growing over Frank Mears's grave and the table talk had lapsed back to bad weather and gated irrigation pipe and bobcat sightings down in Mitchell. Randall had all but forgotten Duncan Simcoe when he received a telephone call from him in early October. He wanted to see Randall the next day, around noon. Would he mind coming in?

When Randall walked into the Sheriff's Office, Duncan Simcoe was working at a card table set up behind the counter. He was wearing the same outfit that Randall had last seen him in – white shirt, dark shoes, pants, and tie. *How goes the mission?* Randall thought of saying. 'You wanted to see me?' he said instead.

Duncan Simcoe looked up and then raised himself from his folding chair. It was the lunch hour and he was alone. He pulled back the short door that swung out from the counter, skidded a chair out for Randall.

Then without small talk he said, 'Your mother and sister are both alive. They live in Florida. Your mother's in St Petersburg, your sister's in Key West. You want the addresses?'

Randall searched in his wallet and wrote the addresses down on a Chadron Implements card, then snapped open his shirt pocket and slipped it in. He thanked Duncan Simcoe, who merely nodded. Randall said, 'Was that all?'

Duncan Simcoe was staring off when he started to speak. 'I was visiting with one of the other men who was out hunting with you that day,' he said. 'This other member of your party said he noticed you were paying a lot of attention to Leo Underwood's nephew.'

'What did he mean by that?' Randall asked and knew at once he'd said it too fast. He needed to calm down.

The agent kept his eyes on Randall. 'I think he meant you were somehow suspicious of him.'

Randall sat fully back in his chair. He made himself speak deliberately. 'He was a creepy kid, was all I thought.'

'Creepy,' Duncan Simcoe said. 'In what respect creepy?'

'Well, he didn't like Whistler's dog. He just seemed to hate that dog, I don't know why, and then later when nobody but the kid was around, the dog was drowned.'

'He drowned the dog?' the agent asked in a gentle voice.

'It seemed possible, yeah.'

Duncan Simcoe tipped his chair back and looked off. 'Do you remember the boy being antagonized by anything or anyone else?'

Randall did, yes, but he waited a few seconds before speaking. Then he said, 'I kind of recall he didn't want to block pheasants with Frmka.'

Duncan Simcoe seemed to be staring up at nothing, at that point where the white wall met the white ceiling. He said, 'Who asked him to do that?'

'Leo.' Randall thought about it. 'But Leo was going to let him off the hook.'

'And?'

With startling clarity, the memory unfolded in Randall's mind. 'And Mears told him he could block or take his skinny little ass back to the truck where he belonged.'

Duncan Simcoe slowly closed and opened his eyes – it reminded Randall of a blink filmed in slow motion. 'Anything else between Frank Mears and the boy?'

'When they were talking about going down to the meadow, Leo told the boy to leave and when he didn't, Mears asked Leo if the boy was deaf as well as dumb. Except he might've even called him a name. He might've asked if the little *something* was deaf and dumb.'

Duncan Simcoe turned now and riffled through his small spiral book. Finally he stopped on a particular page and looked up. '*Bastard*,' he said, half-smiling. '*Pissant* bastard.' He closed his book.

'I don't mean to be rude,' Randall said, 'but if you knew this already, what did you need me for?'

Duncan Simcoe smiled and ignored the question. 'Let me ask you something, Randall. Think of Leo's nephew. Imagine him in your mind's eye. Okay, do you have him?'

Randall said he did.

'Okay, now think of him five years older. Think of him as eighteen-years old.'

Randall did.

'So, Randall, tell me this. Tell me whether you can imagine this eighteen-year-old committing a serious act of violence.'

Randall could of course. 'Him and about fifty other guys in this county,' he said.

Duncan Simcoe stared off as if at some cloud formation he couldn't look away from. 'I'm not telling you this,' he said, 'but what if I was to tell you that this individual belonged to a group that hates every un-Aryan thing in the world, and that predicts great cleansing race wars.'

Randall wasn't sure he was following this. He said, 'Okay, you didn't tell me that, but if you had, I guess you would've lost me.'

'What if this individual figures that by mutilating Frank Mears on an Indian reservation he can repay a personal debt while at the same time firing up some real anti-Indian sentiment.'

Randall waited for more, but nothing more was said. He had a gut feeling that what he was hearing was probably true. He also had a gut feeling that it would never get proved. 'Sounds like a pretty fancy theory to me,' he said.

The agent's face broke into a rueful smile, and he swung his gaze to Randall. 'Yep, that's the problem, all right. In one tough little nutshell.'

Randall tentatively picked up his hat. 'Guess I ought to be getting back to work,' he said.

But Duncan Simcoe wasn't done. He leaned back in his chair, stretched his arms, knitted his fingers behind his head. 'You like it here, Randall?'

Randall said he guessed so, sure.

The agent peered beyond Randall toward the window. 'It's nice country. And kind of a surprise. Before, when people said *Nebraska*, I always thought *flat*.' He stopped then and looked at Randall. 'You know what I mean?'

Randall nodded.

'But you see, it's not flat at all,' Duncan Simcoe said.

Again Randall nodded, but it occurred to him that the FBI man was looking over his sight too much. 'Well, okay then,' Randall said, and when Duncan Simcoe brought his eyes back into focus and stood up, Randall rose, too, and took his leave quickly and without particular care, because he supposed – incorrectly, it would turn out – that he'd be hearing from Duncan Simcoe again.

Randall was driving the straight stretch of Highway 87 south when he saw Marcy's Mercury Cougar approaching from the opposite direction. She was on her way to work, but, almost without realizing it, Randall slightly eased off the gas in order to stretch longer the moment he would see his wife's face behind the windshield. He flicked his hand in greeting, she smiled and waved, they passed and parted, an old coupé and an old pickup truck on a flat two-lane highway in the pale light of October. There wasn't any reason for sadness and yet it saddened Randall. It occurred to him that all the little partings, the ones that ought to be inconsequential, had about them the feeling of preparation for those big, terrible, permanent partings that, because we are blockheads and self-deceivers, we hope to keep pushing before us forever.

At home, Randall walked into and out of the empty mobile home, knocked at the big house – nobody was there – then wandered out beyond the old shearing shed. He leaned against the fence and listened to the crickets and the shush of the river on the bridge piles. From somewhere beyond the water came the smell of woodsmoke, and all at once the season seemed to have turned without his ever getting ready for it. Fall. Then winter. Randall thought suddenly of driving into the TV studio and watching Marcy do the news. He thought of driving into town and playing some pool. He thought of taking his dogs out into the corn to scare up pheasant, but the dogs, when he glanced at their kennel, weren't there. He whistled, and whistled again. Nothing.

Randall followed the smell of woodsmoke toward the barn and, coming through the wide front doors, at once heard the agitated whimpering of dogs, *his* dogs, if he heard right. He followed the sounds along the stalls, past Marcy's mother's horse, toward Lewis's revamped shop. Lewis had repaired the floor, brought in somebody's throwaway divan, and installed a double-drum woodstove, which was now burning. That was the first surprise. The second was that

Lewis was seated next to the stove in a ramshackle chair, lobbing popcorn to Randall's old dogs, Guido and Boo, first to one, then the other.

For a time Lewis didn't acknowledge Randall's entrance into the room, even after Randall said, 'Well, here's a sight to see.'

Lewis flipped the popcorn one piece at a time. The dogs' jaws made snapping sounds as they clamped their mouths over the floating white treats.

'They never miss,' Lewis said, as much to himself as to Randall. 'They're like knuckleballs, and still they never miss.' He waited a moment. 'Know how come?'

Lewis hadn't looked at Randall when he asked this, so it took a second for Randall to realize he was supposed to answer. 'No, I don't,' he said.

'Because before we ever got started I told them I'd shoot dead the first dog who dropped one,' Lewis said and then he let burst a hollow version of the horsy laugh that normally followed one of his lame jokes, the corny jokes, the stale jokes, the ones Randall was used to from Lewis and had grown to like. It occurred to him that if Lewis was here and the main house was dark, Marcy's mother wasn't home. 'Is something wrong?' Randall said.

Lewis made a broad bitter grin. 'Why would you think something like that?'

Randall didn't say anything. The dogs never took their eyes from Lewis's hands, which kept producing the little white fluffs of food. Finally Lewis seemed for a moment to come outside of his mood. He let his face relax into sadness. 'Everything is okay,' he said, almost more to himself than to Randall. 'Everything will be okay.'

III

IT WAS, FOR MOST OF THEM, A BAD WINTER. IT WENT ON AND ON AND ON. Snow began in mid-October, and by late November the downstairs windows were darkened by drifts. Dorothy alone seemed unaffected, and seemed to live in her own placid world. She quilted and – her new project – studied Spanish. '*Es una casa pequeña*,' she would recite. '*Es una chica alta. Es un problema difícil.*' It's a small house. She's a tall girl. It's a difficult problem.

When Dorothy mentioned she was going to buy a used four-wheel-drive so she could get to her language classes, and said that she'd found a nice little Subaru in Chadron, Lewis, who normally would've given a strident speech about their budget before saying no, never, it simply couldn't happen, on this occasion merely said in a dull voice, 'We'll get something safe, if we get anything at all,' and had himself made the purchase for his wife of a massive silver Chevrolet Suburban. Nothing kept Dorothy from going to her classes and conferences although weather occasionally delayed her return. Blizzards came once in January and twice in March, when a dozen lambs were lost. The last blizzard was the worst. Pheasants turned into the wind and died where they stood. 'Imports,' said Lewis – worth noting, because by the end of the winter he had all but given up speech. He meant the pheasants weren't indigenous, had been brought in from China, couldn't cope.

Lewis had turned his shop into his own spartan den, and he spent long days there repairing everything on the place that needed repair, from machinery to old chairs. The routine was slow and steady, returning something fixed and hauling off to his workshop something broken. He never showed off his work, never looked at who was in a room. He'd befriended Randall's old dogs, unpenned them, uncollared them, and they followed him everywhere, strangely quiet without the tinkling of their collars. 'He's like a ghost with pets,' Marcy said one day. 'Ever notice how a door doesn't make a sound when he passes through it?'

Randall said it was just because Lewis had shot all the hinges with oil, but the truth was, Randall noticed plenty. He watched Lewis wearing his greasy down jacket even in the house, moving slowly from room to room, looking straight ahead with half-alive eyes. He'd begun to smell like the dogs. He kept moving about and doing things, but what he did made no sense. 'Let's make some lists,' Randall said one day, but Lewis didn't respond other than bending to let his hand rest on the head of the closest dog.

'He's scaring me,' Marcy said to her mother. 'He's not himself at all,' she said. 'I don't know when he eats and he doesn't even keep himself clean.'

Dorothy didn't want to discuss it. 'It's not like he was always the most fastidious man,' she said. She was sitting up to her quilting frame, working on a series of slanting white lines that reminded Marcy unpleasantly of snow.

'But spending all his time with dogs,' Marcy said. 'And hardly ever changing clothes. It isn't like him at all.' She watched her mother's hand sliding the needle quickly in and out of the gray material. 'Nothing about him is like him.'

Her mother kept quilting.

'He takes those dogs everywhere,' Marcy said. 'I heard he took them into the Dairy Queen.'

Her mother's needle swam through the field of material.

Marcy said, 'If this were a stock animal we'd be calling Doc Parmalee. We'd think it was parasites or something.'

When her mother stilled her needle and looked up, her face was shocking in its serenity. 'Your father's all right,' she said. 'They're calling this the worst winter since 1917. Your father's fifty-nine years old and it's gotten to him a little bit. Dixie says he just waited till the last minute to have one of those mid-life crisis things.' She resumed stitching. 'He'll be okay, Polkadot. You wait and see. Come spring he'll be the first one on the flats out working the dirt. That's what he's in love with – the dirt and what he can coax out of it.' She bit off a new length of thread, slipped it through the eye of the needle, and knotted it. 'Which is fine because in the end we're all responsible for our own happiness anyway.'

'That what Dixie Bailey says?' Marcy asked, but her mother, who'd always been fairly easy to bait, didn't bite.

'She might've,' she said blandly. 'I don't take notes.'

There was something about her mother's expression now, how it had loosened into something not just beautiful but chillingly beatific, that scared Marcy. It was suddenly as if, in her mother's mind, Lewis Lockhardt hadn't gotten sick or even died, but had been somehow erased.

The winter didn't end, it just stretched longer and longer. One night, in town, an old woman, a Whittlesy, under care at Pioneer Manor, put on the coats of three sleeping attendants, slipped out a side door and walked to her old home, inhabited now by a family named Canfield. The door wasn't locked. She went to her old childhood room and slipped into bed with a five-year-old child, who stood waving goodbye when the woman was taken away the next morning. A misdirected salesman got lost in the sandhills, became stuck in a snowdrift and, according to the notes he wrote to his wife on the back of flyers for Monroe metal outbuildings, survived nine days in his car before dying of exposure. Stock died, pipes froze, power failed, was restored, and failed again. There was no news regarding the murder of Frank Mears. Leo Underwood's nephew had been detained for questioning three different times and three different times released. Duncan Simcoe had been transferred to El Paso, Texas. A spokesman for the FBI said that they were developing new leads, that the investigation was ongoing.

Whenever she was blaming weather for a delayed return, Dorothy would call Marcy. 'I tried Lewis at the house, but he didn't answer,' she would say and Lewis, when told his wife would be back a day late, would stare blankly and incline his head in a dim signal of comprehension.

In mid-March, Marcy drove her mother's Suburban to Rapid City to see a doctor, a fertility specialist, who put her into the stirrups and maneuvered what looked and felt like a small microphone into her uterus while watching images float on the screen. Her fallopian tubes, it turned out, were fine, but her egg production wasn't. The doctor was a brusque, hard-charging type (Marcy had overheard her say to someone on the telephone, 'Honey, I can get a *rock* pregnant'). She gave Marcy a brochure for a drug called Clomid and told her to have her husband take a sperm sample to the clinic for testing.

'Well, that sounds like something that isn't ever going to happen,' Randall said.

'And why don't you tell me why not?'

Winter had had its effects on Randall, too. 'Jesus, Marcy, look around you. Your folks have entered opposite ends of the twilight zone and you're at work every day of the week. I'm out here trying to run a farm without hardly knowing how to do it. And you're spending time and money trying to figure out how to make our life more complicated than it already is?'

The force of this speech seemed to push Marcy back into her own little corner, and Randall saw it. He softened his voice. 'Take today, for example. It's time we at least thought about getting ready for drilling corn so today I went looking for Lewis. His truck's at the house but he's nowhere to be found. I went every place once and then I went to the barn a second time, because that's where the dogs are, sleeping in his workshop. So I was standing there just looking at how he's laid out every tool he owns on the counters in neat rows that make absolutely no sense – box wrenches next to putty knives next to drill bits – and trying to figure what he might have had in mind when I get this weird feeling. I turn around and am looking everywhere and finally I look up and there he is, sitting on the edge of the haymow with his legs dangling down just staring at me. I asked him about the corn – should I do this and should I do that and he doesn't say a word, not a word. It finally got so spooky I said, "Well, I guess we'll go over it later then." '

My father is like an iced-over lake, Marcy thought, silence layered over silence. And then she thought that what they were all going through was like some terrible siege, where you're down to eating spoiled fruit and meat and where there isn't enough warmth and light and sustenance to the house, and there hasn't been for so long that it's hard to believe there ever will be again. Marcy went to the kitchen. She told Randall she was going to do the dishes, but that wasn't it. She just wanted her hands under warm water.

In late April the number two and number five alfalfa fields took a hard freeze, the block on the old Case cabless cracked, and the hydraulic on the flatbed truck began to work only sometimes. Lewis had entered a tidying phase, cleaning out the basement, his desk, the kitchen cabinets. Like Dorothy, like Randall and Marcy, he didn't eat much, but while the rest grew lean, Lewis seemed to shrink. His skin loosened and hung. He kept punching new holes in his belt and he let the end loll down like the tongue of a tired dog.

ONE DAY IN LATE MAY, A WARM PLEASANT WEDNESDAY, DOROTHY LOCKHARDT told Lewis that she had Spanish class in Pine Bluff that night, but thought she'd go in early to do some errands. Lewis was sitting in his big chair staring straight ahead. When she'd spoken he'd put his hands on his widened knees, as if he were about to get up and do something, only he'd forgotten what. She fished for her keys and he said something.

'What?' Dorothy said.

'Dodie,' he said in so soft a voice she wasn't sure of it. Dodie. Who'd called her that since childhood?

'What, Sweetie?' she said.

But he didn't speak again and she could see he was somewhere faraway, looking in on some other world. She kissed his unshaven cheek and set the door quietly shut behind her.

After she'd left, Lewis went through his papers again. He stood at the window and watched Randall go off on the 1020. He called the station, asked for Marcy and when she answered, had no idea of what he meant to say and so hung up without uttering a sound. He walked down to the bridge and urinated from its edge. He'd read once that a lot of drowned men had been found with their flies open. They drank, they went to the water's edge, they peed, they teetered, they fell. He stared at the moving water until it almost hypnotized him but didn't. He walked around the place. He sat and picked ticks off the dogs. Some of the ticks were big and crisp and bloated with blood. He cracked them with his boot heel on a piece of concrete. He thought of washing his hands. He turned on the 3 p.m. farm report but didn't hear it. He looked in the freezer. He baked a frozen Mrs Smith boysenberry pie and ate it with a spoon from the center out. He fried two steaks and carried them in the black-iron skillet out to the kennel where the dogs came forward with their tails and whole hindquarters wagging. When they smelled the meat, they sat. When Lewis just stared at them, they lay down. He dropped a steak in front of each of them, then dropped the black skillet into their water bucket. He went into the house and looked through old photographs, reaching into them, slowly running his fingers over Dorothy's young and shining face. Finally it was time to go.

IV

ALFRED JENSEN WAS A BANKER. ELDON ADKINS SOLD UPHOLSTERY FABRIC. David Cowper owned a stationery store.

Not until she'd heard Dixie Bailey refer to men as candidates had Dorothy begun experimentally to view them in that light. Initially it had simply made running errands a little less tedious. The interesting thing about men, Dorothy had discovered, is that a woman possessing even a moderately handsome face and figure, and capable of the simplest forms of flirtation, could gain the attention of almost any man, as long as she didn't overreach too much. All you generally had to do was look a man full in the eye a moment too long. Then, as if catching yourself tempted, you walked away. The next time in, you might let your eyes linger a little longer, and might use a word that would seem exotic to the local shopkeeper. You might remark on the candidate's lovely shirt or his lovely scar or his lovely tattoo. It was dangerous fun and Dorothy knew it, but, still, it was hard to stop. It was like her mare, who, once she'd had sweetener in her feed, wouldn't touch the unsweetened again.

Arturo Solis spoke French and English with the accent of Chichimequillas, Mexico, where he had worked with his five brothers and four sisters until the age of twelve, when, because of early scholastic promise, he had been the single son chosen for a high school education. From there he went to the university in Monterrey to study civil engineering, but instead began taking French and literature classes, and after graduation with marginal marks, too educated to work for a few dollars a day in the broccoli plant near his home and too poorly connected to find professional work in the city, he did what nearly all the young men in Chichimequillas did: he went north. He joined a cousin near Chicago and went to work in a restaurant. Herb and Gina Hammersbacker, on vacation, happened in one night and, after observing how hard Arturo worked (Herb) and how personable he seemed (Gina), they offered him a job at Hammersbacker Hardware in Pine Bluff, Nebraska.

Arturo thought it over and finally broke into a smile. 'It is very beneficial,' he said solemnly to Herb Hammersbacker, and then they all laughed and shook hands.

Hammersbacker's was a good hardware store of the type that pre-dated chain and warehouse shopping. H.O. Hammersbacker, Herb's father, had believed in two things: full stock and hardwood floors. 'Hardware stores should have hardwood floors,' H.O. liked to say. Within his store, the narrow lengths of worn maple had the soft give of a gymnasium, and furnished a pleasant smell that older shoppers, when they entered one of the newer, nationally advertised outlets, would always miss. In Hammersbacker's, the aisles were lined with wooden racks that Arturo tended. He broke small boxes from large ones, affixed prices, and arranged the stock so that it was both accessible and pleasing to behold. He preferred clean tools to dirty dishes, and the Nebraska cornfields turned yellow and dry like the fields of Chichimequillas. He was paid well enough to send home most of his earnings, and the cottage in which he lived had running water and its own bathroom, but Arturo, who had grown up with nine siblings, was utterly alone. Often as he worked he would whistle a ballad from his country, 'Perfidia' or 'La Adelita' or 'El Puente Roto.'

Arturo was whistling 'El Ausente' and shelving machine bolts the day Dorothy Lockhardt came in for picture wire. When he glanced up at her she let her eyes rest on his and said, 'What a lovely song.'

He lowered his eyes and said formally, 'Yes, it is very lovely.'

As Dorothy walked away her whole body seemed to pulse. Color rose to her cheeks, moisture suffused her skin. She turned around and went back.

'Do you have picture wire?' she asked him. He wore a name tag. He was medium height and weight. His cheeks and chin were smooth. 'Allow me to show you,' he said. He laughed and added, '*Allons-y.*'

Dorothy had to laugh. 'Your name is Arturo and you speak English and French?'

'That is correct,' Arturo said and kept walking. 'A little English, a little French.' There was a kind of poised energy that rolled through him that Dorothy lingered to watch. When he stopped and pivoted around, he seemed surprised she was not closer behind him. 'What size is your picture?' he said.

The pulsing within her didn't relent as they chose suitable wire and molly bolts, didn't relent as she followed Arturo up to the counter and paid with cash, didn't relent as she heard herself say in an uncertain voice, 'Arturo, all of my life I have wanted to know a foreign language. I was wondering – would you consider being my tutor?'

When she'd spoken, there was no-one else around – Herb

Hammersbacker was off in garden products, the two other employees were helping other customers – but now, from various aisles, they seemed all to be converging on the cash register. Dorothy felt her face coloring like a schoolgirl's and was wondering if she might actually need to flee when Arturo Solis said, 'Of course. It is very beneficial.'

Beside the Hammersbackers' three-story house, a driveway (two parallel strips of concrete between which bermuda grass grew) led beneath a portico and, finally, to a one-car garage that had been converted into the small three-room cottage where Arturo lived. Dorothy had her head covered with a brown scarf and her eyes covered with dark glasses as she approached the door and knocked.

The door was short – she had to stoop to enter. Within, there was a heavy smell of cooking oil and, beneath that, of mildew. On the walls were provocative hardware calendars – Miss Makita holding a power drill, for example – about which Dorothy felt strangely ambivalent; they made her blood quicken even when she wished they wouldn't. 'It doesn't like you?' Arturo asked.

She was looking at a Milwaukee Sawz-All in the arms of a nearly naked model. 'No,' Dorothy said, 'not very much.'

'Then I should tell you my roommate put it up.'

Dorothy turned quickly. 'You have a roommate?'

Arturo broke into a laugh. 'No. But Mr Hammersbacker told me if a woman comes to my home and sees the calendars I must say my roommate puts them up.' He looked around, found the most offensive of the calendars, and reversed it on its nail. 'There,' Arturo said. 'That is better. Next time all will be down.'

'No, no,' Dorothy said. 'This is your home. You decide on all of the decisions of decoration.' She realized she was constructing odd sentences and speaking them too loudly.

They sat at the kitchen table. Arturo wore a neatly pressed white shirt. In preparation for this meeting, he had written out a vocabulary list and a number of short sentences for her to memorize. *Es mi pueblo.* This is my town. *La habitación esta limpia.* The room is clean. *Mis gafas estan sucias.* My glasses are dirty. When an hour was up, Arturo handed her another pre-written set of sentences and vocabulary words for next time. Dorothy, sorry it was already time to leave, stood, opened her purse, and found a $20 bill.

Arturo laughed and waved it away.

'How much then?' She turned to a playful jocularity. '*Cuánto es dinero?*'

'*Nada,*' he said.

'Why?' Dorothy asked.

'*Porque,*' he said laughing again, but then he became solemn. 'If the lovely American woman would like to learn my language I am happy to teach her.'

He delivered the words as if it were a prepared speech. Dorothy was affected by both the words themselves and the fact that he'd carefully prepared them. She touched his shirt sleeve. 'Well, then, thank you.'

'You are welcome,' he said, and was smiling again. 'Here,' he said. 'You can advise me. All the decorations are mine. That is true. But if this is your house. What will you do?'

Dorothy poked her head into the bedroom, kitchen, and bath – all tiny, all tidy, all decorated with hardware posters and calendars. She said, 'I'd paint everything antique white and replace the mini-blinds with cloth drapes.'

When she next came, on a Wednesday night, church night – Dorothy had learned the Hammersbackers were always gone on church night – Arturo had painted the walls, ceilings, cabinets, and floors an exquisite pale blue. 'White didn't like me,' he explained. He had covered the windows with an inexpensive lace Dorothy had seen in Hammersbacker's. Shadowy light played through. 'Oh, Arturo,' Dorothy said, and stopped. She loved the rooms – they flooded her with a dreamy fluid warmth. They fit someone else's idea of beauty, one that she wanted to make her own. 'It's all absolutely lovely,' she said.

'Absolutely,' Arturo said, laughing, trying it out.

'It's as if I've walked into another country,' Dorothy said.

'Yes,' Arturo said. 'Do you think it is perfect?'

In their sixth tutoring lesson, Dorothy asked him to read aloud to her in Spanish from a book of poetry she had found. Had Arturo heard of the poet? Of course, he said. 'I have an idea,'

Dorothy said. 'I want to lie down with my eyes closed while you read to me.'

This then became the custom before they made love. Often Arturo would hold the book in one hand while undoing her clothes with the other. In time, he became calm and self-possessed, and their lovemaking was unlike anything Dorothy had ever known. Afterwards he would fall asleep and she would smoke a cigarette and look at him in the pale light.

Arturo would stir and say, 'You should sleep now. Sleep and forget everything.' He wouldn't open his eyes. He would merely turn and fit his body close and surround her with his smooth, sweet-smelling limbs.

In an abstract way, Dorothy knew these episodes would end and end badly, so even while she tried to disbelieve in such an ending, she was vigilant for signs of its approach. But the signs, when they came, came too late. Arturo had called one morning to say that he was free that afternoon. Dorothy had told Lewis that she had class that night in Pine Bluff and was running in early to do errands. As she'd left, Lewis had called her Dodie, as he hadn't done since she was a child in her father's house, and this had caused in Dorothy a fleeting pang of melancholy and remorse while she drove south toward Pine Bluff.

When she'd gotten to Arturo's cottage, she'd known something was wrong. Arturo was too relentlessly bright. His voice was stretched too thin, he touched her too quickly and too fiercely. When they were done, he didn't close his eyes. He waited until she had lighted her cigarette and then he said, 'I will go back to Chichimequillas.'

He stopped and she turned from him so that he could speak to her back.

He said, 'I have been fired.'

He said, 'Mrs Hammersbacker saw us through the window.'

He said, 'She has telephoned your *esposo*.'

Mi esposo.

It took a moment for Dorothy to grasp that she was not frightened or even regretful. It was in fact just the opposite. She felt released, suddenly unencumbered. It was as if her head for a long while had simply been too heavy and only when relieved of its extra weight had she become aware of it. She felt lightheaded, without ballast, and she was relieved when Arturo in his deep contained silence slid his arms around her waist and kept her from floating away.

IT WAS A MOONLESS BLACK NIGHT. DOROTHY DROVE THE HIGHWAY SLOWLY, heading north toward home out of nothing other than habit. She thought of driving west or east or south, of driving until she saw a motel she liked, of perhaps pulling off the road and sleeping in the back seat of the Suburban. Cars, when they approached from the opposite direction, startled her. Very occasionally headlights would grow brighter in her rearview mirror, then quickly pass her by.

North of the Hemingford cut-off, as the road rose and fell with the wide rolls of the landscape, a pair of headlights crested a hill behind her, disappeared into a trough, then rose again. The vehicle very gradually drew close and then, after a time, pulled to Dorothy's left as if to pass. But it didn't pass. It simply kept pace, driving alongside, on the left half of the highway. When Dorothy turned, she saw something startling. The interior cab lights of the other vehicle were on. Inside, turning to look at her, was Lewis. They stared at each other for a long time, Dorothy from her dark car, Lewis from his lighted black pickup, until finally he made a small wave and mouthed something – *Hi-dee-ho?* – and without thinking Dorothy's lips in halting mimic formed the words *Hi-dee-ho* and then Lewis's dark pickup was surging ahead and cutting through the black night, until finally his red tail-lights were lost.

She would not go home. She couldn't. She would go back to Pine Bluff, pick up Arturo, and keep driving. Or she would go north to Rapid City, call Arturo, ask him to join her. Or she would call Marcy . . . As one idea generated another, the big Suburban picked up speed.

A few miles ahead, set back a hundred feet from the highway, there stood a white, one-room, clapboard-sided schoolhouse, itself adjoined to a dirt parking lot and poorly equipped playground. The entire half-acre parcel was enclosed by an aged lilac hedge, now leafed out and in bloom. The hedge was just a dark shadow in the night, a shadow Dorothy had seen hundreds of times, thousands, but tonight, as her car hurtled along, something large within the hedge seemed to move, and did move, one shadow sliding out of another and into the highway.

With its lights out, Lewis's black truck had pulled onto Dorothy's side of the road and positioned itself at the end of pre-achieved skid marks, facing south, head-on to Dorothy's headlights. Inside the cab, Lewis's contorted face and wide eyes were illuminated for just an instant before hers, the unbraked projectile with the advantage of mass and velocity and ignorance, slammed into the smaller, and more fragile, stationary object.

DOROTHY WAS ALIVE. SHE CAME OUT OF BLACK LIQUID. SHE WAS ALIVE, she could move, she could feel her entire body. The car was wrongside up. She had to get out. She wriggled, pulled and squirmed to the window. A light bore down on her. She understood it was a motorcycle and would tear her head off if she pushed herself through the window, but she pushed herself through the window. There was no motorcycle. The light shone from a farmer's flashlight. He told his son to stand back. Stand back, he said gravely, the whole thing might blow. When he put the flashlight beam on what had been Lewis's truck, Dorothy slipped again into the black liquid.

Lewis was dead. It was reported in newspapers throughout the tri-state area, this bizarre, unsettling story: MAN AND WIFE IN HEAD-ON COLLISION. There had been no videotape, but Mr Rawley delicately suggested that Marcy's doing the story – though of course she didn't have to – would probably mean national coverage for both her and the station. Marcy declined, and the weekend newscaster was called in.

'Something about it's all wrong,' Marcy said to Randall that night as they sat on the sleeping porch.

'About the accident, you mean?'

Marcy nodded.

'Well, he was never what you'd call a good driver,' Randall said. He thought about it. 'The center line just never meant to him what it means to most people.'

An hour or two earlier, Marcy had gone to the hospital in Chadron to see her mother, who said she remembered nothing. While Marcy held onto her mother's neck and sobbed and made wet stuttering breaths, her mother lay still and kept her eyes fixed on some point beyond the hospital window, even when finally Marcy pushed herself up, and wiped at her face, and looked at her mother, stonefaced, gazing off with dead-alive eyes.

'Know what she looked like?' Marcy said now to Randall. 'Like the direct descendant of Mr Rawley's paralyzed wife.'

They were quiet for a time. A mild westerly carried cottonwood fluff, the sound of slow-moving water, the smell of fermenting silage. 'Forgot the dogs,' Randall said after a while and got up. He dished up kibbles and water and was standing looking out at the river when from the corner of his eye he caught a glimpse of something reaching up out of the water bucket, something black, almost snakelike. He knew at once that he was looking at something he didn't want to see. He moved slowly toward it and lighted a match. It was a black kitchen skillet with the handle sticking up. He stared at it a long moment before pulling it up dripping. It was coated with a thin, slippery layer of fresh orange rust. It smelled faintly of cooked meat. The dogs eased close, nosing at it, beginning to lick. So, Randall thought, leaning against the fencepost. So Lewis had fed the dogs and then Lewis, who took the dogs everywhere, had left them home.

Randall laid the pan down and walked to Lewis's shop. It was neat as a pin. The old sofa had been covered with a clean sheet that was tightly tucked to the cushions. The floor was swept. The tools lay in their weird orderliness on the long shop bench – everything in perfect parallel rows: the crowbars, the levels, the pliers, the punches, the hammers, hand saws, mallets, wrenches, snips, picks, and chisels, on and on, the perfect senseless rows. Randall climbed up to the haymow, looked around, found nothing, and finally seated himself by the ladder, looking down as he'd seen Lewis looking down that day when Randall had come looking for him. Randall's legs dangled and he could imagine, on another day, feeling childlike. While he sat, his eyes rested on the lines of tools and from here, looking down, within the rows was an arrangement of drill bits that unmistakably spelled YOURS.

Suddenly and without warning, Randall felt himself swaying under an old, almost unremembered breeze, felt the facts of his life fragmenting into tiny hollow parts and floating away. He would climb down the ladder. He would go to the closet in the house where the old wooden Roi-Tan box was stored, the one with the *Star Wars* pocket knife and the old .44 cartridges and the unused spring dance tickets he'd once bought for himself and a girl named Anna Belknap. There was also a half-smoked cigar wrapped in yellowed cellophane. He would unwrap the cigar and slide it uncertainly into his mouth. He would go out beyond the sleeping porch and climb up on the fence and light it. He would draw the ancient ghostly smoke deep into his lungs. He would think of how once he'd scooched under a house to see where his father had died. The silence he'd found there was the deep silence of absence, and the silence then was like the silence now. It made loud the rubbings of crickets and the bleating of a ewe. It made the small things large and the large sorrowful.

THE FUNERAL, HELD EARLY SATURDAY EVENING AT ST COLUMBKILLE'S, WAS well attended. When the time came, Randall went up to the front and felt his throat tightening and drying out but managed nonetheless to say that he saw now that Lewis was trying to treat him like a son even though he never said so in so many words because that wouldn't have been Lewis's style, and then, the words starting to kink in his throat, he said he hoped it wasn't too late for Lewis to know that he would like to think of him like a father, and then Marcy stood up and talked about the way her father had always leaned into his life, and trusted in the world, and helped her make every good decision she'd ever made, and would keep helping her still, and when the organist started up on 'That Old Rugged Cross,' men who didn't sing found themselves singing. Everyone sang, except for a few dumbfounded children and Dorothy Lockhardt, who sat silent, untouched by the voices, living now as she would learn to live, within her own dim stillness, hearing, saying, and feeling little, as if parted from the world by a difference in mother tongue.

The news of Lewis Lockhardt's death never reached Arturo Solis. He didn't read English newspapers, he didn't watch television news. Herb and Gina Hammersbacker had learned of the accident, of course, but some quicksilver, self-protective fear of being held responsible made them happy they'd never mentioned any part of the affair to anyone, and made them decide to be shut of it, to mention none of it to anyone, ever. When Arturo needed a ride to the Denver airport, Gina delivered him herself so that no news would pass to or from him. They drove in silence. She didn't ask where he would go or what he would do. 'Goodbye, Arturo,' she said after she'd pulled up to the airport loading zone. When from the sidewalk he bent at the passenger window to look in at her, she averted her eyes. 'I can't get out of the car,' she said. Then she said, 'I can't leave the car unattended.'

Arturo flew to Chicago. Dorothy flew to León, Mexico, and took a delapidated bus to Chichimequillas, not so much because she needed to find Arturo as because she needed to be in motion. 'Arturo Solis,' she said to the first person she saw when she stepped off the bus, not even attempting Spanish, and that first person, a girl with a plastic tub of corn on her head, pointed up a narrow dirt lane. Arturo was not there, of course. His family gathered around Dorothy – the father with the gray, brushy mustache, the wrinkled mother with Arturo's cheekbones and chin, and then, behind and to the sides, the heads of siblings at various heights. They stared until someone after evaluating Dorothy's age and bearing said, *Patrona*, and Dorothy realized they thought she was Arturo's boss. The mother touched her then, pulling her forward, but Dorothy stiffened and stepped away. She couldn't stay, she said in English. She must be going. And she did go, from Chichimequillas to Silao, from Silao to Guanajuato, from town to town and place to place, austerely, intractably, without reason or rest, until she was fluent in a language she no longer loved.

V

MARCY AND RANDALL WENT TOGETHER TO THE FERTILITY CLINIC IN RAPID CITY. the hard-charging doctor prescribed Clomid again and, two weeks later, intrauterine insemination. Their firstborn were twins, a boy and a girl. They named them Jack and Isabella, after nobody. When he was five years old, Jack asked Randall where his missing fingers had gone to and Randall said well, there was a boy in Schenectady who'd only had six fingers so he'd lent him two of his so they'd be even. It then occurred to Isabella to ask about her mother's eye. Randall glanced around at Marcy who turned from the sink with mild alarm. Same kind of deal, Randall said, only your mother lent her eye to a blind doe moose in Juneau, Alaska, and the funny thing was that after the doe moose had the new eye all she wanted to do was go shopping, so if Isabella ever heard of a doe moose browsing in the women's section of a fancy Alaska clothing store that would no doubt be the very same moose.

Later Randall would tell them a series of bedside tales about two kids – pistols, both of them – named Izzy and J.J., who, come to think of it, looked a lot like Jack and Isabella, except Izzy and J.J. were left-handed, not right. Izzy and J.J. had soapboxes that took them to fairs, rodeos, and whatnot, and got their power from no-one knew where – they would just keep running Izzy and J.J. from one interesting place to another. Izzy and J.J. were names their pals loved to call out, because they would get up in the air and carry from county to county and sometimes on cold nights from state to state, which, Randall said, would often scare the citizens in South Dakota. These stories would always end with Izzy and J.J.'s worries melting away like peppermints, at night while they slept, an idea Randall had gotten from a song Lewis used to sing. Randall himself didn't care for peppermints, but whenever Marcy was in Pine Bluff he asked her to stock up from Woolworth's, so that last thing each night, if Jack and Isabella promised not to chew them, Randall would take two peppermints from a tin and lay them on their tongues before saying good night.